CLASH OF HEARTS

The soft glow of the flames caressed her skin. She was achingly beautiful. Any man in his right mind would fall hopelessly in love with her.

Any man except him.

He seized her arm and pulled her close so that she could hear his words distinctly. "I don't want you," he snarled. "The only thing that's important is that I regain control of Castle Fulton."

"I know," she replied.

Her soft voice drove him wild with want. Her large green eyes made him desperate to cast aside every vow he had ever made to himself and to his family.

He gritted his teeth. What was she doing to his mind, to his reasoning? He had to keep a clear head. He had to keep focused on what was important. Instead, all he could think about was Solace. With an anguished growl he pulled her to him, assaulting her lips with an onslaught of kisses. Like an expert in war, he attacked her senses, leaving her powerless against his victory.

When his kisses traveled to her neck, she rallied her final defenses. "I thought you didn't want me."

Her soft-spoken reminder branded him a lying fool. He pulled back sharply to stare into her eyes. "The treasure between your thighs is enough to bring the strongest man to his knees."

A broken sob tore loose from her throat. "But what of you?"

"Is that what you want?" he demanded. "To bring me to my knees?"

"No," she whispered. "To bring you to my side." Her green gems shone at him, pleading in their innocence, dark in their want. "Don't fight me, Logan," she insisted. "I'm not your enemy . . ."

The Lady and The Falconer

Laurel O'Donnell

Zebra Books
Kensington Publishing Corp.
http://www.zebrabooks.com

ZEBRA BOOKS are published by

Kensington Publishing Corp.
850 Third Avenue
New York, NY 10022

Copyright © 1998 by Laurel O'Donnell

Zebra and the Z logo Reg. U.S. Pat. & TM Off.

First Printing: August, 1998
10 9 8 7 6 5 4 3 2 1

Printed in the United States of America

For Mom,
whose courage, perseverance and moral strength
are the inspiration for all true heroines.

For my husband, Jack,
whose loyalty, devotion and love are the heart and soul
of all my heroes. You are them and so much more . . .

Prologue

"Ready or not, here I come!" a young girl's voice cried out in the distance.

Solace Farindale pressed a hand over her mouth and giggled, scrunching lower behind three bales of hay. She didn't know where her friend Gwen was hiding because as soon as Helen had begun counting, she'd run into the barn and had dove behind the hay. Lillian, her maid-servant, would no doubt be angry that she had dirtied her new velvet dress, but Solace couldn't resist such a perfect hiding place. The sweet smell of straw filled her nose, and several strands tickled her back as she settled into her spot. She loved coming to visit Helen on her farm. She and Gwen had begged their fathers to let them go, just for the afternoon, and after much pleading the men had reluctantly agreed. It was half a morning's ride from Gwen's home, but well worth it.

Finally, after a brief moment of expectant waiting, Solace peeked through a slit between the hay bales. The barn was empty. Several stalls that used to house horses now stood vacant. Solace knew Helen's parents had had to sell the beasts off because their crops had yielded a poor harvest last year. Solace scanned the narrow area of the barn that she could see through the opening, but there was still no sign of Helen. She shrugged and settled back to wait.

Then she heard the barn door creak open. Her eyes widened and again she placed a hand over her mouth as she slid lower behind the hay, afraid her giggles would give her away. But there was no scurry of searching feet, no calls of her name.

Solace shifted and peered through the slit between the hay bales. She glimpsed a woman grabbing a rusty bucket from the ground and carrying it to an empty stall across from her. It was only Helen's mother, Anne. Solace's gaze flew to the door. Where is Helen? she wondered.

Anne placed the bucket on the ground next to a small pile of seeds. She scooped up a handful with her cupped palm and dumped them into the bucket.

"Good afternoon, Anne," a man called out. His deep, guttural voice gave the greeting a harshness that belied the innocence of his words.

Solace heard Anne gasp and she tilted her head, leaning closer to the narrow opening between the bales. She saw two men dressed in chain mail lurking near the door and one man standing inside the barn. She nervously twirled a strand of dark hair around her finger as a feeling of fear engulfed her. The tall man wasn't a good man. She could sense the evil in him, as if a dark cloud belonged over his head. His hair was immaculate, styled in a fashionable bowl-cut, black as the night. The red velvet of his jupon was tailored to his chest and arms, padded somewhat at the chest and shoulders to accent their broadness. The collar reached all the way to his neck. He had the coldest blue stare she had ever seen.

"Lord Randol," Anne greeted with a slight bow.

Randol sauntered closer to her. "Looks like you've kept the barn in good order."

"It's our living, m'lord. We take good care of our crops."

"Perhaps you should take as good care of your lord," he grumbled. "Where's your husband?"

"In the fields, of course, m'lord," she replied.

Solace watched Lord Randol nod as if he already knew that Anne would say that. "I'm here for my taxes, Anne."

"M'lord, my husband explained to you that the rains and the flooding have washed out most of the crops."

"You're three months behind in your payments, Anne," Randol interjected.

Solace saw Anne wring her hands and she sensed something terrible was coming, but she didn't know what to do.

"I realize that, m'lord." Anne said. "But we have nothing to pay you with. You have all our animals. We have no coin, no—"

"Coin is not what I'm asking for." He reached out and ran a finger along the bare skin at her throat.

Solace watched with a growing fear as Anne's eyes widened in outrage and her slender fingers slapped Lord Randol's large hand aside.

"You go too far this time," Anne retorted. "You've taxed us until we've become unable to pay. You've taken everything from us. I will not give you myself, too!"

"You have little choice, Anne," Randol said, stepping closer. "With nothing else to give, it's either that or your house."

Anne stepped away from him. "Sleeping in a field is preferable to your touch," she spat out.

"You won't think that come winter," he murmured, but loud enough for Solace to hear. Again Randol reached out to Anne, this time grabbing hold of her dress and yanking it from her shoulder.

Solace wanted to flee, wanted to escape the horrible

man, but she dared not move. The two men lurking in the doorway would surely see her.

Anne bolted for the door. Randol caught her in his arms, pulling her hard against his chest. "Such a willing wench," he whispered, licking her ear.

Anne whirled, striking out at her attacker, raking her nails down his face.

Lord Randol howled his disbelief and rage, and pushed her to the ground. He raised his fingers to his gashed cheek. "Bitch," he snarled, studying the blood on his hand. He undid his belt and let his breeches fall to the ground.

"No!" Anne screamed, struggling uselessly as Randol dropped to his knees.

The hay bales blocked Solace's view of Anne. All she could see was Lord Randol's face, the ugly grimace that twisted his features. She had never seen anything more vicious in her life, the way his lips sneered like a snarling animal's, the way his cold eyes stared like a venomous serpent's, at Anne. She heard Anne screaming and sobbing, saw her hands come up to push Randol away. He ignored her flailing fists and continued to violently thrust himself at her.

Tears came to Solace's eyes. She didn't know what was happening, but she knew that Anne was being hurt. She pressed her hands to her ears, trying to block out the sounds of Anne's cries.

Finally, Lord Randol rose to his feet and wiped an arm across his slashed cheek. Without a word, he turned away.

Hot tears ran down Solace's cheeks. She was trembling all over. She fought to choke back her sobs, terrified of what the man would do to her if he found her.

Anne's moans filled the air. Solace watched Lord Randol take a menacing step toward her, and a bright flash of silver flared across her vision, arcing toward Anne.

Solace blinked. After that, she heard no more sobs. Shivering, she huddled behind the hay, praying that the men would go away, praying that they wouldn't find her. She barely heard Randol's last words. "Never strike a lord."

Solace listened to the silence that followed for a long moment. Her sobs sounded loud to her own ears. She was sure Randol would discover her. Please, she silently begged, don't let him find me.

Then she heard footsteps, booted feet treading over the dried hay of the barn floor. They were getting louder, closer. She hugged her knees tightly to her chest, squeezing her eyes tight. Tears forced their way from the corners of her clenched lids, sliding down her small face, bringing their salty bitterness to the edges of her lips.

The footsteps drew closer. And then stopped. Something called to Solace, compelling her to open her eyes, urging her with an undeniable force to lift her head. Slowly, she opened her wet eyes to stare into the face of evil. Dark, malevolent eyes glared at her, eyes that trapped her in a hypnotic grip.

Something glinted in the morning's sun, reflecting light into her eyes. Her gaze shifted to the sword Randol held in his hand. A smear of blood marred its smooth, flat surface.

Solace couldn't take her eyes from it. She trembled with a ferocity that should have moved the earth. Suddenly, the blade lowered.

Her gaze remained locked on the empty air where the weapon had been.

Then, finally, Solace heard the footsteps recede and the barn door swing closed. Still, she couldn't move. She was afraid of what she would find if she left her hiding spot. What if the men hadn't really gone? What if they were waiting to hurt her?

Finally, after a long moment of silence, Solace pushed herself forward, peering around the hay, her body still shaking with fear. The barn was empty . . .

. . . except for Anne lying on the ground. Solace wanted to see if she was all right. But she was afraid. So afraid. You have to help her, a voice inside her urged. Solace dragged herself out from behind the hay and was surprised to find that her shaky legs held her up. She approached Anne very slowly. Was she dead? Her eyes were closed. Blood trickled from the corner of her mouth. Her chest wasn't moving.

Solace wiped at her moist eyes, trying to push aside her tears so she could see. Suddenly Anne's eyes opened and pinned Solace where she stood.

Solace jumped back, stifling a scream.

"Solace," Anne whispered, a gurgle of blood issuing forth as she tried to speak.

Solace shook her head, refusing to move from her spot. The sight of Anne's blood terrified her. She spun toward the door, wanting to run, wanting to flee and pretend this never happened. But then Helen came to her mind. Helen would want to know why she didn't help her mother. Helen. Where was she? She turned back to Anne and moved stiffly to her side.

Anne reached out to seize hold of the hem of Solace's velvet dress. "Tell your father," Anne coughed. "Don't let Randol get away with this. Don't let me die for nothing."

Solace shook her head again, frightened.

"Please," Anne begged. "Tell Helen that I love her."

Solace watched Anne slump to the earth, saw her hand release Solace's dress and fall lifeless to the dirt. She was dead. Dead. Solace ran from the barn, tears streaming from her eyes, her sobs now loud and heavy in her throat.

* * *

Lord Farindale ran his hands over the parchment, spreading it out on the table before him. He was a tall, imposing man with a thick tangle of brown hair, his full beard flecked with speckles of auburn. He studied the plans for a long moment, tugging at his lower lip in thought. Then, he raised green eyes to the man who stood on the opposite side of the table from him. "This castle will take years to construct," he said.

The man nodded, his bright blue eyes alight with approval. "Yes," he agreed. "It will be a mighty asset. A powerful home for you, my friend. And also one of the strongest fortresses in England."

A smile crept across Farindale's lips. "God's blood, Erickson!" he exclaimed. "I believe you want me to build this for the protection it will offer *you!*"

Erickson chuckled. He was shorter and stockier than Farindale, with a receding hairline that was fast growing into complete baldness. "I won't lie to you," he answered. "A castle this strong will attract many fine knights."

"Not to mention the knights my full coffers will attract."

Erickson continued, nodding. "It would be a relief to know that my neighbor, and my good friend, has such a large disposal of men at his service."

Farindale laughed out loud. He slapped the man on the back. "It's good to see you, Erickson. But come, tell me truly what you think of the plans? Where can I improve them?"

The door squeaked open, and the padding of feet caused the men to turn. Solace raced across the wooden floor and Farindale opened his arms for her. In the flickering light of the room's candles, Farindale made out his daughter's red cheeks and teary eyes. "What's wrong, darling?" he wondered, a tightness constricting his chest at her distress.

She buried her face in his shoulder, sobs wracking her tiny body.

"Where's Gwen?" Erickson demanded. "Where's my daughter?"

Solace turned wet eyes to Erickson. "She's with Lillian. And Helen."

Farindale cast Erickson a glance over the child's dark head. "It's all right, my love," he whispered, turning his attention back to Solace. He sat in a chair to cradle the small girl in his arms. "What's happened?"

"Oh, Father," she wept, clinging to him tightly. "It was horrible."

He pulled back to look into her eyes, scowling. "Tell me," he ordered.

Her lower lip trembled, quivering with anguish. "They killed Anne, Father," she sobbed.

"Anne?" Farindale echoed, casting a confused glance at Erickson.

"One of Randol's tenants. They live on our border. The girls went there this morning to play with her daughter."

Farindale nodded, remembering. "I knew we shouldn't have let them go. There's nothing but trouble to be had in Randol's lands."

Erickson knelt beside Farindale to stroke Solace's soft curls. "Who killed her?"

Solace turned large, green eyes to Erickson. She was crying so hard she could hardly speak. "L—L-Lord Randol and his men." She turned her eyes to her father. "He hurt Anne b-because she couldn't pay her taxes. He d-did something horrible to her. And then he stabbed her with h-his sword."

Farindale clenched his teeth and pulled her head to his chest, trying to calm her, but Solace continued to cry. "Did he hurt you?" he demanded, every muscle in his body tensing.

"No," Solace wept.

Farindale crushed her in an embrace born of relief.

The door opened and a thin woman dressed in black bobbed a curtsey to lord Farindale.

Farindale reluctantly released his hold on his daughter. "Go to Lillian, my love," he whispered, wiping the tears from her red cheeks. "She will get you some warm cider."

Solace refused to let go of him, and Farindale held her tight for a moment longer. He kissed the top of her head, feeling her tiny body shudder. Then, he pulled her arms from around him, and urged encouragingly, "Go with Lillian."

Solace looked up into his eyes. "You have to stop him," she said sincerely. "You can't let him get away with this."

Farindale stared down at his young daughter in shock. Her face was wet from tears, her cheeks and nose red, her eyes swollen, her body trembling with fright. But she was as serious as any adult. He admired her in that instant.

"You won't let Anne die for nothing, will you?" she wondered.

"Hush, child," Farindale said, wiping the tears from her cheeks and stroking her rebellious head of curls. "I'll speak with you later."

Solace nodded softly, and inhaled a shaky breath as she slid from his lap.

Farindale watched her walk to the door and take Lillian's hand. She was a lovely girl, charming and innocent. She was going to grow up to be a beauty. She glanced back at him over her shoulder, those green eyes imploring him. Then, she was gone, closing the door behind her.

Farindale's hands clenched into fists. "That bastard has gone too far."

Erickson placed a hand on his shoulder. "Easy, my friend. Randol is a powerful lord."

"Powerful and evil from all you've told me." Farindale turned to his friend to meet his blue eyes with resolve.

Erickson sighed in resignation. "It's true. He treats his people cruelly. This is not the first time I've heard of his killing a peasant."

"But it's the first time my daughter has witnessed it." Farindale's fists clenched tighter. "I've tried so hard to shelter her from the cruelties of the world. I didn't want her to see this."

"She was on his land," Erickson reminded him.

"Maybe it's time we changed that," Farindale said, moving to the table to stare down at the luxurious plans for his new castle.

Erickson joined him.

Farindale picked up the parchment. "We're not building a castle, my friend." He crumpled the parchment in his fist. "We're taking one."

One

The beautiful fall day was fresh and warm, summer refusing to relinquish its grip. Solace Farindale moved through the grassy field beside Gwen Erickson, their steps leisurely and relaxed. Behind them, Castle Fulton loomed large, its many towers reaching high into the sky. The drawbridge stretched across the deep moat, and dozens of villagers moved in and out of the castle as they saw to the business of the day. A monk passed Solace and her friend on the way to the castle's chapel, his head bowed, his hands clasped in silent prayer. The pious men and their brown robes were a common enough sight at Castle Fulton. The monks stopped at the fortress on their way to the Abbey of St. Michael, sometimes alone, but Solace had seen groups as large as fifteen.

In a field to the left, knights were practicing their jousting skills, their enthusiastic shouts filling the air. Solace turned at the sound of hoofbeats to see a man striking a quintain with his long lance. The counter-weight whirled quickly around and hit the man in the shoulder. The man tumbled from his horse amidst laughter from his fellow knights.

Solace turned her attention back to Gwen. "Is it serious?"

"I . . . I don't know," Gwen replied solemnly, wringing her hands in front of her. "Father just seems so weak."

"I'm sure he'll be fine," Solace said kindly. But she had seen the pale color of lord Erickson's face, the sagging of his shoulders, and knew that his strength was waning. "Have you sought physicians?"

"We've tried everything!" Gwen exclaimed. "They gave him all sorts of herbs. They studied his urine. Even the bloodletting didn't work! More and more of our coin goes to trying to make Father well." Gwen looked up at Solace, her blue eyes dull with worry. "Father doesn't like me to concern myself with the finances, but I know that's why we're here."

"What do you mean?"

"Father was hoping that your father could loan him some gold," Gwen said quietly, glancing around the field, not wanting the others to hear. "But since your father is off with the king . . ." Her voice trailed away.

Solace stopped to meet Gwen's eyes. "Are you in danger?"

"No," Gwen insisted. "It's nothing like that. It's just that our coin is almost depleted. Until the taxes are collected next year, there's not enough to pay the knights who protect the castle."

Solace nodded in understanding. "I'm sure Father would give you the gold without any questions."

"Yes, but will your stepmother?"

Solace opened her mouth to reply when the loud cry of a bird drew her gaze to the sky. A magnificent falcon soared overhead, circling the field. For a moment, she wondered if it had escaped from its owner. But as her gaze dropped back to Gwen, she spotted the falconer in the distance over her friend's shoulder.

A second bird, a peregrine falcon, perched on his fist. The falconer was holding onto the jesses, leather strips attached to the falcon's legs, while offering it a lure. The falcon ate the offered meat, devouring the entire piece. The bird was beautiful, its golden brown feathers shining like expensive silk in the warm sunlight. But it was not the falcon that caught Solace's eye.

Every time she saw him, the falconer's conspicuous good looks totally captured her attention. He towered over the rest of the men by at least a head, and he now stood absolutely still, as if somehow knowing he was being studied. He was marvelous to gaze at, a statue carved by the most skilled artisan. He had an arrogantly symmetrical face that was breathtakingly gorgeous. His aquiline nose was straight, his jaw strong, chiseled by a master sculptor. His lips were firm, strangely . . . foreignly . . . sensual. The sunlight suddenly seemed to be shining for him alone, glimmering over his black hair like a halo, making it gleam like onyx under the sun's bright rays.

A small girl, Mary, ran to him from over the drawbridge. She stopped at his feet, and the falconer turned to her. Solace watched as the girl exchanged words with him. She saw his gaze shift to the falcon on his wrist. Then, he held out a piece of meat to the child. Mary took the meat with a grimace and held it out to the bird with two fingers.

The falcon captured the meat and quickly ate it.

The falconer patted Mary on the head, and the girl beamed at him.

A warm sensation flooded through Solace. There was something about this falconer that wasn't what it seemed.

Gwen turned and glanced over her shoulder. A devious grin stretched her lips as she turned back to face Solace. "He is very handsome."

Solace quickly looked away, blushing.

Suddenly, Old Ben limped by Solace and Gwen, curs-

ing under his breath and muttering, "He's no falconer." Old Ben was the oldest man they knew, his skin
darkened and weathered by the sun. Most of his hair
was gone, and what few strands remained were as white
as lamb's wool.

Solace and Gwen exchanged a look and then smiled
in unison. Old Ben was always complaining about something! Solace knew he took keen pride in his birds, always wanting everything done with perfection. That was
one of the reasons her father had hired him as his first
falconer.

Old Ben waved his arms at the falconer, flapping
them as if he were a great bird himself. "Not like that!"
he called out in exasperation. "If'n ya feed 'er too much
she'll never go after the game! Ya just give her a taste!"
Old Ben took the peregrine from the falconer and
walked away mumbling curses under his breath.

Solace watched the falconer for a long moment. Tales
had circulated about him in the castle, the gossip of
frustrated wives and eager young women. Tales of how
his eyes could undress you with one penetrating gaze.
Tales of how his muscles rippled with explosive energy,
muscles hidden beneath a layer of bronze skin. Tales
of how his deep, confident voice could make your limbs
tremble with the anticipation of hearing your name
whispered by him.

The black falcon cried out again and swooped in for
a landing, digging its claws into the leather patch sewn
on the shoulder of the falconer's tunic. The falconer
barely acknowledged the bird's arrival until Mary
clapped with glee. He smiled down at the girl as the black
falcon shifted its position on his shoulder. The falconer
then set a hand on Mary's shoulder and steered her back
toward the drawbridge.

As he moved, Solace admired the ease, the natural
grace with which the bird rode his shoulder, mildly in-

trigued that it was riding its master's shoulder instead of on his forearm where it belonged.

Gwen gently cleared her throat.

Solace turned away from the falconer. She clasped Gwen's hands. "Don't worry," Solace assured her. "Everything will be fine."

The needle stabbed Solace's finger for the hundredth time, and she silently cursed. She was sure that this embroidery of a flower would turn out much better than her previous efforts. She had been concentrating on it all evening, trying to block out the mundane conversation Gwen was having with her half sister, Beth, and her stepmother. But as much as she tried to focus on her work, the image of the falconer kept haunting each stitch. The beauty of his face, the perfection of his features, aroused her imagination. She continued to try to push the distraction aside, but he kept materializing in her mind's eye like a stubborn phantom refusing to be banished.

Solace glanced across the solar at Gwen to see her head bowed over her work, her fingers nimbly finishing up some fancy mending on her father's leggings. She wondered if the falconer's manly physique was playing havoc with Gwen's mind, too. But as she watched her friend's deft fingers move, she knew Gwen was not thinking of him.

She shifted her gaze to Beth. Her wedding gown cascaded over her lap like a white shimmering waterfall. Solace knew Beth's thoughts would not be interrupted by some mysterious stranger; she was totally devoted to lord Graham Harper, her betrothed.

Her stepmother, Alissa, shifted in her chair, drawing Solace's gaze. Alissa ran a hand over her immaculate brown hair before once again bending over her husband's tunic. She was wearing a new purple houppelande, trimmed with white fur. Alissa was always in fashion. It would be a disgrace for her to be caught wearing one of Solace's favorite dresses, a cotton gown. Alissa's elegance made her beautiful, but her haughtiness made her unlikable. For a long moment, Solace watched her stepmother work. The stitches were perfect, each the exact length of the one before it.

Solace dropped her gaze to her own embroidery. No one in the entire castle would let her do their embroidering. They weren't mean about it, but they always happened to come up with some excuse when she offered her services. This time it would be different, Solace had promised herself. This time she would get it right. Finally, she pulled the last thread through and tied it off. Then, she flipped the fabric over, triumphantly gazing down at the flower . . .

Her expectant smile disintegrated into a disgruntled frown. The flower looked more like a sick, fat snake than a beautiful rose. She didn't understand. She had done everything right! Woefully, she glanced up at the others. Gwen was still bent over her work, her beautiful blond hair falling around the leggings she was stitching as if shielding them from Solace's eyes.

Solace looked over at Beth. Her skillful fingers quickly drew the needle in and out of the silk material, effortlessly creating a detailed floral design of roses and climbing ivy.

Finally, she turned her gaze to her stepmother. Alissa was staring at her. A wicked grin curved her thin lips. "Finished, Solace?" She set aside her husband's tunic and stood.

Solace panicked as all eyes turned to her. She felt Gwen's excited, yet hopeful gaze; Beth's disinterested eyes reluctantly turned to her. "I . . . I . . ." Solace stuttered.

Then, her stepmother was standing before her. She held out a hand to Solace. "May I see it?"

Solace shoved the fabric behind her. "It's not finished," she lied. "I need to . . ."

Alissa nodded patronizingly, her brown eyes shadowed with contempt. "Well, you just take all the time you need to complete . . . your flower."

Beth snickered.

"If you need help, just ask me," Alissa said and turned her back on Solace.

Solace cast a misery-filled glance at Gwen. Her friend stared back, her eyes filled with sympathy. They both knew she could never go to her stepmother for help. Solace's pride wouldn't allow it. Not when she heard her stepmother's laughter behind closed doors, saw the disdain in her eyes. Alissa would never let her forget that she was not her real daughter.

Solace was sure that Alissa would be happier if she were dead—or had never been born. Solace's mother had died when she was two, and her father had married Alissa less than a year later. Beth had been born a year after that.

As Alissa retook her seat and picked up her father's tunic to continue working on it, Solace sneaked the fabric out from behind her back. She gazed down at it dejectedly. It came so easy to the others, she thought sullenly.

Suddenly, the door swung open and a soldier clad in chain mail burst into the room, his breathing ragged and shallow. The candlelight glinted off his damp brown hair, its thin strands plastered to his head with sweat. As his gaze swept over the women, Solace noticed a frantic, if not desperate, look in his eyes and almost stood from her seat.

He approached Alissa, dropping to one knee before her.

"M'lady," he said. "Forgive the intrusion."

"What is it, Fletcher?" Alissa wondered, barely raising her eyes to him. "Aren't you supposed to be off . . . guarding or something?"

Solace stood up, her ruined embroidery forgotten. Yes, she thought, he was supposed to be on guard duty. He was a border patrol guard, keeping watch over the boundaries of Fulton. Her stepmother would have known that if she got up for the weekly reports the guards gave on Saturday morning. But she preferred to sleep in, leaving that one duty to Solace.

"Yes, m'lady," he said, lifting his gaze to her. He cast a sideways glance at Solace, and she read the uncertainty in his eyes.

Solace stepped forward. "What's wrong, Fletcher?" she demanded. "What's happened?"

Fletcher stood to address Solace. "It's Baron Barclay, m'lady. He's amassed an army. I estimate three thousand men."

"Oh, pooh," Beth said dismissively, waving her hand as if to fend off a fly. "Does this mean my wedding will have to be postponed?"

Fletcher's back straightened as he answered with scorn. "He has building materials for siege machines and enough supplies to hold him for months."

"He wouldn't dare," Alissa gasped, bolting to her feet in outrage, clutching her husband's tunic tightly in a clenched fist. She tossed it to the floor, storming from the room, hissing, "Come!"

Fletcher marched after Alissa with Solace following closely.

"Where are you going?" Gwen called.

"We have to prepare!" Solace shouted. "Barclay's going to lay siege to Castle Fulton!"

Two

The darkness of the dungeon surrounded Logan Grey like a dense fog. A stench of decay and urine reached his nose, attacking his sense of smell with an acrid sting, but he didn't flinch. He was used to the smell of the dying, having encountered it numerous times throughout his life in the thick of battle and on the dark, dangerous streets of London.

He sidled cautiously around a corner, knowing that he was nearing the dungeon guard's position. After watching the changing of the dungeon guard for a week, he knew there was no better time to attempt a rescue and escape than at dawn. Now only one man stood between him and his brother. Logan wrapped his fingers tightly around his long, wooden staff. Just a sharp rap on the head would knock the guard out long enough for him to find Peter and escape.

Peter. He had not seen his brother since that fateful day thirteen years ago when Peter had begged him not to leave the castle. All these years . . . He had thought Peter was dead, killed along with his mother and father. Then, a little less than three months ago, a close friend had told him that a friend had spoken with Peter . . . in Castle Fulton. Logan had traveled straight to Fulton and had spent his days and nights seeking out any word, any sight, of his brother. He knew he had to be careful of the questions he asked and of whom he asked them, which made his search all the more difficult. But he had neither seen nor heard any mention of Peter in the week he had spent at the castle. It was as if he were hunting for a ghost. The thought had crossed his mind more than once. Perhaps the man had not spoken to his brother at all. Perhaps it was a different Peter. But Logan could not risk it. He had to know for sure.

A memory flooded into his mind, with images so strong that he was powerless to ignore them—he and his brother pretending to be valiant knights, clutching the wooden swords and shields their father had carved for them, wearing the "chain mail" their mother had embroidered for them, searching the dungeon for spies. Now here he was, skulking through the dungeons like the spies he and Peter had loved to hate.

Logan pushed the memory away and pressed himself against the damp stone wall to slowly, quietly, peer around the next corner. A crackling torch lit the area before him, illuminating the guard who sat in a wooden chair with his back to Logan, his heavy boots propped on a second chair. Logan froze as the guard tipped back on his chair, casually tossing a heavily gnawed mutton bone to the floor. The man stretched, his dull and dirty chain-mail armor struggling to glisten in the torchlight.

Logan moved in, clutching the staff tightly in his hands. He crossed the expanse of the room silently, moving quickly toward the guard. Just a sharp knock and the man would have a headache, but little else to show for his wound. Then a crunch came from beneath Logan's boot and he froze, glancing down at the noise. He raised his foot to see an old crumbled bone from a previous meal lying crushed on the stone flooring.

When Logan lifted his gaze, the guard was standing before him.

"What are you doing here, falconer?" the guard demanded. His gaze flicked quickly to the staff in Logan's hands, then darted back to meet Logan's stare.

Logan remained quiet, certain the guard could understand the resolve that now filled his own eyes, certain he could see his jaw clench tightly, certain he could sense his muscles coiling taut in his body. He sharply flicked his wrist, bringing the bottom end of his staff up into his open, waiting palm.

The guard was just as quick, his hand curling around the hilt of his blade, his elbow bending, releasing the sword from its sheath. He turned the blade back and forth in front of him, the torchlight shimmering on its glossy silver surface, the fire's glare dripping along the blade as if it were freshly drawn blood.

Logan could only think of Peter lying in a pile of his own refuse, chained to the wall like some pathetic caged animal, his skin hanging on him like some ragged piece of cloth as starvation ravaged his body. He let his knees go limp, and his body suddenly dropped toward the floor as he whipped the end of the staff toward the guard's legs. The heavy wooden pole hit the man's right knee. The big man grunted painfully as his legs buckled beneath him, and he dipped his sword to the floor so the sharp edge could prop him up.

Logan swung the staff again, knocking the blade away. The guard plummeted forward, landing on the stone floor with a tremendous thud, the metal covering his arm grating harshly against the rough rock.

Logan brought his staff down on the back of the man's head. The man grunted once and then was still. Logan bent to retrieve the key from the guard's belt. He quickly removed the torch from the wall and disappeared down the dark corridor of the dungeon.

"Peter?" he called into the eerie veil of darkness that lurked beyond the circle of light thrown from his torch. But all that greeted him was an echo of his own voice and the *plip plip* of water dripping somewhere in the distance. Logan stepped deeper into the black heart of the dungeon.

He stopped at the first cell door he came to, stepping closer to the small, rust-covered bars that lined the window opening. He peered through them, calling softly, as if afraid to wake the dead, "Peter?"

A moan sounded from within.

It could be Peter. It could be my brother . . . or it could be some raving lunatic ready to smash my skull to get free. Logan tightened his grip on his staff and stuck the key into the lock. With a click, the thick wooden door opened. He swung the door wide, thrusting the torch into the small cell. The light cut through the blackness like the sun breaking through a hole in a blanket of dark clouds. The occupant groaned, shielding his eyes. He was a skeletal old man, his clothing ragged, sheared away from years of wear. Beneath the ripped and tattered clothing that hung from his thin body, Logan could see open, pustulant sores. Leprosy!

Logan backed quickly out of the cell, closing the door. Dread filled him. What if Peter . . . ? Logan shook his head, refusing to acknowledge the thought, even the possibility.

The next cell was empty, as was the third one, both containing only piles of old bones and scraps of clothing. But as Logan swung the door open on the last cell, he saw a young man sitting cross-legged on the ground, his back to him. His heart skipped a beat. My brother! He thrust the torch at the prisoner, trying to get a better look, taking a joyful step forward. "Peter?" Logan whispered hopefully.

The man didn't answer and Logan felt a tightening of anxiety in the pit of his stomach. He moved closer, stepping around the still form. As the light crept forward to fully reveal the man, Logan's happiness died.

The face that stared at him was not Peter's. The vacant eyes were dull with madness.

Logan backed out of the cell, shutting the door quietly behind him. Bereft, he returned to the land of the living—a living hell for him. His brother was not here. His hopes of the last months suddenly shattered into nothingness. He was the only member of the Grey family left. He cursed himself for even daring to hope. He had learned long ago that hope was the longing of fools, and here he was again proving himself to be just that—a fool.

He returned the torch to the wall and found himself staring down at the unconscious guard. His head was tilted to the side, his neck bared to the dancing torchlight that flickered across his skin. *What are you doing here, falconer?* Logan clearly remembered the guard asking. The man had recognized him. Logan knew he couldn't risk being imprisoned, being the subject of suspicion. He couldn't chance the guard telling anyone he had come to the dungeon.

Too much was at stake.

A strange calm settled over him as he raised his staff over his head.

Logan made his way through the keep to the main door that led outside to the inner ward. He paused in the opening, listening to the calls of the guards from the walkways above. He lifted his head to the sky. It was a bright red as the rising sun stretched its fingers over the world. Even with the early hour there was much activity outside. He heard steady, heavy pounding as scaffolds were being secured to the castle walls. He could smell the acrid stench of burning oil being readied for the siege. People rushed around as if the world were ending.

It brought back the memory of preparations for another siege, a siege from long ago. Logan glanced at the open gate that led to the outer ward. It had been there that his brother warned him not to go. He could still clearly see the image of his brother—that worried expression—in his mind's eye.

Just then the bells of the chapel chimed throughout the courtyard, bringing him out of his reverie. Many people paused in their duties and hurried past him toward the morning mass.

He stepped outside into the morning sun's rays. The smell of burning wood from the Great Hall's hearth filled the air. He could almost taste the porridge that he was certain was brewing in a cauldron over the hot flames. Nearby he saw two men loading a final barrel of ale into a horse-drawn cart. Opposite the ale house, three women were setting their laundry aside, quickly putting their scrubbing boards away.

Logan walked further into the ward, fondly studying his surroundings. One of the biggest fears he'd had of returning to Castle Fulton was that a merchant or a servant would recognize him and call out to him. But that had not happened. No one knew him. And the one or two he remembered probably recalled only a slim boy, not the man he had grown into.

His mind drifted back to his brother . . . to his life here. All the happy days of childhood spent inside these very walls. But he could not remember how happiness felt. He could not recall the joyful abandon of his youth. It had been so long ago, another lifetime. Now all he felt was bitterness. His dreams were filled with regret, and he often awoke in a sweat, cursing himself for his impulsiveness.

Peter is dead, he thought. And nothing can change that. Not the idle gossip of friends, not all my hoping. My family is gone.

The reborn memories of his brother had brought to life the grief he'd thought he had buried all those years ago. He had believed he could control the anguish, but being back home was harder than he'd thought, as the nightmares attested to. Now he would have to push aside the memories again, to concentrate on revenge, the only thing he had left. Thank God, Farindale is not in residence, Logan thought. I would slit his throat on sight. His fists clenched.

"Yes!" he heard a voice call out. "Ask Peter Grey!"

Three

Logan froze. Tingles of bated excitement shot through his entire body. He thought for a moment that it was just his imagination. He thought for a moment that his ears were playing tricks on him. He whirled to search for the person who had said his brother's name.

She stood across the courtyard, her brown hair waving in the wind, her hands resting on a slim waist, a grin curving her full lips. Perhaps he was dreaming and this woman was an angel come to tell him that his brother was gone.

Then, she turned away and headed toward the gate to the outer ward. Anxiety filled him. Could Peter possibly be alive? he wondered, his breath suddenly tight in his chest. This woman might be my only link to him. Impulsively, he found himself racing after her, skirting carts and sheep to keep up with her, fighting to keep from losing sight of her.

Just as she left the inner ward and entered the outer ward, a man grabbed her arm, halting her movement. Logan came to an abrupt stop, his gaze sweeping over him. The man's immaculate, bowl-cut, blond hair made Logan's lip curl in distaste, as did the rich blue velvet jupon he wore, a sure sign that the pompous noble had not done a hard day's work in his life. The nobleman's eyes quickly scanned the courtyard, and Logan's instincts told him to stay hidden. He melted into the shadows of the stone wall.

"You're not at mass this morning," the man said to the woman after surveying the ward.

Even though the wind was blowing toward Logan, pushing their words his way, he still had to strain to hear them.

"Neither are you," she replied. "Perhaps it's an appropriate place for you to be . . . at your betrothed's side."

"There is much work to be done."

"You haven't lifted a finger yet, Graham."

"I didn't say *I* would do the work," the man she called Graham said with a smile.

The woman pulled her arm free. "No, you didn't. But I intend to do as much as I can."

"As always, m'lady, your heart is quite large where the peasants are concerned."

Logan saw her body stiffen, and he was surprised to find he was suddenly clutching his staff so tightly that his knuckles hurt.

Another man, a peasant wearing soiled breeches and a patched tunic, burst through the open gates. The man scanned the area, breathing hard, before running up to Graham and the woman, calling, "Lady Solace! Lady Solace! It's Dorothy!"

"Dorothy?" Solace echoed.

"She's having her baby!"

"Now?" Solace asked in disbelief. "She isn't due for a month."

"Agnes is with her in the village now. But no one else will stay."

As Solace turned to snatch the reins of a horse tethered to a wagon, a tidal wave of dread surged through Logan, so powerful that it left him momentarily incapacitated. Visions of his own impetuousness filled his mind. She was so young, as he had been. So naive.

Suddenly, he was bolting for her, seizing her arm.

The command was out of his mouth before he could stop it. "Don't go!"

She tried to pull her arm free, but his grip tightened. "What are you doing?" she demanded in astonishment. "Let go."

For a moment, Logan didn't speak. She had the largest green eyes he had ever seen. "Think about what you're doing," he finally ordered, forcing himself to look away from her dazzling eyes.

"I have no other choice," she responded.

"There are always choices."

Solace glanced coolly at his hand. After a moment, he removed it from her arm. She turned away from him and hoisted herself onto the horse, settling her petite form on its back. She glanced down at him, her green eyes cool with disdain. "I don't see you rushing to her aid," she snapped and spurred the horse.

"Solace, wait!" Graham called.

Logan watched Solace urge the horse into a run, her brown hair flapping behind her as the animal picked up speed. He heard Graham mutter a curse, then the man raced toward the stables. A second later, the noble was riding out of the castle after her. Logan watched as she disappeared down the road to the village, his stomach churning with dread and frustration. He knew Peter must have felt these same dark emotions as he'd watched him ride out of the castle. Logan set his shoulders, steeling himself against the twisting of his stomach. His jaw clenched so tight that his teeth ached. He had no time to be worrying about some impetuous woman. He had to find his brother.

But how was he going to do that when his only link to Peter was riding out of the castle?

* * *

The nerve of that falconer, Solace thought for the hundredth time, trying to stop me from coming to Dorothy's aid. She knelt beside the small pallet that Dorothy was lying on and smoothed the woman's dark hair away from her sweaty face. Poor Dorothy tossed her head from side to side, as if she were denying the fact that it hurt so badly, groaning as she moved. Solace cast a glance at the only other occupant in the room, the midwife Agnes. Her wrinkled face was puckered in concentration as she waited between Dorothy's spread legs.

A pounding at the door jarred Solace. Is Barclay's army here already? she wondered. But the voice that came from behind the door was not Barclay's, nor that of any other man to be concerned with. "They're coming!" Graham hollered from the other side of the wooden door.

Solace dipped a cloth into the basin of water beside the bed and dabbed the woman's forehead, whispering, "Don't worry, Dorothy. Everything will be fine."

Another pounding sounded at the door. "Lady Solace!" Graham cried out again.

"Agnes?" Solace implored, trying to keep the nervousness out of her voice.

"Not long now," the old woman answered in an excited voice. "I can see the head."

"Solace!" Graham shouted again.

Solace cast an annoyed glance at the door before squeezing Dorothy's hand and saying, "I'll be right back."

"Don't take long, dear," Agnes cautioned.

Solace rushed to the cottage door and threw it open. Graham stood before Solace with his fist raised as though he were going to pound on the wood again. His hazel eyes were filled with desperation and anger. Behind him, the street was vacant and grim, pale moonlight bathing thatch-roofed homes and wooden storefronts in a bleak light. Solace frowned at the sliver of moon. How had so much time slipped away? she wondered.

"They're almost here," Graham exclaimed. "I'm sick of standing here waiting for you. You've been inside all day."

"The labor's taking longer than it should," Solace explained.

"One of the guards passed and told me Barclay was just outside the town. They'll start burning the village any minute! We have to go!"

"I can't leave Dorothy," Solace insisted.

A flush of redness swelled into Graham's cheeks. "Well, I'm not staying! I won't give up my life just for some peasant and her whelp!"

Calm settled over Solace, and a fierce protectiveness filled her. "Then go. No one ever called you a brave man, Graham."

Graham's teeth clenched, and his hand tightened to a fist. "If you weren't a woman, I'd drive my sword through you."

"I don't think you'd have the courage," she whispered, her eyes narrowing.

Graham turned his back on her and headed for the horses.

"Hook the horse to the wagon!" Solace called after him. She cursed her free-speaking tongue as she closed the door. She could have gotten him to stay with sweet words and a stroking of that enormous ego. But she despised his weakness and cowardice. Couldn't he see how frightened she truly was? Yet even though she was scared, she could not leave this helpless woman alone in the throes of childbirth. Not even with Barclay and his army descending on her castle.

Barclay had picked their most vulnerable time to attack—while her father was away at Parliament, planning to conquer the French with King Richard and leaving her stepmother in charge of Castle Fulton. It just didn't make sense, Solace thought. Why was Barclay attacking Fulton? They had never done anything to him. He had never been an ally, but he had never been an enemy either. She wondered what he hoped to gain by laying siege to Castle Fulton. Did he need the lands? Were his crops failing?

A scream from the room behind her jolted her back to reality, and she rushed to Dorothy's side. She grabbed the cloth from the bedside and dabbed the woman's forehead, turning to look at Agnes. That woman's wise old eyes were centered on the new life about to be born. Solace wanted Agnes to leave and seek the safety of the castle. As she opened her mouth to tell her so, Dorothy's cry rent the air and Solace turned to whisper soothing words to her.

It wasn't long afterward that the first cry of life resounded in the room.

"Get them ready to move," Solace whispered hurriedly to Agnes. "I'm going to check on the wagon."

As soon as Solace stepped from the building into the night, the strong scent of smoke stung her nose.

Barclay was in the village!

She spotted the wagon and horse tethered near the side of the house and gave a brief prayer of thanks to God that Graham had not left them stranded. She whirled toward the house to find Agnes helping Dorothy from the building. Dorothy clutched a small baby girl wrapped in blankets tightly to her bosom as she hurried from the cottage. Solace grabbed Dorothy's arm, helping her into the back of the wagon. She turned to assist Agnes, but the woman was already easing herself into the cart.

Solace ran to the front of the wagon and climbed in,

lashing the horse, driving him down the vacant street toward the castle. She gripped the reins tightly, wishing desperately that some of the soldiers or mercenaries had accompanied her, but she had left in such a hurry that the only one who knew she had gone was Graham . . . and that falconer. If handsome looks were bravery, she would be as safe as a kitten curled up beside a roaring hearth.

The wagon hit a bump and Solace was almost knocked from her seat, but she held onto the reins with two hands and drove the horse on with a snap of her wrists. She quickly glanced over her shoulder into the back of the wagon to see Dorothy holding the baby to her breast, shielding the infant from the rough ride as best she could.

Smoke from the burning village swirled around Solace, blown by the fierce winds. The gusts whipped her hair wildly about her. She turned around to face the road, wishing she could make out the welcoming sight of an open drawbridge, but she was still too far away to see in the darkness. Her heart pounded in her chest. She had to make it. If not for her own sake, then at least for the sake of the mother and her newborn babe.

Logan paced the battlements, just as his father must have done all those years ago. He clenched and unclenched his hands. Graham had returned a few moments ago and announced that Solace was still in the village. Where the hell was she? Logan wondered. Around him, soldiers looked for Barclay's troops, but his gaze swept the road before the castle for a glimpse of the girl. In the far distance, a line of fire preceded the attacking army, a line that grew hotter and brighter as the torch-wielding warriors moved closer. Even the falcon at his shoulder constantly shifted position, darting its head this way and that, its large brown eyes wide and alert.

Lady Alissa stood at the walls not far from him. He heard her mutter soft curses beneath her breath. Her hair was hidden by a red-horned headdress, which made her look like the devil himself. Her eyes were narrowed with anger, her hands balled.

Had father been that angry with me? The thought entered Logan's mind unbidden. He tried to push aside his worry for the girl and concentrate on finding Peter. But he needed Solace to know where to begin. A muted curse slipped from his lips.

Alissa placed her fists on the stone wall, her narrowed eyes relaxing as determination filled them. Resolution squared her shoulders, and she raised her chin.

Logan felt the doom settle like a lead ball in the pit of his stomach. He knew the words she was going to speak, had wished many a night that his own father would have made the same command—to save the castle, to save his family.

She opened her mouth just as Logan whirled away in despair to glance at the road. In the soft glow of the moonlight, he spotted a wagon racing toward the castle. He breathed a small sigh of relief and closed his eyes briefly in thanks. But lady Alissa's words brought his eyes wide in shock.

"Close the gates," she said.

"She's there!" Logan shouted, pointing his finger at the wagon.

Alissa cast a dangerous glance at Logan, her brown eyes burning, then whipped her head to face her guard. "Do as I say," Alissa ordered. "Close the gates!"

Solace's wagon came racing out of the village toward Castle Fulton. Her heart stopped and her breath caught in her throat as she saw the drawbridge being raised! It had to be a mistake! Solace watched with horrified eyes as the drawbridge continued to rise, the heavy wooden planks now starting to take the form of an impenetrable door instead of the entrance to safety. The horse snorted gruffly as its hooves churned the ground, kicking up clumps of mud in their wake.

"M'lady!" she heard Agnes gasp from behind her.

"Get down!" Solace yelled back over her shoulder, afraid to take her gaze from the moat for even a second.

The thought of trying to leap the widening gap flashed through her mind, but she quickly realized how dangerous that would be, especially considering the new life lying cradled in a woman's arms a few feet behind her.

The horse raced forward, seemingly oblivious to the danger ahead, the fires burning behind it pushing it on.

Solace pulled back sharply on the reins, but the horse continued to charge forward, fear fueling its speed. "Whoa!" Solace cried out, her arms aching with the effort to keep a firm grip on the thick ropes clutched in her fingers.

The drawbridge continued to rise, revealing the dark waters of the moat hidden beneath it.

"Whoa!" Solace cried out again. She jerked hard on the reins, desperate strength empowering her effort, but the horse raced on.

The wide, deep gap in the earth loomed closer.

Four

"Look!" Agnes cried out from behind Solace.

Solace glanced up from the horse and watched with widening eyes as the drawbridge suddenly, miraculously, began to lower. The wooden planks moved closer and closer to the ground. Someone must have seen them approaching. She again tugged on the reins, but the fires burning in the village behind them pushed the horse on, rendering her efforts useless. They were now only a few dozen feet from the drawbridge. It was coming down slowly. Too slowly! It wasn't going to be down in time! The pounding of the horse's hooves thundered in her ears. She closed her eyes, giving a quick prayer for the baby.

Solace heard Agnes shriek as the wagon hit something and shook roughly from side to side. Then the sound reverberating in her head changed, growing even louder as hooves now pounded on wood instead of dirt.

Wood! She opened her eyes to see the castle entrance looming over her. They had made it! The drawbridge had lowered with only seconds to spare.

Solace maneuvered the horse beneath the gatehouse and into the outer ward, relief washing over her. As soon as the horse stopped, Solace leapt from the wagon, ignoring the outstretched hands of help from soldiers.

The moment her feet hit the ground, Solace raced to the back of the wagon. Agnes and Dorothy were already being helped from the cart by other peasants as Solace reached them.

Dorothy glanced at her, holding her squalling infant to her breast. "Thank you, m'lady. If it wasn't for you—"

"You must be exhausted," Solace interrupted, forcing a smile to her lips. "Go get some rest."

Solace watched Dorothy move away, a crowd of well-wishers surrounding the new mother. As Agnes cast Solace a weary grin of approval before following Dorothy, a proud surge of accomplishment swelled inside Solace. Then, just as quickly, the energy drained from her body. It had been an exhausting day. She turned toward the keep, intending to follow her own advice.

Suddenly, a sharp blow was delivered to her cheek by a horned demon! Shocked into silence, Solace could only face her stepmother with an open mouth, her cheek a bright red with the imprint of Alissa's rage.

"How dare you risk our lives?" Alissa snarled. Solace raised a hand to her stinging skin as Alissa continued, "If Barclay had gained entrance to Castle Fulton because of you, I . . . I . . ." She clenched her teeth with anger.

Solace could see the reined fury in Alissa's balled fists, and she slowly lowered her hand from her burning cheek, raising her chin defiantly before her stepmother.

". . . I would have seen you hung!" Alissa desperately, futilely, finished.

Solace tried to defend her actions. "Dorothy needed help. I knew—"

"You knew nothing except your own selfish needs. When it comes to the welfare of this castle and these villagers you will follow my strict orders, is that clear?"

Solace stood her ground. She had done nothing wrong. She had helped Dorothy and her baby.

"Is that clear?" Alissa demanded through clenched teeth.

Solace was not ready to concede to her stepmother. "What I did was not wrong," she insisted.

"You are a selfish, irresponsible girl," Alissa hissed. "Incapable of thinking about anyone but yourself."

Tears burned Solace's eyes, but she kept them in check. "Dorothy never would have made it to the castle if I hadn't gone to her," Solace answered softly.

"Then you are not only selfish, you are stupid," Alissa sneered. "Stupid to risk your life so easily." Alissa whirled away from Solace, her shoulders rigid, her feet slamming the earth with each step. Her blue samite dress stirred up dust about her feet, little whirlwinds that surrounded a mighty tornado.

When Alissa disappeared into the keep, Solace finally found the strength to move. She took a stiff step and saw that no one had yet tended her horse. She walked to the horse and lifted her hands to the bridle. She tried to remove it, but found that her hands were trembling. Solace glanced over the horse's mane at the castle wall. There, a line of peasants and soldiers stared at her. You should have been here to help with the preparations, a tiny voice inside her accused. But Solace refused to admit that what she had done was wrong. Dorothy had needed her help more than anyone.

Her stepmother always found fault with what she did. Nothing was ever right. Nothing she did was good enough. She had learned to live with that, to accept rejection and disappointment from her stepmother. The things she did were to please herself. Or to help others. Not for her stepmother. Not anymore.

Then why did that woman's words hurt so much? she wondered.

Solace clenched her hands into fists around the bridle.

Warm hands suddenly surrounded hers. She glanced up quickly to find charcoal eyes staring at her. The falconer eased the bridle from her fingers.

"Go," he murmured, and Solace felt the word through her entire body, like a tiny tremor.

She dropped her hands to her sides and stepped back. He wasn't looking at her any longer, but freeing the horse from the wagon. She watched the way his strong, capable hands unhooked and untethered the bridle and the reins, the way his dark hair waved about his shoulders in the soft breeze that blew over the castle walls, the way his shoulder muscles bunched and released beneath his tunic as he tended to the animal.

He stopped moving and turned to stare at her.

Solace smiled shyly like a small child caught in the act of reaching for candy. "Thank you," she finally said.

He didn't reply as he turned back to finish working.

Reluctantly, Solace backed up a few steps and turned away, moving across the courtyard toward the keep.

Somehow the falconer's kindness had taken the sting out of her stepmother's words. Still, she could not help but feel guilty about endangering so many lives. It was something she hadn't considered, but she knew she should have.

She brushed past guards stationed near the doorway and headed into the hall, moving deeper into the keep where the living quarters were. She moved down the torchlit hallway toward her room. She wondered why the falconer's touch had soothed her as it had. His hands were so much larger than her own. But his touch . . . it had been warm and gentle. She grinned at the strength it had given her, the sudden sense of security.

"You find strange things amusing," a thick voice from the darkness whispered.

Solace whirled, gasping, clutching her hands to her

heart. Guilt overwhelmed her, as if she had spoken her words aloud.

"Your cheek is still red with your stepmother's affection, yet you have a smile on your lovely lips." Graham stepped into the light of the flickering torch. Shadows slithered across his face like dark snakes. His blond hair blazed red with the light of the torch.

"You frightened me," Solace whispered, willing her pounding heart to slow. "And yet I should have expected to find you in the keep."

"Just protecting your sister," he said.

Solace thought she heard a mocking tone to his voice. She narrowed her eyes. Graham was betrothed to her sister for six months now. Six months too long in Solace's opinion. She didn't see what her sister saw in him. Graham was a coward, always hiding from battle, always hiring men to do his work. And there were rumors that he had been seen with more than one servant. But Beth professed to love him very much, and Solace was trying desperately to get along with him for her sake. Still, it wasn't easy.

"Yes," she murmured. "That's the perfect place for you. Hiding in her shadow." As soon as the words were out, she cringed inwardly.

She saw him rise up, stiffening under the insult; then she sighed slightly and brushed a lock of dark hair from her brow. "I'm sorry, Graham. You know I didn't mean that."

"Yes," he said after a short pause. "I suppose we're all a little tense. But you must tell me what you found so amusing a moment before. I could use a break from this accursed talk of siege."

Solace's eyes widened slightly. She couldn't tell him she had been thinking of the way the falconer touched her, the way he had soothed her with a simple look from those silver eyes. "I . . . I was thinking of something someone said earlier," she lied. She was never any good at lying and had to avert her eyes, hoping that he wouldn't see through her tale.

"I thought you might have been thinking of some sort of revenge against your mother," he said.

Solace's gaze snapped up to his, and her brows furrowed. He knew very well that she would never do anything to hurt Alissa.

He shrugged slightly, studying his nails. "After the way she degraded you in the courtyard."

Solace raised her fingertips to the mark on her cheek.

"It should have been you slapping her," he added in a whispered tone. "She was, after all, going to have you locked out of the castle."

Solace gasped. "She wouldn't do that."

"Oh, yes," he said. "She had given the order to close the gates, even though we all saw you heading for the castle."

Solace knew Alissa did not hold her in high regard, or even think of her as a daughter, but to do something so cruel was beyond even her. "But the gates were open. Surely she changed her mind."

Graham could hardly contain a grin. "No. She never changed her order. I'm not quite sure how they were opened. I assume you can thank the gate guard for that."

Solace stood dumbstruck, still not believing that Alissa would lock her out of her own home, leaving her to Barclay.

"You poor creature," Graham whispered, placing his hands on her shoulders. "If there's anything I can do for you . . ." He stepped a bit closer to her. "Anything at all, you need just ask."

A prickle of warning went through Solace. "That won't be necessary." He was closer to her than he should be, closer than she ever wanted him to be.

"Graham!" The voice came from down the hallway, and Solace whirled, grateful for the interruption. She stepped away from Graham and turned to see Beth running toward them. Her dark hair flowed behind her, shimmering softly in the torchlight. A samite gown decorated with red and gold embroidered leaves covered her tiny body. The warmth in her blue eyes hardened into cool disdain as her gaze moved from Graham to Solace. She turned away from Solace to hook her arm through Graham's. "I've been looking for you everywhere!"

"I've been speaking with your sister," Graham answered.

"Oh." Beth's words were clipped. "Hello, Solace."

Solace nodded to her half sister, feeling a chill settle around her. How nice it would be to have a sister with whom she could share her secrets. But now that seemed impossible. They had never been very close, and in the last year any semblance of sisterly affection had disappeared completely. A little over a year ago, Beth had been enamored of a young knight who, she said, had pledged his heart to her. She had met him at a Tournament at Court. Then, one fall day he had come to visit Beth at Castle Fulton. Beth had been so excited. It was the first time she'd allowed Solace to share her joy, to be a part of her life. Her half sister had planned to marry the young knight, Robert. Live happily with him, bear him many sons.

He rode into the courtyard with all his armor shining and banners flapping. Solace stood at her sister's side, sharing in Beth's excitement. But from the first moment Solace met Robert, she knew something was wrong. Beth was obviously so in love with the man, fawning all over him, that she was oblivious to the fact that he was not paying her the slightest bit of attention.

It wasn't but a week later that Solace was called in to

see her father. Beth was there, and it was obvious by her red eyes that she had been crying. Her father told her that he had sent Robert away. Solace had turned sympathetic, if confused, eyes to Beth. But when she went to comfort her, Beth had pulled away, snarling that she should not touch her. It was then that Beth proclaimed it was her fault. That Robert had fallen in love with Solace! That she had stolen him away from her!

Solace pushed the memory aside and moved away from Graham and Beth, feeling like an intruder standing before their linked arms, for Beth's narrowed eyes had told her she was not welcome. Solace still wished the two of them to be friends, to be real sisters, and she refused to give up, even in the face of Beth's chilly gaze. "I was just going to change, but afterward I'm going to the Great Hall," Solace murmured. She took a breath, adding hopefully, "Care to join me?"

Beth raised an eyebrow. "No," she answered and turned Graham away to lead him down the hall.

Solace watched them go, and something close to longing filled her soul. How nice it would be to be in love. Unbidden, the falconer's handsome features rose before her mind's eye. She glanced down at her hands where he had touched her, remembering the gentle warmth that had spread through her body as his flesh caressed hers.

How nice it would be to be in love, she again thought wistfully. A winsome smile spread over her lips as she headed to her room.

Beth pulled Graham into an alcove, a tiny arrow slit behind them letting in the only light, a pale sliver from the moon outside. She wrapped her arms around his neck, smiling up into his hazel eyes.

Graham let his hands roam up Beth's shapely figure until they cupped her breasts.

Suddenly, she pulled away from him and presented him with her back. "I've been finding you too much with my sister lately. If I didn't know better, I would say that you were chasing after her."

Graham pressed himself against her bottom, fully aware of the longing that ached just beneath his breeches. "You know there is no one but you, Beth," he cooed, touching her shoulders.

Again, Beth pulled away from him and turned to face him, her pout full and very practiced. "I wish I could believe you."

Graham lunged after her, pressing her back against the wall. "You can believe me. You know I want only you. I would do anything for you, my love."

"Prove it," she whispered.

He began to lift her skirt, his lips nibbling her neck.

She pushed against his chest. "I meant something different," she whispered.

Graham pulled slightly back, confused. Then a wolf-ish smile lit his lips and he began to turn her around, hiking her skirt over her bottom. "You want it like a dog this time, eh?"

"No!" she objected, shoving his hands away. She brushed past him to sit in the window seat. Her eyes flashed with dangerous ideas. "I was thinking . . . if it weren't for Solace, all of this would be ours," she said, indicating the castle. "She is the only one who stands in our way."

Graham quickly joined her. "We knew that when we were betrothed. It matters not to me," Graham exclaimed.

Beth looked at him slyly. "It doesn't? I know you asked Mother for Solace's hand before you asked for mine. Of course, Mother agreed, but Solace turned you down"

Graham gasped. "You know that?"

"I'm not a fool," Beth said. She rose and paced to the other side of the small alcove. "To have Castle Fulton would mean wealth and power for you."

"Beth, all I really want is you, I swear," Graham pleaded.

"Spare me your declarations of love. I care not." Beth turned to Graham, staring down at him haughtily. "Marrying Solace isn't the only way to get Castle Fulton."

Graham's brow furrowed in confusion.

"There is another way."

Five

The late night was disturbingly quiet as Solace walked toward the outer gatehouse. It was hard to believe that just outside the castle walls, thousands of men were preparing to steal her home. Somehow, it just didn't seem real.

She continued on through the courtyard. Her body was urging her to sleep, but thoughts wouldn't stop swirling about her mind. She still couldn't believe her stepmother had given the order to close the gates. But what really surprised her was that Hagen, the gate guard, had deliberately disobeyed Alissa's command, risking his life to help her. Why would he do that? She hardly even knew him.

She opened the wooden door and entered the gatehouse. Two soldiers were stationed near the doorway, both straightening at her entrance. They glanced at each other, and Solace saw the confusion in their gazes.

One of the men stepped forward, shifting his stance uneasily. "M'lady, did you come here alone?"

"Yes," Solace answered, a little baffled by the question. She had traveled to the gatehouse many times alone. And not once had any of the men questioned her.

"Is there something we can help you with, m'lady?" the other guard wondered.

"I'm going to speak with Hagen," she replied, turning to head up the spiraling stone staircase that led to the upper floor of the gatehouse. But then she halted, facing the men. "Is there something wrong?" she wondered.

The first guard ran a hand through his thick sandy brown hair. "Well, no. It's just that . . ." He cast the other guard a glance for help before continuing, ". . . with the Baron just outside the castle . . . well, maybe you shouldn't be walking around alone."

"He's outside," Solace explained, "not inside the castle."

The blond-haired guard bobbed his head. "Yes, m'lady."

Solace turned away from them, moving up the staircase to the second floor. She scowled. Were they truly worried for her safety? Or was it something else? She couldn't help but wonder at their strange behavior. She was safe in her own castle!

Solace entered the second-floor room, nodding to the two guards who stood near the door. They straightened to attention as she walked toward the gate guard.

Hagen was a head taller than Solace, his mass of moppy red hair thick and uncombed. Freckles splashed his cheeks. He stood as she approached him. "M'lady," he greeted with a bow of his head.

"Hello, Hagen," she said. "May I have a word with you?"

He nodded his head and they moved to the far corner of the winch room. As she crossed the room, Solace glanced at the wooden post around which thick ropes were wrapped, the mechanism used to raise and lower the drawbridge under Hagen's orders. She turned her attention back to the red-haired man next to her. Hagen had worked for her father for over ten years. He wasn't a particularly ambitious man, and it had surprised Solace that he had taken it upon himself to open the gates for her, disobeying her stepmother's direct order. "I'd like to thank you," she said softly.

"Me, m'lady?" he wondered.

"For opening the gates for me," she added.

"Oh, 'tweren't me, m'lady," he said, looking down at his boots. "I mean, I woulda if the order was given. Nothin' against you. It was just that . . ."

Solace's brow knit in confusion. "You didn't open the gate?"

"I did," he said. "But I was forced ta, if ya take me meanin'."

"I don't understand."

"I had closed the gate. Me heart was breakin', but an order is an order. When all of a sudden, this demon came charging up the stairs. He knocked over the two at the door and charged directly inta me. Said if I didn't open the gate he was gonna knock me teeth out." He shrugged. "I opened the gate."

"Who was he?"

"Don't know, m'lady. Never saw him before."

"What did he look like?"

"If ya don't mind me sayin', he looked like a bloody demon. Dark as night, except for those eyes. They seemed ta glow!"

Solace nodded slightly, a disbelieving grin twitching her lips. "Thank you," she murmured.

"I'm glad I could do it, open the gate that is," Hagen added. "I'd hate ta see ya hurt."

Solace nodded, calling forth a small smile. To whom did she owe her thanks? she wondered. And for what reason? Was it Graham? She almost laughed out loud. Go against Alissa? That was something Graham would never do!

"M'lady?"

Solace looked up at Hagen.

"Where's yer escort?"

"Escort?" she echoed. "I don't have one."

"Beggin' yer pardon, m'lady. I know it's not me place, but do you think it's safe ta be out alone?"

"We're in Castle Fulton," Solace replied, growing tired of the argument. "There is no safer place."

Hagen glanced at the two guards at the door. "We were informed early this evenin' that there is a murderer in the castle."

Solace straightened. "What?" she gasped.

"We were told to keep a watch out."

"The dungeon guard was killed, m'lady," one of the men at the door added.

Solace's mouth dropped open in shock. "Why wasn't I told?" she asked.

"Lord Harper said it wasn't necessary to worry the ladies," Hagen explained.

Solace's eyes narrowed. "Lord Graham Harper?" she gritted out between clenched teeth.

Steel gray eyes watched Baron Barclay's army solemnly through an arrow slit in the wood hoarding scaffold. The men positioned across the moat, well out of range of the castle's archers, continued construction on a trebuchet that when completed would hurl projectiles over the castle wall.

Earlier that day, messengers from Barclay brought terms of unconditional surrender to lady Alissa. She would have been a fool to surrender on such terms. He was sure that Farindale would hunt her down and kill her if she did. Many a lord would lose his life before losing his castle. Logan knew this from experience. He had been in more sieges than he had cared to think about. Still, the pay had been good, and more important, the loyalties and favors he had gained were invaluable.

The Baron had amassed a good-sized army. The line of soldiers and tents stretched as far back as Sullivan's Hill. Sullivan's Hill . . .

His mind drifted back to another army, another time . . .

Castle Fulton rose up into the sky around him, its gray turrets reaching for the crimson-painted clouds like thick fingers grasping for the safety of the heavens above. On the walkways of the castle wall, soldiers scouted the land for the coming army, their hard, callused fingers nervously tracing the hilts of their sheathed swords. Archers checked their bows, plucking at the strings, and inspected their freshly cut arrows. Around them, at the top of the castle walls, hoarding scaffolds were being built in preparation to drop hot, bubbling oil on any attackers.

He watched as a piercing cry drew the attention of one of the soldiers. The armored man swiveled his head to watch a boy chase after a sheep that had strayed from the flock being herded into the castle. Five other men were having great difficulty keeping the skittish animals in line. Logan looked away from the men to the large carts of food, hay and other supplies that filled the road leading into the castle. Villagers moved with quick desperation into the protection that the large stone walls of Castle Fulton offered.

Nearby another guard directed the incoming carts, his pointing finger darting in one direction, then another, shouting at the top of his lungs to be heard above the din. A small calico cat leapt off of one of these carts and raced through the outer ward, darting between the legs of Logan's horse. The gray-speckled horse whinnied and reared slightly, but he steadied him with a firm hand. He was a young boy of thirteen. His black hair lifted in a breeze that swirled in over the walls and slowly resettled onto his broad shoulders. He turned his gray eyes from the cat who disappeared into the inner ward to his brother who stood beside his mount.

"Don't do it, Logan," Peter begged placing a trembling hand upon the horse's neck.

A smile came easily to Logan's lips; his gray eyes sparkled like the edge of a freshly drawn blade in the setting sun.

"It's too big a risk," his brother insisted, his brown eyes filled with worry. *"You're being foolish."*

"Afraid, Pete?" Logan mocked with a cynical twist to his charming smile.

Peter straightened his shoulders, but refused to give in to the goading. *"You know what Father will say if he finds out."*

Logan shrugged, his black hair waving defiantly in the breeze as he cast his gaze toward the open gate and the steady stream of villagers entering. *"Then he won't find out."* He turned back to his brother. *"Will he?"* Peter turned away from Logan's hard stare. *"Don't worry, Pete. I just want a look. I'll be back before the sun sets."* He turned his steed and headed out through the outer ward gates and down the road into town.

"Be careful!" Peter called after him.

But Logan barely heard. His mind was already on the sight that would greet him. An army! In full plate mail! Riding huge war horses! He had never seen an army. How many knights were there? he wondered. How many foot soldiers? He had accompanied his father to many tournaments, but that was nothing compared to an army! He had to see them, just a peek over Sullivan's Hill. Then, he would return home . . .

But he never made it.

Quickly, he pushed the bitter memories out of his mind. Instead, he concentrated on Farindale's downfall. It wouldn't be long now. He just needed to find his brother.

And to do that he must find her. Solace. But how was he, a common falconer, going to impress the lady enough to get her to tell him where his brother was? Perhaps the best approach was the direct one. "Hello, m'lady. You don't know me, but I'm looking for my brother. Yes, we'd like to kill your father, but pay that no mind."

He groaned softly. How could he ask her when she was the *daughter* of his enemy? Perhaps he could say Peter was a friend. But what if he was locked in the stocks? How would it look for him to be searching for a man who was Farindale's enemy?

Perhaps he should just keep his mouth closed and his eyes and ears open. But where had that gotten him? He could be here for years!

The thought of soft hands and full lips rose in his mind. He cursed silently. The wretched beauty's image had plagued him the entire day. Her stubborn stance against her mother was admirable. And when the woman had struck Solace, a peculiar feeling of protectiveness had surged inside him. Logan had even found himself stepping forward.

And now, late at night, instead of trying to formulate a plan to find his brother, he was thinking of her large green eyes and wondering what her full lips tasted like.

Why did it have to be Farindale's daughter that he thought of? Why couldn't it be some wench who would sate his lusting so he could get on with his mission? Why couldn't it be her sister? She seemed willing enough, rubbing herself along the length of him, making it quite apparent she was more than interested in him. But he was not in the least attracted to her. He had seen her kind before, nobility with no honor, no loyalties. He found himself sneering at the thought of Beth. She was, indeed, beautiful. But her blue eyes held no warmth, no compassion, no sincerity. He could take her and enjoy it as much as taking a warthog.

Suddenly, the falcon on his shoulder shifted its weight slightly, and he could feel its claws press into the leather patch he had sewn onto his tunic. Logan glanced at it for a moment. Its brown eyes were wide and alert.

Logan glanced out of the slit in the scaffold, wondering what had caught the bird's attention. Barclay's soldiers continued their work on their siege machines. Logan took a step to the other side of the hoarding to peer over the crenel of the castle wall. His eyes scanned the courtyard below. Torches hung near the outer gatehouse, throwing patches of light into the deserted ward.

It wasn't until she stepped into a pool of light that Logan saw her exiting the gatehouse. He scowled. Now what would a lady be doing out this late at night? And why would she be in the gatehouse? What was Solace up to?

The next morning, Logan sat alone at the end of a table in the Great Hall, as always. The peasants never sat near him and his bird, leaving him in peace. Which was fine with Logan. Fewer people to have to be cautious of. A serving girl reached around him to refill his mug, then moved on down the table. He dipped a sop into his trencher and chewed on the porridge-soaked piece of bread. The falcon eyed the food with interest and Logan tossed him a small chunk of meat.

The falcon lifted its head, and Logan followed its gaze to see Solace marching up the aisle between the rows of tables that filled the Great Hall. He straightened on the bench as he noticed her tiny fists were clenched, her jaw tight, her eyes narrowed with anger. A grin twitched his lips and his eyes twinkled with amusement as he wondered who was going to be on the receiving end of her wrath. As she marched toward the head table, servants stepped out of the path of the approaching fury and hounds slunk under tables for cover.

She stopped just short of the head table, facing her stepmother, Beth and Graham. The conversation in the room gradually trailed off as everyone in the room waited to hear her flare of temper. Logan leaned forward, not wanting to miss a word. The falcon on his shoulder shifted position, it, too, looking toward the head table.

Solace clenched and unclenched her fists.

Slowly, Graham raised his gaze from the trencher of porridge before him. When his eyes came upon Solace, he smiled beatifically at her.

Solace stepped up on the platform that elevated the head table. "I should have you clapped in irons!" Solace exploded with a barely reined fury.

"Solace!" Alissa hissed.

Solace placed her clenched hands on the table, leaning toward Graham. "What gives you the right to command *my* guards not to tell me about a murderer?"

"A murderer?" Alissa blanched.

Logan froze, straining to hear the conversation as the entire room erupted in a flurry of astonished whispers.

"M'lady," Graham said calmly, "I was only trying to protect—"

"Protect my sister. Protect my mother. But I need no protection from you."

"What is this about a murderer?" Alissa asked, her voice hushed but firm.

"The dungeon guard was found with his head smashed," Graham replied.

The next few exchanges were washed out as murmurs of disbelief swept through the Great Hall. Logan clenched his fists, desperately trying to hear the conversation. The rumblings ebbed quickly, and he heard Solace ask, "Were there any prisoners missing?"

"No," Graham answered, leaning back in his chair. "That was the strange thing about it. The poor man wasn't even robbed."

Solace straightened away from the table. "Did any of the prisoners see or hear anything?"

Logan's hand closed around his mug of ale. If they said anything, he would have to make another, more dangerous visit to the dungeon. He lifted the mug to his lips. He drank the ale, but didn't taste it.

"None of them are talking," Graham said. "My dear, you needn't concern yourself with this. I'm handling it."

"You?" Solace gasped. "You couldn't handle a murderer if you held a sword to his throat!"

"Solace!" Alissa hissed.

"Solace, I'm here and I plan to help with the siege in any way I can," Graham said in a slippery voice.

"Then why aren't you helping guard the castle walls?" she demanded.

"I feel I can be more helpful inside."

"Solace," Alissa said, firmly, "that will be all. Graham is quite right. This is a man's job. You can't possibly handle the guards in a time of siege. Much less a killer. Good heavens, what would you do if you found out who it was?" As she laughed, Logan's spine stiffened. He couldn't stand her condescending tone. "Tell him to stop killing your people . . . please?"

Graham joined in the laughter.

Solace glared at her stepmother. "No," she whispered.

"Go, child," Alissa said, flicking her wrist as if swatting away an annoying fly. "Go practice your embroidery."

Solace stood motionless for a long moment. Logan felt her anguish. He felt her embarrassment. She should say something, he thought. Defend herself.

But she didn't utter a word.

Solace turned away and moved out of the Great Hall, holding her head high. Logan watched her go. Impulsively, he rose and strolled after her into the hallway outside the Great Hall. He found her pacing back and forth, her arms straight as pins, her fists clenched into balls. She was murmuring as she moved, shaking her head and twisting her features in a mockery of someone.

Logan leaned against the wall and crossed his arms. A grin came to his lips as he watched her stomp back and forth, a bloom of hot red coloring her cheeks. She was enchanting in her anger. His eyes devoured her slender form as he heard her mutter, "How dare he? Order my own men to keep secrets from me? My people are in danger!" He watched her storm five steps and spin like a little whirlwind to march the other way. She was one whirlwind he wouldn't mind being caught in.

"Practice your embroidery. I'd like to practice my embroidery—around your neck!" she whispered harshly.

Logan's grin widened into a full-fledged smile. She was spirited! He had to give her that.

"Thinking he could find a murderer!" she gritted out between clenched teeth. "He can't even find his own sword in a siege!"

Logan laughed out loud, his pleasure rolling from his throat in a low timbre.

Solace gasped and whirled to face him.

Logan pushed himself from the wall to approach her. Those brilliant green eyes flashed like precious emeralds caught in torchlight as she glared at him, the remnants of her anger seeping into her whiplash greeting. "Do you always spy on women?"

"Spy?" he asked in shock. Spying was something he had never been accused of where women were concerned. There were so many other things to do with them! Especially women with large green eyes and full, kissable lips. "No," he answered in a low voice.

Solace stepped away from him as a flash of unease crossed her features. "What do you want?"

A dangerous question, Logan thought. His gaze brushed her lips before rising to her eyes. "I came to offer my services," he said softly.

Solace frowned slightly. "Services?"

He would gladly offer her his services—any services—if only she would tell him where Peter was. "Protection."

"Protection?" Solace echoed in disbelief. "You're a falconer!"

"If there's a killer in the castle, it might be dangerous for you to be walking around alone in the courtyards so late at night."

Her eyes widened in surprise. "Have you been watching me?"

Logan's laugh was low. "No. I was in the courtyard and I saw you."

"Oh," she said, fidgeting slightly, averting her gaze at her erroneous assumption. "Well, thank you very much. But I'm safer in Castle Fulton than anywhere else."

The amusement suddenly left Logan. She was too naive, too trusting. "Don't be too sure. A murderer can be anyone. Someone you trust, even." He saw the change in her immediately. Determination clouded her eyes; her chin rose in defiance. He knew instinctively what the little spitfire planned to do. His brows furrowed. "You're going after him, aren't you?"

Shock rocked her body and she stepped away from him, bowing her head to conceal her thoughts. "Don't be silly."

His hand shot out, capturing her chin and lifting it until her eyes met his. Radiant orbs challenged him, dared him to contradict her. They were so vibrant, so full of life and courage. "Solace," he murmured. He'd hate to have to extinguish that life if she got too close to the truth. He dropped his hand. "Be careful."

She nodded once and backed away down the hall. Logan watched her go until she was swallowed by the darkness.

THE LADY AND THE FALCON

wise lady to ask no question were there
Any one they had no answer that was swelled up in the
throat

Six

Solace stared down at the map of Castle Fulton spread out on the table before her.

"All the outer walls are stationed with extra guards," Captain Montgomery said.

Solace watched the captain of the guard's finger trace an area on the map. She turned her gaze to him as he ran his hand over his blond mustache and down his beard. His brown eyes gazed intently at the detailed sketch for a moment before shifting to Solace. "I expect that the arrow attacks will start any time now, and it appears the trebuchet might be ready tomorrow, at the earliest. With any luck it will rain and slow the production."

"You've doubled the men at the gatehouse?"

The captain nodded. "And we have men in the store-rooms listening for sappers. No one's going to tunnel into Castle Fulton without us knowing about it."

"Well done, Captain," Solace congratulated. "I'm certain Barclay will have a very difficult time finding entrance to Castle Fulton."

"Thank you, m'lady," the captain replied.

"Has lady Alissa met with you?"

Montgomery nodded. "She didn't say anything. She knows nothing of protecting the castle."

"Keep an open mind to her suggestions, if she has any. And let's keep our meetings a secret."

Montgomery bowed. "As you wish, m'lady."

"A messenger was dispatched to my father with word of Barclay's siege?"

"He left as soon as we received word that Barclay's army was heading our way."

"Then I'm sure Father will be here with his army soon to stop all this madness, and that coward Barclay will flee into the dark hole where he came from. All we have to do is hold the castle until his arrival."

Montgomery studied the map for a long, quiet moment, his brow wrinkled in concern.

"Is there something else?" Solace wondered at his expression.

He hesitated for a moment. "I don't know what Barclay has planned, but it seems strange to me that he is not building a temporary housing for his men. Usually, by now a siege castle would have been constructed, but I see no sign of one. And they haven't erected any palisades. Something just doesn't seem right." He scowled deeply. "It's as if he doesn't expect to be there for very long."

Anxiety slithered up Solace's spine. "Well, let's just make sure he's wrong," she answered, trying to suppress the uneasiness that gripped her.

After attending morning services at the chapel, Solace strolled into the outer ward beneath a gray sky. The air was fresh with the hint of coming rain. She missed Gwen terribly. She had no one to discuss her plans with. But she understood why Gwen and her father had left Castle Fulton when they'd heard the siege was imminent. They didn't want to be trapped in the castle for months. But that didn't prevent Solace from missing her friend.

As she walked the grounds, she stopped before Tom Reed's pig pen. He was busy feeding a bucket of slop to his sows. She glanced at the nearby wall of the castle, shaking her head and scowling. A simple fence for the pigs wasn't enough. Solace knew that she had to prepare the castle and her people for the arrows and boulders she knew would soon fly over the castle walls.

"It won't do," she said, moving to Tom's side. He glanced up at her. "One arrow attack and the pigs will be slaughtered," she continued. "You have to build an enclosure for them with a sturdy roof."

Tom nodded. "Very well, my lady."

"If you need tools or help, ask Ned," she added.

"M'lady?" Tom called, then hesitated for a moment. "Do you think the Baron is going to try to starve us out, or do you think he's really going to attack?"

Solace stared at him, sympathy tugging at her heart. He had no way of knowing what was happening beyond the walls other than the exaggerated tales that uninformed gossip produced. "We have to be prepared for either," she replied. "So you keep those pigs safe. Our lives could depend on it."

Tom nodded.

Solace continued her stroll through the ward. Her hair was braided behind her, and the dress she had picked out was a simple brown cotton smock with a beige sideless surcoat. It was comfortable, and Lillian couldn't complain too much if she ripped it. She knew she had a lot of work to do today.

Solace lifted her head, and her gaze came to rest on the closed drawbridge, the lowered portcullis. What was once an inviting entrance teeming with visitors was now a formidable blockade, barring the access of any travelers. Solace wondered where the wandering monks would stop on their pilgrimage to the Abbey of St. Michael now that Fulton's gates were closed. She looked around the ward, noticing the absence of the brown-cloaked monks. She felt a surge of anger toward Barclay. Not only had he driven Gwen and her father away, but the monks had also fled. The castle didn't seem whole without them.

She glanced toward the keep and the dungeon. She had meant to get to the dungeon and speak with some of the prisoners, but had not had an opportunity to do it yet.

Solace rubbed a hand over her eyes. She had spent half the night lying awake in her bed. A killer in Castle Fulton. It could spell doom for them. Her people needed to be protected. She had to find him. Her gaze swept the crowd of peasants and soldiers around her. She knew most of the people, and those she didn't know by name, she at least knew their faces. Had Barclay somehow bribed someone? The thought made her scowl. Even though she knew the attraction of coin was strong, she liked to believe that her people and men were loyal and they wouldn't betray Fulton so easily.

But strangely, it wasn't the thought of a killer that had kept her awake. It was the offer of protection. Protection proposed by someone with deep gray eyes.

She wiped a strand of hair from her eyes as her gaze swept the outer ward. She saw the falconer immediately. He stood a head above everyone and wasn't hard to miss as he spoke with old Ben across the courtyard. The falcon perched majestically on the leather patch sewn onto the shoulder of his brown tunic.

A man carrying an armload of wood toward the kitchens crossed Solace's vision. She leaned her head to the side, looking around the man to get a better glimpse of the falconer's powerful physique. Even when he was standing still, the muscles in his arms strained against his tunic. A hot flush spread through her body as she remembered the feel of his hands on hers.

Then, she saw him turn slightly and followed his gaze to see Beth heading in his direction. Her half sister wore the lowest cut dress she had, a pale blue velvet to match her eyes. Her dark hair was curled tightly over her ears in the latest fashion. Beth held out a hand to the falconer, and he promptly took it and brought it to his lips. Solace had a sinking feeling in the pit of her stomach. Disappointed, her shoulders slumped. Was there no man who could resist Beth's beauty?

Old Ben had moved away from the two. Solace could only see Logan's back, his rich, dark hair rivaling the darkest feathers of the falcon on his shoulder.

Beth raised a hand to touch the falcon. The bird nipped at Beth's fingers. Solace found some satisfaction as her half sister quickly withdrew her hand. Serves her right, Solace thought, and was surprised at her own viciousness.

Suddenly, the falcon spread its dark wings and took flight, screeching loudly.

A cry went up from one of the guards stationed on the battlements.

Solace's grin slipped a notch as she saw every muscle in Logan's body tense. He turned and their gazes locked. Solace read the warning there, the alarm. Then, suddenly, a *whooshing* filled the air. She quickly lifted her head to see a swarm of arrows blanketing the sky, heading straight for them!

Seven

Shouts of warning crescendoed around Solace as the arrows descended on their deadly paths. Screams of pain and cries of death rose from all around her. An arrow landed in the ground beside her, scattering the chickens in the coop. A mad dash followed as the villagers raced for the safety of the inner ward.

Instinct told her to run. Instead, she glanced over her shoulder to see the falconer hurrying Beth through the open gates that led to the inner ward.

Solace followed the crowd. Then, she saw a young woman screaming, bending over an older man who had an arrow sticking out of his chest. Solace recognized the miller and his daughter, Jenny. She dodged the peasants running for cover and moved toward the fallen man. Jenny's outstretched hand was smeared with blood, her tear-filled eyes pleading with Solace. Solace turned her gaze to the miller. The blood on Jenny's hand was not from the arrow wound, but from the blood the miller was coughing up.

"Go to the inner ward," Solace ordered Jenny, bending over the miller.

"But my father—" the girl sobbed.

"Go!" she ordered. When Jenny hesitated, Solace turned to her with kind eyes. "I'll stay with him." She wiped some of the young woman's tears from her cheeks before urging her toward safety with a gentle shove.

As soon as the girl was moving, Solace turned her gaze back to the miller. She had seen sword wounds and arrow wounds before, and she knew enough to realize that bleeding from the mouth almost always preceded death.

The miller coughed again, splattering her dress with blood. She took his hand in hers and smoothed some hair back from his forehead. His eyes locked with hers for a long moment, his hand tightening convulsively around hers, before his eyes glazed over and he went limp, his hand slipping from hers. Solace stared at the man for a long moment. Then she lifted a shaking hand and wiped it across his brow in a final good-bye.

Suddenly, she was pulled up . . .

. . . into the arms of the falconer! His gray eyes stared intensely at her for a moment, and strangely, the look calmed her racing heart. Then, he pulled her after him, grabbing a large wooden half-barrel and dumping the water out as he moved. Before she knew what was happening, he shoved her against a building and lifted the barrel before them as a protective barrier. She jumped as an arrow slammed into it, its metal tip erupting through the wood inches from her face! She stared at the sharp, deadly arrowhead for a long moment, fear closing around her heart in an iron grip. She turned a terrified gaze to the falconer.

He threw the useless half-barrel to the ground and pressed her back against the wall, shoving her there with his body. Solace pressed her cheek against his chest and squeezed her eyes closed as he cocooned her head in his arms. She heard the quick beating of his heart, felt the rapid rise and fall of his chest beneath her cheek. Her fingers curled into his tunic, clenching it tightly in her trembling fists.

Loud thunks sounded to her left and right.

Then the falconer pulled away from her. He grabbed her arm and bolted for the inner ward. Solace couldn't match his large strides. If he hadn't been holding her arm, she would have stumbled and fallen. Finally, they dashed inside the inner ward and the gates closed behind them.

Dorothy ran up to Solace, crying, "M'lady! Are you all right?"

The falconer released Solace's arm, and as she turned to thank him, he melted into the shadows. Solace opened her mouth, but a protective crowd of peasants encircled her, cutting her off from him, so her gratitude went unspoken. She anxiously searched the darkness near the wall, but the falconer was gone.

Logan watched the peasants convene around Solace. Like bees to honey, he thought. At least she was all right. And he was surprised that he meant it.

He turned away and moved toward the mews. The falcon floated down from the skies to perch again at his shoulder. He knew that eventually he'd have to seek out the lady Solace and somehow gain her confidence. But he would have to tread carefully. Suspicions were running high since the dungeon guard was found slain. Even old Ben had been looking at him strangely. He would have to wait a few more days.

It will give me time to think, Logan thought. Perhaps too much time.

The image of long dark hair, a defiant upturned chin and shapely body rose in his mind. He cursed silently. Why did Solace have to be so damned. . . . He shook his head fiercely. She was the enemy. She was a Farindale. Still . . .

Fool, he berated himself. He knew he had risked

enough by opening the gates for her. And then, later, he had been ready for a fight, waiting for the castle guards to come and imprison him. But it had not happened. Somehow, lady Alissa had not seen fit to have him clapped in irons for disobeying her direct command. Somehow . . .

He entered the courtyard that housed the mews. Old Ben had the door to the small house that sheltered his prize birds open and was sweeping out droppings and uneaten bits of food. Logan turned and moved toward his small room which was attached to the mews, hoping he could sneak by old Ben. But the man turned to him, calling out. Logan winced. The old man had the blasted hearing of a falcon.

"Out strollin' about again, hey?" the old man asked, scratching his stubbly chin as he approached. "Yer no falconer," he mumbled for the thousandth time.

Logan hid his irritation easily enough. The old man had been suspicious of him from the beginning. But despite his annoying habit of talking too much, the old man was an honest worker and Logan respected him for that. Old Ben worked diligently to keep the mews scrupulously clean and the falcons well fed.

"Are the birds all right?" Logan asked.

"Birds," old Ben grunted. "Me *darlin's* are fine. No thanks to ya. Where were ya? Out whorin'?"

Logan stopped, his back straightening. He had never needed to pay for favors that were freely given. The old man is just irked because I wasn't here with him to protect his *darlin's* from the arrow attack, Logan thought. He turned to Ben, but said nothing.

Old Ben snorted. "Ya know we're in a siege. Need every good sword arm we can get. 'Cause that's what I think you do."

The remark unnerved Logan and he had to turn away, moving toward his quarters.

"It's nothin' ta be embarrassed about. Whatever ya done before coming here is history. Ain't nothin' ta me. 'Sides, I said it before, I'll say it again. Ya ain't no falconer, even if ya do go round with that beauty on yer shoulder."

Logan ignored the old man and continued to his room. It was a small room, not much bigger than a stall. No better than a horse would have, Logan thought grimly. And colder, too. He slept on a bed of old straw in the corner of the room. At least it's private, he thought as he shut the door on old Ben's harangue.

The bird immediately flew to a small wooden perch Logan had carved for it. It fluttered there, watching him with those round brown eyes. He lit a candle and placed it on a table beside the bed. Feeling the bird's gaze on him, Logan glanced impatiently at it. "What are you looking at?" he demanded. But there was no answer. It just continued to watch him.

Of course old Ben was right. He was no falconer. But it was the best disguise he could come up with. And it had worked well enough to get him back into Castle Fulton. He was grateful for the bird's presence, if only because it had helped him fool lady Alissa into hiring him.

Logan sat down beside the candle and removed the dagger from his waistband. He picked up a stone from the floor and ran it along the edge of the blade.

For some reason, his senses were keen now. Perhaps it was the arrow attack. He ran the rock against the blade again.

For some reason, his nerves were on edge. Perhaps it was the battle lust that stirred his blood. The rock sheared across the metal.

Or perhaps it was the soft curves that had pressed against his chest. The lingering scent of roses that filled his nose. The green eyes that radiated enough heat to burn his very soul.

He brought the rock up too far, scraping his knuckles. "Damn," he muttered and shook his hand as burning engulfed it. He stared at his scraped knuckles, allowing the burning to fill his body, to cleanse it of all thoughts but his mission. He had to find Peter. Nothing else mattered.

He put the stone down and picked up a piece of wood. He turned the rough bark over in his hands and studied it for a moment. The crude outline of a girl was etched into the thick branch. He pressed the freshly sharpened dagger to the wood and shaved off a piece near the arm, giving it a slender curve.

Nothing else mattered, he told himself again.

Solace sat in the Great Hall, staring at the trencher of food before her, but not really seeing it. She turned a roll over in her hand again and again. She had eaten late, well after the sun had set. It was the first time she had gotten a break from attending the wounded and comforting the families of the dead. Four people had been killed in the attack, including the miller.

Guilt filled her throughout the day as her mind refused to dwell on the dead and the wounded. To her dismay, her thoughts continued to dwell on steel eyes and the persistent sensation of a hard chest pressed tightly against her breasts. The thoughts were distracting, annoying and . . . totally overpowering.

She wiped a strand of hair from her eyes. She hadn't even had an opportunity to thank him. Solace rose, setting aside her meal, and moved out of the Great Hall. It was late, but maybe he'd still be awake.

She left the keep and headed for the mews. The moon had risen, giving the empty inner ward an eerie, deserted look. As she passed the mews, the silence of the night was loud in her ears; even the falcons were still. She moved toward the sleeping areas next to the mews and entered the small building. She stood in the narrow entranceway, first glancing at the closed door to her left, then to the one on her right. One room would house Old Ben, the other the falconer. She realized that she didn't even know his name. A resolve filled her. She would find out his name. Now. But she paused between the doors. Which one? she wondered. Which was his? She looked at each door as if a simple glance could tell her. Then, taking a deep breath, she raised her fist and knocked on the door to her right. The door creaked open slowly. Solace stood with her hand raised, staring into the darkness of the room. "Hello?" she called, her voice barely above a whisper. The quiet stretched on.

She tried to see into the room, but blackness blanketed it. "Ben?" she queried. She reached out to touch the door. Something seemed strange. Why was the door open? Maybe Old Ben was sick or hurt. Solace eased the door open and stepped into the room. "Is anyone here?"

She stood for a long moment, waiting for her eyes to adjust to the darkness, but without windows it was almost impossible. Then, she noticed a stray moonbeam that shone in through two warped pieces of wood. She stepped into the light. The thin sliver of moonlight illuminated a small table, and Solace could see a candle and flint sitting on its surface.

She lit the candle. As the flickering light spread over the small room, the cloak of darkness fell from it and her gaze moved over to the sleeping area. The bed, a pile of hay covered by a thin blanket, was empty. Beside it was a sack tied shut with a rope. But it wasn't until she noticed the black-winged falcon sleeping on its perch that she knew she was in the falconer's room.

A strange shiver shot through her. I should leave, she thought. I shouldn't be here. She bent to blow the candle out, but a flash of light from the hay caught her attention and she halted. She turned her head to gaze in confusion at the hay where the falconer slept. Was it fire? she wondered. Something was shining dully in the light. But it didn't spread like fire. It reflected the candlelight back at her. She took a step toward the bed, reached out and carefully shifted the straw. For a long moment she could only stare at what she had discovered.

It was the blade of a highly polished sword. What would a falconer be doing with a sword? A shiver of apprehension coursed through her as she pushed the hay farther away from the weapon, revealing the full length of the sword. Solace picked the weapon up, needing two hands to lift its weight, and placed it on her lap to study it. The leather grip covering the handle was well worn. A red jewel adorned the bottom of the handle, its deep color absorbing the candlelight, giving it a lustrous glow. Just above the guard, etched in the silver of the blade, was a crest. Two crossed swords over a full moon. Solace frowned slightly. She had seen that crest somewhere before. But where?

Again the question came to her mind: what was a falconer doing with a sword? Was he a thief? Or a fighter?

Her eyes shifted to the weapon. The sword was beautiful, polished so highly that she could see her reflection in the flat part of the blade. She ran her finger lightly along the side of it. So smooth, she marveled. So . . . sharp!

She pulled her finger away with a start. The blade cleanly cut her skin, leaving a smear of blood along the sword's flawless edge. She stuck her finger in her mouth.

Suddenly, she heard a rustling sound behind her. She shoved the sword back beneath the hay and stood up, whirling to see the falconer standing in the doorway.

THE LIGHT AT THE END... ???

...the floor... Since ... She stood ... has risen in the
... ???

... ... she ... a rustling sound behind her. She
... turned ... back ... saw the ... of ... flashed by
while trying... the lamp at standing on the dresser.

Eight

"What are you doing here?" Logan demanded.

Solace stood motionless, frozen like a rabbit knowing it's been spotted by a bird of prey.

He closed the door behind him, his gaze raking over her, taking in her pale expression, her wild, loose hair, the way she was standing near his bed. He knew an instantaneous, unwanted, stirring in his loins.

"The door was open. I . . . I thought something was wrong," she finally said.

Logan studied her face for a moment; her eyes seemed to be larger than normal, full of guilt. But they were still the most beautiful eyes he had ever seen. It was as if someone had stolen the magic of the sea and locked it in her eyes.

He forced himself to turn away, quickly scanning the room, but nothing seemed to be amiss. He looked back at Solace. "What do you want?"

"I was looking for you. I wanted to thank you. I meant to do it earlier, but—"

"Thank me?" he echoed. His eyes narrowed.

"For saving me," she added quickly.

He watched the way she nervously twisted her hands before her. "And you snuck into my room to do this?"

"I already told you the door was open. I thought Old Ben might be hurt or—"

"So you just walked right into my room?"

"I didn't know it was your room," she insisted.

Logan frowned at her. "Couldn't this wait until morning?"

She shuffled her feet. "I've been so busy all day that I feared I would have even less time tomorrow," she answered, gazing up at him from beneath lowered eyelashes. "And I did want to thank you."

The shaft of moonlight slanted across her large eyes, making them glow with an irresistible innocence. He took a step forward and found himself before her. The scent of roses floated to him, enveloping him in her sweet fragrance. His shadow erased the candlelight, and for one mad moment he wished he could see her eyes again.

"What kind of gratitude are you offering?" he wondered, his voice deep and husky.

Solace opened her mouth to answer, but before she could say a word, Logan placed his hands on her shoulders, gently brushing her silky hair aside. He felt her sharp intake of breath, the press of her breasts against his chest as he stepped forward, drawing her against him.

Suddenly, his boot caught on something. He glanced down to find the hilt of his sword sticking out of the hay. He looked up to find her head bent, her eyes focused on the sword at their feet. When she lifted her gaze to his, he saw a sudden flash of fear flare in her bright green eyes.

Without warning, Solace shoved him aside and bolted for the door. He quickly recovered, spinning toward the door. In one stride he crossed the room, moving with the agility of a warrior. Solace barely opened the door before he slammed it shut from behind her.

"Here to thank me, eh?" Logan growled.

Again, she pulled at the door, but against his strength she was no match.

"What do you want?" he demanded. "Why are you here?"

Suddenly, she straightened and turned to him. Her eyes flashed with defiance. "What are you hiding?"

He slapped his other palm against the door, trapping her between his arms. He leaned closer to her, bringing his face only inches from hers. He could all but smell her fright. He could almost feel her heart beating wildly. "You play a dangerous game, lady Solace."

"Who are you?" she demanded, even though her body trembled.

He had to admire her strength, her spirit, the way her eyes sparkled in the candlelight. He leaned closer, without touching her. Didn't she realize the danger she was in? Why wasn't she pleading with him to spare her life? "The falconer," he whispered.

He watched her swallow hard, the way her delicate throat worked. "Falconers don't have swords," she answered breathlessly.

"And snooping doesn't befit a lady," he retorted.

"I wasn't snooping!" she insisted. "I came to thank you!"

"Then how did you find the sword?" Logan wondered, a mocking sneer curving his lips.

He watched conflicting emotions dance across her lovely face. She immediately opened her mouth to retort, but then a frown creased her brow and she clenched her teeth. Her green eyes flashed with resolution. When she finally spoke, her voice soft, she was begrudgingly relinquishing victory. "I didn't mean to snoop." She dropped her head and wouldn't look him in the eye. "I'm sorry."

Logan's suspicion slipped a notch at her admission. It took courage to admit fault. Not many would acknowledge it. But she had seen the sword, and it had his crest on it. Did she know who he really was? Why he was here? "Let's talk about why you're really here."

Her eyes jerked up to his, and Logan found a moment of delight at seeing those shimmering, heated orbs again. He wanted to kiss that thin-lipped anger into full-blown desire. He wanted to see what those magnificent eyes looked like in the heat of passion. He wanted her to admit that she came into his room in the middle of the night to feel his kisses, his hands, his . . .

"Very well," she said quietly. "I really do appreciate what you did for me this afternoon. You risked your life to help me."

"That's not what I meant," he said.

"But that's why I'm here," she replied.

Logan narrowed his eyes. She was too dangerous. He couldn't afford to have someone discover who he was before he found his brother. He lifted a hand from the wall and moved it toward her neck. Instead, the traitorous hand ran a finger over her cheek. He marveled at the chiseled perfection of her face. His gaze shifted from her cheek to meet her stare. She was watching him in silence with daunting emerald eyes.

What the hell was he doing! Angry, he pushed away from her with a snarl. "Go!" he commanded. He expected to hear the door open and close quickly, to be left standing alone.

She whirled to do just as he expected, but suddenly she was still, her hand on the handle of the door.

Slowly, he lifted his eyes to find her still there. Oh, he thought with a groan. She was tempting him. He could just reach around her smooth, delicate throat and run a kiss . . . a *dagger* across it. She wouldn't even know what had happened. He could just . . .

"Thank you," she whispered.

The sincerity in her voice froze him. It really was why she'd come. She had wanted to thank him.

Then she opened the door and was gone, fleeing into the darkness.

Logan stared at the space she had just occupied. He was a fool. He had risked his freedom by opening the castle gates for her and now he was risking his life by letting her go. Surely she would sound an alarm, call the guards' attention to him.

Disgusted, he sat on the side of the bed, staring at the sword. He pulled it from the straw with one hand, holding it before him. What is happening to me, Father? he wondered as he stared at the sword's gleaming surface. She taints me like a poison, casts a spell over my very flesh. I should keep only my mission in my mind, be pure like this sword.

He turned the blade over, and his eyes narrowed at what he saw. A thin line of dark red on the edge of its surface. Even the sword thirsts for her blood! Logan's eyes rose to the door, to the path Solace had just taken. Then why did his body hunger for something else?

Nine

"I couldn't see much, m'lady," the voice from behind the dungeon-cell door said. "Me old eyes ain't what they used ta be. And that torch was so bright."

Solace nodded, listening to the prisoner's tale. After awakening from a fitful night's sleep, a sleep filled with falcons and silver lightning and horrific beasts lurking in the shadows of the castle, she had immersed herself in the task of finding the murderer. She had come to the dungeon to ask the prisoners about the guard's death. "Was there anything different about him?" she asked the old man in the cell. "Anything at all?"

There was a long silence, and Solace glanced over her shoulder at her escort lounging against the dungeon wall, half hidden in the darkness. When the old man began to speak, she turned her attention back to the door. Two bloodshot eyes gazed at her through the small opening in the wooden door. She could see several pustulant sores ringing the wrinkled skin around his eyes.

"He did carry some sort of stick," the old man said.

"A stick?"

"Aye, sort of like a rod."

"A staff," the man standing against the wall supplied, pushing himself from it into the circle of light cast by the flickering torch on the wall. His brown, bowl-cut hair shimmered in the light. He wore chain-mail armor over his body that cast little pools of reflected light on the murky walls of the dungeon. A sword was strapped to his waist.

"Yes, yes. That's what it was," the old man beamed.

"That must've been how he killed the guard," the man said, leaning close to Solace, reaching out to pull her away from the leper.

Solace shrugged off her escort's hand. "Did he ask for anything? Did he want anything?"

The old leper's eyes narrowed. "I think he was looking for someone. He was calling for someone."

"Who?" Solace wondered.

The prisoner shook his head. "I can't remember who."

Solace scowled. "And you can't remember anything about how he looked?"

"Oh, my lady, he coulda been anyone. Anyone 't all. Except . . ."

Solace placed a hand against the door as if that might coax him.

"Except that he was rather big."

"Heavy?" Solace supplied.

"No. Strong. And tall."

The man accompanying Solace walked to her side as if to protect her. There was confusion in his eyes. He held up a hand about a head taller than Solace. "This big?"

The prisoner shook his head. "No."

The man lifted his hand until it was at his own height. "This tall?"

"Yes," the prisoner said, nodding.

Solace turned to the man beside her. He gazed at her for a moment, then shrugged.

"Thank you, Ed," Solace said to the prisoner. "If you think of anything, anything at all, let the guard know and he'll call me. And don't worry, Ed. As soon as the siege is over I'll make sure you're taken care of."

"Bless you, m'lady," he whispered.

Solace left the dungeon, escorted by her companion. When they entered the keep, her friend spoke. "You're not taking what he said seriously, are you?"

"Why shouldn't I?" Solace wondered. "We've questioned everyone else. He's the only one who saw the killer."

"He's a thief and a liar, Solace!" the man cried. "That's why he's been in the dungeon for the past seven years. You can't trust what he says."

"He's a leper now. And he is very old," Solace said. "He wouldn't lie. I told him I'd free him even if he had nothing to tell me. There's no reason for him to lie."

"I still wish you wouldn't pursue this. It's dangerous, Solace."

"I know. And I promise I'll be careful."

"It's not enough to be careful. This is a murderer. He's already killed the dungeon guard. He might very well kill you, too, if you get in his way."

Solace stopped to face her friend, staring earnestly into his eyes. "No one is safe until we find him."

The man groaned softly. "There is no use talking to you when you get like this. Just promise me that if you find out who this killer is, you'll tell me and you won't go after him alone."

She smiled gently. "I promise. I'll let you protect me and guard my life."

The man softly kissed her on her cheek. "I hate it when you make me worry about you like this. And lately you've been doing it far too much."

"You sound like my father," she chastised playfully.

"If he were here, you wouldn't be doing this."

"If he were here, I wouldn't *have* to be doing this."

The man smiled sadly. "He's been away for a long time."

Solace nodded, an ache tugging at her heart. She missed her father. She whimsically remembered the way his smile curved his droopy mustache. She wondered if the gray peppering through his dark hair had completely spread over his head yet. The few letters he had sent her had been filled with tales of court intrigue, giving only glimpses of the man—the father—she remembered. Yes, she mused silently. He had been away for a long time.

"I have to take my post now," the man said, jarring her from her reverie. "Stay out of trouble."

"Thank you, Peter," she said and watched him walk away.

She thought about Ed's description of the murderer. A strong man. A tall man. Peter's height. She scowled, glancing down the path Peter had taken. Most of the guards were shorter than Peter and almost none were as strong. And none of them, not one, had a staff.

Solace frowned, trying to think. But suddenly the memory of hot hands on her shoulders invaded her mind. She gasped, recalling cold silver eyes staring at her with forging-hot intensity. She had been fighting the images all day, burying them beneath her duty.

Something pulled at the back of her mind, demanding her attention. The image of the crest on the falconer's sword loomed in her thoughts again. She had drawn it on a piece of paper . . . two swords crossed over a full moon. She had seen it before, she was sure of it. But where? She wished desperately that Gwen were still here so she could talk about her turbulent emotions with her.

Solace paused for a moment, her hand outstretched for the handle of her chamber door. She had so much to do. She needed to see to the wounded, had to help the villagers whose animal pens had been damaged in the arrow attack, needed to meet with the servants about the rationing of water and food. She had to find out who the killer was. Then why did she want to return to the mews so badly?

Solace whirled and headed away from her room toward the spiral staircase at the end of the corridor. So much to do. People depending on her. She took the stairs upward. But she needed to think. She needed to be alone. She needed to sort out these new emotions, these strange feelings.

The dust parted beneath her feet, trailing her like the wake of a boat, as she moved down a shadowy hallway. Spiderwebs dangled from the top corners of the door at the end of the hallway. The servants all believed ghosts of the dead lived behind the massive doors. But not Solace. Talk of ghosts was nonsense. She liked coming here because she knew no one else would dare set foot in this room. She stared at the heavy wooden doors, studying the intricate carvings hewn into their surface, an elaborate scrollwork of heraldry shapes and symbols. As she pushed the huge double doors open, they creaked in protest.

Before her stretched a long room. Soldiers lined the wall in silent effigy in the forms of plate-mail suits and pictures of long-dead fighters.

Solace swept into the room, unmindful of the ancient warriors. The sun's rays reached through a large window at the opposite end, stretching across the floor like fingers. She approached the window.

Before her, Fulton stretched, unblemished lands of rolling hills. At this height, she could barely see Barclay's men below. If she tried hard enough, she could almost imagine that it was just another beautiful day, that there wasn't a horde of soldiers below her, that her people weren't wounded and hurt. Solace sighed. No matter how hard she tried, she couldn't escape the siege. All she wanted was to clear her mind, to relax enough to think. Who could the murderer have been looking for? Why was he desperate enough to kill? Would he do it again? She could not let his identity escape her.

A creak sounded behind her and she whirled, her eyes scanning the room. Had someone followed her? But there was no one in the room. That was odd. She shrugged slightly and turned back to the deceivingly serene sight before her.

I suppose anyone would be jumpy with this siege going on, she thought to herself. There was always risk of infiltration and . . .

Footsteps. Solace turned. But the large room was empty. Not a soul in sight. Her heart was pounding in her chest as she took a step away from the window. Her gaze swept the pictures, the suits of plate armor. This had been the ancestral hall of the previous lord. Lord Randol. His family was the one watching her out of unseeing eyes. Her father had wanted the hall cleared and scrubbed clean of any memory of lord Randol and his barbarous history, but her stepmother had convinced him otherwise. She was afraid the angry ghosts would be freed from this room and begin a reign of terror, haunting the entire castle.

The first time Solace had set foot in the room and seen lord Randol's image hanging on the wall, a wave of nausea and a prickling of fear had washed over her. But she bad been determined not to let these feelings get the best of her. She would not let lord Randol scare her again. She was not a child. It had taken her a long time to conquer her fear. And she was not about to take a giant step backward.

Solace placed a hand to her chest, willing her pounding heart to slow. She was hearing things. She didn't believe in ghosts, or she would be afraid that the specter of lord Randol would appear before her, demanding retribution for the loss of his castle. Stubbornly, Solace returned, albeit a bit hesitantly, to the window. Her ears were now finely tuned to every sound, every odd creak.

But there was nothing. Only the dead air of silence.

She laughed silently. Ghosts, she thought, forcing herself to relax.

Then, she heard a rustle and something swept past her shoulders. She whirled, stepping away from the window, demanding, "Who's there?"

Silence answered her. The paintings stared at her with judging eyes, and a chill ran up her spine. She took a step back toward the window, reaching toward the ledge with her hand. But it wasn't the cold stone she touched—

—it was warm skin!

Ten

Solace whirled, stifling a scream, to find the falconer standing before her. The light of the window cascaded over his head, outlining him in a bright yellow halo. Solace blinked and stepped back, gasping. With her movement, the sun hit his shoulders instead of his head, wiping away the angelic illusion.

He stepped toward her and she moved back. The look in his mercury eyes was hungry and dangerous. "You shouldn't be here alone," he said in a quiet voice.

She backed away from him. But he still approached, and there was something predatory in his stance, in his eyes, that frightened her.

"It's dangerous," he added.

His voice rang in her ears, a warning. She backed into a plate of armor and it jangled.

Logan's arm shot out and Solace winced, but he didn't touch her. He placed his hand against the armor, stopping its precarious swaying. His gaze slid to hers.

His arm, so close to her shoulder, was strong, and a warmth flooded her. She raised her chin in defiance of both her feelings and of him. "Are you threatening me?"

"Should I be?"

She swallowed and her gaze lowered to his lips. Then, embarrassed, she looked at his eyes again. There was just a faint glimmer of laughter there, and she scowled at him, wanting to wipe away that smug look. She mustered her courage to retort, "I still want to know what a falconer is doing with a sword."

It worked. Too well.

A dark look clouded his eyes. He leaned closer to her and Solace could feel his breath fan her lips. "It was a gift," he answered. "From a very special person."

"Who are you?" she asked softly.

"Logan," he replied.

Solace's heart pounded, her eyes captivated by the way his lips caressed the word. "Logan," she repeated dully through the haze of fog that had enveloped her. Her gaze shifted to his silver eyes, eyes the color of glinted steel. She could smell the thick scent of leather and something musky and . . . masculine. Even though their bodies weren't touching, she could feel the strength emanating from him, the power. She wanted him to touch her, wanted to feel his fingers on her skin, his lips on hers. The thought frightened her, and she pulled away with such force that her head smacked the plate armor behind her. Even with Logan's hand on it, it swung backward.

Suddenly, she was swept into his arms, and he turned his back to the suit of mail as it lurched forward, clutching her in his embrace and hunching his shoulders to protect her.

The suit of armor toppled around them, crashing to the floor. Solace hid behind Logan for a long moment after the noise had ceased. Then, realizing what had happened, she lifted her head. His arms were still around her, a fact that was strangely reassuring. But it was in his eyes that she found true comfort. There was something tender and caring deep within his orbs, and for a moment Solace thought it was worry as his gaze swept her face, looking for something. So intensely did they search that she believed he could see into her very soul, see the reason why she still clung to him, see the reason for the ease with which her body lay against his.

Embarrassed, she looked away. The scattered pieces of plate mail on the floor caught her attention, and she lowered her eyes to the fallen shield. Blue and gold reflected up at her in the sun's bright light. There was a crest upon the shield, but before she could look at it, Logan's hand was at the nape of her neck, turning her head toward his. His lips descended over hers, desperately, warming hers with his, igniting a fire so hot that it threatened to consume her. She clung to him as if he were her only hope at salvation. She tilted her head to his in an innocent mixture of curiosity and relinquishment. His desperation turned into a slow seduction as he gently coaxed her mouth to open to him with gentle touches of his lips and tongue against her soft skin.

She tentatively parted her lips for him, and he urged them wider, entering her mouth with his tongue, exploring the soft recesses. A groan escaped her lips, and she leaned fully against his strong, hard body.

Logan broke the kiss, pulling back slightly. "You shouldn't be here alone," he repeated.

His body was pressed against hers, and his arms were still securely around her, binding her to him. Solace stared at him through half-opened eyes. She felt she was floating, caught in a foggy dream.

"It's dangerous," he whispered.

Dangerous, her groggy mind repeated. Her gaze settled on his lips, wanting more of the sensual delight they aroused in her. Only then did she realize that the grin on his lips was not a lazy smile of pleasure, but rather a taunting smirk of arrogance. Dangerous. She suddenly straightened in indignation. He was teaching her a lesson!

She lurched away from him, almost stumbling in her hurry to escape him, his mocking tone still stinging her ears. She tripped and almost fell over a piece of the fallen armor, but quickly righted herself and fled the room.

Logan watched her go, feeling a sudden chill as the warmth of her body abandoned him. Desperation had forced him to kiss her. But as the kiss had deepened, his desperation had turned easily to passion. Perhaps too easily. Her lips had been so soft, her skin so hot. She had been so willing!

Logan cursed silently, forcing the unwelcome feelings from his body. He glanced down at the floor where the fallen armor was scattered, his eyes immediately drawn to the shield. The blue and gold of the insignia shone hotly in the sunlight. On its surface was a full moon overlain with two crossed swords. If Solace had seen the shield, he was sure she would have figured out who he was. She had seen the same crest inscribed on his sword.

Logan picked up the shield. He couldn't take it back to his room. He could barely hide the sword there. His eyes scanned the hall. There had to be somewhere to hide it.

Then, his gaze came to rest on a rich, detailed tapestry which lined one of the stone walls.

With a flick of his wrist, the dagger expertly carved out the last strand of hair on the piece of wood. But it was other hair Logan was imagining. Hair that looked as dark and rich as mahogany. He hadn't meant to kiss her. He hadn't meant to hold her so close. But she had been standing just below a picture of his great-great-grandfather. The suit of armor she had knocked over had been his father's.

And the crest on his sword matched the crest on the shield. It was the only way he could think of to distract her. But he had not really been thinking. He had just acted. So often in the past his instincts had saved his life. How could they have been so wrong this time?

How could he have kissed his enemy? He had to find Peter. He needed to gain her confidence. He needed to befriend her.

He needed to get her into bed.

The thought made him grin. He had thought she was untried, a virgin. But then he had seen that man kiss her cheek in the hallway. It had enraged him that she had not even blanched when she'd accepted the kiss. Then, she had let him kiss her, not even protesting when he had violated her mouth . . . She was no virgin. She was a harlot like her sister.

He would savor the seduction. How better to get revenge than to present Farindale with a daughter fat with his babe. And while he was at it, he would find out where his brother was. The problem was, he had been exceedingly cruel to her when he had broken the kiss. It had been days since he had last seen her.

He studied his carving with a satisfaction before nodding and rising. He opened the door to his small room and discovered that it was raining lightly. By the looks of the saturated ground and the dark sky in the distance, there had just been a downpour. The bird squawked in protest and ruffled his feathers, but remained seated on his shoulder. Logan paid it little attention as he walked out of his room.

Old Ben strolled up to him. "Yer falcon's gonna catch his death if ya bring him out in this rain."

Logan grunted. He believed the damned bird would live through anything.

"Well, then don't pay a word of attention ta what I say. I've only spent me whole life attending to these falcons," the old man exclaimed. "I know 'im like the back of me hand. And I know the back of me hand well."

Logan strolled away, moving past the mews toward the courtyard.

"Don't spend the day walkin'. I want yer help with the mending of the mews. Now don't ferget!"

Old Ben's voice faded as Logan walked through the ward. His eyes swept the courtyard for Mary, but there was no sign of the small girl. She loved the birds and often visited, annoying Old Ben. But Logan could tell that secretly Old Ben liked the attention and her constant chattering. She had immediately endeared herself to Logan by bringing him a blanket on his first night at Castle Fulton, knowing the mews were cold.

Busy peasants rushed about to secure their animals. Above the shouts of the villagers and the light pelting of rain, he heard laughter. Frowning at the inappropriate sound, he followed it to the side of the keep. A girl squealed in delight. He peeked around the corner and was shocked at the sight. There, right beside the candle shop, Mary stood laughing. Beside her, Solace stared at the sky, a smile on her face. Both were pressed up against the workshop for shelter, both soaked through to the skin, as if they had been in the brunt of the storm.

Then, suddenly, his falcon took flight just as the skies opened, sending down a new shower of rain that soaked Logan. Solace took Mary's hand and they both dashed out into the onslaught of rain. Logan watched them with amused eyes as they turned round and round, their mouths open and raised to the sky. He watched Solace's face glow with joy, a smile curving her shapely lips. Her dark hair trailed down her back in long, wet strands.

Her drenched velvet houppelande hung heavily on her, accenting her every curve, every move she made.

Solace continued to twirl round in the rain, spinning in joyful abandon. He remembered those carefree days, even though they had been so long ago. And something inside him longed to return to them. He found himself lost in her happiness. The joy on her face almost touched his soul. He wanted to reach out to her, to feel just an inkling of the abandon she felt.

But he couldn't. Not now. Not ever. He had once felt that kind of freedom, and it had cost him everything he held dear. Everything he loved.

He didn't want any part of it. Not at that price.

Logan turned to go. But he couldn't resist one last glance at Solace and those brilliant green eyes that sparkled with happiness. The wet garment clung to her shapely hips like skin, the weight of it pulling her skirt until the bodice was conforming tightly to her shapely breasts.

Longing surged inside him and Logan turned quickly away, clutching the wood carving tightly in his hand. His steps were long and purposeful as he returned to the mews. Drops of rain slid down his head and under the tunic he wore, soaking his skin. He would give the doll to Mary another time. When Solace wasn't there.

He knew he should talk to Solace, should tell her that their kiss was a mistake. But he couldn't.

And now, when his brother should be filling his thoughts, he found his mind occupied by Solace instead. She was becoming too much of a distraction. He had to cleanse his mind of her. He had to put her out of his thoughts.

Logan closed his eyes tightly and sighed, relaxing his body. There had to be someone else in this blasted castle who had seen Peter, or knew of him. Perhaps it was time to ask Old Ben. But the old man didn't trust him now; he would trust him even less if he knew he was searching for someone.

Right now, it seemed, Solace was his only means to finding Peter. But he had to see her for what she was—an enemy with information he needed. He should just capture her, interrogate her and . . .

". . . She needs to be taken care of now," a woman's voice insisted in a barely discernible whisper.

Logan stopped in the middle of the falcon-training ground, in the area bordered by the kennels on one side and the crossbow makers on the other. Something familiar about the woman's voice made him pause.

"What difference does it make if it's today or tomorrow or next week? The siege is going on," a man replied in the same hushed tone.

"We don't know when he'll return," the woman answered.

Logan took a step closer to the kennel, searching for the owners of the voices. They must be in the kennels beside the mews. A rendezvous, perhaps, he thought. Or a plot unfolding. Either way, it didn't concern him.

"I want Solace disposed of," the woman said.

Eleven

Logan froze. He didn't move, afraid the conspirators would hear him. Solace? he wondered silently, his heart missing a beat. Perhaps he hadn't heard right.

"And how do you suppose I go about it, my dear?" the man asked. "Poison?"

"Too suspicious."

"Push her off a walkway?"

"You might be seen."

There was a long, quiet moment in which Logan shifted his stance slightly, moving closer to the open window, easing himself into the shadows of the kennel. When the silence stretched, he thought they had moved on and he had missed them.

But then the woman's icy voice came to him. "No. Slit her throat. There's a killer in the castle. Everyone will blame him."

A chill went through Logan's body. Who was this woman? he wondered. And why did she hate Solace so much?

"You are a genius," the man cooed.

Logan pressed himself against the kennels, tilting his head toward the window. But the voices didn't continue. He heard the rustling of clothing, movement.

Then, Logan realized that they were heading out the door. He looked in the window to see two dogs sleeping on beds of straw, the room otherwise empty. His gaze was drawn to the door as it slowly swung closed. He whirled and raced around the corner of the building, bursting into the courtyard.

The crowd in the courtyard was thick and buzzing with activity. Now that the rain had cleared, there was much to do. Silently Logan cursed. He scanned the courtyard, his gaze darting this way and that, searching desperately for the man and woman. A fat merchant met his gaze while strolling past him with a sack of grain. Another man crossed the yard with an arm full of arrows. A peasant herded his chickens by Logan. A woman shouted, drawing his attention to a spilled basin of water and laundry. Dozens of people hurried around him, busy with their various tasks. It was impossible to tell who the voices had belonged to.

Logan cursed again. He had to protect Solace. He couldn't let her be hurt. Not when she knew where his brother was. But how could he watch her every moment of every day? He would have to warn her.

Solace descended the stairs slowly with a torch in one hand, a bowl in the other. The stairs were so dark she could not see her feet, let alone the steps that descended into the murky blackness. When she reached the bottom, the small circle of light that engulfed her washed over the wooden door of the storage room. She reached for the handle and pushed the door open. The torchlight fell over crates and bags. Solace stepped into the room, moving toward the bags that she knew held the salt. She placed the torch in the sconce on the wall and carefully opened the bag.

A ball of fur rubbed against her leg, and she looked down. She was greeted by a loud caterwaul. Solace bent down to the cat and stroked her soft hair, murmuring,

"Pudding. What are you doing in here?" She sighed slightly, scooping the cat into her arms. "How long have you been locked in here this time?" The cat's soft rumble of contentment was her only answer. Solace grinned and rubbed her face against Pudding's fur. "Oh, Pud. If you're not careful you'll get trapped in here for too long."

"If I were a cat would you show me that kind of affection?"

The voice startled her, and she almost dropped Pudding as she whirled. Logan lounged against the open doorway. His form seemed to fill the entrance. She couldn't help but let her gaze roam over his strong physique.

She hadn't seen him for days. She was purposely avoiding him after being so humiliated. But now, seeing him standing there like some dark god, she felt her body come alive. Dangerously alive. She held Pudding tightly against her chest like a shield. Finally, she caught her breath enough to retort, "If you were a cat, I'd throw you to the dogs." She turned her back to him, trying to hide her body's response to his presence.

She heard his soft rumble of laughter. "I don't think you'd hurt any animal like that," he said.

He was suddenly standing behind her. She could feel him there, without even looking. Her body became warm and flushed, and she wanted him to touch her, even though he had cast her aside like an old blanket.

"What are you doing down here?" he asked, reaching around her to flick the bowl she had rested on the bag of salt.

"Getting salt," she responded instantly, but her hands refused to do anything but hold Pudding. "What are you doing here?" She felt his hot gaze on the back of her head.

"I want to warn you," he whispered.

"Warn me?" she wondered, trying to keep the breathlessness from her voice. "Against what?"

"You shouldn't be alone. Not ever."

He must surely be speaking about himself as the threat. One touch, one kiss and she was doomed. As it was now, all she could think of was the way his lips touched hers, the way he held her tightly to himself. Pudding's head nuzzled her chin, seeking more attention, but her mind was occupied by Logan.

"You're in danger."

It was as if he had poured a bucket of cold water over her. The words mocked her. *You shouldn't be here alone.* She whirled and stepped away from him. Her bottom bumped up against the bag of salt behind her. "You already told me that and quite adequately proved why," she snapped. "I don't need any more of your lessons." Holding Pudding tightly against her pounding, furious heart, she pushed by him and stormed toward the stairs.

Suddenly he stepped in front of her, blocking her way with a wall of solid flesh. "I'm not here to teach you a lesson. Just to warn you. Someone wants to kill you."

"Kill me?" she asked, startled. "But who?"

"I overheard a man and a woman talking. I didn't see who they were."

"That's ridiculous. I don't have any enemies," she snapped. In the torchlight, she watched his eyes narrow.

"I suppose it's one of your closest friends that's laying siege to the castle," Logan quipped.

His sarcasm irritated her further. "No enemy can breech the walls of this castle," Solace retorted.

"You know better than that, Solace," Logan whispered. "That's why you're so frightened."

"I'm not frightened!"

"Then why are you trembling?"

Only then did Solace realize she was shivering. But

she also knew it had nothing to do with being frightened—or with the cold. She was quiet for a long moment, trying to calm her trembling. "Do you think it was some of Barclay's men?" Solace wondered. "The murderer?"

Logan stepped back, into the shadows. "I don't know," he answered. "But I don't see why he would want you dead. You pose no threat to him."

Solace's pride was pricked. "I'm heir to this castle," she said in defense.

"But your father is still alive and so is your stepmother. You're still third in line."

Solace's brow furrowed. "I don't know who would want me dead," she admitted.

"Until we can find out who it was, you'll have to take precautions. Don't take this lightly. They meant business, whoever it was," Logan said. "I'll stay with you until you're done getting the salt, but—"

"You don't have to watch over me like a child," she said.

"Not like a child, Solace," he said patiently. "Like a woman whose life is in danger."

Danger? she thought, a scowl shadowing her brow. The thought seemed too ridiculous. But Logan had said he overheard two people. Why should she doubt him? Suddenly, a tremor of apprehension shot through her. If someone was trying to kill her, what could she do? She couldn't expect Logan to trail her all day. Suddenly, an idea came to her. Maybe there was something Logan could do. She tried to see his face, but could not. The shadows hid him too well. "Do you know how to use that sword?" she wondered.

There was a long moment of silence, and he shifted his weight slightly. "Yes."

She nervously wet her lips with her tongue. "Will you teach me how to defend myself?" When he didn't answer, she continued quickly, "I can't expect someone to be with me at all times. And I might be safer . . . well, I might be better off if I knew just enough to protect myself. It might be—"

His finger touched her lips in a motion to still them. "I'll teach you," he agreed.

The feel of his finger against her lips sent a quivering charge through her. He seemed to keep it there a second longer than need be before he pulled away from her. "Collect your salt," he said. "And I'll meet you."

"Tonight?" she asked, strangely anxious.

"You would train under the moonlight, alone with a stranger?" he wondered.

"No," she answered. "Alone with you."

Solace's words flattered Logan. She trusted him enough to be alone with him. And yet, she was foolhardy to even trust him at all. She didn't know him. She had no clue that he was the one who had killed the dungeon guard. She had no knowledge of what he was planning. What would she think if she knew? he wondered. What would she think about giving him her trust then?

Even though they had agreed to meet behind the mews after the meal, Logan had realized Solace would be coming to him in the dark. That was too much temptation for fate to overlook, too much chance for a murderer to be lurking in the shadows. He had learned long ago to take matters into his own hands, not to wait on fate. She was too cruel too often. So, after his meal, Logan found himself lounging against the wall just outside the Great Hall.

He turned expectantly at the soft tread of footsteps, but felt only disappointment at the sight of Beth approaching from down the hallway. Her face was lit with a sly smile, her eyes lidded with coyness. Logan gritted his teeth as he bowed slightly.

Her grin was annoying. "Looking for me, Logan?" she wondered.

"Alas, no," Logan answered, charmingly. "But had I known you would be up at this late hour, I would have been."

She smiled, batting her lashes at him. "Then you're here to meet with someone else? I'm disappointed."

"You're also betrothed." Logan found himself thankful.

She ran a hand along the length of his arm. "One night of passion does not break a betrothal."

"Unless he finds out."

"And who will tell him?"

"Not I, certainly," Logan admitted. "But there are many eyes and ears in a castle, m'lady."

"We will be discreet," she said, smiling seductively. He felt about as aroused as a dead rat.

He raised his eyes suddenly to glance over Beth's shoulder and caught a movement in the shadows. He saw Solace staring at him with the largest eyes he had ever seen. He saw hurt in them, confusion and pain, before she bowed her head and turned away.

The thought of bedding Beth vanished before the disappointment he had caused Solace. "Excuse me," he said and moved after Solace. He easily caught up with her in the hallway, grabbing her arm gently. "Solace," he murmured. "I was waiting for you."

She looked up at him through thick lashes. "And you found my sister. I understand. If Beth—"

Logan took her hand in his and gently raised it to his lips. "Beth found me. I was waiting here for you." He stared hard at her, his eyes shining like silver. They moved over her face like a caress, touching her eyes, her nose, her lips. "Shall we?" he wondered.

Solace stared at him dubiously. How could she doubt her beauty, Logan wondered. How could she believe he would willingly pick Beth over her? He had seen hundreds like Beth. All fawning about him as if he were a new pup, a prize or even a servant. But never had they looked on him as an equal. Only the peasants had gazed at him as a prospective husband. Logan wondered fleetingly if Solace even knew what she wanted of him. He could show her, take the time to teach her the ways of lovemaking . . . if he wasn't looking for Peter.

Solace cast a glance over her shoulder as if she expected to find Beth watching, but no one was there, just the empty corridor.

Finally, Logan gently tucked Solace's small hand in the crook of his arm and urged her on with one of his most devastating grins.

It worked. She started forward almost immediately, a shy smile lurking at the corners of her lips.

Logan led her back to the mews. As they entered the falcon-training grounds, Logan explained, "The first and most important thing is to scream and kick and do everything you can to get away."

Solace nodded like an obedient student.

"The problem comes when you are caught off guard. So, you have to try to anticipate the unexpected. Notice who is around you, friend and foe alike. Your enemies might be posing as friends. We don't know yet. But let's say you're caught off guard. Your best bet is to try to knee a man between his legs as hard as you can and run. Understand?"

Solace nodded.

"Let's try something. Come here." When she moved in front of him, he turned her around so her back was to him. "Say your attacker approaches from behind." He grabbed her around the neck, not too tightly, not too loosely. He couldn't help but notice how smooth her skin was. Her hair brushed his arm. It was as soft as velvet. "What would you do?" he asked, drawing her close against his body.

For a long moment, she did nothing. Her small hands instinctively came up to grip his arm. Finally, she whispered, "I . . . I would fight and try to scream."

"I don't want to hurt you, but let's say that he tightens his grip and you can't scream." Her hair smelled faintly of roses. He moved his nose closer to her hair to smell the fragrance. He felt her lean back against him slightly, barely noticeably, but close enough that he could feel the length of her against him. His hold on her tightened. His body instantly responded to holding her. Lord, how he wanted her.

One of her hands caressed his arm. He felt the movement even through his tunic. The things he could teach her! "I . . . I don't know," she whispered.

She would die, he thought. And, strangely, it angered him. "You're lucky this man doesn't have a dagger or you would be dead already. Let's say he wants something else." He bent his head to kiss her neck, just behind her ear, and she gasped in surprise. He turned her face to his, claiming her lips in one hungry move. He kissed her with control, with expertise, trying desperately to keep control of his emotions, to teach her.

But she wasn't reacting like a woman trapped by a rapist. She was reacting like a woman who wanted to be ravished. She groaned slightly, and without removing his lips from hers, Logan encouraged, "What do you do?"

Her eyes were closed in languish; she tilted her lips toward his. Logan took the invitation, easily parting her lips with his and thrusting his tongue inside. He reached down to cup her breast, squeezing, feeling the hard nipple beneath her dress. She groaned and thrust her chest into his hand.

Logan could hardly control himself. He ran a palm over her nipple, gently caressing the roundness of her breast. Her mouth tasted like honey; her lips were so soft, so willing! He wanted to taste the rest of her, to let his hands claim her as his own. He ran a hand down her flat stomach, toward the area he knew she wanted him to touch. He felt her thrust her hips and his manhood throbbed against his leggings. "You like this, don't you?" he murmured in her ear. He felt her nod. "Good," he whispered. "Then when the rapist comes to claim you, you don't have to fight. Just enjoy."

He felt her stiffen immediately and was sorry that he had been so cold to her. He wanted to touch her, feel her passion. Instead, he prepared for her reaction. She would struggle or try to elbow him. Logan was caught totally off guard when she stomped down on his foot. Hard.

He released her, trying to hide the excruciating pain that was flaring in his foot.

Solace whirled and stormed away.

"Good!" Logan called out after her. "That's exactly what you should have done in the first place."

But she didn't stop. He watched her until she turned the corner, heading toward the keep. He had gone too far. He knew it then and he knew it now. He shook his head. She had been in his arms, so close. And she'd smelled so damn good, felt so soft to the touch. He wanted more of her. God help him, but he wanted all of her.

Graham grinned as he watched Solace storm into the darkness of the night. For an instant, he envisioned going after her. Instead, he reached inside his leggings and stroked himself.

Twelve

Baron Edwin Barclay glared up at Castle Fulton, cursing for the thousandth time. His long blond hair was tossed about by the wind, the wild strands forming a halo around his head, his pleasant features and strong form giving him the appearance of a saint. He narrowed his eyes, staring up at Fulton's tall towers and gatehouse. He cursed again.

"M'lord!" a rider called as he halted his steed beside Baron Barclay's white warhorse. "There is no sign of the drawbridge being lowered. I'm afraid we've failed."

Barclay's hand was swift and his fist was powerful as he struck the man, sending him rolling off his horse to the ground. "*He* has failed. He must have been discovered and killed. But I will not fail. I will take Castle Fulton and make Farindale grovel before me."

The man wiped the blood from the corner of his lip and stood. "Yes, m'lord."

Barclay ignored him, his cold blue eyes focused on Castle Fulton. "You will fall," he promised, his burning eyes looking more like those of a demon than of a saint.

Late the next day, Solace found herself standing before the chapel. The echo of indiscernible voices drifted out of the church. Often in times of confusion she found herself standing here, as she had when her father had gone to France to fight and left her in Alissa's care. She wanted to go in and find Father Davis. He had always been there to comfort her and to talk with. But she knew he would be busy now with the sick and injured. He wouldn't have time for her. And she needed to speak to someone about . . . about the emotions Logan aroused within her. She wanted to know why he affected her as he did, what the power he held over her was.

With a heavy sigh, she looked away from the towering steeple and was prepared to turn away when a voice called to her. Solace's gaze moved over the entrance, searching for the owner of the voice. It was only when the call came again that she followed it far up into the bell tower. Father Davis stood there, waving down at her, motioning for her to come inside.

With a grin, Solace hiked up her skirts and ran within. She raced up the aisle, moving quickly by the pews, and stopped before the altar to quickly genuflect. She darted to her left, pushing through a door, and climbed the spiraling staircase behind it. The decrepit wooden steps shook beneath her feet as she took the stairs two at a time until she reached the top.

"Easy, child," Father Davis called to her as the bell tower platform rocked slightly from her enthusiastic entrance. He was an old man with a bald head ringed by snow-white hair. He wore a simple brown robe. His gentle brown eyes lit as they saw her.

She smiled at him as she approached, slowing her run to a walk.

"You look like a Gypsy," he said lovingly, "with that glow in your eyes. I always said those were dangerous eyes.

"You always said they were beautiful eyes."

"And they are," he admitted. "It's been a long time, Solace. Why haven't you come up to see me?"

"I know the injured are growing. I know you're busy," she said, leaning out the window and staring down at the inner ward. "I didn't want to disturb you."

"Child," he said patiently, "you are anything but a disturbance."

She cast a grin at him. "I've truly missed you."

Father Davis nodded his agreement. "These godforsaken sieges. It was on a day like this another lifetime ago that I witnessed another siege."

"My father," she said solemnly.

"Your father," he agreed, resting his arms on the ledge beside her and staring out at the cloudy, gray day. "The only good to come from that siege was you. I can't help but wonder about this one, what with your father gone."

"He'll come back," Solace said. "And trap Barclay's army and wipe them all out. All we have to do is hold the castle until then."

Father Davis stared at her for a long time. "This is a messy business, Solace. I want you to promise me that if they enter the castle, you'll run."

"Run?" she turned to him, shocked.

"Run to safety. I want you out of the castle if they enter. You are the heir to Fulton, Solace. It will be you that Barclay is looking for."

She waved the issue aside with a disbelieving flick of her wrist. "And where am I supposed to run?" she wondered.

Father Davis seized her arm, squeezing it firmly. "To your father, Solace. You must find him. And trust no one. No one, do you hear?"

"You're scaring me," she admitted, trying to pull her arm free.

"Good. That's exactly what this stubborn little head

needs. A good dose of reality." His eyes grew distant as a faraway look seeped into them. "These days, it's hard enough to find good fighters, let alone men who won't turn their back on you for a gold piece. And gold is something that Barclay has plenty of."

"Father, are you . . . feeling all right?" Solace wondered. It was odd for him to be so concerned with matters of warfare and not matters of the spirit.

Father Davis nodded. "Yes," he said, rubbing his bald head. "I'm sorry."

Solace knew she could not talk to him about Logan, not now. He had too much on his mind. Perhaps the tide was turning. Perhaps now Father Davis needed her to listen to him for a change.

He suddenly seemed so old, so tired. Solace stayed and comforted him, listening to his concerns. By the time she left the chapel an hour later, the sky had darkened. She felt as lost as when she had entered. She needed to talk to someone. Alissa wouldn't understand. Beth wouldn't take the time to listen. She wished her father were in the castle; even though he was seldom home, she had always been able to talk to him.

Then, her eyes lit and her gaze turned up to the battlements. There had always been one person with whom she enjoyed spending time, who was like a brother to her, who always took the time to listen.

She headed toward the walkways, knowing that Peter was on guard duty.

Logan stared out through an arrow slit in the hoarding. The full moon illuminated the scene below in a pale glow. Beyond the moat he could see that the siege tower was almost complete. He knew he had wasted enough time, too much time. He had to find Peter before it was too late.

He cursed silently. Solace had become too much of a distraction. Whenever he was with her, all thoughts of his brother simply disappeared. Even when he was alone, despite his resolve to stay focused on Peter, his mind filled with images of holding her in his arms, caressing her tender flesh, kissing her hot mouth.

He glanced over to his left, studying the damaged wall of the hoarding. It looked as though a boulder thrown by the trebuchet had knocked a two-foot hole into the wood.

Suddenly, a faint glow of light drew his gaze, growing brighter with each second. The fool! Logan thought. Whoever it is is bringing a candle up here!

As the person rounded the corner, Logan barely had time to notice it was a woman before he threw himself at her, knocking her to the ground. The candle fell from her grip and dropped to the wooden floor of the hoarding. Logan smashed his hand down on it, snuffing out the light beneath his open palm. A small *wheeze* and then a thud broke the silence.

For a long moment, they lay together, his weight pressing her down to the floor. Her breasts pressed against his chest again and again as she gasped for air. Then she began to wriggle, her hips grinding against his own. His body's response to her movement was instantaneous. He pressed a hand over her mouth, hissing, "Shhh!"

Moonlight streaming through the arrow loop washed over the woman's face and his eyebrows rose in surprise. Solace. It was as if his thoughts had conjured her.

The light made her face as pale as the moon itself. He wondered how he could have missed those eyes before; they were so large, so green, so haunting. Even though he had seen her numerous times, he still marveled at the delicate sculpture of her high cheekbones. Her full lips were warm and wet against his hand.

She began to struggle, her small hands pushing at his chest. He removed his hand from her mouth, and she quickly demanded, "What are you doing? Get off of me." He slid off of her. He watched her sit up, keeping the moonlight to his back so he could see her more clearly.

"What kind of fool are you to come up here with a candle?" he retorted.

Solace was quiet for a long moment. "Logan?" Solace asked. "Is that you?"

"Who else would it be?" he snapped.

"Well, I . . ." Her voice trailed off and she looked away from him. "Never mind."

"Fire on this hoarding is not a smart idea."

He watched her large green eyes glance down at the floor. "I . . . I couldn't see," she defended, lamely.

"Then you shouldn't be up here," he said.

She clenched her jaw and began to rise to her feet, but Logan closed a hand over her arm, keeping her before him. "And it's not a good idea to show them that you are here."

She wrenched her arm away from him. "Their aim is not that good."

He pointed to a wooden beam above her. An arrow's metal tip was embedded inches from her shoulder. The highly polished shaft shimmered in the moonlight. "At least one of them is good enough," he said.

She straightened her spine, trying to appear noble in a kneeling position. The moonlight washed over her, bathing her skin in an iridescent glow. There was hurt in her eyes and embarrassment.

Suddenly, she stood, moving away from him, out of the shaft of moonlight. "What are you doing up here?" she wondered.

"I couldn't sleep," he answered tersely. "What are you doing up here?"

"I was looking for a friend."

A friend, he thought. A lover? Why else would she be walking the hoardings alone, so late at night? Logan turned away from her to gaze out the arrow loop at the army below, not wanting her to see the tightness in his set jaw. "Instead, you found me," he retorted and was surprised at the bitterness in his tone.

Solace joined him, following his stare. "Can you see the army? What are they doing?"

He stiffened. Her words were tinged with awe and excitement. Instantly, he was transported back thirteen years . . .

He raced his horse through the emptying streets of the village, heading toward Sullivan's Hill. Lord Farindale's army! The thought sent a forbidden thrill through his body. Logan knew that just the thought of an army attacking his home should have filled him with outrage, and he knew full well there was a very strong possibility that many people would be killed, but the excitement simmering in his blood burned away all such rational thought. He would finally get to see a real battle! And besides, he had all the faith in the world that his father's knights would be victorious.

Logan jerked the reins and the horse changed direction, taking a quicker route through Millie's Field toward Sullivan's Hill. By now, the land was strangely empty and quiet. There were no children's squeals of delight, no stray geese to scatter. Everyone had moved into the safety of the castle wards. Only the pounding of his horse's hooves on the ground reached his ears.

Within moments, he could see Sullivan's Hill before him, a large rise in the earth that obscured the road behind it from view. Logan urged his horse on, and the animal raced up the hill. As he came to the top, he was momentarily blinded by the flare of the sun as the blood-red sky splashed across his face. He blinked his eyes clear and lowered his gaze to the road. The sight that greeted him caused his heart to falter.

They were marching in pairs down the road. Knights on horseback in gleaming armor, footmen behind them. Logan became increasingly uneasy as his eyes followed the line down the road, far, far back. He could not make out the end of the line of approaching warriors.

He had never seen so many knights! The excitement withered and died from his spirit. When Peter told him there were five thousand men coming to lay siege to Castle Fulton, he'd thought he understood. But his mind couldn't, until now, comprehend just how many men that was. I have to get back to warn Father, Logan thought.

He reined in his horse, but in his urgency to return to the castle he jerked too roughly on the reins and the animal spooked, rearing high into the air with a panicked whinny. Logan felt himself sliding from the saddle, and he clutched desperately at the reins as the thin ropes tore free from his grasp. The horse reared higher and Logan lost what little balance he had left, tumbling backward from the saddle. His shoulders hit the ground first, whipping his head sharply back onto a large rock . . .

Logan shook his head, ridding himself of the painful memory. He struggled to hold the anger he felt toward Solace inside him. He wanted to throttle her, tell her how foolish her excitement was—tell her what she could lose.

Instead, he turned his back to her, his fists clenching. After all this time, he had been positive that he had his emotions under control. But her innocent curiosity made him angry. Didn't she understand what those men were out there to do? Didn't she realize what could happen? Didn't she know they would stop at nothing to enter her castle?

"It's a grand sight," she murmured.

Logan suddenly grabbed her arm and pushed her back against the wooden wall, pressing her there with his body. "A grand sight?" he echoed angrily, his face an inch from her own. "They're here to take your castle from you! You shouldn't be in awe of them! You should hate them with every ounce of your being, with every breath! You should want every last one of them dead for daring to lay siege to your home, for daring to want to take what is yours! But never, ever admire them!" He was breathing hard, his words churning from lips curled in an expression of hate. His hands clutched her shoulders tightly.

"Logan." The word was almost a plea on her lips.

He removed his trembling hands from her shoulders and took a step back. I should follow my own advice and hate her with every breath, he thought. I do. I hate her. But the thought made him angry because he knew it was a lie. "I told you not to roam the castle alone, especially at night. Someone wants to kill you."

Solace reached into a pocket in the skirt of her dress, drawing forth a small dagger, its blade shiny and clean. "I have this," she said hesitantly.

His eyes shifted to the dagger. "What's that, a dinner knife?" he mocked. With a quick swipe of his hand, he easily batted the utensil from her fist, sending it skittering across the hoarding.

Her mouth dropped open in shock. His gaze was drawn unwillingly to her parted lips. Like a sweet flower budding with nectar, they beckoned to him. He could think of nothing but kissing those enticing lips, stealing the honey they hid in their depths. The urge was overpowering. "Damn it," he muttered and grabbed her shoulders, pulling her roughly against him, claiming her lips with an urgency and need that was not to be denied.

Thirteen

Swirls of desire coursed through Solace's body as Logan's lips devoured hers. His tongue flitted over her lips, enticing her to open her mouth wider for him. Flames exploded through her body, igniting a passion that only he could arouse. She parted her lips and he lunged into her, driving his tongue between her lips, tasting every corner, every succulent recess of her mouth until she was left breathless.

She gasped for a breath and he moved on, his kisses moving over her jaw, down her neck, fanning her skin with light, teasing strokes of his lips and tongue. His mouth was hot against her flesh, leaving warm, lingering memories of its path as it spiraled downward to the soft hollow of her throat. He sucked her flesh gently, teasing her delicate skin with his teeth. She heard a low, guttural moan escape from his lips, and for a moment she thought he would bite her like some savage animal attacking its freshly captured prey.

His hand moved from her shoulder to cup one of her breasts. He squeezed it firmly, relentlessly. Her nipple hardened instantly under his touch. Involuntarily, she ran her nails over his back, pulling him against her. She threw her head back, exposing her pale throat to him.

Logan plunged a hand beneath the satin fabric of

her dress to fondle her bare breast. Solace gasped, arching her back, filling his hand with her skin. A raging flood of liquid fire swept through her, enflaming her already-blazing passion.

With a skilled hand, he undid the buttons at the back of her dress, almost ripping the last button free in his haste to rid her of her clothing. He yanked sharply down on her dress, exposing her breasts to his heated gaze. With a guttural growl, he then attacked her nipples, kissing and sucking with a frenzy that swept her up in its relentless fury.

His fingers skimmed her clothing, moving down to her thigh, squeezing and teasing her, urging her legs to part. Weak from the onslaught of emotions and feelings that battered her, Solace obeyed his silent command. Logan immediately cupped her womanhood through her clothing. She opened her mouth to gasp, but his lips seared across hers, sealing her moan beneath his passion.

Solace reached down to touch his hand, but she wasn't sure whether it was to stop him or to encourage him. She knew she should stop him. She knew the way he was touching her, the things he was doing, couldn't be right, that she shouldn't do this, but somehow the feelings that were spreading through her were so new, so pleasant, so . . . exciting.

Disappointment flooded through her as he removed his hand.

He reached down to lift the satin material of her dress up over her hips. His hand blazed a path from her breasts to her thigh. She instinctively arched toward him, wrapping her hands around his neck, entwining her fingers in his hair.

He touched her womanly hair, moving lower and lower through her dark curls with an agonizing slowness. Solace groaned, wanting him to stop the fiery flames that ignited inside her, to quench the fires that he had ignited. Finally, he touched her on the bud of her womanhood. Spirals of ecstasy shot through her, and she reached down to grip his hand tightly, afraid of the sensations she was feeling, afraid he would move his hand away. But he didn't. He caressed her in slow, tight circles, rubbing his finger round and round over the delicate skin until she thought the world would end in a bright explosion of blinding light.

Solace realized she was clinging to him, clutching his shirt in balled fists lest she crumble to the ground. He scooped her up into his arms and lay her gently on the floor of the hoarding, desperately kissing her lips, warming them, enflaming them.

Logan pulled back to gaze upon her body. The intensity and pure longing in his eyes ignited a desire so great in her, so irresistible, that it was unlike anything she had ever known before. She reached for him, but he pulled back, ripping his belt from his body, shedding his tunic and hose with a manic intensity.

Solace had never seen a more beautiful sight. His body was hard and firm, carved from granite. The muscles in his arms rippled with power as he held himself over her. His chest was so strong, his stomach ribbed with muscle.

She reached up to caress his face, lifting up on her elbows to claim his lips. She wanted to be a part of him, to feel his touch again. She wanted him to ease the urgency that tormented her.

He lowered himself over her, the entire length of his hot body pressing against hers. He parted her legs with his knee and moved between her thighs. She felt something press against the most intimate part of her and groaned slightly. Logan gazed into her eyes, and in their misty grayness Solace saw his passion burning brightly, mirroring her own. Then he parted the delicate folds of her womanhood with his shaft, entering her.

Solace stiffened as his manhood filled her. Then Logan was kissing her mouth, her eyes, her neck with urgency and desperation, enflaming her soul with a contagious plague of want. She returned his kisses with an equal fervor.

He began to move inside of her, thrusting slowly at first, the tempo increasing as their passion built.

A carnal hunger raged through Solace, a building tension racing through her veins. It claimed every portion of her body until she thought she could take no more. She cried out for release. Logan answered her cries, driving his manhood deeper and harder into her.

With each thrust, Solace rose in swirling clouds of rapture, soaring higher and higher, until she reached the stars, adding a glow to the night that had never been there before. Waves of ecstasy washed over her again and again until she lay still, sated and fulfilled.

She opened her eyes and stared at Logan in awe. A strange grin tugged at his lips before he began to move again, thrusting deep into her until his body stiffened and shook.

Solace felt his shoulder muscles coil tight beneath her palms before he slumped forward with a satisfied sigh. They lay together for a long moment, the sounds of the night returning them to reality. Voices calling out in the distance. The *clip-clop* of a horse trotting by.

Solace caressed his shoulders, winding a lock of his hair around one finger.

"Solace," Logan finally said, pushing himself up onto his elbows to stare down at her.

She gazed at him, a small grin turning up the corners of her lips. Absolute bliss lingered in her veins. She felt somehow free and uninhibited. She had never realized it could be like that. That a man, that Logan, could make her feel this way. Solace's grin turned into a full smile.

Logan pressed a kiss onto her open mouth, before climbing to his feet to pull up his leggings.

She sat up, gazing at him with beguiling delight. She didn't even bother to cover her exposed breasts.

Logan chuckled softly and held out a hand to her. She took it, and he pulled her into his embrace. Her breasts tingled as they brushed his chest. He righted her dress so it covered her chest. But when his hand lingered over one of her breasts longer than it should, Solace looked at him from beneath her eyelashes.

With a growl, he gently shoved her back against the hoarding wall. "We could easily be discovered up here," he whispered. "But if you keep looking at me like that I'm going to take you again anyway."

Solace couldn't move when he was so close. Her senses left her, disappearing under the promise of one of his kisses, a caress. He lowered his hand and Solace held her breath, thinking, hoping he would touch her again. Instead, he gently smoothed out her skirt, pulling it down to cover her legs.

He took her hand in his and began to turn away, heading toward the stairs.

Solace halted, whispering, "Just one more kiss."

Logan groaned slightly, but turned to her, wrapping his arms around her. "Wanton wench," he murmured, pressing his lips to hers.

The still smoldering passion flamed to life in Solace. She melted against him, giving in to his expertise, allowing him complete reign over her senses.

He pulled away, backing quickly from her as if she had burned him. He held her hand tightly and pulled her toward the stairs. They descended the steps to the courtyard. There, he released her hand, but continued at her side until they reached the keep.

He stepped in front of her, so close that Solace could feel his breath on her upturned lips. The tips of her breasts were almost touching his chest, and they hardened in response to his closeness.

"Come to me in the morning," he whispered. "I'll be free after I've trained the falcons near the mews."

"I will," she promised.

Logan stepped around her, his gaze searing her to the spot. He backed away from her, a sly smile on his lips. Solace watched the falconer until the darkness swallowed him.

Hagen, the gate guard, watched from the battlements as Logan moved toward the mews. He was sure that he was the man who had forced him to open the gates. But who was he? Suddenly, from the darkness of the night, a large falcon descended to land on the stranger's shoulder.

Hagen's eyes narrowed.

Fourteen

Logan dropped the last piece of meat and the gyrfalcon quickly snatched it up, tearing into it. He knew she was coming to him. He knew that after he finished training the birds she would be there. He was actually looking forward to her visit. He grabbed his glove and the lure as he moved out the door.

As he walked outside, he saw that the courtyard was full of merchants opening their doors to begin the day. Across it, the kitchen servants were collecting some vegetables from the garden. A small child ran toward the keep with a large sack slung over his shoulder.

He rounded the corner to the kennels, heading to the training grounds . . .

. . . and slammed into a little whirlwind! He barely flinched, but the impact sent the other person to the ground.

Logan stared down at Solace. She looked a little dazed and utterly beautiful. He couldn't stop the grin from spreading across his face. "Don't you ever walk?" he wondered, holding a hand out to her. Solace grasped his hand, and he pulled her up with a little too much force so she landed tightly against his chest. "You're early."

She gazed into his eyes for a long, heated moment before stepping away from him and nodding.

His stare swept down her face, from her deep green eyes, over her pert little nose, to her lips where his hot gaze lingered. After a long moment, Solace parted her lips slightly and dropped her head, but not before Logan noticed the red in her cheeks. He smiled slightly. "Have you come to help me now?" he wondered.

She lifted her gaze to meet his eyes. "Do you need help?" she asked.

His eyes burned into hers. "I can always use your help," he said, brushing by her, moving toward a white falcon that was sitting on a perch on the edge of the training grounds. Lord, how his body ached for her. He had thought of her through the entire night and now found he couldn't concentrate on the falcons. He wanted to be inside her again.

"Logan," she whispered.

Logan half turned to find her standing close behind him.

"Why didn't you tell me?" she wondered.

"Tell you?" he questioned, frowning at the seriousness of her tone.

"Did you think I wouldn't find out?"

Logan stiffened. His heart was suddenly pounding in his chest. How had she discovered the truth? How much does she know? he wondered.

"You didn't have to keep it a secret. At least not from me."

Logan turned away, nervously gathering the jesses in his hand.

"Logan, I don't understand why you did it," she said softly.

He shook his head. "You're making this out to be bigger than it is," he said, hoping to bluff his way through.

"It's treason! If my stepmother finds out, you'll be thrown in the stocks. Or worse."

He clenched his jaw as dread shot through his body. "Are you going to tell her?"

"Of course not," she answered, and Logan heard the hurt in her voice.

It must be the dungeon! She had found out he killed the guard! "I had no other choice," he said.

"But to disobey my stepmother . . ."

Logan frowned, his eyes narrowing quizzically. "Disobey?" he echoed and turned to her.

"That was very brave of you. If those gates had closed, I would have been in Barclay's hands now."

"The gates," he breathed. Relief flooded every fiber of his body. She was talking about the gates! The damn gates! He almost laughed, but she looked so serious, so damned kissable, that he hid his laughter behind a wide grin. "I guess you owe me your life."

She nodded once. "And my gratitude." Her gaze dipped to his lips.

Desire washed through him. God's blood! She could arouse him with a mere look. No, he amended silently. With her mere presence. Quickly, he turned back to the falcon. The sooner he finished the training, the sooner he could be alone with Solace. His entire body ached with wanting. No woman had ever affected him this way. No woman had consumed his thoughts, his mind, like Solace did.

He took the lure and stepped away from the post, passing close to Solace, very close. She didn't back away, but he heard her slight gasp as he came within touching distance. Could she want him as badly as he wanted her?

"What do you want me to do?" she asked.

He cast her a scorching look and a grin tugged at her lips. "Don't tempt me," he replied in a deep, guttural voice.

Solace bowed her head, a smile spreading over her

face, and walked to an overturned crate. She boosted her bottom up on it and turned to watch him.

Logan reached the middle of the training ground and stopped. He planted his booted feet apart and lifted the lure, whirling it above his head.

The white peregrine falcon sat on its perch, staring at Logan with small black eyes.

A caw sounded in the air, and Logan raised his gaze to see his black falcon sitting on a nearby crenel, studying the lure with hungry eyes.

Logan swung the sand-filled leather bag in slow, looping circles above his head. He knew he should have been paying attention to the white bird, but Solace was much more attractive to look at. She sat so demurely on the crate, a royal princess on her throne. And she looked like one, dressed in a rich blue velvet houppelande, which he couldn't wait to rid her of. Her hair was braided tightly and wrapped around her head. He was dying to free her luxurious mane and sink his hands into its lush fullness.

The lure spun faster and faster, whistling as it whipped through the air. "Chase it, you damn bird," Logan muttered. The falcon puffed up its white feathers as if in indignation.

Solace's grin grew as the bird hopped on its perch, turning its back to Logan.

Logan continued swinging the lure at a furious pace until his arm tired. Finally, he stopped and threw the lure to the ground in disgust. "Fine. Then don't learn to hunt," he whispered harshly.

"You can hardly blame the falcon," Solace called. "It can't possibly fly that fast."

Logan turned to her, his eyes dark and flashing. He grabbed the lure by one of the limp feathers sewn onto the bag and held it out to her. "Perhaps you'd like to try it, m'lady."

Solace hopped down off the crate and approached him. She took the lure from his hand and shook the string out before her, turning her back to him. All Logan wanted to do was wrap his hands around her and pull her against him. Damn, he thought, as his body responded instantly to the picture, his manhood stirring in his leggings.

Solace whistled softly, catching the falcon's attention; the bird looked over its shoulder at her. Solace cooed, "Come on, darling. You'll get fat if you sit on your perch all day." She began to twirl the lure in the air in wider and wider circles. The white falcon hopped on the perch, turning full face to Solace.

Solace mimicked Old Ben's call, urging the bird to attack its fake prey. The bird's black eyes locked on the lure, watching it circle. Solace continued to twirl the lure in slow, but steady circles. Then, suddenly, the falcon launched from its perch, circled the sky once and dove, catching the lure in midair. It landed on the perch, the lure secure in its sharp claws.

Solace stared at the falcon for a long moment before turning to Logan with a smug look of triumph. Her large green eyes glittered like emeralds.

Her grin was contagious. "We could have saved a lot of time if you trained the bird in the first place," he said. He marched past her, moving toward the white falcon.

"Are you in a hurry?" she asked.

He cast a hungry glance at her over his shoulder.

She approached behind him, leaning close to murmur. "You're not a falconer, are you?"

Logan froze. God's blood! Did she know all his secrets? he wondered.

Her soft laughter reached his ears. "At least not a very good one."

Logan snapped on his thick leather glove. "Where

did you learn how to handle a lure?" He approached the white falcon, holding his covered forearm out to the creature. The bird was still holding its prize enthusiastically, if a bit possessively. Logan moved his glove closer, touching the leather to the bird's chest feathers. The bird instantly pecked hard at the glove, angry at the intrusion.

Solace lowered her gaze to her clasped hands. "I hung around Old Ben long enough to learn."

After the rebuff from the falcon, Logan moved to a nearby pail and drew out a piece of red meat, tossing it to the peregrine. The bird immediately dropped the lure and clutched at the food, snatching it easily out of the air. Its sharp beak tore into the meat, easily ripping off a small portion.

Logan picked up the fallen lure and turned to Solace.

Shyly, she turned her stare to the ground and Logan's gaze settled on her lustrous hair. It shimmered in the sunlight, beckoning to him. He moved toward her, his steps full of purpose. Solace lifted her gaze to him as he stopped just before her. He stared into her beautiful green eyes for a long moment before reaching toward her. Her lips parted as his hand touched her temple, skimming over her hair, his fingers moving toward the back of her head. He pulled the pins from her hair and her braids tumbled down her back.

Solace didn't move as he reached around to the back of her head, entwining his fingers in her hair, loosening the braids until her sumptuous locks hung in riotous waves along her back. He ran his hand through her hair once again, enjoying the feel of it, the way tiny tendrils curled about his fingers. Then, his gaze returned to hers. "So you think you know a lot about falcons."

"A little," she admitted breathlessly.

"They can be very unpredictable," he said.

"I know," Solace said.

Suddenly, he grabbed both of her wrists in his hand, holding them firmly against his chest. "We have to tie jesses around their legs so they can't fly away. This is how we keep the falcons from escaping." He felt her heart hammering in her chest. He allowed one of his fingers to snake out and touch the rounded portion of her breast.

He felt the tremor shoot through her body at the caress.

"Logan," she whispered.

He knew he could take her right there and she wouldn't object, would probably encourage him. But as much as he wanted her, he wanted to love her slowly and thoroughly this time. And here was not the place. He ran a finger over her lips. "Not yet, my lady," he said. He could have sworn he heard her groan in protest as he stepped away from her and turned back to the falcon.

The bird had finished eating the meat and was now staring at him with black eyes. Logan put his gloved hand to the bird's chest, and this time it hopped up on his wrist.

"Where are you from?" Solace asked softly.

Logan grabbed the lure and headed toward the mews. Solace followed. "Cavindale," Logan answered.

"That's a long way from here. What are you doing here?"

"I'm a wanderer," he lied, elegantly. "I go where I want to go."

"Why settle here?"

A grin stretched his lips as he turned his gaze back to her. I'm looking at the reason. "Coin," he said. "Wandering pays very little." He entered the mews and put the falcon on its perch.

"But you know how to use your sword. Can't you—?"

Logan interrupted her, knowing what she was going to ask. "Just because I know how to use it doesn't mean I like to."

Solace leaned against the doorframe, watching him put the lure away. "Where did you learn how to use a sword?"

"When you have traveled as much as I have, you find many . . . opportunities . . . to learn how to wield a blade. You either learn or you die. It's that simple."

"And your falcon?" she wondered.

He turned a quizzical gaze to her.

"Where did you find him?" she inquired.

"I didn't find him. He found me." Logan paused in his work for a long moment, thinking about the first time he'd encountered his feathered companion. "The damned bird hasn't left my side for five years."

"Where did he come from?"

Logan looked out of the mews to see the black falcon, "his falcon" as Solace had called it, watching him with its dark, keen eyes. For the first time, it struck him as odd that he had never given the bird a name. He just hadn't thought the bird would shadow him for five years, so he hadn't bothered to think of one. Well, now's not the time to give him one, he thought. He turned back to Solace. "I was out in the woods hunting for my supper, looking for rabbit mostly," he said, beginning his tale. "I spotted one hiding in the brush and nocked an arrow in my bow."

"A hunter, too," Solace mused softly to herself, but loud enough for Logan to hear.

"I took aim and just as I let the arrow fly, a flash of black raced across my vision and a rush of air swept past my face. I saw that it was a falcon diving for prey," he paused and looked toward the falcon. "My prey!" he shouted at the bird.

The falcon ignored his outburst.

Logan turned back to see Solace grinning gaily at him. And he completely lost his train of thought. "Your prey . . ." she supplied.

"Right," Logan said with a nod. "He was going for the rabbit, but my arrow struck the rabbit first, knocking it to the side. The falcon was surprised by a move the rabbit wasn't supposed to be able to make and faltered in its dive. He hit the ground hard."

"Did he get hurt?"

Logan shook his head. "I don't think so. Just mad. Because then he shot up into the sky and circled high above me as I gathered up my kill. I lit a fire and was preparing to cook the rabbit when I looked up to see the falcon staring at me from only a foot away with those damn beady eyes. It was the most foolhardy thing I have ever seen an animal do.

"The bird inched closer, and I just stared right back. I had to admire the bastard's courage. I mean, he was close enough that I could grab him and have him for dessert. Then he tried to grab a piece of meat right out from under my nose, but I pulled it away just before he took any. He barked at me like some wild dog, and darted off into the sky." He paused, then smiled softly, remembering. "He just kept circling and circling while I ate."

"Then what happened?"

Logan shrugged, still unable to understand the bird's behavior himself. "From that day on, the bird's always been somewhere close by. I suppose it's his way of getting revenge . . . by annoying me until the end of time."

Solace was staring at him with rapt fascination. She was so damn beautiful. Who cared about tales of hunting or falcons or prey or supper when she was near? Or revenge, a small voice inside him added. But the voice was so faint now it was easy to ignore its feeble attempt to be heard.

Suddenly he grabbed her arm, pulling her into the mews. He clasped her against him as he leaned into the wall. "Are you through asking me questions?" he wondered.

"I—" She opened her mouth to answer, and Logan pressed his lips to hers, hungrily stealing a kiss from her parted lips. He tasted the sweet honey of her mouth, pressing against her, wanting so much more than this. He pulled back from her to gaze into her eyes and saw they were clouded with aroused passion. Her lips were slightly swollen from being kissed so thoroughly. He cupped her chin.

"Will you come with me?" he asked.

"Yes," she replied instantly.

He chuckled deeply. "You don't know where I want you to go."

She gazed into his eyes with the sultry passion that enflamed his own. "Where do you want me to go?"

"To my room," he whispered, nuzzling her neck.

"Yes," she answered, just as quickly.

Logan took her hand in his and kissed her knuckles, before pulling her out of the mews. Together they headed for his room, their steps anxious and hurried.

A call from the battlements halted them. "We're under attack!" They both raised startled eyes to the walkway to see a swarm of men battling.

Around them, chaos erupted, villagers charging for the protection of the keep, merchants shutting their doors and windows against the intruders, mothers screaming for their children! The clang of swords resounded through the ward, the thundering clatter drowning out the panicked cries of the people.

Logan glanced at Solace and saw the concern etched on her face. She moved toward the stairway that led to the battlements, but Logan pulled her roughly back to him. "You can't go up there!" he said.

"I have to," she answered, her gaze pinned on the walkway.

Logan grabbed her shoulders, shaking her once, forcing her gaze to meet his. "Those are armed men. Just what do you think you can do?"

"They're my men, Logan," she answered with firm resolve. "I have to see what's happening."

Logan cursed silently. He cursed her honorable dedication. He cursed Farindale's men. But mostly he cursed the timing. "I'll go," he said. A tortured scream ripped through the air, and Logan knew the body count was growing by the minute. "Go back to the keep," he ordered, releasing her hand and heading for the stairs. "I'll come for you when it's safe."

Solace moved to obey him. She had taken one step toward the keep when a man fell with a scream over the battlements, to land at her feet. He clutched at a gaping wound in his chest. Blood oozed through his fingers. But it wasn't the blood that horrified Solace. It was the thought of Logan lying at her feet instead of one of Barclay's men.

Her gaze whipped back to the stairs Logan had taken, but he was already gone. Logan! Without a second thought, she raced toward the stairs.

Fifteen

Solace skidded to a halt when she reached the battlements. The long walkway was jammed with Barclay's men and Fulton's knights, battling desperately with maces and swords and axes. The clashing of weapons and the shouting were deafening,

Through the crenels of the castle walls, Solace saw a large wooden attack tower pulled up against Fulton's outer wall. The side of the tower burned, shooting bright orange flames into the air. Solace quickly scanned the perimeter of the walls, looking for another of the siege engines, but she could see none. She had to get help. But where was Logan? Her eyes frantically searched the walkways, the fighting men, but she couldn't see him. She couldn't find him!

Suddenly, someone grabbed her arm, spinning her around. Peter gazed at her with concern. "What are you doing up here? Never mind," he amended. "Get out of here."

But Solace didn't move; she wanted to help, but was unsure of what to do. She watched Peter brush by her with a small garrison of guards. She backed slowly away, walking down the stairs, heading to the courtyard. She hadn't taken more than two steps into the ward when she spotted a man in armor looking around near the mews.

Solace ran toward him, but as she came closer and he turned toward her, she realized with a jolt that he was one of Barclay's men. She stopped abruptly, but her foot slid on loose gravel and she lost her balance, landing her on her bottom. She quickly turned over and pushed herself to her feet.

The soldier's arms closed around her from behind.

Solace struggled and opened her mouth to scream, but his gauntleted hand rose before her, clutching a dagger, silencing her protest.

"Let her go." The powerful voice issued forth from the deep shadows near the wall.

Solace looked up to see a shifting shadow, then a solid wall of man as Logan materialized from the darkness like a phantom. He held a large piece of wood before him, gently pounding his open palm with it. He moved toward them with deadly intent, his look dark and foreboding.

Suddenly, the soldier whipped the dagger at Logan, its sharp tip moving toward his neck with the speed of an arrow. At the last moment, Logan lifted the wood and the dagger slammed into it, imbedding itself deep in the plank.

Barclay's man whirled away, pulling Solace toward the stairs. Two more of Barclay's men appeared from the stairs to block Logan's path, swords in hand. Logan did not even hesitate; he kept coming, weaponless, his face twisted into a grimace of loathing.

Solace threw a desperate look over her shoulder to see one of the intruders swing. Logan easily deflected the blow with the wood, quickly swinging the plank around to knock the soldier in the jaw, sending him sprawling backward. Then Logan whirled with the agility of a cat and blocked a blow from the second soldier. The sword stuck in the wood, and Logan punched the man in the face, sending him to the ground. "Damn fool, Barclay," Logan muttered.

Logan continued after them, undaunted. He came at them like a storm cloud, steady and sure of his path. Suddenly, there were voices and Solace raised her head to see five more of Barclay's men running down the stairs.

Her captor bent to scoop up a fallen sword from the ground. Solace took the opportunity to lurch away, but he reached out, catching her hair in a fist. He yanked her back against him, pressing the tip of his sword to her neck.

Logan paused, his eyes narrowing dangerously.

Solace knew she had to free herself. How could Logan stand against five men?

"Solace!" a voice cried from the stairs.

Solace shifted her eyes, afraid to move her head for the pressure of the sword against her throat, and saw Peter leaping over the stone rail of the stairs. Distracted, the soldier eased the pressure of the blade against her neck. She raised her hands and pushed the sword from her throat, lurching forward to escape.

Logan caught her easily, and set her behind him, using his body as a shield. Peter reached Logan's side, putting his shoulder to Logan's, his sword poised.

Standing side by side, Peter and Logan were like a wall; Solace could see nothing beyond their thick shoulders. They were exactly the same height and build. She could hear the clash of metal against metal as Peter engaged an enemy.

As he moved, Solace caught glimpses of Barclay's men around them. Logan was dodging the blows with a grace and agility that belied his large frame. They fought with unerring accuracy, Peter with his sword, Logan with the piece of wood. Suddenly, a soldier lunged and Logan swiped at the sword with his makeshift weapon, sending the blade spinning off into the air.

Then Solace's view was blocked again as the remaining soldiers moved in. She pressed herself against the wall, the clang of metal and the bang of the wood ringing out in the air.

Suddenly, one of the soldiers broke away and raced through the courtyard, charging toward the gatehouse. Logan took a step forward, ready to bolt after him, but then stopped, letting him go. It was Peter who broke off from the fight and dashed after Barclay's man, shouting for Fulton's archers to cut him down.

Some of Fulton's own troops moved in to join the fight, quickly finishing off the remainder of the invaders. Solace spotted Captain Montgomery leading them. "Captain!" she shouted, gaining his attention.

Logan grabbed Solace's arm and held onto her, pulling her quickly toward the keep.

"Is the castle secure?" she called, resisting Logan's attempts to get her away from the scene of the battle.

"Yes!" Montgomery shouted back. "We were ready for them! Only twenty men got over the wall. We burned the siege engine!"

Logan walked briskly forward, and Solace had to quickly pick up her pace to match his.

As they reached the keep, Solace noticed that the sounds of battle were gone, replaced by an eerie silence. As her heartbeat began to slow, she realized she was trembling all over. She turned her gaze to Logan.

He paced the doorway, his hands on his hips. His muscles bunched and released beneath a sheen of perspiration. He flung the wood aside, mouthing a silent curse.

Solace reached up to swipe a strand of hair from her forehead, but before her hand touched her hair, she noticed a red drop trailing a path down her arm onto her sleeve. Curious, she turned her palm over . . .

. . . and gasped! Blood was dripping over the side of her palm, oozing from a slash mark in the center. She turned her other hand over to see blood pool in her cupped palm. With this discovery came an onslaught of pain.

Logan seized her wrists in his hand, studying the wounds on her palms. "What happened?" he asked urgently.

"It must have been when I pushed the soldier's sword away." She watched the blood drip through her fingers. "Am I going to die?" she asked. She had treated many wounds, but seeing her own blood sent her mind reeling. Darkness edged her vision.

The question brought a grin to Logan's lips. "No. Far from it."

He gently pulled her with him, leading her back to the mews. She half-heartedly tried to pull away from him. "I should make sure the castle is secure," she said, looking toward the battlements.

"The fighting is over," he replied. "Castle Fulton is safe, for now." He opened the door to his chambers and gently pushed her back onto his mattress of hay. Then he bent over the sack near the table and pulled something from the interior before turning to her. He knelt before her and took her hand into his, carefully wiping the wound and then wrapping a fresh cloth around her cut.

Solace raised her eyes to study his face—his bronze skin, kissed by the sun; his long lashes; his perfect features; his dark, wavy hair. She could gaze at him all day and feel peaceful and contented. And yet something was bothering her. The way he fought . . . he was no falconer. He was as good, if not better, than Peter—with just a piece of wood. Could he have been a knight at one time? Did he have training? She knew she should be cautious, that she didn't really know him.

He finished bandaging her palms and stood, guiding her up with him. They found themselves just barely touching. She could feel the heat emanating from him, and it filled her own body. His look was lidded, as if he had just awoken from a pleasant dream.

But then, she realized, she had never known a man better.

He lingered near her. She could feel his breath on her lips as she lifted her eyes to his. He was looking at her as if she were a rare delicacy to be slowly enjoyed. A blush crept up her neck to her cheeks.

Logan ran a finger along her jaw, a grin twitching the corners of his lips.

Solace smiled, playing with the edge of his tunic near his neck. He lowered his mouth to hers and gently kissed her lips, then pulled back slightly and his mercury eyes filled her vision. His hand slid over her shoulder to her nape and tilted her head up, exposing her slender neck. He dropped a kiss there, and she swore she could hear a guttural groan as he trailed a path of playful nibbles to her jaw and across her lips. When he claimed them again, his kiss was full of burning need, branding his desire on her skin.

Logan pressed his lips against hers, hotly, feverishly, drinking of her sweet innocence, promising her of things to come.

Solace responded to his kiss with a need of her own, her hands pulling him close. She pressed herself against him and a soft groan issued from deep within her.

He pushed her back against the wall, his hands kneading her breasts. The flame within her grew until it was a roaring bonfire. She ran her hands down his strong back, marveling at the strength, the power of him. She needed him so desperately that she wanted to cry. She wanted him to fill the aching, lonely part in her life. Solace pulled him closer, whispering, "Logan."

He lifted her dress and touched her leg, caressing the smooth length of it. His palm was so hot against her skin. She grew anxious for his touch, their bonding.

Boldly, she reached down and cupped his manhood. Shocked, he grabbed her hand, halting her movement. "Brazen hussy," he growled playfully, a sly grin curling his lips. He looked her in the eye, a smoky brilliance dancing in the secret depths of his gaze.

He moved her hand over his bulge, and it grew hard and stiff at her touch. The magical member that had driven her to heights she had never known responded to her touch like a live animal. "I want to see it," she whispered.

Logan pulled her tight against his rock-hard chest. "God's blood, woman!" he said in a light voice that was somehow deep and primeval. "Where did you learn to be so forthright?"

"Well, I—"

"Then release it," he murmured, pulling back.

Solace's eyes scanned him. She stepped forward, barely able to keep her hands from touching every inch of him. She reached out to clutch his tunic and lifted it over his head, revealing his hard chest muscles. She glided her fingertips over his skin, over his naked torso, from the very edges of his shoulders, down to the tops of his leggings. She admired the smoothness of his skin, the utter perfection of it, until her exploration brought her to a ragged scar that stretched from the bottom of his ribs to his leggings. "What happened?" she gasped.

"I was careless and didn't guard my back," he replied, directing her hands to the laces that held up his leggings.

Solace pulled the strings and his leggings slid from his body like a cloth falling away to reveal a masterpiece.

His legs were strong and lined with well-defined muscles. His member stood straight and when her hand accidentally brushed it, he hissed with enjoyment.

"It's so . . . big," she whispered in awe. Tentatively, she reached out and stroked the tip with her fingertip. It jumped at her touch and she almost laughed.

Logan grabbed her by the elbows. "You won't think it's funny when it's inside you," he promised huskily. "My turn."

His arms reached around her, and his hands deftly undid the buttons that lined her back. He pulled the houppelande from her shoulders and pushed it down her waist until it pooled on the floor in a cloud of blue velvet. Logan's gaze devoured her from head to foot as she stood before him in nothing but her chemise.

Solace felt the desire grow inside her at his mere gaze. She reached out to him, but he caught her wrists and gently eased them back to her sides.

Logan lifted his hands to place his fingertips at her cheeks and then trace the curves of her face, moving them down her cheekbones, over her chin and down her neck. He leaned close to her, and heated kisses followed his touch, flitting over her already-burning skin, sending sensations of pulsating passion flowing through her.

Logan unlaced the chemise and slowly pulled it down her bare skin, sliding it over her breasts. The cloth grazed her nipples, and she felt a flash of heat between her legs. He gazed at her breasts in absolute admiration. "Lord, they're perfect," he gasped, reaching up to cup them. They filled his hands and he began to stroke them, stoking the fire that was already ignited inside Solace. His thumb ran over a nipple and then again, encircling the precious peak in slow, undulating circles.

Solace groaned softly, delighting in the sensual torture.

Laurel O'Donnell

Logan lowered his lips to one of her mounds, his tongue circling the nipple as his thumb had done. His hands eased the chemise over her flat stomach and down her hips until it fell away from her body and she stood before him, naked.

He stared at her for a long moment, his reverent gaze sweeping her body, lingering with heated intensity at her breasts. Solace felt his stare searing through her, and every fiber of her yearned for him, for his touch, his caress.

Finally, after what seemed like torturous hours, he pulled her to him, claiming her lips in an urgent plundering of her mouth. His hand cupped her buttocks before moving around her hips to gently graze her velvety-soft curls. Solace groaned and thrust toward him. He eased his finger down her forest of curls, and spread the petals of her womanhood, searching for the bud that would release her ecstasy. When he discovered it, Solace felt a sharp stab of rapture spear her body.

"Tell me you like it," he whispered into her ear, teasing her skin with his teeth.

Solace's knees buckled and it was all she could do to support herself by clutching at his strong shoulders.

"Tell me you want me to touch you," he urged more desperately, his spiraling strokes raising her higher and higher on a cloud of exhilaration.

"Oh," she groaned, barely managing to open her mouth to speak.

"Tell me you want me."

"I want you," she gasped and Logan thrust his finger inside her. She shattered into a million glowing stars as shivers of utter delight tore through her, sending her exploding over the brink of pleasure into the gates of heaven. Wave after wave of sensational delight splashed over her, again and again, buffeting her with ecstasy.

Slowly, the feeling abated and she opened her eyes,

sated and fulfilled, to gaze into Logan's shimmering orbs. They shone like stars at her, shining on her new-found delight with approval.

He eased her back onto his mattress of straw, delicately holding her in his arms. He moved over her, bearing his weight on his arms, refusing to take his eyes from her. He parted her legs, and she eased her thighs open until she felt his manhood against her. Solace groaned, anticipating their joining.

He slowly moved into her, sheathing himself inside her folds. A sigh escaped from his lips, and Solace reached up to run her hands along his cheeks. When he opened his eyes, he was staring at her with an intensity that touched her soul.

Then he began to move. Slowly at first, but his tempo quickly built as their lovemaking intensified. He thrust into her again and again until his body stiffened, growing taut with exertion, and his face flooded with release.

Logan rolled off Solace, scooping her up into his arms, and pulled her tight against him. They lay together for a long, quiet moment. Solace listened to the beat of Logan's heart, the sated bliss in his breathing.

Finally she sat up, reaching for her clothing.

Logan grabbed her wrist. "Where do you think you're going?"

"To check on the castle," she said.

"I don't think so," he replied, pulling her back down on top of him. "I'm not through with you yet."

With a delighted squeak of protest, Solace felt him growing stiff once again . . .

It wasn't until much later that evening that Solace sneaked out of Logan's room, leaving him sleeping peacefully. She gazed at him for a long moment in the doorway. He was sprawled on the straw, his body curled around the spot she had just vacated. In a beam of moonlight that peeked in through two boards of wood, Solace could see his peaceful face. His head was cushioned on his arm and his dark hair spilled over his skin to the straw mattress.

She stared fondly at Logan for a moment longer before quietly closing his door, then eyed the courtyard to see if anyone had seen her. But the ward was empty. Her stomach rumbled, and she remembered she had had nothing to eat since early that morning. A cool wind encircled her, but she barely noticed as her heated flesh remembered their day of lovemaking. Solace looked contentedly up at the starry sky. Suddenly, impulsively, she spun around, her hands outstretched at her sides, a blissful grin lighting her face. She had never felt this way before!

Solace rounded the corner, moving past the training grounds. Suddenly an arm jutted out from the shadows and caught her wrist! She stifled the scream that immediately came to her lips when Graham stepped from the darkness.

"Now what might a proper woman like you be doing in a man's room so late at night?"

Solace tried to pull away. "Let me go this instant," she commanded.

"Pretty imperious for a slut," Graham retorted, but dropped her hand.

She displayed her bandaged hands impatiently. "He tended my wounds," she snapped.

"Is that all he tended?" Graham took a step toward her, and she retreated. He reached out and touched her lips, but she jerked her face aside. "You seem to be giving away your kisses rather freely."

Solace was so shocked that she couldn't reply. Anger vied with fear in her.

"What else are you giving away?"

Solace opened her mouth to respond, but Graham seized her waist, pulling her to him. She fought against his hold, but he managed to lift her skirt and touch the inside of her thigh. A crooked, horrible smile twisted his lips as he released her to rub his moist fingers together. "His seed."

She tried to run past him, but he grabbed her arm, whirling her to him, pressing her against his chest.

"Why settle for a man like that when I would be more than happy to oblige you?" Graham pressed his lips against hers.

In a moment of sheer terror, an image from her past blazed across her memory. She saw lord Randol forcing his lips to Anne's, saw him pawing at her flesh with groping hands. Only now did Solace realize exactly what she had witnessed all those years ago. The thought sent her into a frenzy, and she lashed out at Graham, drawing three ragged claw marks down across his cheek. "Get away from me!"

His reaction was quick and instantaneous. He smashed a fist into her cheek, knocking her to the ground. Then he was on top of her. She opened her mouth to cry out, but he pressed his arm into her neck, almost choking her. She tried to fight, but he pinned her with his weight, "Let's see if you're as wet for me as you are for him."

She struggled, but against his warrior-trained strength she was no match.

Sixteen

The howling of the dogs filtered into Logan's sleep-filled mind. He bolted up in his bed, his heart hammering in his chest. His eyes darted around the darkness.

Then he noticed that Solace was gone. He flew from the bed, stopping only long enough to don his leggings.

Outside, the dogs were barking and growling fiercely, scratching at the walls of the kennel. Something was wrong. Terribly wrong. He looked to the skies, expecting a hail of stones or a swarm of flaming arrows, but the night sky was clear and empty. So what was spooking the dogs?

He glanced around the mews. Where the hell was Solace? But again he saw nothing.

Suddenly, his black falcon swooped in and landed on his shoulder. It cocked its head to the side, listening. Logan strained to hear. Beneath the raucous barking of the dogs, a cry rent the air. A scuffling sound. It sounded like a struggle. Logan grabbed his staff, which had been leaning against the side of the mews, and dashed toward the noise.

The falcon on his shoulder took flight again as he rounded the kennels, coming to the training grounds. There, in the shadows of the wall, he could barely make out a woman with a man on top of her. Fierce, protective anger consumed him as he recognized her even in the darkness. Solace! Instinctively, he charged forward and swung his staff sharply, striking the man beneath his chin. The man flew backward and landed roughly on his back a few feet from Solace, his breath exploding out of his lungs in a loud grunt as he struck the earth.

Logan dropped to one knee, pulling Solace into his embrace. She fought wildly to get free, pummeling him with her fists. "Solace!" Logan called, seizing her wrists. "It's me. You're safe. It's over."

"No!" she cried out, trying to break free of his hold. Logan tightened his grip. "Solace! It's Logan. Stop!"

"No! Don't!" she sobbed.

Logan seized her shoulders and shook her. "Stop it!"

Sobbing, she looked around with wild eyes until he locked gazes with her. "You're all right," he soothed. "You're all right."

Solace collapsed against him, sobbing even harder. As Logan felt her tremble, a need to again bash the head of the man who'd attacked her struck him. He held her firmly to his chest, stroking her hair. He felt her curl against him, push her face into his neck, felt her hot tears on his shoulder.

"You'll pay for that," the attacker snarled as he rose to his feet, wiping blood from the corner of his mouth.

Logan swung a dark gaze to the man. His fingers curled tightly around his staff, and his eyes narrowed to dangerous slits as he recognized Graham.

Solace continued to sob softly against him, her warm tears trickling down his chest. He stroked Solace's soft hair again, trying to let the anger inside him fade, knowing that she needed him to comfort her, but the rage wouldn't subside. It only grew. Finally, he gently gripped Solace's arm and eased her away from him. He set Solace behind him, touching her tear-streaked cheek with the tips of his fingers, before turning to face Graham.

The thought of his vile body pressed intimately against Solace's struggling form made Logan furious—savage.

Without warning, Logan lashed out with his staff, catching Graham on the side of the head. When the nobleman staggered, Logan came after him with a blow to the jaw. Graham went down hard on his bottom. Logan charged forward, throwing his staff aside, and grabbed Graham's velvet tunic. With a violent tug, he dragged the man up until his face was mere inches from Logan's. Fear haunted the cur's eyes. But it wasn't enough. The urge to smash his head in with his bare hands consumed Logan, and he raised his fist.

"Please," Graham gasped out.

"Logan," Solace pleaded, her sobs still catching in her throat.

Logan froze. His jaw clenched. And then he slowly lowered his fist. "If I see you touch her again, I'll let the birds have you for their next meal," he snarled. He brought his fist back up and slammed his clenched hand into Graham's nose.

Graham howled as blood erupted from his nostrils.

Logan dropped him to the ground before turning to Solace. Her cheeks were pale, her green eyes wide with fear. He moved to her, putting his arms around her shoulders. "Are you all right?"

She pressed her wet face to his bare chest.

Feeling her tremble, Logan squeezed her tightly, soothing her. Behind him, he heard receding footsteps and knew that Graham had fled. As he stroked her hair, his fingers brushed against a stray piece of straw trapped in the rich velvet of her hair. He gently untangled it and let it float to the ground.

Solace raised her eyes to him, and the moonlight reflected off the misery in those large orbs.

"Did he hurt you?" Logan demanded.

Solace shook her head. "I couldn't get him off of

me," she told him in a ragged breath. "He was so strong and—"

Logan pulled her tight against him. "It's all right," he whispered. "You're all right." He squeezed his eyes shut. If he had lingered in his room for just a moment longer, he would have been too late. The thought sent immobilizing fear through him. He opened his eyes, and they burned with rage.

That was when he saw something in the dirt. He focused his eyes on the object. The clouds parted and the moon shone down on it. A dagger. A gold-tipped dagger, its handle etched with flowers. Did the dagger belong to Graham? Or had it inadvertently been dropped by someone else? His eyes narrowed suspiciously.

Logan moved to grab the dagger, but he felt Solace's fingers dig into his shoulders and he returned his attention to her. With a backward glance at the dagger, he guided her toward his room, whispering comforting words to her.

Logan pulled her with him to his mattress. They lay together, she on top of him as he held her against his heart. "It's all right," Logan whispered to her. "I won't let anyone hurt you. Not ever." Logan let her cry, stroking her hair. After a long while, he realized she was asleep. He smiled against the top of her head, pressing a kiss to her scalp.

With a violent crack, the door to Logan's room exploded open and three soldiers stormed inside! Startled from sleep, Solace quickly sat upright, trying to get her groggy mind to function. Was the castle under attack? The men quickly descended upon Logan as he reached for his sword hidden beneath the hay. They pulled him to his feet, wrenching his arms behind his back, quickly binding his wrists with thick ropes.

"No!" Solace screamed. "What are you doing?"

She recognized two of the three men as castle guards and ordered, "I command you to stop this."

"Now isn't this a compromising situation?"

Solace glanced up to see Graham lounging against the doorframe, his lecherous gaze plundering her body. A cloth stretched across his nose, the fabric stained with blood.

Logan lunged toward Graham, but the guards easily caught him and shoved him toward the doorway.

Graham took a step to the side, letting the guards roughly usher Logan outside. He glanced at Solace. "What will lady Alissa say?" Graham asked.

"You can't do this," Solace retorted.

"It's already done."

Graham approached Solace, but she slipped by him to race after Logan. She quickly reached his side, and cried, "I won't let them get away with this."

"Just stay away from Graham," Logan ordered as the guards shoved him forward. "Do you hear me?"

Solace nodded to Logan. She whirled on Graham. "Where are you taking him?"

"The dungeon, of course," Graham answered.

Tucked neatly into Graham's belt was a gold-tipped dagger, its handle etched with flowers.

Seventeen

The next morning, Solace waited at the back of the courthouse beside Logan. He was flanked by two guards, his wrists bound behind his back with thick rope. She cast a nervous glance at him to find his cool, metallic eyes on her. She tried to force a smile to her lips, but found she could not.

His eyes lidded just a little, and a warm flush swept through Solace. A shy smile formed in her heart and worked its way up to her lips. She quickly looked away from him. She couldn't think about how he made her feel. She couldn't think about kissing his lips, nor about his hands on her body. She had to concentrate on getting Logan set free.

She lifted her gaze to the platform. Alissa was seated at the head of the courthouse, listening to Captain Montgomery reporting on the current security of Castle Fulton. She barely stifled a yawn as she nodded to him, waving him away. Then her eyes locked with Solace's, and a stern look of disapproval thinned her lips and eyes.

To Solace's left, a few villagers stood in a line, awaiting their turn to voice their complaints.

Graham lounged against a pillar not far from them, gingerly rubbing the cloth that covered his nose. Despite her best resolve, fear surged within Solace at the memory of his body pressed to hers, his hands moving up her thigh. She shivered and glanced away . . .

. . . to lock eyes with Logan. His brows furrowed, and he looked in the direction she had been gazing moments before, his eyes searching the faces until he saw Graham's. His frown deepened and his body tensed before he returned his look to Solace.

She read the anger in his slitted eyes, the hatred in his clenched jaw. During the battle, she had seen that same look on his face, that same single-mindedness of purpose. She had seen that look before, thirteen years ago when Peter was a prisoner. He had looked at her father with the same fury and loathing, with an intensity that was so disturbing she had not forgotten it in all these years. They were very much alike, Logan and Peter, the same build, the same height. Why, they could be kin . . . Something tugged at her mind. A distant memory. But just as a picture began to form, the guards urged Logan forward.

Solace quickly took up pace with him, as if she, too, were a prisoner. She tried to keep her chin up and her back straight as the courthouse became hushed and all eyes turned to them. Graham stepped before them, leading the way up the aisle.

Alissa's gaze swept over Logan, then moved by Solace to land on Graham as they halted before her. "What is the complaint?" she wondered.

Solace glanced at Beth. Beth was seated with her long legs crossed, leaning back in a chair beside her mother.

"He struck me," Graham answered, indicating the bandage on his nose.

"You struck a noble?" Alissa exclaimed in disbelief.

"I did," Logan replied.

"He was defending me," Solace proclaimed, taking a step forward, placing herself before Logan. "Graham attacked me."

A murmur spread through the courthouse.

"It's a lie!" Graham replied. "I found them together. Apparently the falconer didn't like being interrupted."

Solace's mouth dropped and a blush rose to her cheeks. "That's not true!"

"Then where did you get those scratches on your face?" Logan wondered.

Graham's eyes pivoted to Logan. "From our battle."

"Women scratch," Logan pointed out. "I use my fists."

"Enough!" Alissa shouted, standing. When all eyes turned to her and the room quieted, she continued with a regal air. "It is very clear to me that someone is not telling the truth." Her gaze burned into Solace. "To discern the truth, I have no other choice but to proclaim a trial by fire."

Solace stiffened. Trial by fire! It hadn't been done in years! The accused had to carry a piece of red-hot iron in their bare hands over a long distance. If there were no burns, then the accused was innocent. No one ever passed this test.

"If the falconer's innocent, God will surely protect him," Alissa said.

Solace cast a nervous glance over her shoulder at Logan. Her mind worked furiously. She had to do something to help him! She caught the smug look in Graham's eyes, the smile twitching his lips. Bastard! Coward!

Suddenly an idea came to her and she turned back to her stepmother. "Why not make it trial by combat?"

"Surely you jest," Alissa said in disbelief. "You're giving your falconer no chance at all. He knows nothing of the art of fighting. Graham is highly trained."

"You're right, Mother," Solace said, quickly, slyly, and looked away. "Forget I even mentioned it."

Alissa stood silent for a moment, thinking. Beth

leaned over to whisper something into her mother's ear. Alissa's face darkened with a cunning sneer, and she nodded at Beth's comment. She then turned to face the assembly. "The guards need a distraction, as do the peasants. It shall be trial by combat," she proclaimed. "They shall fight until one yields."

An hour later, the castle courtyard was overflowing with expectant onlookers. Soldiers packed the battlements. Villagers watched from their shops. An alewife moved through the crowd, collecting wagers on the coming fight. She had to stop as Logan was ushered through the crowd before her by two guards. Graham awaited him in the makeshift circle the crowd had created.

Logan couldn't help but overhear that the odds were not in his favor. His eyes scanned the crowd. He didn't care about the damn odds. He had faced far worse before. He continued searching for Solace, knowing that she would be here somewhere. Then his gaze came to rest on her. She stood near the garden fence, her hands folded, her eyes on him. It had been a stroke of genius to suggest trial by combat. No one knew him as a fighter. He felt a strange stirring of pride.

He lifted his gaze to the sky, having to shield his eyes with his hand from the glare of the sun to see the falcon circling high overhead like a vulture. "Damn bird," Logan grumbled. It seemed even the falcon was betting against him.

Alissa stepped forward. "Let the trial begin!" she announced. Then she turned to Graham, bowing slightly. "At your leisure, lord Graham."

Logan caught the handle of the blade Graham threw to him, but didn't have time to inspect it as Graham attacked immediately. Logan blocked his blow, feigning a stumble backward. He was far too good a warrior not to expect an immediate attack. But Logan also knew that if he didn't pretend unease with the sword, his cover could be blown. He stumbled again, allowing Graham to push him back.

The crowd parted as the two fighters moved too close. Graham was a weak fighter. Logan saw it immediately, the way he struck and pulled back in case Logan attacked. The man was incapable of anything but a one-swing attack. He was doomed.

Logan felt the press of a wall behind him. A grin stretched Graham's lips taut. The image of those lips pressing on Solace's flesh distracted Logan for a moment. Graham sliced at Logan and was rewarded by a slash on his arm. Logan grimaced, pushing aside any thoughts of Solace.

Then, more confident, Graham swung a blow at Logan's head. Logan ducked and sidestepped, the blade whizzing in the air just above his head. He quickly moved around Graham to trap him against the wall, raising his weapon to attack. He lunged, pinning part of Graham's tunic to the wall.

The crowd gasped. All around him, Logan heard shouts of encouragement, but none directed at him.

Logan withdrew the blade in time to block a frantic swing of Graham's. There was panic in the noble's eyes, and it would have been Logan's turn to grin, if he were prone to that sort of thing. He stepped forward, arcing the blade toward Graham's neck.

Desperately, Graham brought his sword up, blocking the blow. As the blades hit, Logan's gave way, splitting cleanly in half.

Again the crowd gasped, this time louder than before. Coins began to exchange hands as murmurings of the falconer's imminent defeat swept through the crowd.

Logan stared in shock at the straight break in the

blade. Then his eyes lifted to Graham's. There was no surprise there, only acceptance. He had planned it this way! That was why he hadn't given Logan the chance to look at the sword. Logan threw the useless blade to the ground.

He then backed away as Graham waved his blade before him, toying with him. Logan doubted the man would stop with a yield, and he'd be damned if he would give him one.

Graham chuckled low in his throat as Logan retreated. He swung his sword, and Logan leapt aside. The man was out for blood.

"Logan!"

Logan turned and Solace tossed a piece of wood at him. He caught it easily and turned back just in time to block Graham's swing. With his new weapon in hand, Logan attacked relentlessly, driving Graham back to the herb garden fence near the east wall. He was tired of this game, tired of this man. He wanted to bash his head in and spill his brains into the earth.

Suddenly, Logan stepped on the pointed tip of the broken blade and his ankle twisted. He fell to the ground, the wood tumbling from his hands, sliding across the courtyard.

In the next instant, Graham was standing over him, his blade raised. Logan reached out to his sides, groping blindly in the dirt, searching for something, anything. His fingers closed over the handle of the broken blade. He raised it to protect himself just as Graham plunged forward to slam the sword at his skull.

Eighteen

Logan moved his head to the side and Graham's sword plunged into the earth beside his cheek. Grimacing, Logan thrust his broken blade up.

He stared at Graham's shocked face. Graham coughed, spraying Logan with blood, before he slowly slumped to the side. Logan sat up and was greeted by absolute quiet. Hundreds gaped at the bloody scene, their eyes wide with shock and disbelief. Slowly, Logan stood and looked down at Graham, who lay unmoving, blood soaking through his tunic.

A scream pierced the silence like a clap of thunder, and Beth shoved her way through the crowd, rushing to Graham's side. She dropped to her knees, sobbing.

Logan cast a look at Solace who stood motionless, as stunned as everyone, her hand planted firmly over her mouth, her green eyes wide.

"Murderer!" Beth hissed at Logan, her eyes full of real tears.

"Guards!" Alissa screamed.

Two men appeared at Logan's side, both holding swords.

"Take him to the dungeon!" she shouted.

Logan made no attempt to resist as he was led away. He turned one last time to glance over his shoulder at

Solace, to see her slowly drop her hand from her mouth . . .

Solace watched the men take him away, her heart breaking. Guilt washed over her. It was all her fault. She was the one who had suggested trial by combat. She was the one Logan was protecting when he hit Graham. She was the one Graham had lusted after.

Beth's wailing broke through her fragile shell of remorse, and she turned her eyes to her half sister. She was sobbing onto Graham's bloody chest, her fingers clutching at his tunic. Alissa was at her side, whispering soothing words to her, gently patting her back.

Immediately, Solace moved to Beth. She knelt at her sister's side, despite the warning glare from Alissa. Solace put a hand to Beth's shoulder, offering her comfort.

But the scathing eyes that rose to her caused Solace to snatch her hand back as if she had just been burned. "You," Beth snarled with contempt and pure hatred. "You little bitch!" She lunged at Solace, catching her around the throat. Solace fell back, trying to fight her off, but Beth's grip was tight and unrelenting. It wasn't until Alissa grabbed Beth's shoulders and hauled her away from Solace that she was able to back away from her sister. She put her hands to her throat, massaging the tender skin, her eyes wide with disbelief.

"It isn't enough to be heir to Fulton," Beth hollered. "You've always wanted what was mine! You've tried to steal away the men I love."

Her mouth dropped in shock. She continued to rub her neck slowly, realizing for the first time the depth of hatred Beth felt toward her. "I only wanted you to be happy. I never tried to hurt you, Beth," Solace said, her voice heavy.

"Hurt me? You stole Robert away from me! And you took Graham from me!"

Solace straightened her back. "Graham was attacking me near the mews," Solace said, raising her gaze defensively to her stepmother. "He tried to rape me."

Beth's peal of deranged laughter echoed through the ward. "Of course he did!" she chortled. "Every man wants you! Why, you're the most beautiful woman alive. No man can withstand your charms!" She picked up a lock of Solace's dark hair, toying with the rebellious curl. "Why your hair is always tucked neatly under a headdress or combed to a brilliant glow." Her voice was filled with mocking sarcasm. Solace always wore her hair down or braided.

Solace brushed her hair from her sister's hand.

Beth snatched at Solace's blue houppelande. "You're always clothed in the latest fashions!"

Solace stood, her brows drawing together in a frown. Beth pursued her, pinching Solace's sun-kissed cheeks in a mock kiss. "Your skin is as white as the limewash. You're never in the sun! Your lips—"

Solace pulled her face free of Beth's hold.

"Solace," Alissa said patiently, "you must be mistaken. Graham wouldn't have wanted you."

Solace's anger deepened. "Why?" she demanded. "He had been following me around the castle for months."

Beth snorted in disbelief.

"Regardless of what you believe," she said to Beth. "Graham attacked me. That was why he had those marks on his face. I did it, not Logan."

"Logan," Beth cooed in a strangely sensual way, before turning her gaze to her mother. "He killed Graham!" A sly smile twisted Beth's lips. "I want him executed, Mother!"

"No," Solace gasped, stepping toward Alissa. "You can't do that."

"He killed Graham. Of course he will be executed."

Horror filled Solace as a smug, vindictive look crossed Beth's face. "It was trial by combat. He won. He proved his innocence."

Alissa turned dark eyes to Solace. "Because of your interference, he dies at dawn," she said.

"Interference?" Solace echoed in confusion.

"When he was defenseless you gave him the piece of wood."

"No!" Solace gasped.

"Burn him, Mother," Beth suggested in a retaliatory voice.

Alissa nodded in agreement.

"Please, Mother," Solace begged, grabbing hold of her hand. "He was helping me."

Alissa's eyes narrowed to cold slits and she pulled her hand free. "Yes," she murmured. "Helping you become a whore."

"Looks like you'll have to find someone else to spread your legs for," Beth hissed, joyfully. "Harlot."

"Mother . . ." Solace pleaded, glancing at Alissa.

"Slut," Beth called out.

Solace stumbled back, horrified at the sudden turn of events, fearful that she couldn't stop them. She turned and fled from the courtyard to the keep, racing through the hallways of the castle, not seeing the faces of the villagers who watched her run past them. She didn't know where she was going, only that she had to get away from their accusations.

She wasn't a harlot. She wasn't a whore.

Solace found herself standing before the large wooden doors that led to the old hall. Cobwebs still hung thick in the corners; the dust stirred around her, making her sneeze.

She pushed the doors open, and this time they didn't seem to give as easily as they had before. She raced to the window and dropped to her knees before it, resting her forehead against the cold stone of the ledge. Its coolness felt soothing to her hot brow. It was almost as hot as her guilt. Logan had helped her, saved her from Graham. And because of that he was going to be executed.

She could not let him die. But what could she do? If only she could postpone his execution until her father came home. She would do anything to spare Logan.

She turned around to stare at the pictures against the wall. "Tell me," she challenged them. "Tell me the secret. How shall I help Logan?"

Her voice echoed through the room, answerless.

She shook her head and wiped a strand of hair from her eyes. She couldn't get over the fact that Alissa didn't believe her. Solace had expected as much from Beth, but not Alissa. Perhaps if she were a man things would be different. A brother to Beth. Then there wouldn't be any competition between them. She had always wanted a brother, or a sister for that matter. The closest thing to a brother she had was Peter. He had always been there for her. More like a family than her stepmother and half sister.

Then an image came to her mind. She again remembered Peter fighting side by side with Logan. They had been built so much alike. So very tall, so broad. It was strange. Why, if she didn't know better, she would think they were . . .

Solace straightened, her face dawning with realization. That was it! That was where she had seen the crest before! She pushed away from the window, her heart hammering. The crest! Her mind kept screaming. She knew she had seen it somewhere before.

She approached the plate armor that she had knocked over and noticed that no one had reassembled the fallen suit. Her eyes scanned the floor, looking for the shield. But it was not there. It was gone.

Solace scowled. It had been here. The final piece to the puzzle. She searched the floor, but it was nowhere to be found. Frustrated, she stepped back, sighing.

She was sure it had been here. Perhaps the crest was somewhere else. On a tapestry, perhaps. Her gaze moved to the tapestry on the wall behind where the suit of armor had been.

The tapestry depicted two mighty warriors on horseback. Their swords crossed as their animals reared in combat. But nowhere on the entire tapestry was there a crest.

Solace hung her head. She had been so sure she could find answers here, so sure. She was about to turn away when something caught her eye. There was a strange bulge beneath the tapestry. She stepped closer and noticed that something was hidden beneath the fabric.

She eased the tapestry aside and released a curtain of dust that assaulted her. She swatted aside the annoying cloud, moving closer, refusing to give up her pursuit of the answer. When the dust settled, Solace gasped.

The shield that had been hidden by the tapestry glinted in the sunlight! On its surface she could see two crossed swords upon a full moon . . . the Grey family crest. The same crest she'd seen on Logan's sword!

Nineteen

The constant *drip-drip* was going to drive Logan insane, he was sure. He was bound by a metal collar around his neck that was attached by a thick chain to a large bolt on the wall. For the first few hours, he had paced the cell, trying to relieve the battle lust that surged through his veins, trying to tell himself that Solace would get him out of here. She was his last hope. His only hope. The irony wasn't lost on him.

He sat on the dirty ground, his forehead resting on his bent knees. There was no sunlight in the bowels of the castle, no way to tell exactly what time it was. He had slept once, restlessly and shivering. In a rough guess, he figured half a day had passed because they had brought him two meager meals. Earlier he had searched the cell for a means of escape, pulling his chains until his wrists were raw and chafed. Now he began to doubt he would ever see the light of day again. His only hold on sanity was a pair of bright green eyes—and the hope that he would see them again.

As the hours inched by and the *drip-drip* was drowned out by another prisoner's moans, Logan began to doubt that he would be able to finish his mission. Peter would never know that he was here, looking for him. Solace would never truly know how much she meant to him. He hadn't realized it . . . until he had seen Graham on top of her. Then, when his opportunity came to destroy the monster, he had taken it, forsaking all else to save Solace. To exact his revenge.

Revenge. It was the wrong revenge. He forced himself to think back, trying to clear his mind, trying to focus on his mission. He closed his eyes and he could see Sullivan's Hill as if it had all happened yesterday . . .

Dark. It was so dark. Then, Logan realized he was lying on his back in the grass, staring up at the starless night sky. A strange light flickered at the edge of his vision, but he paid it no mind as he boosted himself to his elbow. A sharp spear of agony cut through his head, and he raised a hand to his forehead. His hair was plastered to his skin in thick clumps of wetness. Logan knew it was blood. Slowly, he sat up, gently probing the cut on the side of his head.

Burning wood. The smell wafted to his nose, and he snapped his head up to see the castle—his castle—burning! Thick, consuming flames billowed out from the interior of his home.

"Father," Logan whispered, a frantic feeling knotting the inside of his stomach.

He was on his feet instantly. The world swam before his eyes and he staggered, battling off the effects of his wound. When the dizziness retreated, Logan searched the hill for his horse, but the animal was nowhere to be found.

He walked down Sullivan's Hill, resisting the urge to run, knowing he would stumble and fall if he did. How had the castle fallen? How could his father have been beaten so quickly, so easily? They had had food and reserves prepared for nearly a year!

His step quickened, his stomach twisted and every one of his muscles corded tight. Something had gone wrong. Terribly wrong.

He moved through town, fighting off the throbbing in his head, moving from shadow to shadow until the castle loomed before him. Smoke churned skyward from inside the walls in thick black clouds of destruction. As he came to the main road he had to pull back quickly.

Armored men were moving in groups along it.

Logan pressed himself close to the walls of the tailor's shop. The flickering red of the flames burning behind the approaching men swayed over their tunics. Logan's eyes gaped. Lined with gold, the white tunics bore the symbol of the lion—Farindale's crest!

His jaw tightened as he watched the soldiers disappear into the blacksmith's shop at the end of the street.

Suddenly, a movement across the road caught his attention. Logan swiveled his gaze to the shadows. He made out the figure of a man stumbling along the road. He was dragging his leg behind him, hurrying to escape.

Logan glanced one way along the street and then the other, making sure it was clear of guards, before racing across. He ignored the throbbing in his head as best he could, knowing he had to find answers. As he neared the bent man, Logan could see he was severely wounded. The man clutched his arm to his chest where his torn chain mail hung from his body, groaning with each step he took. Logan recognized the man's crest immediately, two swords crossed over a full moon. His family crest.

Logan caught him by the shoulder and turned him. The man whirled with a gasp. When he set eyes on Logan he sighed slightly, but none of the tension left his body and his gaze darted anxiously down the street.

"What happened?" Logan demanded looking at the castle.

"Lord Farindale defeated us. They burned the apartments and all who were within," the soldier answered.

Logan's eyes riveted on the soldier's like hot metal. "My mother?" he gasped.

"Dead, my lord," the man answered grimly.

Logan's lips parted in disbelief. Dead. "Father?" he asked, almost desperately. "Where is he?"

"Killed defending the castle."

*Suddenly, anger burned across his vision and he grabbed
the man, shaking him for speaking the words he didn't want
to hear, refused to believe. "This can not be! Farindale could
not have gained entrance to the castle so easily!"*

"The main gate was open!" the man hollered.

*Stunned, Logan stopped shaking him. His fingers dug into
the man's shoulders. "What?"*

"Your father refused to close the gate, my lord," the man said.

"Refused? But why? He knew Farindale was coming."

*The sounds of voices came from down the street and Logan
ignored them, glaring at the man. The man tried to move from
Logan's grasp, but his grip tightened.*

"We must go," the man pleaded.

*Logan's hold was relentless. "Why were the gates open?" he
demanded.*

The man shook his head. "If we stay, it will be our heads!"

"Why!"

"He was waiting."

*"Waiting?" Logan repeated gravely. "For what? What could
be so important to keep the gates open?"*

"You."

*Utter horror swept through Logan. The soldier easily broke
away from him and scampered away, casting only one backward glance at his former lord who stood unmoving. But
Logan did not see him. His mind's eye saw Castle Fulton falling, his friends and family butchered. He felt as though the
life had been cut out of him. He felt numb. His father. His
mother.*

All because of him.

*The shock of guilt held him immobile in its clenched fist.
Finally, a consuming grief filled him and he fell to his knees,
pressing his palms to his teary eyes, his body trembling with
remorse.*

Behind him, the castle burned . . .

Logan had spent years waiting and planning to return
to Castle Fulton and seek revenge. He clenched his fists.

And now that he was here, all he could think about was Solace. Her innocence. Her pure beauty. He cursed silently.

Then the door opened. Even as his hope soared, Logan turned his head from the torchlight that was thrust into the cell. Solace had come for him! He was free. Slowly, he rose to his feet, waiting for the manacle around his neck to be removed. But as the moment stretched out and his binding wasn't removed, Logan lifted his gaze. As he raised an arm to shield his eyes from the blinding light, a shadow formed in his vision. A woman's shadow.

But it wasn't Solace's.

Beth stared at him through icy blue eyes. They glittered like frost in the torchlight. She stood a few feet from him, well out of his reach. Logan straightened his back, lowering his arm.

Finally, she clucked her tongue. "You, my dear falconer, are in grave danger."

Logan remained silent. If she wanted the satisfaction of seeing him cower, she had come to the wrong man.

"You're to be executed at dawn," Beth added.

Logan tried to remain placid, but couldn't quite stop the clenching of his jaw. "So, you've come to gloat?"

"No," she replied with the same nonchalance. "Actually I'm here to save your life."

Logan's eyes narrowed suspiciously.

"All you have to do is say that Solace concocted this entire thing. That she paid you to kill Graham. That's why she threw you the piece of wood."

Logan's heart skipped a beat. "And what will happen to her?"

"She will take your place in the dungeon," Beth said, shrugging slightly. "Possibly banishment."

"Not execution?"

Beth scoffed. "Even my mother would not dare to risk Father's wrath."

"Why do you hate her so?" Logan wondered.

Beth raised a dainty eyebrow. "All my life she has gotten whatever she's wanted with an innocent look, a sweet, sickening smile. It's time she received what is rightfully hers."

The description sounds more like Beth than Solace, Logan thought disgustedly. But Beth had a good idea. He *should* implicate Solace. She was his enemy. She was Farindale's daughter. He opened his mouth to tell Beth what she wanted to hear . . .

. . . but nothing came out. No words of accusation. Nothing. He could only remember Solace's upturned mouth when she spun in the rain, her fierce determination as she raced out of the castle to rescue the pregnant woman, her soft curves enfolded in his arms.

"So, what do you say, falconer?" Beth demanded. "Your life for hers."

The way she said it sent a shiver of dread shooting up Logan's spine. "I don't think so."

Beth's eyes slanted as she grimaced with contempt. "Fool," she spat, stepping aside.

One dungeon guard entered the cell, followed by another. They grabbed his arms, pulling him back against the wall.

"I hope your sense of misplaced honor comforts you when your face is no longer so handsome and my whoring sister refuses to part her legs for you," Beth hissed.

Logan scowled at her words, the first inkling of anxiety beginning to creep into his stomach. Through the open door, the executioner entered the cell, in his hand was not a sharp-edged ax but a red-hot branding iron.

Twenty

"Solace!"

Solace looked up to see Peter walking through the Great Hall toward her. He reached the table where she sat and slid into the chair beside her. "I thought I missed you. Sorry I'm late." He picked up a piece of bread from the trencher awaiting him and began eating.

Solace had long since finished her evening meal, or rather had not even touched her food. She had thought Peter wasn't coming. But now that he was here, she was nervous. She wasn't sure how she was going to attempt this line of questioning. She wasn't sure how the shield or the sword fit into the scheme of things, let alone Logan. "It's all right," she said, lifting a mug of ale to her lips. She hardly drank. Was Logan some family member? A cousin perhaps? Or had he stolen the sword from some man, making the whole thing just a coincidence?

"Barclay tried another assault," Peter was saying. "But we repelled it, thank the Lord. I just wish your father would hurry and get here."

Solace wet her lips with her tongue. "Peter," she said. "Tell me about your family."

Peter straightened slightly and looked at her. He

shook his head, his short cropped hair shaking. "You've been up in that dusty old room again, haven't you?"

Solace shrugged helplessly.

Peter dropped his head. "I don't know why you keep digging up the past."

She gently placed a hand on his shoulder, her eyes full of concern. "I don't mean to hurt you. I just want to know. Those people in the tapestries . . ."

"It doesn't hurt me. That part of my past is long gone. Dead and buried."

Solace dropped her hand from his shoulder as he took a long sip of ale. She wondered if he even realized how much of a lie that was.

"What's there to know? I already told you everything," Peter explained.

"Do you have any cousins?"

"Only a few. I believe one is in Cavindale. But I never heard from them." He bit into a piece of venison.

Cavindale. Shivers of anxiety shot through Solace's body. Logan had said that he came from Cavindale. "And what about brothers?"

Peter's hand dropped slightly; a distant, hard look edged his brown eyes. "I had one brother."

"You never told me you have a brother."

"*Had* a brother. He's long dead now, too."

"What happened to him?" she wondered.

He looked at her and Solace saw the pain in his eyes. "He abandoned his family."

"What?"

Peter glanced at her with burning, reproachful eyes. "He left us," he said vaguely. "I never saw him again after the siege."

Peter's voice was cold, the frostiness of his tone chilling her. Solace's anxiety spread, encompassing her entire body. She refused to look at Peter, locking her gaze on the blazing hearth at the far end of the room. "What was his name?" she asked.

"Name?" Peter said, as if shaken from a bad memory.

"Your brother's name," Solace entreated. "What was it?"

"Logan," Peter replied. "His name was Logan."

Logan awoke to a burning pain in his cheek. He struggled to sit up, wincing as he moved. He raised a hand to his face. The charred flesh of his cheek was painfully tender to even the most delicate probing of his fingertips. He remembered the x-shaped brand moving toward his face, the iron glowing an evil red. He had struggled, but against the guards' holds and his steel manacles, his efforts were useless. He didn't remember much after the brand touched his cheek.

He scanned the cell. The torchlight from the hallway flickered in through the bars on the cell window, falling across a tray of food near his feet. He could still smell the sick scent of charred flesh. His flesh. Suddenly, he lashed out with his foot, kicking over his meal. Immediately, he heard the scurrying of the rodents as they rushed forward to take the scraps of food. His neck burned from chafing. He tugged futilely at the chain, but the movement caused the pain from his cheek to flare up.

He cursed Solace for entering his life. He cursed her for being so curvy and soft as to attract Graham's attention. To attract his attention. But most of all, he cursed himself for getting involved.

The *drip-drip* rang in the quiet dungeon again, sending the dull ache in his head flaring to a steady pounding. Logan hung his head, resting his neck on the edge of the metal manacle. His cheek throbbed in a grotesque, pulsating rhythm.

The clang of the lock echoed in his cell. The guard coming to take his food tray, no doubt. He did not look up as a circle of torchlight probed his cell. He watched with dull eyes as the light moved to barely touch the tips of his black boots. Then, strangely, he heard the rustle of silk. I must truly be going mad now, he thought. The beat of his heart rose in his ears, in cadence with the quick *drip-drip* sound in the distance.

Then a skirt moved to the very edge of the circle of light, the hem of the dress just touching his boot. Was it Beth coming back to gloat? Or was it . . . ? It couldn't be hope that made his heart pound so madly. It couldn't be hope that made his breathing stop. Hope had been extinguished in him a very long time ago. It couldn't be Solace; he refused to believe it was.

Then why couldn't he lift his head to prove himself wrong?

The specter before him knelt. He saw the skirt bend, and then gentle hands took his. His gaze lifted over perfectly formed breasts to a slender neck, past full red lips to bright green eyes. All the anger that had burned in him was extinguished at the sight of her. She was lovelier than he remembered. And he wanted nothing more than to bask in her radiance, her innocence, to feel her kindness touch his wounded spirit.

She moved toward him and the circle of illumination moved with her, as if the light were coming from her. As it engulfed him in its warmth, washing over him like a warm blanket, he lunged for the shimmering splendor of her, capturing her in his arms, crushing her against his breast. Her hair was so soft against his cheek, her body so warm in the coldness of the cell.

"I'm so sorry," she whispered.

"Sorry?" Logan wondered in a dry throat.

"It's all my fault," she told him, trying to pull free of his hold.

Logan refused to let her go. "It's not your fault. That bastard got what was coming to him."

"Oh, Logan," Solace pulled back slightly and lifted a hand to his cheek. It froze in midair, her eyes going wide with shock. She gasped and pulled her hand away.

For a moment, Logan was afraid the light would recede with her, but it didn't.

"Your face . . ." she moaned.

He had forgotten. For one wonderful instant, he had forgotten the horrible X that had been burned into his skin. He raised a hand to his cheek as if to shield it from her view. He felt a moment of panic. Would she reject him now as Beth had prophesied? He fought the panic with the only weapon he had. Anger. He hardened his heart to her, lowering his hand obstinately. "Come to stare?" he asked.

"Who did this?" she agonized, reaching toward his face.

Logan pulled away from her touch, afraid it would burn him worse than the branding iron had.

A wounded look crossed her face, saddening those large translucent eyes. Then the look disappeared, replaced by determination. She slowly stood, towering over him like an inquisitor. "Tell me who you are and what you're doing here."

"You know those answers already," he said, tearing his eyes from her perfect face to look on the soiled ground near his feet.

"Did you kill the dungeon guard?" she wondered

"Have you come to interrogate me or get me out of here?" he asked.

She ignored him, continuing, "Were you looking for someone?"

Logan's entire body tensed. She knew. He was sure of it. She knew why he was here, who he was looking for. He knew for certain that he would never see the light of day again.

"Is Logan your real name?"

His eyebrows furrowed, and his eyes rose to lock with hers. "What's that supposed to mean?"

"What are you doing here and who are you, really?" she demanded.

Logan narrowed his eyes. Did she know the answers already, only wanting the truth from his lips? Or was she searching, probing him for the answers? How much of it did she know?

"Did you come for Peter?" she wondered.

A shiver of trepidation shot down his spine. Should he tell her? Dare he tell her? Would she call to the dungeon guards? Was this some elaborate trap set by Beth? "Where is he?" he couldn't help but ask.

Her eyes scanned his face, and he saw doubt there. "What do you want of him?" Solace questioned.

She had to tell him! He had to know! "Where is he?"

"Are you here to hurt him?" she asked.

The question surprised him. Why would he hurt his own brother? "Is he a captive?"

He saw the shock on her face, or was that surprise that he had guessed the truth? He pushed himself to his feet. "Tell me. Tell me where I can find Peter." Logan took a menacing step toward her. He grabbed her shoulders and was surprised to find that his own hands were shaking. "Where is Peter?"

"Right here."

Logan looked past Solace. A dark form stood in the doorway, outlined by a flickering torch from outside the cell.

The man took a step into the darkness, seizing Solace's arm and pulling her from Logan's hold. "Are you all right?" he asked her.

Solace nodded.

Peter set Solace aside and stepped forward. The light washed over his face, and it was all Logan could do not to gasp. He knew that face! He had fought beside this man just days ago and had not even realized who he was. But as Logan looked closer, he could see the boy he once knew in Peter's features, even through the lines of hardship around his mouth and at the corners of his eyes. His face had matured, and his features had become pronounced. He was a man now. "Peter?" Logan asked. He stood up straight, his heart stopping, for even though he stood face-to-face with his brother, he couldn't quite believe it was him.

"Yes," Solace breathed. "Logan, I'd like you to meet Peter Grey. Peter, your brother, Logan."

Logan watched Peter's face transform from frosty anger into anguished confusion.

"Logan? Is it really you?" Peter asked in a thick voice.

Logan saw Solace slip out the door, leaving them alone, and he was grateful to her. Tears came to Logan's eyes as he nodded his head. He couldn't believe his brother was standing before him after all these years, after all the dashed hopes, the years of planning for revenge. He wanted to embrace him; he wanted to touch him and make sure he was really there.

But before he could move, Peter cocked his fist back and delivered a blow to his chin.

Logan jerked back. Pain seared through his jaw and through his burned cheek.

"I told you not to go!" Peter hollered.

Another blow to his stomach doubled Logan over.

"I cursed your name, Logan! I thought you were dead," Peter snarled. "And I'm going to make you wish you were."

Twenty-one

"I am dead," Logan answered his brother, clutching his stomach against the pain that Peter's blow caused. "I've been in hell for thirteen years."

"Good!" Peter shouted. "You should have been. After what you did. It was your fault. Mother and Father . . ." He stopped, his voice cracking, and he turned away from Logan.

Logan lifted his head, staring at his brother. He had thought this would be a joyous occasion, to find the last of his family. He'd imagined embracing, slapping Peter on the back. He had even imagined Peter helping to exact revenge. But he had never imagined this reunion, had never realized the extent to which his brother would hate and blame him . . . almost as much as he himself did.

"Damn it, Logan," Peter said in a heavy voice. "I thought I'd never see you again."

Logan stood, head bowed, allowing his brother to vent his hatred, his anger. Everything Peter had said was something he had already told himself over and over.

"You were supposed to come back," Peter told him. "You told me you would. And then you didn't show up."

Would it matter if I told him that it hadn't been my

fault? Logan wondered. That the damn horse threw me. That the damn rock smacked my head so hard . . . He shook his head sadly. It would still be my fault. It would not bring our parents back.

Peter grabbed him by the front of his tunic and shoved him back against the wall with enough force to make him gasp. "Father was worried sick. He blamed me! Because I was the responsible one. And I had let you go."

Logan saw the pain in his brother's eyes, the grief. "I'm sorry, Peter. I was wrong," Logan confessed.

"Wrong?" Peter released him and stepped back. "Is that all you can say for yourself?"

"What do you want me to say?" Logan cried. "Don't you think I've gone through it over and over in my mind? How foolish I was, how naive! What I could have done differently!"

"You should have stayed in the castle!"

"Yes. I should have. But I didn't." Logan looked away from his brother toward the cell door. "I thought you were dead. I'd given up everything, all hope. I had only revenge to concentrate on." He swiveled his gaze back to Peter. "Then I found out you were alive. I came as soon as I heard."

"It wasn't soon enough," Peter retorted.

Logan ignored him. "I had visions of you in chains in the dungeon. But the dungeon was empty. I looked in the stocks, everywhere I could think a prisoner might be. But you weren't there." Logan's brow furrowed with confusion. "Where have you been?"

Peter turned his back on his brother. Logan saw the corded muscles of his neck tighten as he crossed his arms. "I work for Farindale now."

Outrage seared through Logan, hotter than the branding iron that had scorched his cheek. "Farindale?" he gritted out. "After what he did?"

Peter whirled on him, shoving a finger into his chest. "No, what you did."

Logan batted Peter's arm away, furiously. "He invaded Fulton! Do you think I made him do it?"

"It was your fault that the gates were open. We would have had a fighting chance against him if it weren't for you!"

"That doesn't explain why you're working for him!" Logan shouted. "Why you're working for our enemy!"

"It was a long time ago!" Peter answered hotly. "I *was* a prisoner at first. I refused to be cooperative." He glanced about the dungeon. "So I was locked in here for months. Do you know what this place can do to a man? Do you know what this place can do to a *boy?*" Peter laughed harshly, more a bark of agony than a chortle of merriment. "I couldn't stand it anymore. The darkness. The gloom. The silence. So I gave them my word I would not try to escape and Farindale let me have the run of the castle."

"And then you just decided to work for him?" Logan asked incredulously.

"It wasn't like that," Peter answered, some of the fire leaving his voice. "It was a long time. Years passed. And it was still the home I had grown up in."

"Minus your family," Logan answered bitterly.

"Yes. But the Farindales were kind to me. Solace in particular. She was so gentle and smart and patient. And beautiful."

Logan froze, dreading his brother's next words.

Peter continued. "Even though I spurned her efforts at friendliness, she kept trying." He chuckled softly, remembering. "I said some mean things to her. But she has the patience and persistence of a saint. I found myself looking forward to her visits. We would take walks every day."

Logan's body trembled. He didn't want to hear anymore. He didn't want to know how friendly they had become. He could see himself in Peter. And for the first time, it became clear to Logan how Solace had manipulated him, working her way into his life just as she had Peter's. He, too, looked for her every time he entered the courtyard, found his eyes following her when she walked.

"And then they offered me a position as a guard."

"What better way to be near her," Logan murmured, understanding.

"And protect her. They gave me a sword, armor." Peter looked into Logan's eyes. "I love her, Logan."

Stunned, Logan could not move. Another man, his *brother*, loved Solace. A fierce, sudden anger consumed him and he grabbed Peter's shirt, shoving his face at him. "How could you love her?" He shook him, hard. His fists knotted in the fabric of his tunic. "She's our enemy!" Finally Logan shoved his brother to the ground, snarling, "Traitor." He stood over Peter, his fists clenched so hard his knuckles were white, his jaw clenched so tight that his cheek flamed with pain. "You traitor!" Logan sneered, looking down at Peter's ashen face. "Get away from me!" He whirled away, pacing the cell, keeping his back to his brother.

He had fallen into the same trap Peter had! He had looked forward to seeing Solace every day, sought her out at any excuse. Kissed her and made love to her as tenderly as if she were his wife. Within months, would he be working for Farindale, too? The thought enraged him, and he slammed his fist into the wall with a fierce cry.

Suddenly, he heard a lock being undone. He turned to find Peter standing near the dungeon wall, the padlock of his captivity swinging open. Logan raised startled eyes to his brother.

"I'm not a traitor," Peter declared and tossed Logan a key.

Logan caught it in his open palm. He saw a dagger drop to the ground near his feet. When he looked up, Peter was leaving the cell. Quickly, Logan unlocked the manacle around his throat and tore it off. He moved to the open cell door.

Peter loved Solace. Logan had come all this way, put his revenge on hold for a traitor! How could Peter love her? Her father had killed their parents. How could Peter hold her in his arms, knowing that it was her family that had murdered theirs?

You did, a tiny voice inside him accused.

Logan moved out into the hallway, sneaking up on the unsuspecting guard as he bent to take a bite of his bread. He slid the dagger across the guard's throat.

I'll show them, he thought. I'll retake Castle Fulton and . . .

Peter loved her.

Logan snuck out of the dungeon, the shadows of the night hiding him like a cloaked spy.

. . . and reclaim the castle for my own. I'll rule in my father's name and . . .

Peter loved Solace.

Logan moved through the courtyard with the agility of a cat, moving from shadow to shadow like a thief.

. . . and bring honor to myself.

Peter loved Solace!

Logan kicked open the door to his room with a howl of rage. How could he have let a Farindale get the best of him? How could he have let her manipulate him like that?

Furious, he shoved a blanket into the sack beside the table. He whirled on the table and swept it clean with his arm, pulling his belongings into the sack. He turned to survey the room when a gleam from beneath the mattress caught his attention.

He reverently bent and retrieved the sword, his father's sword. He ran his hand lovingly over the crest. Peter was a traitor. How could he work for Farindale? How could he have turned traitor? How could he love her? The same questions refused to stop swirling about his mind.

"Logan?"

Logan whirled, bringing the sword around, finding it pointing at his enemy's chest.

Solace froze with a gasp.

He rose, keeping the sword aimed at her heart. "What do you want, witch?" he asked from between gritted teeth. "How did you know to find me here?"

"Peter told me. I wanted to see if you were all right," she answered, eyeing the sword.

"What's your real reason for coming here?" he demanded. "Did you hope to bewitch me as you have my brother?"

"I don't understand," she said.

Logan eyed her. Her long, brown hair was unleashed about her face in a flurry of curls. Her cheeks were smooth and touched with pink, kissed by the sun. Her large emerald eyes stared up at him in confusion. Her lips were full and kissable.

Logan tossed aside the sword. It clanged against the wall and fell to the straw mattress. He was before her in one step, grabbing her shoulders. "Why have you come? What do you want of me?"

She opened her mouth to reply, but in the next instant his mouth was covering hers, plundering hers with a hunger, a vengeance, a longing that consumed him. He felt her stiffen and try to pull away, but he held her still against him, kissing her savagely.

Solace yanked her head away from him, shoving at his chest.

Logan thought to punish her for being so pure, so beautiful, as to lead him away from his mission. Instead, he felt utter horror and complete embarrassment over what he had just done to her. He stiffened in fury at himself, his face twisting in an ugly grimace. "Get out," he snarled.

Her large eyes pooled with shock and then confusion.

With a savage cry, he shoved her away from him. She landed in the dirt just outside his room, stunned. "Get away from me, witch!" he hollered.

She stumbled back and tears entered her large eyes. Then she turned and ran.

As she fled, she took with her any compassion he had left. A coldness spread through Logan, leaving a desolate wasteland inside him. He turned back to his room and picked up the sack and the sword.

He marched out of his room, through the courtyard, clutching his sword. His vengeance was just beginning. It was time to finish it.

It was time to retake Castle Fulton.

Twenty-two

Solace ran to her room and threw herself onto her bed. Tears streaked from her eyes and she found she was unable to stop them. Why would he hurt me that way? she wondered. Why would he push me away? There had been no tenderness in his touch, no kindness in his eyes. Only anger. Only hate. With that realization came a searing pain through her heart as if he had slashed it with a sword.

She trembled at the haunting look she had seen in his eyes. She couldn't believe it was the same man who had kissed her so passionately, touched her body with such devotion, brought her to such a sweet explosive release . . . the same man she had fallen hopelessly in love with.

She sat up, wiping a sleeve across her runny nose. How could she have allowed herself to love him? Because he was strong and handsome—even with that horrible burn now branded into the side of his face. Did Logan somehow blame her for his branding?

Suddenly, a disturbingly familiar noise rang through the air, a sound that sent shivers up her spine. She stiffened, listening. The clashing of metal echoed distantly in the otherwise silent night air. Solace tilted her head, straining to hear. Like an approaching storm, the sound came closer, and with it screams and shouts. It sounded more like . . .

Dread filled her so completely that for a moment she couldn't move. Then she bolted into action, running from her room. A feeling of doom seemed to shadow her steps as she moved toward the Great Hall. She glanced over her shoulder, searching for someone. But no one appeared, no page, no servant, no knight.

She reached an alcove where a large window stood shuttered against the night's cold. She could hear the muffled sound of clashing swords from behind the shutters. The sound was close. Too close. Solace reached for the shutters, but then pulled her hands back, afraid of what she would find. Hesitantly, she reached again for the shutters and pushed them open. Below her, her soldiers were battling a swarm of purple and black tuniced men, obviously outnumbered. No, her mind screamed. It can't be!

Slowly her gaze rose and through the open outer ward gates she saw that the castle gates were wide open, inviting the steady swarm of attacking soldiers that poured in. A shudder shot down her spine. Open? But . . . how? Had Barclay bribed one of the guards to open the gate? She had heard of such a thing in a siege at Williamsburg.

A chilling scream sounded from down the hallway. Solace spun toward the cry, but stood for a long moment, indecision plaguing her. What could she hope to do against a barrage of enemy soldiers? They were attacking her people! Her heart ached and despair consumed her. I can't leave the villagers to Barclay, she thought and grim determination filled her as she ran toward the scream.

Then, Father Davis's words rang in her head. *I want you to promise me that if they enter the castle, you'll run.* To her father. How could she run? How could she leave her castle? Her people? She couldn't.

The clunk of armored boots reached her ears. She whirled to see Barclay's soldiers behind her! But where had they come from? It was as though they had materialized out of thin air. Was Barclay using some sort of black magic?

Frightened, she bolted out the open doors into the courtyard. And raced into—

—chaos! Flames engulfed the blacksmith's shop, its heat threatening to sear her skin. The desperate shouts that came from the battlements thundered in her ears. Smoke billowed out from the doorway of the arrow maker's shop, the thick black cloud blowing around her, stinging her eyes and stealing the breath from her lungs. All around her, Solace heard the clang of metal against metal. She stumbled from the black cloud, disoriented and scared. Fear made her run through the night, through the turmoil. She had to find . . . She needed . . .

She found herself before the mews, racing toward the sleeping compartments. She threw open a door. "Logan?" she asked in a shaky voice.

But his room was empty. Everything was gone. His sack. The table was bare. She ran to the side of the bed and dropped to her knees. With trembling hands, she lifted the straw. It was gone. She stuck her hands beneath the straw, searching frantically.

No. No! It wasn't there. It was gone. Logan's sword was gone. He had left. Tears welled in her eyes; her throat constricted painfully. Slowly, she rose to her feet. At least she knew he was safely gone. At least she knew he was alive.

Why should he have stayed? He had done what he came to do . . . he had found Peter.

Her body trembled and she wasn't sure whether it

was because he was gone or whether it was because her castle was lost. She stepped out into the night, trying to think clearly. But all around her, she heard defeat, the cries of the dying, flames spitting at the night sky, screams of her people.

"What do we have here?"

Solace whirled to see one of Barclay's men staring at her. He clutched a bloody blade, which he lowered slightly. His face was red from exertion. "It looks like it's time for my reward," he said with a grin.

Solace straightened as he took a step toward her. Think, she told herself. But she couldn't. Her mind wouldn't function. She knew that look in the soldier's eyes. She had seen it before. In Graham's eyes. In lord Randol's eyes. An all-consuming fear began closing in on her mind, fogging her thoughts.

"Wait," she pleaded desperately, holding her hands up before her, trying to ward off the evil gleam glowing in the soldier's eyes.

"I've waited long enough," he growled and lunged for her, catching one of her wrists in his hold.

Images of lord Randol ripping Anne's clothing filled her mind. Memories of Graham's body pressed against her own.

The man pulled her to him, slamming her hard against his chest.

No, she thought. It seemed to be the only word her mind could focus on. She tried to speak it, but the horror of what was happening kept her voice frozen inside her.

"The Baron said whatever treasure we find is ours," he whispered hotly in her ear. His hands roamed her breasts, squeezing them savagely.

Solace tried to shove his hands away, a growing desperation surging in her soul.

"And I think your treasures will be a mighty fine reward," he chuckled.

"I've got gold," she said, trying to buy herself a moment.

The soldier paused, pulling back to look at her. "Gold?" he asked, his eyes twinkling with a different kind of lust.

Solace nodded. "I'll give it all to you if you let me go."

"You'll give it all to me anyway. Where is it?" the soldier demanded, his eyes narrowing.

The moment of reprieve set her mind working furiously. Over his shoulder, she spotted a pile of wood. "Over there." Solace pointed a trembling finger to the stack of logs. "I hid it beneath the wood."

"Show me," he commanded.

Solace knew he probably didn't believe her. But he didn't have to. All he had to do was look for it. The moment he was distracted, she would break free of him and run to the keep. She led him to the pile, pointing at the bottom.

His dark gaze narrowed, and he seemed to sum her up with one glance. Then he turned his back to her, bending toward the bottom of the pile of wood. "Where?"

Run! her mind screamed. She moved to obey, but her gaze alighted on a loose piece of wood on the ground at her feet. A piece of wood just like the one Logan had used to defend himself against Graham. Slowly, Solace bent to retrieve it. "Right there at the bottom."

As the soldier ducked his head to peer between the logs, Solace raised the wood above her and brought it down over the soldier's head. She quickly retreated, shocked at what she had just done. The soldier staggered back against the pile of wood, sending the logs tumbling to the ground with a loud clatter. He shook his head clear and turned to face her, snarling.

Desperate, Solace swung again. The soldier caught the wood in his palm, yanking it from her grip. He threw the wood to the ground and raised his blade over her head.

Solace instinctively raised her hands to shield herself and squeezed her eyes closed against the impending blow. She felt something hit her shoulder and wondered why there was no pain. Then a loud thump jarred her eyes open.

Solace lowered her arms to see the soldier lying prone at her feet.

"Nice try," a familiar voice said.

Solace snapped her head up to see Logan standing before her, a staff held easily in his palm. Relief crested the tidal wave of joy that surged through her body.

"You're too small. You have to hit him with all your strength or else—"

She threw herself into his arms. "Oh, Logan," she whispered. She pressed her cheek against his chest, felt his free hand encircle her waist, his cheek brush the top of her head.

"I thought . . ." It didn't matter. Nothing mattered except that Logan was there.

And that Barclay had entered her home. Her head snapped up to look him in the eyes. "We have to get out of here. Barclay's gotten into the castle. We need to—"

"It's all right," Logan said, smoothing her hair away from her face.

Something in the way he said it made her believe him. Everything would be all right. He took her hand in his and led her out of the mews, past the burning blacksmith shop and back into the keep.

Solace went without a fight. Maybe he was going to

get them food before leaving. Or maybe the only escape left open was the secret rear exit. But how would he know about that?

He led her back through the double doors of the keep. He was a Grey. Maybe he knew about the secret escape passage from living at Castle Fulton before.

He led her through the empty corridor toward the Great Hall. One of Barclay's men stood guard at the entrance. Solace squeezed Logan's hand tight, anticipating another battle. But Logan did not even pause in his stride as he marched past the man.

Something was wrong. Very wrong. She could feel it. She tightened her grip on his hand. "Logan . . ." she said as they entered the double doors of the Great Hall.

Her words died on her lips. Barclay's men were all over the hall! They encircled the room, lining the walls like statues. Solace's heart pounded madly in her chest, and she pulled at Logan's hand, trying to get him to leave.

But Logan continued on, tugging her along with him. He stopped a few yards before the flaming hearth. His hand bound hers like a manacle. She looked up into his face, to find it devoid of emotion. She followed his cool gaze to see Beth and Alissa standing near the hearth, its gentle light flickering over them, casting them alternately in shadows and in light. Beth's face was tear-streaked, her blue eyes red and swollen. Alissa held her hand, her face pale against the darkness around them.

A man stood before the dancing flames with one arm resting on the mantel. He was nudging a log with his plate-mail boots, sending sparks shooting up as a larger log smashed a smaller one. He wore a black cape and his blond hair billowed over it in sharp contrast. He stiffened, raising his head as if sniffing the air, and spun to face them. His stark blue eyes narrowed like a fox's when sighting a rabbit. Solace knew instinctively that she faced her enemy—Baron Barclay.

She glanced desperately at Logan. Surely he had a plan. Had he come to kill Barclay?

"Could this be Solace?" Barclay asked, drawing her gaze back to him.

Solace raised her chin slightly as his gaze ran slowly over her body, a grin curving his thin lips. What was Logan's plan? Why had he brought her here?

"I am pleased to finally make your acquaintance. I'm sorry it must be under such unpleasant circumstances," Barclay said in a sly voice.

Solace's jaw clenched. Barclay surveyed her and Logan with a cool stare that made her shiver, stopping on their hands. She still clutched Logan's hand with fear and desperation. A low rumble of amusement issued from Barclay's throat.

"Well done, Logan," he said. "Very well done, indeed."

Solace wavered, trying to comprehend what she was hearing, but not wanting to understand it, refusing to believe it. She looked to Logan for answers, but he refused to meet her gaze.

"It was you!" Alissa accused, stabbing a finger at the falconer.

Solace's bright eyes shimmered with the tortured dullness of disbelief She was frozen in some bizarre limbo where all actions and decisions were impossible. She could only stare at Logan, waiting for him to deny Barclay.

But he never did.

"Logan and I have been friends for years," Barclay explained.

His words didn't register on her dazed senses.

"He gave us detailed plans for all the secret passageways leading into Castle Fulton," Barclay was saying.

Solace's heart refused to believe what her mind was telling her, what her ears were hearing.

"He opened the gates for us," Barclay gleefully explained.

The screams of frustration remained at the back of Solace's throat as she snatched her hand from Logan's grip.

"Secret passageways?" Alissa echoed, casting a confused glance at Barclay.

"Oh, yes. They were elemental to the overtaking of Castle Fulton. We were able to infiltrate from inside, as well as outside."

Solace backed away from Logan. She felt as if her heart had been ripped out of her chest, cast to the ground at his feet and trampled. Her vision blurred beneath the onset of tears as she stared at him. But he would not meet her gaze.

"Without his help, we never would have taken Fulton this quickly," Barclay said, drawing his sword and glancing at himself in the flat edge of the blade.

Solace drew herself up proudly, but her spirit was dead.

"A pity about your face," Barclay commented. "What were you punished for? Striking a noble?"

Logan shook his head, his dark hair swaying over his shoulders. "Killing one."

Barclay's chuckle rumbled through the room.

Solace's throat closed around unshed tears. She tried desperately to cover her agony and wrenched her gaze from Logan back to Barclay, only to find his gaze locked on her.

"Did you find your brother?" Barclay asked Logan.

"Yes," Logan said, a bit stiffly. "Your efforts are greatly appreciated, but your work here is done. I can handle the situation now."

"Of course," Barclay murmured, shifting his gaze

back to Logan. He turned the blade over in his palm.
"You know, it would have been so much easier to kill
Farindale."

Solace felt numb. The pain of betrayal engulfed her.
She tried not to think of it. She tried to ignore it. She
had to focus, to shake herself out of her tortured self-
ishness by concentrating on her family, but she could
not. It had all been a lie. The way he'd looked at her,
the way he had loved her. He had used her.

"The time will come," Logan replied.

Solace shivered at the coldness in his voice.

"What should we do with them?" Barclay jerked his
head at Alissa and Beth.

Logan turned and Solace saw his profile. His gaze
was icy, his jaw clenched.

"You know how I hate loose ends," Barclay said.

"They're my problem, Edwin," Logan said, stepping
forward. He placed his staff on a table as he approached
the hearth.

"This is your fault!" Alissa snarled at Solace. "He
should be in the dungeon!"

Guilt overrode Solace's feelings of betrayal, but she
raised her chin slightly in the face of her stepmother's
accusation.

Logan rebuffed Alissa. "It's not her fault."

"Is that any way to speak to your daughter?" Barclay
reprimanded Alissa.

"She's not my daughter," Alissa snarled. "And you.
You are a barbarian, and I demand you leave my home
this instant!"

Barclay's eyes narrowed. "You, my dear, are a bigger
thorn in my side than either of your two lovely daugh-
ters." Suddenly he whirled, his sword raised, and, with
one mighty blow, cut Alissa's head off. "The thorn has
been removed."

Beth's anguished cry rent the air.

Solace covered her mouth in sheer terror, her eyes wide with disbelief. She raced forward and reached her stepmother's side just as the body fell before her. Blood splattered her dress, gushing from her mother's fatal wound like water spouting from a fountain.

Solace screamed in horror, clenching her fists at the sides of her head.

She turned tearful, hate-filled eyes on Barclay. "You monster!" she cried. "You bastard!" She launched herself at him, her fingers curved into claws. She never saw him aim his bloody sword at her abdomen.

Twenty-three

Logan lurched forward, catching Solace around the stomach, and pulled her away from Barclay's sword. Beth's hysterical cries resounded all around them, echoing off the stone walls.

Logan saw the evil enjoyment glittering in Barclay's eyes and stepped in front of Solace, trying to protect her from the sight of her slain mother. The blood from the dead woman spilled over the rushes on the floor, soaking them. "What the hell are you doing, Edwin?" he demanded. "There's no reason for this! The castle is taken."

Logan felt Solace try to twist free of his hold, but he tightened it. She was trembling with grief and anger. And his own heart twisted. He couldn't look at her face, couldn't look into her eyes for the anguish he would see there. He steeled himself against the attack she was waging on his emotions, emotions he never knew he had.

Barclay removed a bloody rag from his belt and slowly wiped the sword's blade free of blood. His eyes followed the red cloth with obvious enjoyment as it trailed over the stained sword. "These people must be taught their place. It will be a difficult job."

"I'm fully aware of the difficulties I face," Logan said.

"We've discussed this. There was nothing said about murdering women."

Barclay resheathed his sword and bowed. "A slight change of plans, old friend."

Something was wrong and every instinct Logan had was telling him to run.

"You know, Logan." Barclay strolled over to the fire again. "When you didn't open the gate at our appointed time, I feared that you had died or had been captured."

"I needed more time to find my brother," Logan explained.

"Well, I must say that I had time to think. To consider our arrangement."

Logan opened his mouth to respond, but Barclay turned to him, his gloved hands calmly clasped before him. "The heir to Fulton is a beautiful girl, one I wouldn't mind taming."

Logan tensed immediately. He didn't like where this was headed. "I opened the gates as soon as I could." His hand tightened convulsively around Solace's wrist.

"And there are the lands. You *did* neglect to tell me how rich they are."

"They were not your concern. They are mine."

A cold smile spread over Barclay's lips. "Castle Fulton is a mighty fortress. A powerful addition to any lord's lands. I really do thank you for all your help. You've saved me weeks, perhaps *months* of siege."

Logan quickly scanned the room to see row after row of Barclay's men.

"Did you really think I would just hand the castle over to you? I'm not a fool," Barclay said calmly.

Four knights came up behind Logan. "You treacherous bastard," Logan growled. He cast a quick glance at his staff. It was lying on the table, where he had tossed it just before he'd grabbed Solace. He needed to get to

it. But he also knew the odds of getting out of this alive
if he attacked the Baron were very slim.

"But rest assured I *do* have other plans for you. We
can't leave a member of the Grey family alive with some
silly notion of revenge. You see, I tie up loose ends,
unlike Farindale. Sloppy job, there."

"What do you want from me, Barclay?" Logan gritted
out.

Barclay inclined his head and the four soldiers put
their sword tips to Logan's spine. "The dungeon," Barclay said. "Until we find your brother."

Logan glanced at Solace. "What are you going to do
with her?"

Barclay's eyes shifted to her. "She will make a fine
bride. After I wed her, I will be legal heir to Fulton.
When Farindale is dead, no one will argue my claim."

Logan cast a glance over his shoulder at Solace. Her
dress was splattered with blood. Her face was pale, her
cheeks wet with tears. She refused to look at Logan,
and he was momentarily thankful for that. He didn't
want to see the pain and betrayal that he was sure would
be mirrored in her bright eyes. Where before there was
joy and happiness, now there would be hatred and anguish. He had seen the look before. He had seen the
same look when he'd glanced into a mirror. He couldn't
let Barclay have Solace. But first I have to find some
way to save my own neck, he thought as four guards
escorted him to the dungeon.

Solace stood stoically in the Great Hall, surrounded
by the victorious faces of her enemy. She tried to push
aside her swirling emotions to draw forth anger. But it
wouldn't come. All she could think of was Logan's betrayal. She had been a fool to trust him, a fool to give

herself to him. An even bigger fool to let him take her heart.

Sobs filled the air and Solace turned her head to see a hysterical Beth, her large blue eyes focused on Alissa's body. She instinctively moved toward her half sister, gently taking Beth's arm to pull her away from the grisly sight.

But Beth yanked free of her hold.

"Give me your word that you won't try to escape," Barclay said. "Otherwise I'll have to keep you under lock and key."

Solace's gaze swiveled to Barclay. He elegantly removed his black cape, draping it across one of the chairs near the table. "I'll give you nothing but my contempt," Solace sneered.

"Tsk, tsk," Barclay admonished. "I won't tolerate disrespect from my betrothed."

Solace swallowed down her bruising retort at seeing the strange gleam in his eyes. It sent a shiver of loathing through her.

"It's a shame about Logan, wouldn't you say?" Barclay wondered. "He's such a *treacherous bastard.*"

There was a sly grin on his lips. Solace looked away from him, afraid he'd read the anguish on her face.

"Don't tell me the cur charmed you, too?" Barclay shook his head. "You mustn't feel bad, Solace. I've seen him work his talents on many women. Some much more experienced than you. You mustn't blame yourself."

She remained silent.

"Tell me where his brother is," Barclay crooned.

Solace froze in horror. She would never tell Barclay where Peter was! "I don't know the exact location of every one of my guards!"

"A guard?" Barclay smiled. "It's somewhere to start."

Solace winced. She had fallen into his trap and, in doing so, endangered Peter.

Barclay walked up to her, a smile lingering at the corners of his lips. "Thank you. You've been most helpful." He placed a finger at her jawline, but she pulled her head away from his touch. "I hope your accommodations won't be too . . . confining." He raised a hand and two guards moved forward to flank her. "To her chambers."

Solace stared at the shuttered window of her room. The weather had suddenly turned cold. There was a brutal nip in the air that hadn't been there before. She had changed her clothing immediately, donning a black dress of velvet. She had cleansed her arms and face of Alissa's blood, replacing the horrible red smears with patches of skin scrubbed raw.

What does Barclay have planned for me? she wondered. Is he truly going to wed me as he told Logan?

Logan. She clenched her teeth against the fresh onslaught of tears that threatened to break through her resolve. Everything was suddenly making sense. He had been the killer searching for Peter in the dungeons. He had opened the gates for her, not out of honor as she had thought, but because he had wanted her to tell him where Peter was.

Traitor! her mind kept repeating. But her heart did not repeat the bitter rhythm of her mind; it lay shattered in thousands of pieces inside her chest.

She had trusted him. Hadn't it been her father who had said she was too trusting, too naive? Fool! She had actually thought she loved Logan.

She pushed Logan's image to the back of her mind. She didn't have time to dwell on her pain. She had to concentrate. What was she to do? She couldn't just wait for Barclay to force her into marriage. She had to leave Fulton. She needed to find her father.

Images of Barclay's brutality plagued her. The blood haunted her. Who was to say when Barclay would behead her, too, having decided he didn't need her.

One thing stopped her from taking action. Beth. She couldn't leave Beth to Barclay. She had to free her somehow!

Solace moved to her window, shoving open the shutters. A cold breeze lifted the ends of her hair and touched the nape of her neck, making her tremble. The rising sun stretched over the sky, blanketing it in a pink glow. But she didn't see the beauty of the sun; her eyes were locked on Barclay's guards walking the battlements.

Solace bent her head into her hands. She had not slept at all. A sensation of desolation swept through her. She was suddenly overwhelmed, struck immobile by the torment of the past night. What was she to do?

She had no time for self-pity. She needed to come up with a way out of here. But how?

Where is Father? she wondered. When will he come for us? Why hadn't he responded to the message he was sent?

She knew she couldn't wait for him. If she or Beth were still in Barclay's hands when her father arrived, he would not be able to do anything. He would never risk their lives.

Suddenly there came a knock at the door, jarring Solace from her reverie. "Yes?"

The door opened and a guard stepped into the room. "The Baron requires your presence in the Great Hall to break your fast," he said. He stepped aside and waited for her to approach.

Solace cast one last wistful glance at the freedom the new day taunted her with before closing the shutters and moving past the guard.

The hallways were filled with Barclay's men, laughing

and gambling away their newly stolen coin. As she walked by, groups of men hooted at her, chortling drunkenly. Solace continued on without casting them a glance.

When she entered the Great Hall, she saw Beth sitting to one side of Barclay at a long table. Her dainty fingers held a piece of venison. Solace swallowed hard. Beth looked . . . glowing. Her cheeks were pink with color; her hair was immaculate; her dress fit her slender figure perfectly, accenting her breasts.

A feeling of doom settled in the pit of Solace's stomach. What had Barclay promised Beth to make her so . . . vibrant?

The guard behind her cleared his throat, drawing Barclay's attention. A smile stretched across the Baron's mouth and he stood, inviting Solace forward with an outstretched hand.

Solace's jaw clenched and she refused to budge, until the guard shoved her forward.

"I'm pleased you could join us," Barclay cooed, making Solace almost retch. He signaled the empty seat beside him.

The guard escorted Solace to the chair and remained stationed just behind her as she sat.

"Please," Barclay said, pushing his mug of ale toward her.

Solace did not move.

Barclay sat back in his chair, his eyes perusing her face. "I see you're not thirsty," Barclay mused. "Perhaps venison?" He gently offered her some of his meat.

Solace turned away.

"Has the taste of falconers soured your lovely lips?" Barclay inquired.

Solace cast him a surprised glance.

"I assure you the taste of a Baron is far superior," he mocked.

Solace threw Beth a condemning stare, but her sister didn't bother to glance at her.

"We're to have a guest this morning," Barclay said, gnawing on a bone. He wiped a sleeve across his mouth.

A prickling of warning shot up Solace's spine.

Suddenly the doors at the far end of the room opened and two guards led a chained Logan into the room. His shoulders were bent in supplication, his head was bowed. They pushed him to his knees in front of the table.

Agony tore through Solace at seeing the bruises on his face.

Barclay was suddenly standing behind her. He placed his hands on her shoulders, and she stiffened. "Your sister told me that you and Logan were almost inseparable."

Solace forced herself to be nonchalant. "I hate him," she professed.

Barclay bent to whisper. "Now. But I hear that at one time Logan's charms were quite . . . penetrating," he murmured, nuzzling her ear.

"You wretch!" Solace accused, standing and whirling on him. "How dare you speak to me that way?"

Barclay took a step forward and Solace retreated, but came up short against the table. He continued to approach until she had to reach back, supporting herself with her arms on the table. "How would it look for my wife to be anything but a virgin?" Barclay wondered in that disturbingly gallant voice. "I'm going to take you now," he told her, pressing up against her. He forced her knees apart until her velvet dress was the only barrier between them. "And if I don't see your virgin's blood, I will give you to the men like a common whore."

Solace's hand closed around the mug of ale behind her as he began to draw her dress up. She swung it forward. Barclay caught it in his palm, his eyes glowing with rage. His retribution was as quick as a flash of lightning. His fist struck her soft cheek, spinning her half around. Barclay flipped her over onto her stomach, forcing her to the table with strong hands, pushing down on her shoulders. "If you choose to act like an animal, you shall be treated like one," he snarled.

Solace's gaze searched one soldier's face. But all she saw in his eyes was burning lust. Her frantic gaze shifted to the other soldier, only to find a hungry grin curving his lips.

Barclay threw her skirt over her hips.

Solace's terrified gaze locked with Logan's. Strands of dark hair had fallen over his eyes, eyes that fumed like swirling clouds of vapor from hell itself. "Barclay," he warned from behind clenched teeth. "Let her go."

Barclay put a hand to her head, forcing her face down into the table. "You should enjoy watching your enemy's daughter be taken like an animal. Retribution for what he did to your family."

Understanding coursed through Solace, even while Barclay's hand held her firmly in place. That was why Logan had made love to her! He did it as vengeance, not as love or even desire. Utter desolation swept through her, sweeping her soul like the barren winds of a desert. Hope abandoned her. She clamped her eyes shut tightly, her hands gripping the edge of the table. A lone tear was squeezed from between her clenched lids.

Twenty-four

"What is going on here?"

Solace's eyes flew open as she recognized Father Davis's voice. Immediately, Barclay released her. But she could only lie on the table, shaken and scared.

"Father!" Solace heard Barclay say, his tone overly boisterous. "Welcome!"

Solace pushed herself up from the table with shaky arms, her trembling hands adjusting her skirt, pulling it down over her bare skin. She watched Father Davis approach, his brown eyes locked on her, his brow furrowed with concern.

Logan's gaze was on her, also. She could feel it, but she was afraid if she looked at him she would crumple into the trembling, fearful child she was fighting to keep at bay.

"What do you think you're doing?" Father Davis demanded.

"Why, just eating," Barclay exclaimed, a note of nervousness in his voice. "Won't you join us?"

Father Davis scowled at Barclay for a long moment, causing the Baron to shuffle his feet and shift uncomfortably from foot to foot.

Father Davis passed Logan, eyeing him sympathetically. Solace saw something cross his face, but it was gone before she could figure out what it was. He continued to approach the table.

"Return the prisoner to the dungeon," Barclay said quickly with a flick of his wrist.

The two guards hauled Logan to his feet, pulling him back toward the double doors.

"How dare you treat that man in such a way?" Father Davis scolded.

"Surely God will forgive me if I donate another two bags of coin to the Church."

Father Davis ignored Barclay's comment and put a kind hand on Solace's shoulder. "Are you all right?" he inquired.

Solace opened her mouth to reply, but Barclay motioned her guard forward.

"Lady Solace looks a bit weary," he said. He cocked an eyebrow at her. "Return her to her room."

Father Davis raised suspicious and angry eyes to Barclay, but he withdrew his hand from Solace's shoulder.

The guard took her arm, leading her away from Father Davis. And Barclay. For that she was grateful. She glanced over her shoulder at Father Davis to find Barclay's head bowed while Father Davis raised a hand to bless the food. His eyes were locked on her as he said, "May God watch over you."

The door shut behind her, and she heard the lock slide into place with a loud *clink*. Solace paced the room, hugging her elbows. She had to get out of there. And she had to do it quickly. But how? There was only one door out of the room. Or was there?

Her eyes drifted to the wall. Barclay had said something about secret passages. She walked to the wall, running her hand along the masonry work, wondering if there was a passage in her room.

Logan would know. She pushed the painful image of him from her mind. She couldn't think about him. She couldn't dwell upon his betrayal, not now.

She had to escape the castle. And she had to take Beth. Where were those passages? Did they connect her room with Beth's? Could she use them? How complicated were they? And how much did Barclay know?

Again the thought—Logan would know. He could tell her. But why should he? Why would he help her? And why should she want him to? She couldn't trust him any longer.

She bowed her head as images of the past weeks came back to her. She had trusted him, befriended him, loved him. And now . . . Now she was a prisoner in her own castle.

Solace wiped at her eyes, refusing to shed the tears of betrayal brimming in them. She wouldn't let him win. She wouldn't let Logan defeat her. She had to fight. She had to get Barclay from her castle. But how?

Her gaze came to rest on the wooden chest at the bottom of her bed. Her eyes narrowed. She ran to it and opened it, searching through the dresses and gifts her father had bestowed on her over the years. Silk dresses that glistened in the candlelight. Rich velvet houppelandes that were the softest in the land. Deep emerald rings. Red ruby necklaces. But she shoved these aside, digging deep down into the chest, almost to the bottom. She parted two silk chemises and stopped. There, cushioned on the sleeve of an embroidered dress, was what she was searching for.

Solace reached into the chest and cupped the blade in her hand lovingly. Her father had given it to her, but she had had no use for such a deadly weapon and had put it away in her chest long ago. She thanked her father for his foresight, then grabbed the pommel of the dagger and brought it forth into the candlelight. Its golden blade shone. It was untouched by scratches, had never tasted the blood of an enemy. But all that was to change.

She stood gazing at her weapon.

A whistling sound caused her to whirl, her eyes scanning the room, the walls. Were they watching her through some hidden hole in the passageways? She quickly hid the dagger behind her arm, its blade brushing her wrist. She reached down and hid the weapon in the folds of her dress.

A loud caw caught her attention, and she turned to the shuttered window. She walked over to it and pushed it open. The black falcon swooped down to perch on the sill.

She stared at the beautiful bird for a long moment. It watched her with large, unblinking eyes.

Suddenly Solace called, "Guard!"

The door opened and the guard appeared. "What do you want?" he asked.

She rose up before him, lifting her narrowed gaze to meet his. "Take me to the dungeon," she announced. "I want to spit in the face of the man who betrayed me," she proclaimed.

He began to shake his head "Baron Barclay—"

"The baron told me I deserve at least that much," she lied.

The guard stared hard at her. "I was ordered to watch you."

Solace met his gaze unflinchingly. "You can watch me. I don't care. I just want to see Logan Grey chained to the walls like the animal he is."

"But the Baron—"

"Will not appreciate being bothered," Solace again interrupted the man. "He has given me permission. If you want to seek him out, that is your decision."

After a long moment, the guard nodded and turned, leading the way out of the room toward the dungeon.

Logan angrily rattled the chains that bound his arms. The heavy metal links were attached to the handcuffs biting into his wrists at one end and imbedded into the stone wall of his dungeon cell at the other. His legs were securely bound as well.

Damn that lying bastard! Logan cursed silently; the image of Barclay's hands on Solace scorched his mind's eye. He cursed again, his voice echoing in the cell. If it hadn't been for Father Davis . . . Father Davis. Why hadn't he thought of the priest earlier? Davis could have helped him locate Peter. Father Davis had been loyal to his father when Logan was growing up, always chastising Logan for whispering to Peter in chapel. And the priest had taught Logan how to read and write. He was a patient man, devoted to his faith.

It had only been luck that Father Davis had come to take his meal at that moment. Barclay was a very Christian man, believing in prayer before battle, in thanking God for everything. Logan knew that deep inside, Barclay was afraid that God would turn against him for his barbaric acts, so he loyally gave staggering amounts of gold to the Church to cleanse his spirit, to buy his way into heaven.

Logan gritted his teeth for the thousandth time. Barclay had been his friend for years! The man had fooled him completely. I should have been suspicious of his easy acceptance of my request for help. Curse me for a fool. I was too caught up in my own quest for vengeance to question any help I was getting.

He shook his chains violently, the small cell filling with the sound of clanking, grating metal. Barclay will kill me soon, Logan thought. There is no reason to keep me alive much longer. He will realize that Peter is no threat to him. What could a vengeful brother do against Barclay's army anyway? Look where vengeance got me.

Rage exploded through him and he again shook his chains futilely, growling like some wild bear caught in a trap.

The clang of the lock being undone echoed in the small cell, silencing him. Then, the door swung open.

A torch blinded Logan for a moment, and all he could see was a shadow move toward him. A familiar scent wafted to him on a slight breeze . . . roses! As the pain from the light lessened and his vision cleared, he saw Solace standing before him. One of Barclay's soldiers stood behind her, holding a torch.

"Solace," he said, trying to hide the surprise in his voice.

But before he could say another word, she slapped his face as hard as she could.

The soldier behind her chuckled, relaxing somewhat.

Even though she had struck his other cheek, the branded cheek flared and pain pierced his skull. Logan let the stinging of his flesh subside before he turned cold eyes to Solace. "I'm pleased to see you, too, m'lady."

"You bastard," she sneered, stepping closer to him. "I despise you for what you've done to me and my family."

Logan felt the leather hilt of a dagger pressed into his hand. He quickly glanced up into Solace's eyes, but he could read nothing there.

"Help me!" she suddenly cried. "He has me!"

The soldier stepped toward Logan, chuckling. "Let her be, dog!" He raised a fist to strike Logan.

Solace stepped out of the way.

Logan struck quickly, sinking the blade deep into the

soldier's gut. He then quickly withdrew the blade and slit the enemy's throat. The man gurgled and dropped to the floor.

Logan fell to his knees beside him. Searching his waist until he found the keys, he quickly unlocked the manacles.

The torch flickered in the water of the dungeon floor and went out, casting the room in darkness.

Logan glanced up at Solace. She was just a shadow against the light from the open door. "Are you all right?" he demanded.

She didn't answer for a long moment, and he wished he could see her face. When she did answer, he heard the ache, the bitterness in her voice. "I want you to take Beth and leave Castle Fulton."

"Solace," he said in a tortured voice. He stood, grasping her arms, pulling her close to him. "Did Barclay touch you? Did that bastard hurt you?"

She shook her head and eased herself from his grip. The anguish her silent rejection caused him was worse than anything Barclay could do to him. "I didn't mean to hurt you," he said quietly.

He saw her turn her head away from him, tried to discern her features in the darkness, but couldn't. Guilt settled on his shoulders. He had felt guilt for years, but never like this. She had shown him what he had been missing. He had tasted her innocence, basked in her kindness and love. And the only thing he had shown her in return was how to hate. "Solace, it wasn't supposed to be like this," he said desperately.

"You didn't mean to open the gates?" she asked, and there was a bitterness in her voice that hadn't been there before.

"I was supposed to have Fulton. Barclay was to give me the castle, and in exchange I would give him some of the northern lands and a percentage of the crops."

"It doesn't matter," she murmured.

"It *does* matter." Again Logan reached out and grabbed her hand. "Had I known what he intended, I never would have brought you to him. You have to believe me. I wanted to protect you. I wanted you by my side."

She was silent for a long time, and Logan could feel the warring emotions inside her. He could feel her hand trembling. He thought he heard her swallow hard. When she spoke, her voice was thick and strained. "And you thought that once I learned what you had done I would want anything to do with you?"

He dropped her hand. "It appears I hadn't thought things through."

"Will you take Beth and leave the castle? Will you do this one thing for me?" she asked.

Logan turned away from her, unable to face her sorrow any longer. "Yes," he answered quietly.

"There's one more guard, the dungeon guard, the one that gave us the keys," Solace told him. "He's at the entrance to the dungeon."

Logan glanced past her to the door. "Call to him," he told her. "Get him to come in here."

There was a moment of silence before Solace cried out, "Help! Help me!"

Running feet sounded in the dungeon, and a silhouette of a man appeared in the doorway.

An awkward moment of silence stretched on. "He's got me!" Solace shouted. "Help!"

"Where's Pavia?" the guard demanded.

"Help!" Solace screamed.

The guard stepped hesitantly toward her voice.

Logan lunged forward, catching the guard around the waist and tackling him to the floor. He plunged the dagger into his stomach and then lurched for Solace's hand, leaving the guard for dead. He pulled her toward the stairs and stopped just beneath a torch. Logan chanced a look at Solace. There were rings under her eyes, and her lids were swollen from crying. Her usually bright eyes were dull with sadness.

He looked away from her. All these years he had seen the world through angry eyes. For one brief moment, she had allowed him to see it through her eyes. Now, he had made those once bright eyes as angry and bitter as his own. "Where is she?" he asked.

"This way," Solace said, and led him up a spiral staircase, then down a hallway. She stopped in the shadows of the staircase when she saw two guards standing outside Beth's room.

"I'll distract the guards," she said. "Get Beth and leave the castle."

As she began to move away from him, Logan grabbed her wrist and pulled her back against him. "What about you?" he demanded.

She looked into his eyes for a moment and he saw her resolve, her willingness to sacrifice herself for her sister. Finally, she looked away.

"I won't let you stay," Logan said. "He was going to rape you just hours ago. You can't possibly be thinking of staying!"

"And the alternative is trusting you?" she asked bitterly.

"I know how you're feeling. But you have few other choices."

"You're wrong," she answered and tried to pull away from him.

Logan saw determination burning in those weary eyes. Even after the horrors of the night, she still had spirit. He refused to release her wrist. "What are you going to do, Solace? You can't marry Barclay."

"Don't you mean you won't let me?"

"He'd have control of Fulton then," Logan retorted.

"And that would just kill you, wouldn't it?"

Logan's jaw clenched. "Fulton is my birthright. I've waited thirteen years for my revenge."

Solace stared at him for a long moment. "Then you must be a very bitter, angry man." She turned her back on him.

"Solace, sacrificing yourself isn't the answer."

"You have a better one?"

"Join forces with me," he said.

For a moment he swore he saw longing wash over her face, but then it was gone and in its place was a cold anger. "Oh, that's promising!" she laughed bitterly. "Let's see. My choices are to marry a man who killed my stepmother or to become allies with a man who betrayed me."

I deserved that, Logan told himself. "I want to help you."

"Help me what? Help me betray my people, my family? You've done quite enough already."

"Help you get Fulton back," he said sincerely.

"Liar!" she hissed vehemently. "You would only help me because you think it easier to steal from a woman. I trusted you before, Logan, and you taught me that there is no compassion in the world." She yanked her arm free. "It's a lesson I won't ever forget." She whirled, her long hair slapping his face.

Logan stood, watching her. He gritted his teeth against the guilt that suddenly rose in him like bile. I have done nothing wrong! he told himself.

He reached out, clamping a hand around her mouth, and dragged her back into the hallway with him. Then, with her struggling against him, he pushed a rock and a panel of the wall swung open. He pulled her into the darkness. The wall swung shut behind them, sealing them in.

He released her. "You can't stay here," he insisted.

"I can get you and your sister out of the castle safely."
He felt her eyes on him, sensed the indecision that
plagued her. He knew how she must feel . . . betrayed,
hurt. But Castle Fulton was his. He would do everything
in his power to get it back. She would do the same. He
stiffened slightly. Yes. She would do the same. He had
turned her into him. The animosity, the bitterness. He
feared he had just created something very dangerous
and unpredictable in Solace Farindale.

She turned away from studying the small, hidden
walkway she now found herself in and looked at Logan.
"Give me the dagger," she finally said.

"Why?" Logan asked.

"Because if you're lying to me I want to be able to
plunge it into your cold heart."

Logan grinned. "Fair enough," he replied.

Logan pushed open the wall just enough so that he
could see into the room from where he and Solace
were lurking in the hidden corridor. It was dark except
for the soft glow of a candle that washed over a form
in the bed. Logan's eyes narrowed. There was something . . .

Solace moved to step around him, but Logan's arm
shot out, covering her mouth. When her eyes turned
to his, he put a finger to his lips in a motion for silence.
Then, he removed his hand from her mouth.

It took only a moment for the form to shift and separate into two bodies, one moving off the other. The
light washed over Barclay's features.

And Beth's.

Logan heard Solace stifle a gasp and felt her stiffen.
She leaned into him for support. He kept a firm hold
on her. Had the blackguard raped her sister?

Beth's hair lay in dark strands across the pillow. Her

face glowed. "You see, darling," Beth cooed, "I can be most accommodating. You needn't dispose of me. I can make myself most indispensable." Her hand snaked beneath the blanket toward his manhood.

Barclay chuckled, seizing her wrist and withdrawing it. "What a lusty wench you are."

Logan jerked forward. Now was his moment. Barclay was defenseless. He could easily strangle the life out of him. Break his neck. Bash his skull into the stone wall. Logan's eyes narrowed. But Beth would call out for help, and two armed guards lurked just outside the room. He glanced at Solace. He had to see her safely away from the castle. His revenge would have to wait. Again.

Logan slowly pulled Solace from the room, quietly closing the secret passage's door. He had seen enough. Seen enough to turn his stomach. That woman had no morals! The man had just killed her mother and she was lying with him!

"Why?" Solace asked. "Why would she do that?"

Logan had to admit that he didn't have the answer. He shook his head. "We can't stay here," he advised.

For a long moment, Solace said nothing. Logan tried to see her face, tried to read her dilemma. He knew she didn't trust him. And he knew he should trust her even less. Could he travel with a companion who might turn him in at any moment? Knowing that she might stab him in the back? God's blood! He had given her the dagger! Still . . .

He knew he could never leave her here.

Finally, she nodded her head. "Yes. We have to leave."

Relief coursed through Logan. But it was tinged with something else. Warning. Was she coming with him to seek her own revenge? Did the same vengeance that had consumed him in the past now eat away at her?

He took her elbow and guided her through the dark

passages, then down a narrow stairway that led straight into a solid stone wall. He was grateful that he and Peter had played games in the hidden tunnels, pretending they were chasing down villainous thugs, because now all the twisting turns easily came back to him.

Peter. Logan hoped that he had survived the attack. He thought how ironic it was that he had spent months agonizing over his brother's safety only to find that Peter had chosen to work as a soldier in the enemy's army. Peter has chosen his own path to travel, Logan thought. As have I.

Logan quickly pushed one of the stones set into the wall, and the wall slowly moved away from them, revealing a crack just wide enough for a man to pass. Logan moved through, pulling Solace with him.

His pace increased as he moved through the new set of tunnels. Barclay must know we're gone by now, he thought. It won't be long before he has men searching these corridors.

Finally, Logan pushed a wall open an inch, scanned an empty room and shoved the wall open farther. He signaled for Solace to wait, then dashed into the room and quickly grabbed a rope that hung on the wall before rushing back into the corridor.

When they finally emerged from the darkness of the secret passageways, they were in Alissa's room. Logan quickly tied one end of the rope around the bedpost and fastened the other end around Solace's thin waist. He couldn't help but notice the curves of her shapely hips as he secured the rope, but he forced his attention to the window. He grabbed her arm and led her over to it.

"What are you doing?" Solace asked, a note of panic to her voice.

"I'm going to lower you down," Logan told her. He felt her apprehension as if it were a tangible thing.

"Don't be frightened. I won't let go." He patted the window ledge.

She looked at the ledge, then at him. Her eyes narrowed slightly. Just when Logan thought she was going to protest, she stepped up onto the ledge. "Feet first," he instructed. "Then just hold onto the rope. And whatever you do, don't look down."

The sounds of booted feet in the hallway caught Logan's attention. He heard doors being opened and closed. "There's no time," he said. He quickly untied the rope from her waist. He turned his back to her and pulled her roughly against him. Logan had to fight the jolt that speared his body at contact with hers. He could feel her breasts pressed to his back, feel her small hands clutch his tunic.

"What are you doing?" she demanded.

"Just hold onto me," he said.

"Why?" she wondered.

"Do it. There's no time to argue."

She slid her hands beneath his arms and clutched his shoulders. Logan wrapped the rope around their waists and tied it tight, effectively binding her to him. "Hang on tight," he advised, hoping the danger would ease the passion that was beginning to stir his blood. He gripped the rope tightly, climbed onto the ledge and turned to face the room.

Solace's feet hung over the side. She squeezed her eyes closed, whispering, "Don't fall."

Every muscle in Logan's body strained as he lowered himself and Solace over the window ledge. As they descended the wall, Logan felt Solace's grip tighten. He tried to ignore the scent of roses that teased him as a cool breeze blew a strand of her hair before his face and around his neck.

The rope burned into his palms, and he struggled to keep his grip. He used his feet to guide them down the wall. Halfway down it, the muscles in his arms and shoulders felt as if they were on fire. He paused to glance down at the ground and muttered a curse when he realized how much farther they had to go. His palms began to sweat. In the moat below, he saw rows of logs spanning the brackish waters. He knew that during the siege Barclay's men had filled in part of the moat with sand and rock and had created a bridge with the logs so they could cross. He never thought he would be thanking Barclay for their escape route.

Solace gasped loudly and he felt her grip falter. She slipped down an inch, jerking him hard.

He braced himself against the wall, stopping their descent. "Hold on," he commanded through clenched teeth.

Solace clutched desperately at him, grabbing at his tunic.

When Logan had his balance again, he continued downward. Finally, after what seemed like hours, his feet touched the ground. He quickly undid the rope, freeing Solace.

Suddenly the cry of his falcon sounded in the air above him, its shrill call sending a shiver of alarm racing through him. Without thinking, Logan grabbed Solace's hand and dashed for the logs that filled the section of moat in front of them. The logs shifted beneath their feet as they raced across them.

The first arrow missed Logan's head by inches, lodging in a log at his feet.

But the second came closer to the mark.

Twenty-five

The arrow pierced Logan's tunic, ripping through the fabric near his ribs, barely missing his skin. Logan pulled Solace close as they cleared the moat, quickly leading her into the trees that bordered the west end of the castle. But he didn't stop there. He continued his breakneck pace through the woods, dodging trees, sidestepping bushes, splashing through small brooks. All the while, Solace followed silently, keeping pace.

They reached a stream and Logan plunged into the water, planning to throw any pursuers off their trail. He trudged a great distance in the chilly brook before he glanced back over his shoulder to see how Solace was faring. She had raised her skirt up to her shins, the hem of which was soaked. Her slippered shoes were heavy with water, and her bare skin was pink from the cold.

Logan glanced down at his warm, booted feet. He quickly moved back to her, scooped her up into his arms and continued on despite her protests.

We need to find horses, Logan thought. He chanced a look at the woman in his arms, only to find her staring at him, a scowl on her face. When she saw him looking at her, she glanced away, into the direction they were heading. He caught himself studying the soft outline of her face, the delicate arch of her neck. The dark rings underlining her eyes were in sharp contrast to the pale complexion of her face. We need to get sleep, he thought. For, even though adrenaline pumped through his veins, he felt the beginnings of fatigue sapping his strength.

Suddenly, Solace turned those brilliant green eyes to him and it was Logan's turn to look away.

"Where are you going?" she wondered.

"For now, just trying to make a path that the guards won't be able to follow," Logan answered, emerging from the stream and setting her feet on the ground beside an old oak tree.

"Westhaven is only a day's walk that way." She pointed south.

Logan's gaze followed her finger as if he could see the town.

"I have friends there who might be able to help," Solace added.

Help. Every nerve in Logan's body tensed. Yes, he thought. Help you. Leave me to rot in some dung heap. "I think we'll head in this direction," he said, moving north.

"What's wrong with you?" she asked. "I said I knew people who could help hide us."

"I'm not here to escort you to your destination," Logan snapped angrily. "And I don't intend to hide like some frightened kitten."

"You said you would see me to safety!" Solace shouted.

Logan spread his arms wide. "Here you are."

Solace gasped at him, anger flaming her cheeks. "You're going to leave me here?"

He shrugged. "You can travel with me."

"You . . . you unchivalrous lout!" she shouted. "I

should have known I couldn't trust you! Not after what you did!"

Logan approached her, his jaw tight with leashed fury. She backed away from him until she bumped into a tree and could retreat no further. "Let's get one thing straight. I did what I had to do. The same thing you would have done had you been in my place."

He expected her to shiver and cower before his rage as he towered over her like some angry ogre. What he didn't expect was the sparkle of tears in her bright eyes.

"I never would have betrayed someone I . . ." Her words faded.

A frown creased Logan's brow as he found himself gazing into the most spectacular eyes he had ever seen, eyes bright with courage and defiance. A shadow of sadness haunted them, and something else. Fear? What had she been about to say?

Her tongue traced her lips before she finished with, "I never would have done that to you."

Her declaration cut into his resolve, slashing a hole in the wall he had built around his heart. No, he knew with certainty that she never would have done that to him. With the realization came a tidal wave of regret. He battled through the wave with his anger, trying not to drown in those green waters that flooded from her eyes.

His gaze lowered to her sweet lips. He had tasted their honeyed depths before, had sought comfort in her arms as he'd devoured them. But he knew that he could never do that to her—or himself—again.

"I don't need your friends' help," Logan snapped, turning away from her and heading into the forest again.

"We're in no position to turn down any kind of help. We have no food, no water, no—"

"I've gotten along fine by myself," he said, fighting the logic to her thinking. She wanted him captured. Would her friends set a trap for him? Protect her and send him to Barclay? Could she now betray him? Had she changed that much? He knew that was what *he* would do if he were in her position. "Are you coming?"

For a long moment, he didn't hear anything. Then, he heard her footfalls and knew she was storming after him.

Solace shivered as the night wind snaked its cold fingers around her. She glanced for the thousandth time at Logan. He sat across from her, his back to a tree, his long legs stretched out before him. He had found a long, thick branch on their travels and now his new staff lay at his side within easy reach. Darkness had fallen over an hour ago. If she weren't so cold, Solace knew that she would be able to sleep, regardless of whether or not she was in her own bed.

But she was freezing. Logan had informed her that there would be no fire so as to not attract any unwanted attention. In addition to being cold and tired, she was hungry. She had been trying for what seemed like forever to dig out a root with the dagger, but the stubborn thing wouldn't let go of the ground. She had pulled at it, chopped at it, but she just wasn't strong enough. The relentless wind laughed around her, encircling her in an icy hug. She shivered, sitting back, exasperated. A root! she thought. I can't believe I can't get the thing out of the ground. I've dug up thousands . . . okay, hundreds . . . all right, a few.

She looked at the dagger in her hand. It wasn't enough. She blew a strand of hair from her eyes, wishing she had some stronger tool. She needed help. She needed . . .

Solace glanced over her shoulder at Logan. Then she frowned. There was no way she was going to ask him for help. No way!

A rumble moved across her stomach as if it were alive.

She gazed at Logan, rubbing her stomach. Well, maybe just this once . . . Solace stood and stared down at the root. Damn thing! She kicked it before turning and heading for Logan.

She wiped the dirt from the dagger on her black skirt as she moved closer to him. His hands were folded over his stomach, his head resting comfortably against a tree, his long legs outstretched as if he were in a bed. She stopped at his side, gazing down at him, watching the slight rise and fall of his chest. She absently turned the blade over in her palm. A breeze ushered her forward, and she swallowed her pride as she bent down to touch his shoulder.

Logan's eyes flashed open, full of suspicion and recrimination. He snapped his wrist toward her and easily slapped the dagger from her hand. "Branding's not good enough, eh, Solace?"

She pulled back, surprised and shocked. She rubbed her smarting fingers, staring at him in total bewilderment.

Logan grabbed the dagger off the ground and stood, slipping the thin blade into the belt at his waist. "You don't mind if I hold onto this for you, do you?" He tapped the dagger's leather-bound handle. "I wouldn't want you to accidentally cut anything you weren't supposed to."

Confusion washed over her. "Why did you hit my hand?" she asked.

"Did you think I would just lie here while you slit my throat?" he growled.

"What?" she gasped. "I—I wasn't going to slit your throat. I wanted . . ." His words penetrated her bewilderment. She clenched her jaw and narrowed her eyes. "I'm afraid I'm not as bloodthirsty as you." How could he accuse her of a thing like that? She wasn't the one who had betrayed him! She smiled coldly at him. "Although, it's not a bad idea."

Logan took a threatening step closer. "Then what were you doing with the dagger? Contemplating giving me a shave?"

Solace raised her chin, refusing to budge a step. "How dare *you* accuse *me* of lying! All you have done is lie to me. Use me for your own vile purposes. It must have been very hard for such an accomplished lover to pull the wool over a virgin's eyes!"

"Virgin!" Logan exploded. "You were no virgin."

Solace tried to keep his hurtful words from cutting her. "I have been with no other man," she proclaimed, facing his accusations with all the bravery she could muster.

"There was no blood," Logan said, but doubt had crept into his words. "All virgins bleed."

"Not this one," she replied and turned away from him. *Whore, harlot, slut.* The words of her sister and her stepmother echoed in her memory. She couldn't explain the fact that there had been no blood. And she knew that Logan would never believe her. He would think the same thing Alissa and Beth had. So what did it matter?

Everything.

She returned to the tree, sat down and drew her knees up to her chest. She was just as cold and hungry as she had been when she'd approached Logan. But now she was without a dagger.

The root sat there in the ground at her feet, half dug out, refusing to release its hold on the life-giving earth.

As Solace lay her head on her knees, a tear trickled over her cheek.

Logan stood over her, watching her sleep. She was curled tightly in a ball, on her side, shivering. Most women would have broken down by now, crying out against the injustice of the world. They would have lost their will to fight.

Moonlight washed over her small frame, caressing her with a pale kiss, giving her more warmth than her mother and sister. More tenderness than he had bestowed upon her. In the shadows of the night, he felt hidden, free to explore his feelings. And as he stared at her, an emotion rose within him, so strong that it threatened to choke him. In her small body, Solace possessed more courage and determination than most knights he had known.

Logan thought back to her declaration of innocence. He had never heard of a virgin who did not bleed. But as he thought back on their encounters, there were other things, other signs, that now seemed to confirm her inexperience. The way she had first kissed him, with reserved passion. Everything she had done had been filled with an innocent curiosity. That was what had drawn him to her. Now it was more than that. He admired her defiance, her will, her strong spirit.

Solace's breathing was shallow, seemingly closer to death than slumber.

A chill breeze wrapped Logan in a blanket of cold. They had brought nothing from Castle Fulton. No blankets, no food, no water. They had fled only with the clothing on their backs.

A caw came from the tree above him, drawing Logan's attention. His falcon was perched on a branch to their right, drawing one of its legs up under itself to sleep.

"Wretched beast," Logan grumbled, even though he was secretly glad to see the falcon. "I was wondering when you'd show up."

He turned his dark gaze back to Solace. She was everything a man could learn to love, to care for. But he was not any man. He had no time for tenderness, no time for love. He had to get his castle back. He wouldn't let himself fall under her spell, not the way Peter had. Peter. Had he survived yet another siege? Logan's heart ached for his brother, for the kinship that could never be.

He turned his back on Solace, but as he walked away he couldn't resist a glance over his shoulder.

The warm sun streamed in through Solace's bedroom window, warming her face. She turned her head to the sunlight and a sharp pain flared in her back. Something was sticking her in the spine. She reached under her to discover that it was a solid chunk of earth. Her arm brushed the dirt from beneath her. Then she realized that in her room the sunlight didn't reach her bed. She opened her eyes to see a canopy over her, but it was not the soft velvet canopy of her bed; it was a crisp canopy of leaves.

She had not been dreaming. Her castle was in the hands of Baron Barclay. Alissa had been brutally killed. Beth had welcomed the enemy into her bed. But isn't that what I had done? Solace wondered.

The wind whistled around her, its icy breeze kissing her body, weaving its way beneath her skirt. She pulled her skirt over her feet to block it out. Then she sat up, her gaze searching the trees for Logan.

He wasn't there. He had left her. The thought didn't shock or surprise her. Then why did she feel disappointed? She rose, using the tree as support. Logan had done what he said he would. He had seen her safely away from Fulton. There was no reason for him to remain with her. There was not an ounce of chivalry in him. In that strong body. The body that had hovered over hers before he'd filled her with his manhood, sating the desire and passion that had seized every part of her. The body that had protected her from the arrow attack.

"Solace?" Logan called.

She whirled, surprise and guilt written on her face. She gaped for a moment, then masked her look, afraid he was able to read every one of her thoughts.

Logan walked up to her, his hands cupped in front of him. But it wasn't his hands she was looking at, it was his lips.

"Here," he insisted, nudging her with his fingers.

She dropped her gaze to his hands, her cheeks flaming. Her mouth dropped open. But not in agony or embarrassment. In wonderment. In his cupped hands were berries. She pooled her skirt into a pocket and Logan deposited them into her lap.

Her stomach grumbled in anticipation as she popped one into her mouth. Sweetness exploded on her tongue, and she chewed the berry slowly as if she were savoring the most delicious delicacy from France.

When she opened her eyes, she found Logan gazing at her. The smoldering flame she saw in his eyes confused her. She hadn't seen that look since he'd bedded her in his room days ago. A heated flush crept into her cheeks. She quickly indicated the berries with a nod of her head. "Eat," she suggested.

A wry smile formed on his lips as he studied her berry-stained mouth. "I already have," he replied.

It was the way he said it that made her blush darken. His deep voice had suggested something other than partaking of the fruit.

They stood, staring at each other for a long moment, sharing another place in time. Around them, the leaves wavered in the gentle breeze. Birds sang to their mates.

Solace knew it could never be the same for them. He saw her as a whore and his enemy. She lowered her eyes and turned away from Logan.

"I'm going to Cavindale," Logan finally said. "I think you should come with me."

It was the way he said it. It was not a request. The decision had already been made. Suddenly, the berries didn't taste so sweet. "You won't make it to Cavindale. Winter's coming."

"It won't be here in a week."

"Be reasonable, Logan," Solace pleaded. "You have no food, no shelter, no coin and no blankets."

"The food is there," he said, pointing to the berries in her skirt. "The shelter is the forest. What do I need coin for?"

Solace stared hard at him, trying to see past the stubbornness. Finally, she asked, "What do you need me for?"

"Need you for?" Logan echoed. "I don't need you. I thought you had nowhere else to go. I know what that's like."

"I won't die with you. I'm going to Westhaven."

She saw his jaw clench, his fists twitch. "Then go," he said.

A twinge of pain flared inside her, but she refused to acknowledge it. "I can't go alone, Logan. It's too dangerous. Please. Westhaven is a day's walk. Take me there." She straightened, pushing aside the sudden onslaught of tears that threatened her. "Leave me with my friends. Then you don't have to trouble with me anymore."

Logan bowed his head, considering her words.

She watched the breeze blow through his soft hair like fingers raking through the strands. Longing and sadness filled her. "I think you owe me that much," Solace whispered.

Logan stiffened. He raised dark eyes to her. "Westhaven it is. Then I never have to lay eyes on you again."

Solace nodded and turned away from him. She hadn't realized she'd released her skirt, dropping the berries, until she stepped on one, smashing it beneath her foot.

The town of Westhaven was aglow. The afternoon sunlight shimmered on the stone-and-thatch buildings that made up the heart of the town. Patches of clouds drifted languidly across the sky, but somehow always seemed to leave a wide hole above Westhaven for the sun to shower the town in its golden streams. It's some kind of beacon, Logan thought. But is this heavenly sign meant for Solace or me?

He cast Solace a sideways look. She was gazing on the town from their crouched position behind some bushes with more excitement than he had seen on her face since before Castle Fulton had been taken. If she wanted to go, let her. He struggled with uncertainty, as he had since that morning. Uncertainty and anger. He didn't need her, he told himself for the thousandth time. He gazed at her profile, that straight nose, those high cheekbones, that sensual mouth, those large eyes filled with such joy, and he wondered how such perfect beauty could make him so sad.

Logan turned his gaze back to the town. At midday, Westhaven was a gathering of merchants and craftsmen. He watched the activity from a distance now, waiting for nightfall. His original plan was to walk into town at midday, well hidden in the crowd. Then Solace reminded him about the cross on his cheek. Every person in the town would notice it.

He was a criminal, a man marked for what he had done. Some townspeople would steer clear of him, some would mock him, others would throw stones or pelt him with rotten food. He had seen it happen to others. Logan found himself rubbing the tender skin on his face. As the pain built, he rubbed it harder, as if trying to erase it. The damn thing was a guide for Barclay. He knew he could no longer walk through the streets unaccosted. He would have to become a creature of the night.

Perhaps getting away from him was best for Solace. He couldn't ask her to share his nocturnal life. And he didn't want to! he told himself emphatically. He had more important things to think of.

His gaze shifted to her again. She had sat back against a tree and pulled her knees to her chest. Her tiny feet were tapping the ground beneath the dirty hem of her gown. Her head was buried between her knees, the black material hiding her face.

She would be gone soon.

The thought had come unbidden, though Logan had tried to push it aside all day. Now, with her departure so close he found he couldn't rid himself of it. She would be gone. A pang of remorse shot through his chest. He didn't want to leave with her hating him. He didn't want her as an enemy. He opened his mouth to tell her . . . But what could he say to her? She wouldn't believe him anyway. Slowly, his mouth closed and his chin dropped to his chest.

It was useless to try to make amends. He remembered the fierce anger that had coursed through him when he had found his home taken, the insatiable need for vengeance. No one could have talked him out of his hate. No one could have taken his pain away.

He felt a prickling along the length of his neck and lifted his eyes.

Solace was staring at him, quietly surveying his face, each of his features. Her brow was furrowed slightly as if she were trying to figure something out. Then she looked away toward the village.

A coldness settled around him as if a biting wind had suddenly lashed his cheeks. There was a wall between them, one as thick and impenetrable as the walls of Castle Fulton.

He followed her stare to the town. From their spot behind the bushes, Logan could smell the loaves of bread that one of the merchants had just pulled from his oven. Pickled fish wafted to him on a small breeze. He was hungry. He glanced at Solace. She must be just as hungry as he, even though she didn't show it. Possibly more so. She hadn't eaten the berries that morning.

They waited in silence, trying their best to ignore each other's presence. Finally the sun dipped below the horizon. Just a few more minutes now and they would sneak toward the blacksmith's shop. They had seen no sign of Barclay's men, but Logan knew they were there.

His falcon landed on his shoulder, but Logan took little notice. He watched a group of men saying good night to each other as they moved into their houses. Shops closed their windows. Mothers called to their children to come home. Husbands went to share their beds with their wives. Again, Logan couldn't resist the urge to glance at Solace. She had put her face back into the rich darkness of her dress.

"Solace?" he couldn't help but call.

For a long moment, she didn't raise her head, didn't reply.

He scowled and crawled toward her. "Are you all right?" he wondered, a knot closing around his throat.

She nodded her head, a strand of her dark hair falling forward to brush the leaves on the ground. He wanted to capture it in his palm, to hold its softness one last time. And even though he knew he shouldn't do it, his traitorous hand shot forward to cup the silky strand. He rubbed it between his thumb and forefinger as if it were spun gold. His throat closed around the despair that engulfed him.

He turned his gaze to her to find she had lifted her eyes enough to look at him. In the fading light he could see they were ringed with redness, and for a moment he couldn't tell if the rays of the setting sun or tears had caused it. The light from the dying sun turned a tear golden, and he followed its lonely path from her eye to her cheek.

Anguish overwhelmed Logan, and he reached forward to brush the golden drop from her skin, only to find that it was not alone. She lifted her head from her dress, revealing to him her complete sadness.

Grief and shock washed over Logan. Had he done this to her? The thought tore at him, and he turned away from her. "We'll start toward your friends in a few minutes," he murmured.

Suddenly, she was on her feet behind him, and before he could stop her she was racing out of the cover of the bushes toward the village.

"Solace!" He lunged forward to grab a hold of her dress, but was too late.

As she ran toward the village, he heard her heart-wrenching sobs and her muttered cry, "I hate you, Logan."

It was as if a sorcerer had cast a spell over him. He

could not move. He lay on his stomach, the branches of the bush digging through his tunic into his ribs, his arm outstretched before him, his hand closed around nothing. He watched her small, fragile form race toward the blacksmith's shop and disappear into the blackened doorway.

It doesn't matter what she thinks of me, he told himself. She *should* hate me.

He pushed himself up onto his hands and then onto his feet. He cast one last look at the town.

It blurred, and he blinked quickly to clear his eyes before turning and moving away into the woods.

Twenty-six

The sunshine was bright as Logan entered the village of Cavindale. It had been a long time since he had been there. As far as he could see, there were seven or eight new farms. The village has changed, he admitted grudgingly. But my memories have not.

The tree just beyond Marion's farm was where he had watched as his cousin, William, had carved his name into the tree with a heart and Elizabeth's name. Logan had been too busy with thoughts of vengeance to care much for girls. He had carved a name into the tree, too. But it had been Farindale's, with an x through it. Logan lifted his hand to his cheek. Now, he was the one who bore the mark.

Logan moved through the village, his head swiveling to the west. The windmill was on the outskirts, near the stream. He and William used to go swimming there. William for fun, Logan to strengthen his body. Logan turned his head to the east. The meadow just past Widow Jane's shop was where they used to practice sword-fighting.

He kept to the shadows when he entered the main part of town, kept his head lowered, a hand across his cheek to hide the brand.

The streets were crowded and memory upon forgotten memory invaded Logan's mind. The stand of apples was still in front of Copplepot's. Years ago, Logan had knocked the cart over and gotten a sharp reprimand from old Copplepot, as well as Uncle Hugh.

At the thought of Uncle Hugh, Logan's eyes rose to the distance. Cavindale Manor stood like a great rock, its square structure looking sturdy and strangely comforting. A fond grin spread over Logan's lips. What would they think upon seeing him? It had been so long. All the tension suddenly drained from his body, like a sigh. He was home.

A part of Logan still seemed empty and this surprised him. There was something missing. He knew what it was, and before he could block the vision, a pair of brilliant green eyes came to his mind. He pushed the image aside.

As Logan neared the home, he saw an old man speaking with a younger man. The older man's hair was completely white, and he was very thin. Logan narrowed his eyes slightly. Could it be?

As he moved forward, he heard the man's droll voice and he smiled. Crox! Logan stopped just behind the white-haired man. After a moment, the man turned familiar blue eyes to him, assessing him. Then a scowl creased his wrinkled brow. "Can I help you, sir?" he wondered.

He belonged in court, Logan thought as he had all those years before. Always so proper. But Crox hated it there. Preferred the countryside . . . Logan smiled. "After all this time, you're still a rambling old man," Logan said, jovially.

Crox's eyes slowly lit with recognition. Then a smile came to his weathered face. "Logan, old boy, is that you?"

Logan embraced the man. "Good Lord, Crox, don't you change at all?" he asked.

Crox slapped Logan on the back. "No need to change

perfection," he answered, stiffly. When Logan released him, he stepped back to look at him. "It's been years, lad. We were starting to wonder if you were dead." A caw sounded from the sky, and Crox raised his eyes to it. "Oh, good heavens! You don't still have that wretched bird!"

Logan shrugged. "Can't seem to get rid of him." He started toward the large wooden door of Cavindale Manor. "Where's Uncle? And William?"

"Master Hugh is at the castle, not to return for two days. Master William is in the fields."

"Thanks," Logan said.

"Logan," Crox called. "Might I inquire what happened to your face?"

"You might," Logan answered evasively and continued inside.

The Great Hall was strangely empty. It was as large as he remembered. To his right, the stairs to the upper apartments disappeared into blackness. Two tables lined the back wall and behind these were the kitchens. The walls of the room were whitewashed and bare. Logan felt like a stranger. He was not the same man . . . boy . . . who had lived here.

"May I help ya?" a voice wondered.

Logan turned to find a young boy standing beside him, staring at him with large dark eyes. This child was new to Cavindale Manor. Logan hadn't seen him before. But before he could answer, a booming voice came from the table at the far end of the room.

"There's no help for the likes of him!"

Logan squinted at the man clothed in a black tunic and leggings, tipped back in one of the chairs. There was something familiar about him. Logan stepped by the boy, moving toward the man. Slowly, a grin slid across Logan's face; the same grin that faced him.

"Just get him an ale," the man instructed. "From the looks of him, he hasn't tasted one for quite some time."

"What are you doing here, Alexander?" Logan wondered.

"Heard about Fulton and knew you'd come here," Alexander replied, placing a booted foot on the table.

"No jobs available so you've come to harass me?" Logan asked, sitting in a chair beside him.

"I was in Lexington when Barclay's men arrived," Alexander explained. "Apparently, you've made yourself quite indispensable to the Baron. He's willing to pay a pretty sum for your return."

Logan shrugged slightly. "He won't find me here."

"Are you so sure? I did."

"You know I grew up here. He doesn't," Logan explained.

Alexander shook his head in disapproval. "Nothing's a secret if you have enough coin. There are men willing to sell you out."

"Only friends know about Cavindale."

"Friends like Barclay?" Alexander wondered.

Logan clenched his teeth and looked away from Alexander toward the door. "I already told you, he doesn't know about Cavindale."

Alexander's eyes narrowed slightly. "Is that mark on your face a gift from your friend?"

"No," Logan replied, raising his hand to absently message the scar. "Barclay didn't do this."

"That's going to make it harder with the ladies, eh?"

"Perhaps one," Logan murmured.

"Solace?"

Logan glanced up sharply at Alexander.

"Barclay's men were looking for a branded man and Farindale's daughter," Alexander said.

Logan grit his teeth, staring off into the distance. Solace's large eyes appeared in his mind's eye, as bright as the most precious of gems. They were beguiling in an innocent, sultry way. He remembered the way her lips curved in a tender smile that seemed to brighten his day. He clenched his jaw tight against the images that threatened to chip away at the wall he had erected around his heart. *She hates you, remember?* he asked himself.

"Why didn't you ask me, Grey?"

Logan glanced up to see Alexander staring into his mug of ale pensively. "Ask you?" Logan echoed.

"I kept waiting for you to ask me to help you retake Fulton."

The thought hadn't even crossed his mind. Logan had no gold, nothing to offer Alexander as payment. Besides, he had Barclay to help him. "I didn't think I would need you," Logan said.

"Didn't think you needed me?" Alexander echoed in disbelief. "The man who saved your hide from that axeman at Willow's Ridge? The man who took that arrow in the shoulder for you at Woodland Hills? You didn't need *me?*"

Logan shrugged. "I heard you were doing pretty well with your Gypsy hunting. And still making good coin from it, I warrant. You certainly dress better these days."

Alexander's look sobered. "You could have used me to watch your back," he said. "I could have helped."

Logan stared at him for a long moment. Yes. He should have asked Alexander. He should have asked Blade or Goliath or McColl. But he had looked to Barclay, and all of Barclay's resources.

The boy brought an ale and some bread, and placed them in front of Logan. He immediately took a long drink of the smooth ale. It wet his parched throat. Then he wiped at his lower lip with the backs of his fingers. "Yes, you could have." Logan took another drink.

"A guest?" a voice called from the doorway. A man

about Logan's age rushed in. "Why didn't someone tell me?"

Logan stood, knowing the man immediately, even though he was gazing upon William for the first time in years. A slender man, but happy and jovial. When he entered the room, it seemed to come to life. A servant appeared from the kitchen, wiping her hands on her apron. Crox followed William into the room with a grin on his face.

William approached Logan. "Good day, sir," he greeted. "I don't believe I've had the pleasure . . ."

"Pleasure? Last time I was here, you called me a warted piece of dung before shoving me into a trough."

William slowed as recognition dawned on his face. "Logan? Is that you?"

"Didn't you see the falcon?"

"Ha ha!" William leapt over the table to embrace his cousin. "It's been years! Years! We thought you were dead!"

"Crox told me," Logan said.

William pulled back to gaze at Logan's face. His smile vanished beneath a scowl as he saw the brand. "A criminal?" he wondered. "For what? Striking a noble?"

"For killing one."

"I warned you," William said. He shook his head, and his mane of golden hair shook with the movement. When he next locked eyes on Logan, there was sincere concern in his gaze. "Are you in danger? Do you need shelter?" he asked.

"Not hidden, but not announced either," Logan said, glancing at Alexander meaningfully.

Alexander grinned. "I'll keep quiet."

"Of course," William said. Then he threw back his head and laughed. "What are you doing back here anyway? I thought you weren't returning until you could say Fulton was yours."

The gentle mocking tone in William's voice irked Logan, and the dark cloud that had hovered about him since leaving Fulton returned. Logan took a long drink from his cup. He sloshed the liquid around in the mug. Barclay that cur, he thought. I'll have Fulton back, this I vow. It was a long moment before Logan realized that William was staring at him. He raised his eyes.

"You're still obsessed with reclaiming the castle, aren't you?" William wondered.

Logan grunted softly.

"You would have been a lot more fun if you weren't so single-minded."

"I'll have plenty of time for fun once Fulton is in my hands."

"Logan, give it up, man!" William pleaded. "It's been thirteen years! Get on with your life!"

"I can't. Not when my mother and father were murdered. Not when—"

"It wasn't your fault, Logan," William said softly. "How could you have known?"

"It *was* my fault!" Logan said slamming the mug of ale onto the table. "If I had been there . . ."

Alexander lifted the mug of ale to his lips, ignoring their fight.

"You're wasting your life! Don't make it one of hate," William said.

Logan glared at William. Some things never changed. Finally, he looked away from his cousin, battling his anger. "I don't want to fight with you again, William."

William sighed. "What will it take to make you see how few days we really have?"

"Don't you think I've seen it? I've been in wars and sieges that have killed hundreds of men. I've seen people killed in the streets of London for nothing more than the clothes off their back. I've wasted enough time sitting and waiting. I have to get Fulton back now."

William stared at him until Logan turned away, his fists clenched, his jaw tight. William leaned in closer to Logan, gazing at him with an intense frown.

Logan's fists tightened as he prepared himself for one of William's lectures. Finally, he turned to his cousin, fighting the anger that was racing through his veins.

"God's blood!" William exclaimed. "That's an ugly mark! Matches your ugly face!" A smile eased its way across William's good looks.

Surprise rocked Logan and he burst out laughing. Alexander sputtered with a mouth full of ale before his guffaws joined the merriment.

It was good to be home.

Despite William's best attempts to draw Logan into the celebration of his homecoming, including a game of chess and a lusty wench, Logan resisted, choosing to separate himself from the others.

Alexander watched Logan's brooding, pensive mood with curiosity. All the while Alexander had known him, Logan had a single purpose, a focused goal. There was only one thing he wanted, and that was Castle Fulton. Women, for instance, never held the same appeal for Logan as they did for other men. He never wooed women. When they sought him out, he used them to satisfy a need, never bedding one more than once, never thinking back upon the night of lovemaking.

Alexander had to admit that he had never seen Logan like this. It was as if he were at odds with himself. And Alexander knew it had nothing to do with Fulton.

It wasn't until everyone had retired for the night that Alexander approached Logan as he sat before the hearth, the light from the flames flickering over him. Alexander seated himself in the empty chair to Logan's right and stared at the fire for a long moment. "You miss her, don't you?" he asked, tipping back in his chair.

"No," Logan snapped. "She can do whatever she wants. It's of no concern to me."

The force of his denial told Alexander he had hit the mark. "You know I stopped over in Westhaven on my way from Lexington." He watched Logan's expression harden, his eyes flash with just the right amount of interest and coolness.

"What's your point?" he demanded.

"I just thought you might want to know there's some boy in Westhaven you might consider joining forces with."

"Boy?" Logan echoed.

"Or should I say a woman disguised, very badly I might add, to look like a boy."

Logan's fingers tightened over the arm of the chair, his eyes pinning Alexander with a hot glare. "Is this one of your poor jokes?"

"She tried to hire me for the army she was mounting against Barclay."

Logan's face paled to an ashen gray.

Alexander scowled at him, feigning ignorance. "Do you know her?"

"Solace," he groaned.

"Very courageous. It's too bad she won't get to see her plan come to pass."

"What do you mean?" Logan wondered.

"She's trying to recruit mercenaries, Logan. With no coin. She doesn't know what she's doing. And not all mercenaries are as fine and respectable as I."

Logan rose from his chair, moving toward the hearth. He grabbed a stick that was resting against the brick wall of the hearth and absently rolled it between his fingers. "She's going to get herself killed."

Alexander shifted slightly in his chair. "I thought you didn't care."

"I don't," Logan snarled. He shoved the stick into the burning logs and the flames exploded upward with a hissing screech.

Twenty-seven

Solace sat in the far corner of the Wolf's Inn, staring at the motley assortment of men who inhabited the tables. One, a hooded monk garbed in a dark brown robe, probably on his way to the Abbey of St. Michael, sat at the table closest to the door. Another was a peasant with a mug of ale clutched tightly in his fist as he lay slumped over a table, sleeping soundly. A third man was a fighter, from the looks of his scarred face. He ate with his head down, shoveling the food into his mouth.

Solace stared at the man, ignoring the rabbit stew in the bowl before her. She gently bit her lower lip, pulling the cloak around her face. She hated having to bind her breasts, but she kind of liked the breeches. They had been itchy at first, but two weeks later she had become accustomed to them and was enjoying the privacy they offered. Her friends, Mitch and Geoffrey, had taken her in immediately, and she had come up with the disguise of an apprentice.

Now, if she could only recruit a mercenary, she would be on her way to taking back her castle. She knew that she had to be careful. She couldn't just walk in and hire the first mercenary she saw. She had developed a plan. She would sum up the inn early in the evening, before most of the patrons had retired. Then she would approach one man a night until she had an entourage.

The door opened, letting in the last rays of the setting sun. A chill wind weaved its way into the inn, twirling around Solace until the fire warmed it and it disappeared. Autumn was coming to a close; winter was almost here. Solace knew she couldn't mount a successful attack against Fulton in the dead of winter. Her time was running out.

A man filled the doorway. He was two heads taller than the innkeeper who greeted him. His face was hidden by a hood. Solace's eyes narrowed slightly. He had a sword strapped to his waist. One of Barclay's men? Solace wondered. But he wore no colors, no crest.

The innkeeper pointed to a table just in front of her. The man made his way toward her, and Solace's breath caught in her throat as he moved. Each step was filled with graceful power. He paused just before he got to her table, and Solace could have sworn he brushed her with a guarded look before he swept his cloak out and sat in the chair.

She couldn't see his face at all, but she could see his hands as they eased his sword to the side.

He must be a mercenary, she thought. Wearing a sword and chain mail. A mercenary who was doing quite well. He would be an asset to her army.

The innkeeper brought him an ale.

Solace waited until the man had a few sips of his drink, then stood and approached him. His face was hidden in the shadows cast by his hood, as she imagined her own face was. She noticed how his large hands encircled the mug. The image of those hands around a neck came to mind, and she shivered. But she needed him. The moment stretched out, and she indicated the empty chair across from him. "May I?" she inquired.

She saw the hood move and took it as a nod. She slid into the chair opposite him, folding her hands in front of her. She tried to see into the recessed depths of the hood, but couldn't. She should have taken comfort in knowing this because that meant he could not see beyond her disguise, but somehow not being able to see his face made her all the more cautious. She could be dealing with the devil for all she knew.

"You're a mercenary?" she asked, knowing the answer.

Again, he nodded his head.

Solace frowned slightly. Couldn't he talk? "I'd like to hire you," she added.

The man was silent for a long moment, then slowly lifted his head a bit higher.

Solace could feel the gaze of his hidden eyes penetrating her to her very soul.

"I'm a killer," he told her, his voice a deep, menacing rumble. "I'm just as likely to slit your pale throat as to have a cup of ale with you." He took a drink from his mug. "Depends on my mood."

The timbre of his voice shook her from head to toe. "And . . ." she started, somewhat hesitantly. "Do you feel like another ale?" She placed a coin on the table top.

He slammed his hand down atop hers, trapping the gold beneath her palm.

Unnerved by his actions, Solace yanked her hand back, hiding it in her lap.

He took the coin and put it into the worn leather pouch at his waist. "I'm not thirsty," he said.

Solace swallowed hard, her stomach knotted tight with trepidation. She dredged up every last ounce of courage to ask. "Are you for hire or not?"

"Maybe I've already been hired. Have you thought of that?" He took another drink of ale and slowly set the cup down on the table.

A feeling of alarm made the nape of Solace's neck tingle. "Then, if you're already hired, I'll be going," she said and rose. There is no way he could know who I am, she told herself, trying to calm her pounding heart.

The man thrust his arm across the table and grabbed her wrist, forcing her back down onto her seat. "I didn't say that I wasn't available." He released her wrist and tapped the leather pouch at his waist. "Besides, where there's one, there's usually another."

Solace took a deep breath. She wasn't going to tell him that she had no coin to pay him with . . . yet. "Are you for hire or not?" she demanded a bit sharply. He was making her nervous, and she wasn't sure why.

"Let's just say I'm intrigued." The man flashed her two rows of white teeth in what could have been either a snarl or a smile; she wasn't sure which. "You obviously haven't done this kind of thing before," he told her. "Terms aren't discussed in a public place. You never know who might be listening or watching. Do you have a place where we can talk?"

His words bothered Solace more than she was willing to admit. It was true, she knew nothing of hiring men. Nonetheless, she wasn't a fool. She wasn't going anywhere with this man. It was too dangerous. "No," she said, trying to sound sure of herself. "This place will do fine."

Suddenly, she felt the sting of a sword against her belly beneath the table. "Listen . . ." The man paused. ". . . *boy*. Put all your gold on the table or I'll run you through."

Solace gasped, her mouth falling open. The tip shoved into her belly and she blurted out, "I—I don't have any gold. I don't have any coin at all. You took the only one I had."

The man again flashed his teeth at her, and this time she was certain it was a snarl. "You want to hire me with no coin! Are you mad, boy? Does a demon afflict you?

I ought to run you through just for aggravating me. I've killed men for less."

"Please," she whispered, a note of fear edging her voice. "I'm desperate. I can feed you for however long it takes. I can give you all the gold you want when my task is complete."

Even though it was dark beneath the man's hood, she could sense his eyes narrowing. "How can an ugly boy like you pay me all the gold I want? What kind of task will reward you with untold riches?"

She opened her mouth to tell him her father was rich, but closed it immediately. This man would, no doubt, take her for ransom. She could tell him who she was, but that might be even worse. With the price Barclay put on her head, he might very well hand her over to him. The tip of the sword pressed against her abdomen. "I plan to take Castle Fulton," she finally whispered.

The man was silent for a long moment. "Would you mind telling me that again? I think my ears must be full of wax. I could've sworn that you, an ugly boy with no coin, just told me you are going to attack Fulton."

The words spoken back to her sounded utterly ridiculous. Everything he said was true. She had no coin, no army. A sense of defeat swelled inside her, but she pushed it back with a strong sense of determination. She refused to be ridiculed and intimidated by him. She straightened her shoulders, drawing forth all her courage to face him. "That's what I told you," she retorted. "Rome wasn't built in a day. Either join my cause or let me get on with my recruiting."

"You're a damn fool!" the man hissed. "Rome was built by breaking the backs of thousands of slaves."

"The men I employ will not be slaves," she reminded him. "They will be well rewarded for their efforts. Now remove your sword."

The man hesitated for a long moment, then abruptly removed his sword and set it on the seat next to him. He looked out into the tavern at the patrons, the fighter, the monk and the drunk peasant. "Gather round, men!" he called out. "The boy here promises us all gold! Bags of gold! All we have to do is risk our lives without pay! He assures me we shall all be rewarded in the end!"

The monk raised his head slightly, but then turned back to his food. The fighter eyed the pair with disinterest.

"Bastard," Solace hissed, rising. "I wouldn't call food and board 'without pay.' " She had to get out of there. She couldn't be seen dealing with mercenaries. All sorts of suspicions would be aroused.

The man dismissed her with an impatient wave of his hand.

Solace quickly took the rear door out of the Wolf's Inn. A cold breeze accosted her as she exited into the street behind the inn, catching her hood and almost pulling it from her head, but she grabbed it before it could blow off. Damn, she thought. Now I'll have to wait a couple of days, perhaps a week, before I can return to the inn. She paced two steps one way and whirled, pacing the other way.

She paced for a few moments longer, trying to get rid of the fear and anxiety and anger that gripped her. The honorless blackguard! How could he rob some helpless boy? This was the type of man she was dealing with. She rubbed her hand along her forehead. Where is Father? she wondered. Where could he be?

Solace turned toward the blacksmith's shop. The streets at this time of night were vacant, the shops that lined them all closed. She refused to give up her plan— no matter how outrageous it sounded!

"It isn't safe to be out alone after dark. Even for a

boy who thinks he can command an army of mercenaries."

Solace whirled, hearing the voice. She couldn't see where it was coming from, but she was sure it was the mercenary from the inn! What did he want of her? Whatever it was, she wanted no part of it! A shiver of dread shot up her spine. She took a step backward, scanning the dark street, the shadows near the shops for the owner of the ominous voice. But it was useless. The night's blackness was all around her, enshrouding her in its impenetrable cloak.

Solace turned and ran.

A dark shape stepped in front of her, moving out from behind a store front, and she slammed into a solid wall of flesh. Terror seized her in an icy hold. She barely noticed that her hood had slipped from her head. She jerked back from the man, trying to move around him.

The man clamped a hand over her mouth and ensnared her waist with his free arm, trapping her against his body. "Barclay has a very high price on your head," the man whispered hotly in her ear.

Twenty-eight

Solace struggled uselessly against her captor, pushing against his strong chest with powerless fingers. The heavy hood he still wore hid his face deep in its black shadows, giving him the appearance of an executioner. Finally, desperation overpowering her fear, she brought her knee up, driving it into his groin.

The man doubled over, releasing her mouth for a moment. Solace inhaled for a scream, but the man shoved his hand over her mouth again, grabbing the nape of her neck roughly. Cursing, he pulled her toward a dark alley, stumbling as he moved. She tried to fight, but his hold tightened, bruising the back of her neck. He stopped in the darkness of the alley, gasping and still partially bent.

Solace pulled at the strong fingers clamped over her mouth, trying to break free of his hold, trying to call for help. He pushed her back against the rear of the inn, snarling, "Shut up!"

For a moment Solace could barely breathe. He held her still, one hand clamped over her mouth, one at the back of her neck. Solace watched him with wide eyes. But his gaze was not on her. It was on the street.

Then she heard it. Footsteps. Had someone else been following her? What was going on? The footsteps faltered just before the entrance to the alley.

The man released the nape of her neck, and his hand dipped to the handle of the sword at his waist.

For a moment everything froze. She instinctively knew the danger was not from the cloaked man who held her against the wall, but from the person at the entrance to the alley.

Then the footsteps moved off. With a sigh that sounded more like a groan, the man dropped his hand from her mouth and leaned against the wall beside her. "That was a pleasant greeting," he murmured.

Solace straightened, instantly pulling away from him. "Who are you?" she demanded.

"It's only been a month, Solace. You can't tell me you've forgotten already." He brushed off the hood. The moonlight fell over his dark, wavy hair. His gray eyes shone like silver, gleaming like the eyes of some nocturnal animal. The once black x on his cheek was healing, becoming a permanent fallen cross etched in his skin.

"Logan!" Solace gasped. A tumult of emotions flared within her. Disbelief. Anger. Joy. She didn't know how to react. She wasn't really sure he was standing before her. She had missed him so much. An overwhelming sadness filled her. Every night she had replayed the events that led up to his opening the gates, the way he had looked at her, the warm feeling that had encompassed her when he was near. Now it started somewhere deep inside of her and raced through her veins. She knew with certainty that she would do it all again, just for those few days with him.

"That's a new look for you. Do you think it fools anyone?" His words were cold and clipped.

She refused to be baited by his anger and smiled grimly in the face of his irritability. "It's the same look for you, Logan. Scowling brows and all."

He pushed his face close to hers. "This isn't a game,

Solace," he snarled. "Do you know how dangerous it is for you to be walking the streets at night, not to mention trying to recruit mercenaries!"

"Have you come all this way to lecture me?"

"I came to make you stop this crazy plan of yours," he snapped. "And you *will* stop."

"When I get my army," she responded.

"Damn it, woman!" Logan snarled. "Do you have a death wish? Didn't I just prove to you that you're risking your life?"

Solace stared at him for a long moment. She wished he would smile at her. She wished she could touch that soft wave in his hair. She wished he had greeted her with a warm hug, a gentle kiss. A somber feeling settled over her. "All you've proved is that you're an expert at deceiving me," she retorted.

Logan exhaled slowly, raking a hand through his dark mane. "Look, I didn't come here to argue with you."

"Then why did you come here?" Solace demanded.

"Because someone has to tell you what a foolish thing it is you're doing," he said. "You don't know how to go about this. It's dangerous business. You could get hurt or killed."

"I can't let Barclay harm my people. I have to get my castle back." She turned her gaze to the stars. They splattered the sky like freckles across a lad's face.

Logan stood for a long moment, and eventually she turned her gaze to him. He reached out, slipping his hand around hers.

Solace watched the way his large hand enfolded hers, the way his thumb easily, comfortingly, slid back and forth across her knuckles.

"I want you to come with me to Cavindale."

Solace began to shake her head and opened her mouth to object.

But Logan continued quickly, "I have an army waiting there."

Logan saw the greedy light in her eyes even in the darkness, saw her green orbs spark like fire when he mentioned the army.

"An army?" she asked. "But how?"

Logan called forth a grin. "A month is plenty of time to put out the word," he said.

"An army of mercenaries?" she inquired.

He nodded.

"And you'd let me command your army?"

He couldn't help admiring her bravado. She was a courageous woman. "With my help," he said.

Logan prepared himself for her anger, but it never came. Instead, a look of weary sadness crossed her features.

"I wish I could believe you," she said in a thick voice, and dropped her gaze to the ground.

"You *can* Solace," Logan said desperately.

She turned to look at him over her shoulder, a guarded skepticism in her lidded eyes. "Then what do you need me for?"

He opened his mouth and then closed it, setting his jaw.

Solace turned away from him and started out of the alley.

"I don't want to see you hurt again," he called. When she didn't stop, Logan cursed and rushed after her. He reached her before she entered the street, stepping in front of her to block her path. "Why do you think I came all this way to stop you?"

"I think you did it to keep me out of the way," she replied.

"Do you think that one woman is going to make a

difference in this battle?" Logan wondered, sternly. "Think about what you're saying. Think about what you're doing. It's madness!"

"Because I'm a woman."

"No. Because you don't know how to go about hiring mercenaries. You don't know what kind of men you're dealing with."

"I don't need your help, thank you." She moved around him.

Logan blocked her path with his body again. "All it takes is one man. Maybe the next one you approach. He'll follow you through the streets like I did, then pull you into a lonely alley, a vacant field, a dark corner." He watched her fight the horror that threatened to engulf her and knew that this was his only weapon. "He'll take your body in ways you can't even imagine! Then drag you back to the inn and share you with his friends. When they're done playing with you, he'll slit your throat and leave you on the dirty floor of the inn."

Solace swallowed hard.

"If you're dead, it won't really matter who has Castle Fulton, will it?"

She raised that stubborn little chin, fighting to find her voice. "And you know mercenaries so well?"

Logan pushed his face close to hers. "I'm one of them."

Solace reared back, a tremor shuddered through her. She pushed past him, moving down the street.

Logan watched her for a moment, wondering if it had been enough, wondering if the foolish chit would cease trying to raise an army. He knew his answer immediately. She was far too stubborn to leave her people and her castle in Barclay's hands. He had to convince her to come to Cavindale with him.

He raced after her toward her friend's shop. He caught up to her as she rounded the last corner before the blacksmith's. Voices floated to him on a dark breeze, prickling the back of his neck. His arm shot out, grabbing her wrist. When she turned to him, he put his finger to his lips in a motion for silence.

He led her into the shadows of a nearby building.

"What?" Solace asked in a whisper.

Logan's eyes were locked on the blacksmith's shop. Three horses were tethered out front. The window covering flickered with light from a burning candle inside the shop. Something was not right. His senses tingled with warning. Something . . . smelled strange. He knew the smell, but the wind dragged it away from his nose before he could place it. He strained to hear the voices again, but could not make out a sound.

From the outside, everything looked calm and normal.

Solace yanked her arm away from him, taking a step forward.

Logan seized her shoulder and dragged her back into the shadows. "Wait," he whispered urgently in her ear.

The door to the shop opened, and the voices floated out into the night air. Logan couldn't hear the words, but one melodic voice set his teeth on edge.

A scream ripped through the night, erupting from the open door. The stench assaulted his sense of smell again and Logan reeled back, recognizing the pungent odor of burning flesh. The brand on his cheek throbbed as the unwanted memory of his own agony lurched to the front of his mind.

Solace pushed forward, but Logan caught her around the waist, pulling her farther away.

Two of Barclay's men exited the shop, carrying a body between them. Inside, the screaming continued.

Logan placed a hand over Solace's mouth to stifle her horrified gasps of disbelief.

A third man appeared in the doorway, his face hidden

in dark shadows. But Logan could still see his features in his mind's eye. Thin, cruel lips. Cold blue eyes. A once handsome face turned ugly from inside. Logan froze, his muscles tensing, his jaw clenching so tight that his teeth ached.

"I want her found," the man ordered, stepping into the street.

Logan's eyes narrowed as the moonlight struck Baron Edwin Barclay's face.

"She's in this village. Seal off all the roads. No one is to leave without my knowing about it. If she escapes, I will burn the town to the ground." Barclay whirled, but suddenly halted. His billowing cape settled around his shoulders. Then he swiveled his head, pinning Logan and Solace to the spot.

Twenty-nine

Logan felt Solace stiffen in his arms. He tightened his hold on her to keep her absolutely still.

Barclay's blue eyes seared into the spot where they were standing as if he were able to see into the darkness. Finally, he turned and went back into the shop.

For a long moment Logan couldn't move. He watched as the soldiers threw the body over one of the horses and reentered the blacksmith's shop. Then three mounted soldiers appeared from behind the shop and, before riding hard into the night, passed not five feet from where Logan and Solace had stood.

Logan exploded into motion, pulling Solace with him. He moved with precision and purpose through the streets. He knew he didn't have much time. Barclay's soldiers were setting up guards at the roads even now.

They quickly reached the Wolf's Inn to find Alexander waiting for them, the horses untethered and ready to ride. "Looks like you stuck a stick in the hornet's nest," Alexander mumbled. Logan took the reins from his friend's hand, and the two of them mounted their horses.

Logan reached down to help Solace mount, but she didn't offer him her hand. "I can't leave," she said.

"What do you mean?" Logan demanded, his horse dancing anxiously beneath him.

"They killed Geoffrey," she said softly. "I have to help Mitch."

"What do you think you can do against an armed garrison?" Logan demanded. "You exposed yourself at the inn. What did you think was going to happen? Any fool could see that you weren't a boy!" He extended a hand to her. "Come on."

She shook her head stubbornly, glancing back at the village.

Alexander's mount pranced nervously.

Logan saw the tears in her eyes, but there was no time for sympathy. He knew if they stood around much longer they would be trapped. His anger rose. "You should never have gone to the inn. It wouldn't have taken much to ask a few questions, or follow you and find out where you were staying. It could have been one of the villagers that gave you away. It could have been a mercenary." He shoved his hand toward her. "Come on!"

"It's my fault," she whispered. "I should never have gone to them for help."

"It's not important whose fault it is. What's important is that you're still alive to fight Barclay."

Solace raised her eyes to him. Logan saw the pain there, and then he saw her lips clench in firm resolve. She grabbed his hand and he pulled her up behind him, spurring the horse hard toward Cavindale.

Castle Fulton's towers appeared red in the setting sun, as if blood ran from the turrets. The red light splashed through a small arrow slit in one of the towers, casting a bloody cross over Nolan Ryder's body. He gazed down upon the land with apathetic black eyes.

His long black beard nearly touched the thick leather belt around his waist. "I don't like doing business like this."

"Take the terms or leave them," a woman's voice said from behind him. "I can find others who will take the job for half the coin."

Ryder knew this was true, but none were as skilled as he. He rubbed his hand across his mouth, massaging his red lips. "You say she was last seen in Westhaven?"

"Two days ago. It shouldn't be hard for such a talented tracker as you to pick up her trail." She jingled the pouch of gold in her hand slightly.

Manipulative bitch, Ryder thought. "I'll have to bribe many men. There'll be lodging and food to pay for." He turned to her. She was a beautiful woman, but there was a coldness in her blue eyes that he found even more intriguing. "I need more up front," he finally said.

Her eyes narrowed. "Fine," she snapped. "I'll get you what you need. But not a shilling over half of what we agreed to."

"I haven't agreed to anything . . . yet."

A grin curved her full lips. "But you will."

"I don't like killing women," Ryder professed.

"I don't give a damn what you like and what you don't. If you want the gold, you'll do as I tell you. Do we have a deal?"

Ryder pondered the offer. Kill the girl and get the gold. It shouldn't be hard. For the coin she was paying, he could hire a man to do the work and oversee the job himself, still have enough to buy a sturdy steed and a wench when it was all over. A grin curved his lips and he bowed slightly. "You have yourself a deal."

A smile darkened the woman's face. She pulled a gold-tipped dagger from her belt. She held it out to Ryder, handle first.

"What's this?" Ryder wondered, taking the dagger

from her, studying the finely etched flowers in the black
handle.

"You'll need it," she answered.

Suspicious, Ryder lifted his gaze to meet hers. "For
what?"

"I want her blood on my dagger," she murmured
with a strange glow of excitement in her eyes. "I want
you to bring me Solace Farindale's head."

Solace sat near the bank of the small stream where
they had stopped to rest. They had ridden relentlessly
for two days, stopping only when necessary. Logan had
offered no words of sympathy, no condolences, for the
loss of her friends.

Geoffrey's death had been her fault.

The thought sent prickles of pain throughout her
body. She had grieved for her friends the first day, silently shedding tears as the horses rode. Now, as she
stared down at the clear, calm water, she said a silent
prayer for them.

Solace bent to splash water over her face. It was icy
cold, but she couldn't resist the refreshing feeling it
gave her. She rubbed the water from her eyes and
splashed some of the chill liquid over her neck. A cool
breeze whipped around her and she shivered slightly.
The Yuletide would be here soon. She wondered how
Barclay would treat the pilgrimage of monks that would
soon arrive at Castle Fulton. Every year, for as long as
she could remember, scores of monks had stopped at
Fulton on their way to the Abbey of St. Michael for the
holiest of celebrations. Her father had always welcomed
them with open arms and tables full of food. Barclay
seemed to have respect for the pious. Solace remembered how he treated Father Davis. Maybe the monks

would fare well with Barclay. For their sake, she hoped so.

The cloth that bound her breasts was tight and itchy. She longed to remove it and had come to the stream to do just that. Solace lifted her tunic and fumbled with the knot at the front of her chest.

She turned her thoughts to that other man. The mercenary. Logan's friend. Alexander. He must have been the first man she had approached in Westhaven. She now understood how Logan had found out about her plan to recruit an army.

She pulled the cloth off her chest, freeing her breasts. They tingled, and she rubbed the circulation back into them, groaning softly. It was pure pleasure. She splashed water over them, cleaning her body.

Logan had an army. The thought rose unexpectedly to her mind. An army. Dare she believe him? Dare she hope that she could trust him? But she didn't. Not with his betrayal so fresh and painful in her mind.

Solace wanted to believe in him. She pulled her shirt back over her torso.

Feeling a chill at the nape of her neck that had nothing to do with the wind, she turned her head. Logan was leaning against a nearby tree, his arms crossed over his chest. A shiver shot through her body at his smoldering gaze. She watched the slow, predatory way he approached.

"How long have you been standing there?" Solace wondered.

"Long enough to tell you that it's about time you took that ridiculous thing off," he replied, gently kicking the cloth that had bound her breasts.

Solace blushed slightly. "You shouldn't spy on people," she chastised.

"I wasn't spying," he said in a husky voice.

A warmth flooded through Solace at the deep timbre

of his voice. She did her best to ignore the traitorous reaction of her body. "Do you really have an army?" she asked quickly, changing the subject.

His eyes darkened, and Solace felt a door closing somewhere inside him, sealing off some part of his soul. "Yes."

"Tell me about it," she encouraged.

Logan's gaze swept the distant horizon, his look was lidded and somehow secretive. He crossed his arms over his chest again. "There aren't a lot of men, but they're good. Only the best."

"Are there enough to retake Fulton?" Solace wondered, searching for something that would reveal the truth to her. It would be foolish for Logan to lie to her. They would be at Cavindale in a few days. She would see his army for herself.

"Not yet."

His words confirmed her suspicions, and she glanced sharply at him.

"But soon," he added quickly.

Her brow remained furrowed. There was something he was not telling her.

"It takes time to build an army," he defended.

Solace nodded, looking away from him. "We'll attack before winter?"

Logan wet his lips. "It might be better to wait until spring."

Solace objected, "It will give Barclay more time to settle into the castle."

"If winter hits when we're laying siege, we'll lose. It's as simple as that."

Solace stood before him, looking deeply into his gray eyes, wishing she felt as sure about the plan as he did. Suddenly, and quite unexpectedly, pride rose in her breast and she realized that she was glad he had returned. His dark hair fanned across his face as a whispered breeze slipped by. She reached up and gently brushed it away from his cheek, unveiling the brand.

A criminal, her mind said. A man wrongly punished, her heart countered. He saved your life more than once.

Only to shatter it.

She dropped her hand. But he caught it in his and brought it to his lips, pressing a kiss to her knuckles. There was an intensity in his eyes, a fevered desire that was more than lust, more than truth. It penetrated her skin, soaring through her blood to her spirit. But before she could figure out exactly what it was, he turned away, leaving her alone and more confused than before.

Solace finished up at the stream before following Logan's path back to the horses. He was nowhere to be seen. Alexander was checking the shoes of his horse. Solace walked up to him, her gaze scanning the forest for any sign of Logan. She chewed her lip gently, debating the best way to question him.

"What do you want?" Alexander demanded, making her jump slightly.

"Well," she said hesitantly, "I was wondering how long you've known Logan."

Alexander didn't look up from his work. "Why?"

Solace straightened her back. "Because I want to know if you're close."

"Close enough for me to accompany him to Westhaven to find you," he retorted.

"Oh," she said casually. "I see. So, you're part of his army." It was a bluff and she didn't know whether it would work or not. But she had to try.

He finally raised his eyes to her. But they were blank and unrevealing. He didn't say a word, just regarded her coolly.

Solace scowled at him, unnerved by his distant demeanor. "You should try to smile sometimes," she snapped. "It might improve your disposition."

She whirled and stormed to the other horse to await Logan's return.

That night, after a hard day's ride, Logan sat with his back against a tall oak, dragging his dagger along a thick piece of wood he had found. His eyes, however, were not on the chore. They were locked on Solace as she slept. She had kicked free of the blanket, even though the night wind was cold. Golden-, red- and orange-colored leaves lay scattered around her. One red one had entangled itself in a lock of her hair which fanned out beneath her.

She was beautiful. The most beautiful woman he had ever laid eyes on. With every ounce of his being he wanted to kiss her, to touch her, to make her the center of his universe. But he couldn't. Not yet. Not until he got Fulton back. Not until his revenge was complete.

Besides, what would she want with a man like him? Not even a knight. He found himself absently rubbing the brand on his cheek. A marked man. Could she ever love him? No. Not after what he had done to her home, to her. Logan was sure of it. She was using him to get to his "army." He almost laughed out loud at the thought.

His army. The mighty, grand army that awaited him at Cavindale. He shook his head. He would have said anything to get her out of Westhaven. She was in danger, attracting attention to herself. Any fool with two eyes could see the gentle sway of her hips as she walked.

And Logan was the biggest of all fools. He was allowing himself to care for her again. She was getting in his way. A distraction of the most dangerous sort. That was why he had come a week's journey from Cavindale. Two weeks of valuable time away from his mission. Time that could have been better spent making contacts, gathering much needed allies. From what he had learned before leaving Cavindale, Barclay was not a well-liked man. Logan had known that years ago when he'd allied himself with Barclay, but they had gotten along well enough. He had trusted Barclay. It seems that I am no good at putting my trust in the right place, he thought. He vowed not to make that mistake again.

Solace turned her head, calling his attention to her. Her soft lips parted slightly and something inside Logan softened. The joy he had seen for a moment on her face when she knew it was him was worth the time he had taken from his revenge, and more. He watched the slight rise and fall of her chest, and suddenly had the strongest desire to see the unbound treasures that lay beneath that tunic. The leggings she wore curved around her hips and thighs, arousing him every time he glanced at her.

Logan cursed silently and looked away. Too dangerous a distraction, he reminded himself.

Suddenly, a hand clamped over his shoulder and Logan whirled, bringing the dagger up.

"Whoa!" Alexander cried, backing up a step.

Grumbling, Logan lowered the dagger. Damn, he hadn't even heard him coming. Too much of a distraction, he thought again.

"A little jumpy today, hey, my friend?" Alexander wondered, squatting beside him.

Logan scraped the dagger across the wood again.

"We should be at Cavindale the day after tomorrow," Alexander said, his eyes shifting to Solace. "I like her," Alexander murmured after a quiet moment. "She had the courage to tell me I should smile more."

Logan almost laughed out loud. "You mean she didn't tremble under your glowering?"

"Tremble?" Alexander rumbled. "She didn't even blink. She must be used to dark looks by now." He cast a telling glance at Logan. "She's worth giving up a lot for."

"She's dangerous," Logan insisted.

"Dangerous?" Alexander echoed in disbelief.

"Because she *is* worth giving up a lot for. I don't trust her."

"Don't, or can't?"

"I don't even trust you," Logan replied.

"Stop flattering me," Alexander said.

"We've been through a lot together," Logan said. "You've got morals and as much as you'd hate to admit it, you have honor."

"And she doesn't?"

"*I* don't. I would do anything to get my revenge. I can't help thinking that if it were me in her position, there would be no way in hell that I would trust me. Not after what I did to her."

"She's not you. Maybe she has more confidence in you."

Logan stood up, his eyes darkening. "Maybe she shouldn't."

Alexander shrugged. "She'll find that out when your *army* of farmers and alemakers welcomes us home, won't she?"

Thirty

Logan rode his stallion into Cavindale with Solace sitting sidesaddle in front of him. He was pensive and quiet, waiting for her warmth and growing excitement to change into bitter hatred. He had told himself that he wanted to tell her the truth about his army, but he couldn't. Not until they reached Cavindale.

Now that they were here, his dry mouth wouldn't say the condemning words.

He could feel the anticipation simmering inside her. She didn't want to believe him, he knew, but something inside her was trusting and naive . . . and very foolish.

As they approached Cavindale Manor, Alexander spurred his steed on ahead of them.

Solace craned her lovely neck. "Where's the army?" she wondered, scanning the surrounding hills.

Was that anxiety in her voice or was she mocking him? Logan wondered if *she* even knew which it was.

The roads remained empty.

Logan knew he had to tell her. He couldn't let her go on believing. She would find out soon enough. And then it would be too late to redeem himself. It was his only chance. "Solace . . ." he began.

"Over there?" she asked, pointing to a slight rise.

"Solace . . ." Logan was shaking his head, but she

seemed oblivious. She slid off the horse. Her feet barely struck ground before she proceeded toward the rise.

He couldn't move for a long moment. He hung his head. He would hear her disappointment soon, the hurt in her voice.

"Oh, Logan," she sighed.

He closed his eyes for a moment. Then he dismounted and walked to her side, expecting to see sorrow in those brilliant green eyes, expecting to see disappointment. "I wanted to tell you . . ." he started to say as he came to stand beside her.

She launched herself into his arms, her hands encircling his neck. "It's wonderful!" she murmured.

Logan's eyes swept the valley before him to see tent upon tent cradled between the rises. Men and horses milled about everywhere. Weapons of all kinds sparkled in the sunlight.

Logan's mouth dropped and he gasped, "My God."

Solace lurched forward, running to greet her army. An army Logan knew nothing about. He reached out to stop her, trying to grab her arm, but she was too far away. What if it were Barclay's army? Logan wondered fleetingly. But he knew it wasn't. There were no colors on the tents; there were no banners flapping in the breeze.

His eyes scanned the tents again. There was nothing. No heraldry, no crests, nothing.

Suddenly, a large bellow resounded across the valley. Logan turned and drew his weapon instinctively . . .

Solace had reached the bottom of the small hill when she heard the war cry and turned to see a giant man racing toward Logan, a sword raised high above his head. He had tight curly red hair crowning his massive head. His thick arms, covered with numerous scars, bulged with muscle. Solace gasped as Logan and the man collided, and she swore the ground beneath her feet trembled with the impact. She could see the strain in Logan's corded neck as he locked swords with the man, holding him at bay.

She bolted back up the hill.

Logan almost fell over as the giant pushed off with his sword. Then the huge man grumbled and swung. Logan ducked and Solace's heart stopped as the blade barely missed his head.

She started forward, but an arm on her wrist stopped her. She glanced up to see Alexander. He had a strange grin on his face as he watched the two men fight.

"Help him," Solace begged Alexander. Logan's friend didn't move.

Logan glanced at her and the giant man punched him in the jaw, sending him back onto his bottom. Logan raised his sword in time to block the next blow. He rolled out of the way as the giant swung again. The giant's sword lodged in the earth as Logan jumped to his feet to face the man.

Solace forced herself to relax and wait. Her eyes scanned the field for a weapon.

With a growl of rage, the giant man ripped his sword from the earth, sending a clump of dirt flying through the air. Logan sidestepped to the right as the giant swung. He deflected the next blow, losing ground to his opponent.

Alexander relaxed his grip and Solace pulled free. She ran to Logan's horse and flipped the backpack open. She rifled through the leather pouch, searching around a blanket, finally grabbing the large stick Logan had been working on.

As she turned, she saw that Logan and the giant man

were battling on the top of the rise. A crowd of specta-
tors had gathered around them. Determined to help
Logan, Solace slowly climbed the hill, careful to stay
out of the giant's sight.

The giant lurched forward and Logan caught the
blow, grabbing the giant's arm.

Solace approached the giant from behind, the stick
raised.

Logan's eyes locked on the raised log and the giant
kicked him in the stomach, sending him flying back,
just as Solace slammed the wood over the giant's head
with all her might. He toppled forward to his hands
and knees.

For a long moment, all was quiet. Solace ran to Logan's side. "Are you all right?" she asked, helping him
to sit up.

A crooked grin curled Logan's lips as Solace helped
him to rise. He gazed into her eyes and ran a gentle
finger across her jaw. "You're getting pretty good at
that," he murmured before turning from her to approach the giant. "You must be slipping," he told the
big man. "This is the first time I've beaten you."

The giant raised his eyes to Logan and Solace saw
the trickle of blood from a cut on his head. "Ya didn't
tell me you had an accomplice."

Logan offered the giant his hand.

"Goliath this is Solace," Logan introduced. "Goliath
is a friend."

"A friend!" Solace repeated in disbelief.

"I tried to stop you," Alexander murmured.

"Do you always greet friends like this?" Solace asked
with chagrin.

"Goliath and I do. We always have. Ever since we met
on the battlefield."

Goliath staggered and Logan placed a hand on his shoulder to steady him.

"The little weasel kept ducking me best blows," Goliath complained, swiping the blood from his head with his sleeve. "If he'da kept still I woulda won."

Logan chuckled. "We were the last ones standing. We fought until we were too exhausted to finish each other. So, instead, we became friends."

Solace stared at them in disbelief "And you greet each other like this all the time?"

"All the time," Logan said, swiveling his gaze to her, a wry smile on his lips.

Solace looked away from Logan's stare to Goliath. The trickle of blood dripped down his forehead. "I'm so sorry," she whispered.

"It's all right, lass," Goliath responded.

She felt Logan's gaze on her, and she looked at him again. His eyes seemed to deepen to a cloudy gray, and her blood began to boil.

Logan stepped up to her. She felt protected by his closeness, his strength. But his gaze wasn't on her; he was scanning the crowd. "Blade. McColl. John Jones. Doric. What are you doing here?"

A light-haired man grasping a hunter's bow stepped forward, offering Logan his arm. Logan grabbed it fiercely. "Blade," Logan greeted with a smile. "Good to see you."

"We came when we heard about Castle Fulton," Blade said.

"All of you?" Logan gasped in disbelief.

"One by one," the man replied, a smile on his handsome face. He turned his beaming gaze onto Solace as Logan stepped away from her to greet more of the men. "Who do we have here?" he asked, taking her hand in his and pressing a kiss to her knuckles. "My name is

Blade." He was a tall man, slightly taller than Logan, with deep blue eyes. He adjusted the bow slung over his shoulder, smiling pleasantly at her.

Logan intercepted her hand, sliding it from Blade's hold. "This is Solace," he said. "Solace Farindale."

"Farindale?" Goliath echoed.

Solace heard the crowd of men grumble as if they were tethered wild beasts sniffing an approaching enemy. Hostility shone in the eyes of some, confusion in those of others. She swallowed down her trepidation. She was here to lead these men, and she couldn't show fear. She had to be brave. "Yes," she said, stepping around Logan. She had to look up to meet the shortest man's gaze, but she did it unflinchingly. "I'm here to lead you against Baron Barclay."

"Solace . . ." Logan began.

A couple of men's brows rose in disbelief. A few others chuckled. And some shifted their gaze in silent query to Logan.

"You?" a man with a dark gruff beard and scraggly hair asked in disbelief.

"Solace, I have to talk to you," Logan said.

A caw sounded from above him, and Solace craned her neck to see Logan's black falcon.

"Logan!" The voice boomed over the valley.

Solace followed its source to see an older man strolling toward them over the rise, his look dark and harried. "Logan! You'd better have an answer for all of these . . . these . . . men trampling my fields and harassing my people!"

Logan's falcon alighted on his shoulder, but he barely acknowledged it as he winced at the man's tirade, raising his eyes to Blade.

Blade shrugged. "I'm not their keeper."

Logan shook his head and turned to greet the man. "Uncle. This wasn't my idea. I—"

"They're your friends, aren't they?"

"Yes, but I had no idea they would all come here." Logan splayed his fingers before him in a helpless gesture.

"No idea?" Solace echoed. "You knew they were here. You told me so."

"He had no idea," Blade said patiently. "We arrived after he left."

An ill feeling settled unsteadily in the pit of Solace's stomach. "After?" she murmured, turning to look at Logan. "He told me he had an army—"

"An army to eat me out of my home! If they stay, we'll have no winter storage! We'll starve," Uncle Hugh ranted, his hands on his hips as he glared at Logan.

"Relax, old man," a gruff-looking short man said. "We already told ya we don't need yer food."

"Don't call me an 'old man,' you worthless codger!"

The falcon nipped hard at Logan's shoulder, drawing blood through his tunic. He shrugged his shoulder so hard the bird took flight.

Alexander chuckled. "It looks like your feathered friend didn't like being locked up for two weeks."

Solace pulled at Logan's arm, confusion knitting her brows. "Logan, you said you had an army."

Logan suddenly yanked his arm free of her hold. "There is no army!" he hollered, standing amidst the group of men. "I lied to you to get you to Cavindale. To make you stop that stupid plan of yours!"

Solace pulled back as if he had slapped her. She had known he was lying, but to hear it from his lips wounded her as no dagger ever could.

Logan whirled on his uncle, his face a mask of anger. "They'll restock your stores! They'll replow the fields!

They'll stop harassing your people!" His fists were clenched tightly, his jaw taut with fury.

Everything stopped, everything froze. Logan's friends stared at him in shock; Uncle Hugh's mouth hung open. Logan stood under the gazes of all for a moment before whirling and heading down the hill.

The falcon flew to a nearby tree and perched on a branch, watching Logan storm off with impassive eyes.

Stupid! Solace berated herself. Fool! She was humiliated. With a snort, she turned and walked, with as much dignity as she could, away from the direction in which Logan had headed. She didn't know where she was going. She just knew she was going away.

There was only one thing that calmed Logan when he was angry.

"You ready?" Alexander wondered.

Logan stared at the blade in his hand. He had dragged Alexander into the field near Cavindale's northern border, desperate to vent his raging anxiety. He twisted the sword slightly, watching the sunlight reflect off the polished blade. He thought about—

—striking. He swung the weapon at Alexander, aiming for his head. Alexander easily blocked the blow with his own blade. "Why so angry, Grey?" Alexander taunted, sidestepping another swing. "Because Hugh is so furious with you?"

Logan grunted. "Hardly," he snapped, arcing his weapon toward Alexander's blabbering mouth.

Alexander caught the blow and deflected it. "Because you made an ass of yourself?"

Logan thrust toward Alexander's stomach, only to have his sword swiped aside. "It wouldn't be the first time."

"What then?" Alexander wondered.

"Are you going to talk or fight?" Logan demanded.

Alexander cocked his head slightly. "The girl?" he wondered. He thrust at Logan. "You can't tell me you actually care for the daughter of your enemy?"

Logan just barely parried the blow. "She hates me for lying to her," Logan said in a rush.

"What do you care what she thinks?" A swing.

"She should have known better!" A block.

"So what?"

Logan raised his blade and then drove the sword deep into the earth. He threw back his head to holler at the sky. "Why does she keep trusting me?"

Alexander set a hand on his friend's shoulder. "Because she loves you."

Logan shrugged Alexander's hand from his shoulder. "You're wrong. How could she love me? I let Barclay into her home."

Alexander chuckled. "Love is blind, dear fellow. Or she'd certainly see that ugly scar on your cheek and seek a more dashing companion . . . like Blade."

Every muscle in Logan's body stiffened. Blade. God's blood! Blade! They had competed for many women in the days they had worked together. Blade found it amusing, and Logan had played along good-naturedly, not really caring one way or another. But now, for some reason, his insides twisted with fear and dread. "Oh, Lord!" he half cried, half groaned. He pulled the sword from the ground and headed toward Cavindale Manor, hoping he wasn't too late.

With each step, visions danced mockingly in his head. Solace sobbing by the hearth, all his friends gathered around to offer their sympathies. Solace crying on Blade's shoulder. Blade's hands caressing her back, moving upward to caress her breast.

Logan broke into a run.

He swung the door to the Great Hall open, expecting anything. But he wasn't prepared for the vision that greeted him.

Thirty-one

When the door to the Great Hall slammed opened, all eyes turned to pin Logan where he stood. Solace stood in the middle of a group of his friends, Blade at one side, Goliath at the other. They had been bent over one of the tables quietly discussing something. Logan's gaze locked on Solace. She raised that defiant little chin, her deep green eyes flashing with challenge.

Logan approached the group with large strides. His friends parted for him like a curtain until he stood beside Solace, glaring at her. What was she planning? A secret rendezvous with all of his friends? He glanced down at the table.

There was only a sketch of the borders to Castle Fulton. Solace was planning an attack, with his own friends, against Barclay! They were planning to retake *his* castle!

He dropped his head, and the laughter churned in his throat. The little vixen had not seduced his friends into her bed, but into her allegiance.

"Go ahead and laugh," she challenged.

Logan heard the daggers in her voice and wondered if she had a weapon hidden beneath her tunic somewhere to cut out his heart. She didn't know she wouldn't find a heart.

His eyes rose like the moon to gleam at her. There was accusation and rebellion in her large eyes. Logan realized, perhaps for the first time, that this was not the same woman he had met at Fulton. She had changed, grown into a woman capable of many things. A woman capable of taking back her home. He could not laugh at her. He could only admire her.

Finally, he stepped away and turned his back on them, moving silently to the hearth. She had gotten her army, it appeared. And he had handed it to her. What a fool I've been! he thought. A small army has been within my reach for years, and I haven't even seen it.

Solace's gaze returned to the paper laid out before them, and slowly, each of his friends turned with her. Damnation! With friends like that who needed Barclay? Logan thought.

Logan's eyes narrowed as he saw Blade ease a hand to her lower back. Logan grumbled and called for an ale. Goliath leaned closer to the paper, brushing her arm. Logan's look darkened as Alexander moved over to the group. He listened for a moment, and then a smile lit his usually pensive face. To him they looked like a group of moon-eyed admirers.

Logan clenched his teeth so hard that it hurt. Well, he wasn't going to be one of them! he vowed. He had other more important things to do. He threw back a drink of the ale a somber servant had just delivered.

He could not tear his eyes from the sight of Solace surrounded by his own friends. Traitors, he thought. Every one of them. Sniffing about her skirts like rutting bulls. That's fine. Let them entertain her, he thought darkly. It'll give me time to plot my revenge.

But the only revenge he was able to come up with was the attack he planned on her sweet body.

It was very late that night when Solace snuck out of the room she had procured from Logan's uncle. Cavindale Manor was quiet, most of its occupants asleep. She had waited to emerge again until she was sure that Logan was not in the Great Hall. She descended the stairs toward the flickering darkness below, peered around the wall to see the Great Hall was empty. The flames of the hearth were dying, but there was still a flame that danced over the last log and the embers glowed with heat. She moved toward the warmth, instinctively stretching her hands out to it. It bathed her fingers with heat and she reveled in the warm feeling. The last time she had stood thus was at Castle Fulton.

Slowly, she dropped her hands, seeing different flames. Flames of destruction.

"Are you cold?" a voice asked.

Solace whirled to see Logan sitting in a high-backed chair, a mug of ale dangling from his fingers. Solace straightened her back and raised her chin. "Yes. I find the atmosphere chilly," she replied.

The grin that spread across his lips sent a tremor through Solace.

"I'll have William bring you a blanket," he finally said.

The cordiality of his response did not match the blatant desire written on his features. She tried to peer through the darkness that surrounded Logan, but couldn't. Like the veil of vengefulness and anger that he had lived in, the darkness made it impossible to see the real Logan. The one she had trusted. Fool that she was. Solace wished she could see the Logan she trusted one more time. Coming to Cavindale had been a mistake. But she couldn't leave. Not with the army, her army, here. Well, it wasn't quite an army, yet. But it was a start. Many of Logan's friends had vowed to help in her quest against Barclay.

"Why did you come to Cavindale?" Logan asked.

Solace turned back to the flames. She hugged her

elbows, a shiver running up her spine. "You know why I came," she said. "You told me you had an army."

"Did you come for vengeance?" he demanded.

"Vengeance?" she asked, whirling to face him again. Her back straightened, her eyes narrowing slightly.

"To slit my throat as I slept?"

"The thought never crossed my mind."

Logan was out of the chair, closing the space between them in two large strides. "Maybe you had some other reason. There was no one in Westhaven to cure your chill? Is that why you were sneaking down here in the middle of the night? Were you hoping to find me down here? Or someone else?"

Her mouth dropped. He still saw her as a whore, a tramp, a—

Suddenly, he swept her against his rock-hard chest and her every argument vanished beneath his closeness. He stared into her eyes for a long moment; the flames of the hearth reflected back from their depths. Then his lips were against hers, ruthlessly plundering, stealing every ounce of resistance until she responded by pressing against him, wrapping her arms around him, kissing him with the desperation of weeks of loneliness, weeks of missing him.

Suddenly, he released her and she almost fell, but caught herself.

A smile snaked over his lips. "I'm sure you're much warmer now," he said.

Tears burned her lids. Why was he hurting her like this? What had she done? Then, her jaw clenched. She refused to stand passively by while people hurt her. All her life Alissa had done it, and now Logan. It was time to end it. Instead of withdrawing, she launched herself at him, pressing her lips against his, holding herself against him by locking her arms around his neck. She tried to imitate his actions, tried to ravage his mouth with her tongue, but somehow it didn't work that way. Their tongues warred, battling for control. His arms went around her, his body sought the length of hers. But, just as his hands began to roam lower, she pushed away from him.

"Two can play at that game," she said.

Shock flickered across Logan's face like sparks shooting across a roaring fire. Then, his jaw clenched tight and he came forward, a shadowed look to his eyes.

Solace realized, perhaps too late, that some things could only be pushed so far. She retreated until she bumped into the wall. He stopped close to her, very close. He raised a hand and Solace inhaled sharply, thinking he was going to touch her. Instead, he laid it beside her head on the wall. "And a very dangerous game it is, woman," Logan warned her. "Play with caution." Then he broke away from her, pushing from the wall, and strolled off into the darkness of the Great Hall.

Solace was surprised to find that she was trembling. But it wasn't from the cold. She realized with a start that she had as much power over him as he did over her. But fire was a strange thing to play with. She might get burned just as badly as Logan.

She walked to the chair that Logan had vacated and fell into it. It was still warm from his body and she curled up in it, raising her knees to her stomach, resting her feet on the chair. It smelled of leather and ale.

And him.

"He can be a bastard at times, can't he?"

Solace started at the voice, raising weary eyes. She placed her feet on the ground. Blade emerged from the blackness of a shadowed wall like a dark angel.

As the candlelight washed over his features, Solace realized that many women would consider him handsome with his bright blue eyes and blond hair. "At times," Solace agreed.

"I didn't tell you before how devastated I was to hear about your castle," Blade said.

Solace nodded. Her castle.

"A tragic thing, really, when a beautiful woman is put out of her home."

Solace nodded again. A bigger tragedy was coming all this way to find that Logan had lied to her again.

"It wounds my sense of honor to see a lady such as yourself so put out, so . . . lonely." He stopped just before her. "If only women knew how to fight," he said. "It might be an entirely different matter. But they are defenseless, helpless."

If only she knew how to fight. Then she could knock some sense into Logan. Then maybe he would notice her. At least not take her for granted. Her eyes lit up as an idea struck her. She turned to Blade. "Yes," she said. "If a woman knew how to fight, she would have a chance against the world. If she knew how to protect herself."

"Ah, yes," he lamented, reaching to massage one of her shoulders.

Solace realized she suddenly had a use for Blade and his gallantry. "I need you," she told him.

"I would go to the ends of the world for you. I would give you the moon on a golden platter."

When she told him what she needed, a grin slid across his lips. "Absolutely," he replied. "It would be a great pleasure. My *greatest* pleasure."

Thirty-two

Logan worked up a sweat out in the field with his new staff, jabbing, swinging, ducking until he thought his lungs would explode. He rested the staff against the ground, leaning heavily on it. It was no use. Her soft lips still haunted him. The memory of her body pressing tightly against his own drove him wild with want. No distraction was strong enough to drive the image of Solace from the forefront of his thoughts.

Suddenly he straightened. She was here. He could feel her eyes on him. Slowly, he turned his head to find Solace standing at the edge of the field. For a moment, he couldn't breathe, couldn't move. She was the loveliest creature he had ever seen. Her cheeks were flushed with color. Her hair hung in thick curls around her shoulders, flowing down her back in sumptuous waves of silk. Those large green eyes were fixed on him.

Logan turned to face her. He wore no shirt, only leggings and boots. For the first time all afternoon, he felt the cool air against his skin. A sudden twinge of pain in his fingers made him realize he was clutching his staff too tightly.

Solace lowered her head and moved past him, cutting through the field.

Logan watched her for a moment, then his eyes narrowed to tight slits and his jaw clenched. He intercepted her, moving in front of her to block her path. "Where are you going?" he demanded.

She raised her gaze to his, opened her mouth as if to reply, but promptly shut it.

She was going to meet Blade. Logan was sure of it. The thought brought an ache like a dagger wound to his heart. But that should have been impossible. He had to keep reminding himself that he didn't care about this little chit. Then why was he grabbing her wrist and pulling her close to him, close enough to smell the fragrance of roses in her hair?

"Do you know what he wants of you?" Logan whispered through clenched teeth.

"Who?" Solace asked, stunned.

"Blade," he retorted, his blood boiling at the mere thought of Blade laying hands on her.

"Of course I know," she replied, trying to pull free of Logan's hand.

His grip tightened. "You know?"

She stilled her fight. "I asked him to do it."

Shock and surprise filled Logan before complete and utter rage engulfed him in an inferno of betrayal. He shoved her away from him, hard.

She fell to her bottom, stunned.

"You asked him?" Logan demanded, his brow knitting in dark fury as he towered over her.

"Well, you wouldn't do it!" Solace shouted.

"I wouldn't . . . ?" He took a threatening step forward. So that was what last night was about! His blood pounded in his ears, his fists clenched. The little tart had asked Blade to take her to his bed! She'd asked him! God's blood! "Then, go to him!" Logan shouted.

Solace rose to her feet, confusion written on her face.

Logan refused to see the astonishment; he turned his back on her. "Go!"

She hesitated a moment before taking a step toward him.

If she touches me, if she so much as looks me in the eye, I'll do her all right. His manhood throbbed and pulsated with the thought. "Get away from me!" he hollered at her.

Solace ran past him, racing through the field.

Logan didn't move for a long moment. She had asked Blade to take her. She had asked him to touch her, to kiss those lips. Logan bowed his head. If that was what she wanted, then he didn't care. He didn't need her. And he'd be damned if he would let it eat away at him.

Logan resumed his workout, swinging his staff with angry energy, attacking an invisible foe that slowly took on Blade's image.

Later that day, Logan sat near the hearth with Goliath and Alexander, watching the wavering flames. His body ached from the staff practice, and he vowed to continue it. To at least try to keep his mind clear. Clear of unwanted things. He lifted the mug of ale to his lips.

Goliath cast a concerned look his way, but Logan ignored it, keeping his gaze on the flames as if trying to warm himself. The air was chill. The snows would start any day. Winter had arrived. Ice had closed around his heart, sealing it from the warmth of Cavindale Manor.

"Logan!"

Logan cringed, recognizing Blade's voice. He couldn't help but turn, searching for Solace. He briefly saw her climbing the stairs to her room. Couldn't let the others see her disheveled appearance, no doubt,

Logan thought, returning his glare to the fire. It might cast her in a less than favorable light.

Logan's jaw clenched as Blade joined them.

"In bad sorts today, old friend?" Blade asked Logan.

Logan shifted in his seat, turning away from him.

"I don't blame you," Blade said. "She's a lovely woman. Smart, quick to learn."

Logan clenched his teeth.

"You've never been a sore loser, though, old boy," Blade added, picking up a mug of ale. "What is it about Solace that irks you?"

Logan remained quiet. He lifted his mug to his lips, only to find it empty.

"Logan? This is a friendly little game, isn't it? If she means anything to you, I'll break off now, before—"

"She means nothing," Logan insisted.

Blade licked his lips, pondering Logan's statement. "I believe by tomorrow I should have her—"

"Tomorrow?" Logan interrupted before Blade could finish. "You're seeing her again tomorrow?"

"Yes. She rather values my company. Do you want to know what happened today?"

"No," Logan snapped.

Blade laughed. "You've always wanted to know! Don't be shy now. She enjoyed handling my sword. And did quite well at it for a beginner. I plan—"

"I said I don't want to hear!" Logan snarled, rising. He stalked to the door and flung it open.

"What's wrong with him?" Logan heard Blade ask Goliath as he headed out into the night.

Logan stood outside the inn, staring at the wooden structure in the moonlight. He didn't need Solace to satisfy him. He had learned long ago that one woman was as good as the next, as with the times when he had lost to Blade after a long pursuit. And like now. But he hadn't been pursuing Solace. Why did he feel so . . . so . . . betrayed?

He entered the inn, shoving the door so violently that it smacked hard into the wall. All the patrons looked up. Logan paid them no heed; he stalked into the room, taking a seat at the rear of the inn.

His eyes scanned the small room. The other patrons resumed eating and talking. A woman made her way over to him and boosted herself onto the table, her legs dangling from the side. He didn't need to raise his eyes to know who it was.

"It's been a very long time, Logan," the soft voice said. She was an expert in pleasing a man. She had done it years ago, and he was sure that she was still quite proficient at it.

He nodded. "Marcie."

She bent toward him, and before Logan raised his eyes to her face, he saw the swell of her breasts all but bursting from her excruciatingly tight dress. When he raised his eyes, he noted that the face from so long ago had barely been changed by time. But something had changed. The eyes he had once found flawless were now but a dull blue compared with the bright green gems that haunted his nights. The lips he had so wanted to kiss were now thin and pale compared with the full kissable red lips that taunted him in his dreams. Even the face itself was plump and blemished compared with the tanned, flawless complexion that had burned itself into his brain.

Cursing, he rose, taking her hand in his. He didn't care if she wasn't Solace, he told himself. He dragged her from the inn, but once they got outside, she pulled free.

"Hey!" she objected. "I'm not some whore you can simply throw to the ground and ravish in the middle of the night."

Logan stepped toward her, grabbing the nape of her neck and drew her lips to his. He would prove to himself it didn't have to be Solace, that it didn't much matter who it was. Her lips parted beneath his, and he drove his tongue into her mouth, wanting to prove to himself it didn't matter. But the taste of her mouth wasn't the taste of sweet honey. It was the taste of stale ale and rotten meat.

Logan pulled away from her, just as she began to wrap her arms around him, to push her hips against his. He stepped farther away from her, horrified at what he had learned.

It mattered. It mattered very much that she wasn't Solace. For the first time in his life, something mattered other than his revenge. And it scared him.

Logan returned late that night, after aimlessly wandering the streets, trying to sort out the emotions that swirled through him. As he entered the Great Hall, he saw Solace slumped over the table. Immediately, fear gripped him. Had someone murdered her? He knew that many of his friends fed off of his hatred for Farindale. Would they have killed her to hurt Farindale? He raced toward her and was ready to take her in his arms when he noticed her peaceful face. She wasn't hurt, he realized. She was sleeping. Her head rested upon folded arms. He saw the sketching of Castle Fulton laid out beneath her hands.

Logan stood, staring at her for a long moment. Breathtaking. Beautiful. He wanted nothing more than to stand there and watch her sleep. Her unbound hair

cascaded over her arms like a dark waterfall. Her long
lashes rested against her creamy skin. Her red lips were
parted slightly. Beneath all this softness and innocence
was the plan for Castle Fulton.

She was as determined as he was. She wanted her
home back.

And Logan wanted her. With all his heart, he wanted
to hold her and touch her. And kiss her. He reached
down to softly stroke one of her silken tresses.

"Logan?"

He jerked his hand back, glancing at her face to find
her large eyes open. "What are you doing up?" he
asked, sitting down on the bench beside her.

"Waiting for you," she said, sitting up.

Waiting for you. The words echoed in his stunned
head. Was that what she would say when he came home
after surveying the lands? When they were safely nestled
in Castle Fulton? He tore his eyes away from her. Was
that what she had said to Blade?

"I can't do it alone," she admitted quietly. "I need
your help."

Logan shifted his position slightly. He didn't know if
he should encourage her. It was ridiculous for her to
think she could do this. "How many men do you have?"
he asked.

"About fifty," she murmured.

Fifty! God's blood! Logan thought. What a smile will
do to turn men's hearts. To turn his friend's heads! He
wondered how many were helping Solace under some
misguided notion that it would benefit him. Still, fifty
was more than he would have given her credit for. That
was almost all of his friends!

"Logan," she said, drawing his gaze to her. "This has
to work."

The desperation in her voice twisted his heart, and

suddenly he understood how his friends could so read-
ily give their allegiance to her.

She bowed her head. "I don't want Barclay to have
my home," she whispered.

There was something in her he recognized. Something he sympathized with. He himself had said: *I don't
want Farindale to have my home.* Every muscle in his body
went taut. It took all his willpower not to clench his
fists. "What do you want my help for?" he demanded
through clenched teeth. "It seems you have all the help
you need."

"You know the secret passages," Solace explained.

"Why would you trust me after everything I've done
to you?" he sneered. "If you were smart, you'd stay away
from me."

She raised her eyes to his, and he saw the anguish
there. The torment. The indecision. "I know," she whispered.

He wanted to take her and shake her—shake her until she saw what a worthless, lying, betraying dog he was.
Shake her until she said she didn't need him. Until her
beauty faded from his mind. He stood. "I can't help
you," he said, steeling himself against her wiles. He
turned to walk away.

"Logan," she called after him.

He paused, but did not turn.

"Where were you?" she wondered.

"What do you mean?" he demanded, in no mood
for her games.

"When my father took Fulton. Where were you?"

His back muscles stiffened, his jaw clenching until his
face hurt. "None of your damned business," he snarled
and stormed away, leaving Solace alone.

Logan crossed the yard to the barn, quietly cursing

her curiosity. What business did she have questioning his past?

"Grey!"

Logan paused, recognizing the voice. He lifted his gaze, scanning the blackness of the yard. It wasn't until a shadow separated from the darkness near the barn and moved toward him that Logan recognized another one of his comrades. A grudging smile stretched over his face. Another friend to aid Solace.

He extended his hand. "Nice to see you, Ryder."

Thirty-three

Solace shivered, sitting up in her bed, her arms peppered with goose bumps. She wrapped the covers tightly around her, wondering why it was so cold. Then she looked at the window to find one of the shutters had blown open during the night, letting in a chilling draft. She swung her legs out of the bed and padded to the window, keeping her blanket curled around her. But as she reached a hand out to close the shutters, she halted. A winsome smile grew on her lips, and she threw the shutters wide. Joy soared through her. Large flakes of snow were falling from the gray sky, tumbling end over end, floating earthward with silent grace. The ground was covered in a downy white blanket. The trees were splashed with a shimmering coat of ivory.

The cold abruptly vanished from her body as an excited warmth consumed her. The laughter of children sang to her from somewhere outside, their sweet voices filling her with comforting cheer. She threw the blanket from her body and quickly rummaged through a chest at the foot of the bed. It was overflowing with dresses that Uncle Hugh had told her had belonged to his late wife. She quickly donned one of them, pulled on some shoes and raced down the stairs, out into the chill morning air. She turned her face up to the sky, letting the large snowflakes kiss her skin with cold lips. She laughed out loud and held her hands out to capture the elusive flakes.

"Are you mad?"

The voice startled her and she whirled to face Logan. Slowly, a grin spread across her face. "Isn't it beautiful?" she cried. Another snowflake kissed her lips, and her mouth shimmered in the sun's morning light.

"You have no cloak on. Your shoes are soaked through," Logan answered darkly, approaching her from the barn. His angry breath was clearly visible, white puffs of air erupting from his mouth and nose like the outraged snorts of a disturbed dragon.

"You're one to talk," she said, looking over his disheveled white tunic, black leggings and black boots, which he had obviously just thrown on.

As she turned her back to him, she heard him retort, "That's because someone's insane cackling woke me and I came out to see who was up so damn early."

She moved to a tree stump covered with snow and bent over the wood, slowly gathering a handful of fallen flakes. "Yes. Laughter is such a strange sound around here," she said, hoping to distract him for a moment.

"Get inside this instant before you catch your death," he ordered.

Solace whirled, letting the snowball fly. It sailed through the air, spinning straight for its intended target, but Logan easily sidestepped it. His face darkened with outrage and disbelief as he continued to approach her. She burst into giggles and stooped to grab another handful of snow.

"Don't!" he warned.

Splat. The ball of snow hit him squarely in the chest, spreading a dark smear of cold wetness across his tunic.

Solace clapped in glee. Ignoring the frigid chill in her reddening fingers, she bent to retrieve another snowball. The insolent dog deserves to have an entire avalanche of snow fall on his stubborn head, she thought. And I'm going to start it! As she straightened, she saw Logan was only a few feet away from her. She quickly pelted him with the next snowball. Without seeing where it hit, she turned to race away.

Logan launched himself at her, catching her around the waist, tackling her. Snow billowed up all around them as their bodies hit the ground. He pinned her in the snow, his body pressing tightly against hers.

Solace laughed, soft, white clouds of happiness slipping out from her lips as her warm joy mingled with the cold air.

Until he picked up a handful of snow.

Then her laughter trailed off as her eyes widened incredulously. "You wouldn't!" she half laughed, half shrieked, grabbing his hand and holding it away from her.

A smile crossed his handsome face, lighting up his features with a warmth she had always hoped to see again. Surrounded by freezing wind, entrapped in a frozen cocoon of snow, Solace's heart melted. His smile was the most devastatingly beautiful thing she had ever seen. Her hold on his hand eased, and the laughter left her face. "You should smile more often."

He sobered, his smile fading as he stared down at her, inspecting her face closely. His gaze caressed her cherry nose, her red cheeks, and finally came to rest on her moist, parted lips.

Her lips parted even more, obeying the command his eyes were giving them, inviting entrance to their temptation.

A trickle of icy water traced its way from the snow in Logan's hand down Solace's wrist, disappearing beneath her sleeve. She didn't want to move, didn't want to breathe for fear he would leave her, but the snow melting in his palm was a temptation she couldn't resist.

She shoved his hand into his face, smearing the frozen white rain across his skin, breaking the spell they were falling under. He hissed steam and she squirmed wildly, trying to get away from him, but his weight effectively held her hostage. He wiped the snow from his cheek with his shoulder and scooped up another handful. "You'll pay for that one."

"Don't! Don't!" she squealed as an evil smile crossed his face. He easily held her hands aside with one of his, trapping them above her head. He touched the snow to her lips and slowly made a cold, wet line from her chin to the top of her dress. Solace squirmed helplessly in his clutches. He paused at her neckline, then lifted the fabric and tucked the snow down the front of her dress.

Gasping in disbelief, Solace shoved him from her and stood, arching her body away from the snow in her dress, dancing like some mad drunk in her effort to escape the stinging cold. The ball of melting snow traced an icy path down her body, dipping between her breasts, then rolling across her stomach and finally out her skirt. She shivered and glared at him. "This is war," she vowed.

He approached her, and she backed away from him. "You want a war," Logan murmured, "you've got one."

She backed up slowly, stopping short as her back touched the stone wall of Cavindale Manor. "Wait," she said, holding up her hands and pressing them tentatively against his chest. His muscles were hard. "I was just kidding. I don't want to be at war with you." There was honesty in her voice.

Snowflakes swirled around them, drifting lazily through the morning air, sparkling as the sun bounced off their delicate shapes. For a moment, Solace felt a stirring of magic in her soul, and she wondered if it was from nature's wintry gift or from the look on Logan's face as he gazed tenderly at her.

He reached a hand to run it down her nose and over her cheeks. "You're freezing. Let's get inside and warm up."

The sudden thought of curling into a blanket beside Logan warmed her spirit as well as her body. She allowed him to take her hand in his and lead her inside Cavindale Manor.

"Go upstairs and get changed," Logan instructed as he closed the door behind them.

Something like alarm flared through her. She felt so close to him now, so at ease. She was afraid that if she left him, if she even let go of his hand, the distance would somehow be in his eyes when she returned.

"Go on," he ordered, gently disengaging his hand from hers.

"Wait for me by the hearth," she replied.

His lips curved in a warm promise and Solace turned, fleeing up the stairs.

Logan leaned against the roaring hearth, spreading his fingers before him to warm them. As the snow melted from his chest and hair, the magic began to fade and Logan's old, cynical mood returned. Finally, he heard the rustle of cloth and turned to see Solace crossing the Great Hall toward him. He saw her tiny toes appear and disappear with her steps beneath her blue gown; she hadn't even taken the time to don a pair of shoes. She wore a blanket around her shoulders. Her hair was wild and uncombed, a tangle of rebellious curls. But it was her large emerald eyes that kept his gaze riveted.

When she joined him, Logan turned his gaze back

to the dancing, twisting flames, flames that ate away at his soul.

She stood beside him for a long moment, staring at the wavering flames. "When I was young I was never allowed to play in the snow or in the rain. Father said I had too many other, more important things to do," Solace explained.

Logan shifted his gaze back to her face. So, now she is making up for the denied pleasures of her childhood, he thought. I wish I had time to do the same. And for a moment—under her guidance, he realized—he had.

"Now he's not here to tell me I can't do it." She stared down into the hypnotic flames.

Logan watched the reflection of light shimmer on her face. The soft glow of the flames caressed her skin. She was achingly beautiful. Any man in his right mind would fall hopelessly in love with her.

Any man except him.

He seized her arm and pulled her close so that she could hear his words distinctly. "I don't want you," he snarled, his anger directed more at himself than at her. "The only thing that's important is that I regain control of Castle Fulton."

"I know," she replied weakly.

Her soft voice drove him wild with want. Her large green eyes made him desperate to cast aside every vow he had ever made to himself and to his family and love her.

He gritted his teeth. What was she doing to his mind, to his reasoning? He had to keep a clear head. He had to keep focused on what was important. Instead, all he could see, all he could think about, was Solace. With an anguished growl, he pulled her to him, assaulting her lips with an onslaught of kisses. He reached around behind her, coming up from the rear like a vanquishing army, trapping her tightly against his body. Like an expert in war, he attacked her senses, leaving her power-less against his victory.

When his kisses traveled to her neck, she rallied her final defenses. "I thought you didn't want me."

Her soft-spoken reminder branded him a lying fool. He pulled back sharply to stare into her eyes. "The treasure between your thighs is enough to bring the strongest man to his knees."

A broken sob tore loose from her throat. "But what of you?"

"Is that what you want?" he demanded. "To bring me to my knees?"

"No," she whispered. "To bring you to my side, as my ally."

Her green gems shone at him, pleading in their in-nocence, dark in their want. He could see her desire in them. He knew he would give her the world, the heavens, the stars. But he could not give her his alle-giance. The only allegiance he had was to his family. His dead family. But they were gone and she was so very alive. With a groan of despair and indecision, he pushed away from her.

"Don't fight me, Logan," Solace insisted. "I'm not your enemy."

He stepped away from her. Logan Grey had never been truly frightened of anything in his life. He knew his future, knew his destiny. He knew that someday he would regain Fulton. It was all he had ever wanted, all he had ever needed. But now, staring down at this woman, the woman who should be his enemy, he doubted his destiny. He doubted his duty. He would push it all away to spend an eternity at her side. He had fallen into the same trap as Peter, and he would not let it consume him. "No," he whispered hotly. "I will not let you destroy everything that I am."

"I don't want to destroy you." She reached for him.

Logan moved away from her touch.

"Don't shut me out," Solace begged. "Don't do this."

Logan heard the anguish in her voice and steeled himself.

"Let me help you."

"You can't," he whispered hoarsely, turning away from her. "No one can."

Solace stared out over the hills, gazing down at a farm at the outskirts of Cavindale. She had walked a great distance that morning, trying to clear her mind. Most of the first snow had melted, leaving behind a soggy, mud-filled land. Despite the bright sun, her feet were cold, her hands red from the biting winds. She pulled her cloak tighter around her neck.

She wanted Logan's friendship desperately, but he refused to have anything to do with her. Solace knew that it was she who should be wanting nothing to do with him. She needed someone she could depend on. Someone who would be there for her.

And that wasn't Logan.

Then why did she feel so empty? She didn't know what to do, who to turn to. She rubbed her red hands as the wind whipped about her body, trying to blow the cloak she wore from her shoulders. It was hopeless. Simply hopeless. Even the elements attacked her, refusing to give her a moment's respite.

A caw made her lift her gaze to a young tree near where she stood. Logan's black falcon perched on a branch, watching her with his keen eyes. "Go back to your master," she spat out, then immediately regretted her harsh tone.

The laughter of children drew her attention, and she turned her head to see a farmer's wife near the small creek washing clothes. Two children were running around behind her, chasing each other, their smiles wide and bright. It was so peaceful. She watched them all with a longing that she hadn't known she possessed. Children. Assuredly a fine husband, too. A family.

The falcon cried out again, this time in a shrill, excited voice, and took to the air. Suddenly, the ground seemed to tremble beneath Solace's feet.

Horses! And they were coming in fast! A tremor of trepidation raced up her spine as she turned to see two riders approaching her, charging over one of the rises. Solace squinted, shielding her eyes from the glaring sun, straining to see who they were. They wore no heraldry, no colors. It wasn't until the two horses drew closer that she recognized one of the men, the newest member to her army. Nolan Ryder. Solace stepped up to greet the man as he reined in his horse. The other man circled behind her.

"You shouldn't be out here alone, m'lady," Ryder said.

Solace scowled at him, remembering the same warning issued from Logan's lips a long time ago. A nervous chill swept through her. She glanced back at the man behind her. "Is something wrong?" she wondered. She hadn't acquainted herself with him and didn't like the way his horse danced anxiously beneath him or the hungry look in his eyes as he gazed at her. She looked back at Ryder.

"Wrong?" he asked in a strangely businesslike tone. "No, nothing's wrong."

"Then what are you doing out here?" she asked, turning once again to look at the man behind her. Her eyes dipped to his waist. He wore a sheathed sword and had a large club in a pouch at his horse's side. She lifted her eyes to see an unsettling smile split his lips.

Her gaze turned back to Ryder. "What's going on?" she demanded.

She heard the horse move forward behind her and instinctively stepped away from it. Suddenly, a blinding pain flared in her head. There was a flash of white light before darkness came. She fought the black abyss, even though her body wanted to leap into the peaceful darkness. Her knees gave way and she dropped to the ground, falling hard onto her back. She forced her groggy eyes open. The bright blue sky swayed above her. Too bright. She squinted and rolled onto her side, pushing herself up onto her feet. Her head was pounding and something thick wet the side of her face.

She turned in time to see that the man had dismounted and was approaching her. He tossed the club aside and drew a dagger from his belt. Solace backed away, trying to focus on her attacker, stumbling slightly as she retreated. She bumped into Ryder's horse, and the animal whinnied and pranced away from her.

Solace turned and desperately clutched Ryder's leg, looking up at him through pain-fogged eyes. "Help me," she managed to gasp.

Ryder's black eyes narrowed. "Finish her," he commanded.

Thirty-four

Laughter floated around Logan, but somehow he felt removed from it. Goliath and Blade were practicing their sword skills in the Great Hall. Logan could only feign interest. His gaze continued to drift up the stairs. Where was Solace? Why wasn't she down here watching her men practice their maneuvers? *Her* men. Even he was thinking of them as hers now.

"Distracted, old friend?" Alexander wondered, taking a seat beside him at the table.

"No," Logan answered, tearing his gaze away from the stairs to look at Alexander.

Alexander chuckled softly, knowingly. He suddenly found something very interesting in the bottom of his ale mug.

"Mind your own damn business," Logan snapped.

Alexander threw his head back, taking a long drink of his ale, a smile twitching his lips.

Logan's gaze wandered again to the stairs.

"She's not there," Alexander said. "She left awhile ago."

"Left?"

"I saw her leave Cavindale Manor."

An irrational fear twisted Logan's stomach. "On foot?"

Alexander nodded.

"Grey!" Goliath called, resting his sword point on the floor and leaning toward him. "Are you going to observe all day or do we get a taste of that famed weapon?"

Logan looked toward the main door that led outside. His skin prickled, setting his nerves on edge.

Just then Crox came in, and as the door began to swing closed behind him, the falcon swooped in through the narrowing gap and circled the Great Hall, screeching.

"Logan!" Uncle Hugh screamed almost as loudly as the falcon. "Get that thing out of here!"

Logan grunted. "Like I have any control over it," he muttered.

"Maybe we can shoot it down!" Blade called, raising a bow.

"Try!" Logan exclaimed. The damn bird would easily evade Blade's arrow, even though he was an accomplished marksman. The falcon was too stubborn to die.

Suddenly, the bird dove, its claws outstretched for Blade's head.

"Hey!" the fighter called, ducking, shielding his face with his bow.

Logan bolted upright, scowling. He hadn't seen the falcon act this way since he had captured the rabbit that very first day he had set eyes on the cursed thing. Something was wrong. The tension strung his body tight as a bowstring. Something was very wrong. Without realizing what he was doing, he suddenly found himself out of his chair, running across the hall.

Alexander chased after him. "What is it?" his friend called. "What's wrong?"

Logan opened the door and the falcon swooped out. Logan ran after it, ignoring his friend's concerned questions. He raced into the stables, disregarding the surprised groom as well, and swung himself up onto a horse, bareback. The animal whinnied and circled toward the door as he tugged on its mane.

"Open the door!" Logan ordered the groom.

The frightened man shoved the door open, and Logan whipped past him in a blur of speed.

"Logan!" his uncle called, lumbering uselessly after him.

As Logan followed the falcon over the rises in the hills, a prickling sensation of impending disaster slithered across his spine. He clenched his jaw, his hands knotted tight in the horse's mane as he rode. Solace, his mind kept repeating. Solace.

Logan saw the falcon moving away from him in the distance, a dark speck against the blue sky. He was flying toward the outer reaches of Cavindale. Logan spurred his horse over the last rise that bordered his uncle's lands. The sight that greeted him sent horror spearing through his body.

Solace stood, wavering before a man who stalked her. The tip of the dagger he clutched winked evilly as the sun glinted off its metal surface. Blood covered the side of Solace's head. Dark, wet blood.

Ryder was there, sitting atop his horse. He locked gazes with Logan for a long moment before dismounting and running toward Solace's attacker.

The man lurched toward Solace, the dagger outstretched toward her.

Ryder's not going to make it, Logan thought. He's still too far away. Logan leaned forward over the horse, urging the animal faster. Faster.

The man lashed out.

No, Logan thought. No!!

Solace stumbled back, out of the dagger's range, but turned, and in doing so the dagger sliced her shoulder.

"Ahhhh!" Logan shouted in dread and anguish as she went down to her knees.

Ryder seized the man from behind and quickly drew a dagger across his neck.

Logan leapt from the horse, running to Solace's side, dropping to his knees beside her. She lay still on the ground. Agony and fear swelled inside him. He was afraid to touch her, afraid to move her, afraid she wouldn't respond.

She groaned and tried to push up onto her hands, but fell weakly to the ground again.

Logan seized her in his arms, rolling her over onto his lap so he could see her face. The left side of her head was covered with blood, plastering her dark hair to her cheek. Logan tried to move some of her limp, wet hair aside to see how bad the wound was, but his fingers trembled fiercely and he couldn't stop their shaking.

"Logan," she whispered, drawing his gaze to hers. Her eyes were strangely bright and clear.

"I'm here," he said, drawing her close against his chest. It was impossible to steady his frantic pulse.

"I knew you'd come," she said softly.

Logan couldn't help but grin. "Perhaps a little too late." His voice sounded thick even in his own ears.

Pain flared in her face and her eyes closed.

"Solace," Logan demanded, shaking her gently, afraid that if she closed her eyes for too long she would never open them again. "I'm sorry," he whispered.

Her eyes opened wide, the sparkle of tears filling them. "I love you," she murmured and her eyes closed again.

Logan felt her body go limp. For a long moment, he couldn't move. He couldn't breathe. Then he leaned over and gently kissed her lips. As he pulled back from her face, he felt her breath touch his mouth. Relief flooded his body, dousing the fiery anguish that had been burning in him. He leaned his head over hers, rubbing his cheek across her forehead. A tear escaped his closed eyes, trickling down his cheek to mingle with the blood on her forehead. "What have I done to you?" he murmured.

Logan carried Solace back to Cavindale Manor, cradling her as tenderly as a child in his arms, refusing help from anyone, not letting anyone touch her but him. As he walked through the fields, his friends joined him, a procession of silent followers.

He walked the steps to her room like the grim reaper, his face pale, his mouth set in a thin line. His muscles should have ached with the effort of carrying her so far, but they did not; she had been as light as an angel's wings in his arms. He lay Solace on the bed, growling at William as he tried to peer over his shoulder at Solace's wounds.

Logan gently wiped the drying blood from Solace's face, her cheek, her neck with his tunic. Still, she didn't move. Her eyes remained closed.

"Logan," William said softly from behind him, "let Beatrice stitch her wound."

Logan's eyes moved to Solace's shoulder. Her clothing was saturated with darkening red liquid. His heart clenched. He didn't want anyone else touching her. He didn't want to move away from her. But he knew he had to. Especially if he wanted her to live.

"You can't do it all by yourself," William added.

Logan rose stiffly and took a step back, his jaw clenched tight. Beatrice moved in front of him.

As she began to cut the fabric from Solace's shoulder,

William grabbed Logan's arm. "We'd best wait outside," he said softly.

Logan ripped his arm free of William's hold. "I'm not going anywhere," he replied with stern determination.

"It's not going to help her if you stay," William said.

"Come on, boy," Uncle Hugh encouraged. "It's best if you don't see her wound."

"You'll make poor Beatrice nervous," William added.

Logan's shoulders straightened. "I'm not going."

There was a moment of uncomfortable quiet before the door opened and closed, his uncle and William departing in the silent wake of his stated resolve. Logan's gaze locked on Beatrice's hands as she peeled back the cotton dress, revealing the wound in all its evil, ugly and gaping and dark. It was still bleeding.

Logan realized then why his uncle had said that he shouldn't see the wound. His anguish was so fierce and so sudden that he had to clench his fists and keep his arms tightly pinned to his sides, lest he lash out and destroy everything around him to vent his rage. She wouldn't die, he told himself again and again. But the seriousness of her wounds made this a possibility. And Logan knew it. His stomach clenched as tightly as his hands and his jaw. I won't lose her, he whispered quietly to himself. He stood guard over Solace like a stone gargoyle protecting its territory.

William descended the stairs beside his father, his expression glum.

Alexander sat in a chair in the Great Hall, running a rock across his sword to sharpen it. Blade paced before the smoldering hearth. Goliath held a stick and was sharpening the point with his dagger. Ryder sat at the table, rummaging through the leftover dinner bones for scraps of meat. At William and Hugh's approach, all eyes lifted to them.

"How is the lass?" Goliath wondered, his deep voice resounding through the Great Hall like a trumpet.

Uncle Hugh shook his head and William lowered his gaze.

"And Grey?" Blade asked.

"Worse," William said. "Won't leave her side. It's like the dagger sliced him as well."

"Perhaps it has," Blade said, knowingly. "A deadlier dagger than that of steel."

William joined Alexander at the table, leaning against its edge. "He's a stubborn man."

"He doesn't even know, does he?" Blade asked.

William shook his head.

"Perhaps now he has an inkling," Alexander suggested.

"Perhaps now we all do," Blade said, regretfully.

"If he ever understands, his obsession for revenge will change to a different kind of obsession. A saner kind."

"If she lives," Uncle Hugh added.

All eyes turned to Hugh. William sighed. "If she lives," he agreed.

Silently, Ryder fingered the flowered handle of the gold-tipped dagger in his belt.

Logan splashed water onto his face from the basin on the table. He moved to the window to stare at the night sky. Dark clouds drifted by the moon like thick wisps of black cotton, obscuring the stars.

It made no sense. How could a killer have found Solace? He pounded the ledge with a clenched fist. She was safe at Cavindale! Perhaps not so much as you would have liked to believe, a voice inside told him. If Ryder had not reached the man first, she would have been dead.

A groan from behind him caused him to cast a glance back at the bed. Solace was still, her soft skin as pale as a moonbeam. He moved to her side and settled into a chair.

As he expected, there had been two wounds. The dagger wound, which he had watched Beatrice stitch, and the head wound. It was the head wound that caused him the most concern. He had seen men die of head wounds less serious than what Solace had.

He bent over and touched her forehead, smoothing back her dark hair. He wished he could see her eyes, wished she would open them so he could look into their emerald depths once again. He ran a finger along her lips. He wished she would smile again. He wished he could take every single one of her wounds into himself so she wouldn't have to endure them.

I love you. Her words haunted his every thought. She couldn't love him. Not after everything he had done to her. She must have been delirious.

Logan sank back into the chair. God's blood, he thought, closing his eyes tightly. How could I be so blind? I didn't ride back to Westhaven to stop her from her foolish plan. I rode back to see her again. Damn my stubbornness. My destiny was right before me all this time and I didn't even see her.

He took her hand in his. It looked so tiny and small in his large, callused palm. I should have been there, he thought. I should have been at her side. None of this would have happened. The words resounded in his head just as they had for thirteen years. *I should have been there. It seems I can never do the right thing.* He ran a hand over his eyes.

"Logan?"

He sat upright quickly, leaning toward her voice as if it were the source of his lifeblood. "Solace?" He clutched her hand tightly, refusing to release his hold on her. A shaft of fleeting moonlight shimmered in her open eyes.

"Logan, don't leave," she murmured in a thick voice.

His heart twisted. He had abandoned her before. He leaned forward, closing the distance between them, until his lips were almost brushing hers. "Never," he promised. He was so close to her face that he could feel her gentle breath fan across his lips. He felt a familiar stirring, too familiar when he was around her. "You'll have to kick me out."

Her gentle smile was his reward. It was the most glorious reward he had ever received. Does she have to make all my wishes come true? he wondered bemusedly.

Suddenly the clouds thinned and the moonlight shone fully in, casting her face in a pale glow, giving her eyes a deep green luminescence. He touched her cheek. She was all any man could want. He brushed his lips against hers. "Are you hungry? Thirsty? Can I get you something?"

"Everything I want is right here," she whispered.

Logan gazed into her eyes. He had been a fool. Why couldn't he see how much . . . ? God's blood! he thought. Let her live and I swear I'll give up my quest for revenge. Just let her live.

She lifted a hand to touch her bandaged forehead. "My head is pounding."

"He hit you pretty hard," Logan said.

"Did you get 'em?" Solace asked.

Logan nodded. "You're all right now. Everything's fine. You don't have to worry. Just rest. I'll tell you everything later."

Solace nodded, struggling to keep her eyes open.

His attention was drawn to her mouth as her tongue slipped out to wet her full lips. He found himself leaning forward to taste those lips, to see if they were as sweet as he remembered. He shook himself. She is wounded! he thought. And still I find myself incapable of breaking the spell she casts over me. Logan stood up unsteadily. "Rest," he said. "I'll come back tomorrow."

He stood and moved to the door. He gripped the handle and opened it a fraction of an inch before pausing. A tingling sensation shot through his body and he turned. Solace was gazing at him with a wistful expression. Her large luminescent eyes shone brighter than the sun, calling to him.

In the next instant, he was beside her. She stared up at him, breathlessly. She lifted her hand, reaching out to him.

Logan captured her fingers in his. He bent, gently scooping her up in his arms and eased himself into the bed, delicately pulling her against him so her head was pillowed on his chest. He rubbed his cheek against her head as she settled against him.

He felt the heated length of her along his body and knew that there would be no sleep for him this night.

Within moments, Logan sensed the steady breathing of a deep sleep as Solace drifted off into a healing slumber. Still, selfishly, he held her against his heart and waited until the sun began to peek over the horizon, waited until there was no time left and Beatrice would soon enter the room. Only then did he slide slowly from beneath Solace, being careful not to wake her.

He stared down at her for a long moment. She had curled into the warmth of the spot he had just vacated. Her soft face was peaceful, worry free. His eyes instinctively scanned the room, looking for . . .

He smiled to himself. Looking for what? he wondered. Killers lurking in the shadows? Murderers crawling from beneath the four-poster bed? Even as he smiled and chuckled, he knew that had been exactly what he was doing. He rubbed his eyes. He needed to get something to eat, but he was reluctant to leave her.

He thought briefly of Blade. His jealousy was nothing next to the pain of losing Solace. He would not lose her—not even to Blade.

Suddenly, a knock sounded at the door. Logan opened the door to see Ryder standing in the dark corridor just outside the room.

"How is she?" Ryder inquired.

"Better," Logan replied. He stepped aside, allowing Ryder entrance into the room, and closed the door behind him. "I didn't get a chance to thank you for stopping that bastard."

"You don't have to," Ryder answered, his stare settling on Solace.

Logan extended his arm. "I do," he told him sincerely. "It means a lot to me."

Ryder clasped Logan's arm, gripping it tightly. For a moment, their eyes met. It triggered a memory in Logan's mind. A memory of Ryder sitting atop his horse in the field while the killer headed toward Solace.

Ryder dropped his arm and turned back to Solace. "It's been a long night," he said. "Go get something to eat. I'll stay and watch her."

A prickling of anxiety snaked its way up Logan's spine. He dropped his gaze and something in Ryder's belt caught his attention. The flowered handle of a dagger. Logan scowled slightly.

Ryder put a hand on Logan's shoulder, jarring Logan's thoughts. "It's all right," he soothed. "I'll stay with her."

Logan nodded. He was being foolish. Ryder was a friend. Solace would be safe with him. Again he nodded and headed for the door. As his hand closed over the handle, he turned back to cast a glance at Solace. She will be fine with Ryder, he told himself, and quietly closed the door behind him.

Thirty-five

Logan stood for a long moment outside Solace's door, his fingers curled around the handle, his head bent. He didn't like leaving Solace. Not even with Ryder.

Ryder. Sitting in the saddle atop his horse, while the other man went after Solace with a dagger. Logan shook his head. You're being overly suspicious, he thought. Not everyone is out to kill her, even if she is Farindale's daughter.

Logan released the door handle and moved away from the room, forcing himself to descend the steps. When he reached the Great Hall, he paused, his gaze scanning the room. It was empty and Logan realized it was still very early.

Why had Ryder been up? Logan wondered. He sat heavily on a wooden bench, every one of his bones aching. Then his gaze drifted up the stairs toward Solace's room. But instead of Solace's image, the picture of a flowered-handled dagger came to his mind. The dagger had been tucked into Ryder's belt. Logan knew he had seen it somewhere before. He looked down at the rushes on the floor. But where?

Suddenly, he shot to his feet with such force that he knocked over the wooden bench. He bolted up the stairs, taking them two at a time and practically knocked the door down in his hurry to enter Solace's room.

One of Ryder's hands was clamped around Solace's neck. The other held the gold-tipped dagger, its blade reflecting the warming red rays of the rising sun and spitting them back into the room in glaring slivers of blood red light. An image flashed through Logan's mind. The dagger glinting in the dirt of the courtyard near the mews of Castle Fulton. The dagger Graham had attacked Solace with! He hadn't meant to rape her, but to kill her.

Ryder lifted his head at the sudden interruption, snapping it toward Logan's violent entrance. Solace's small hands pulled at the thick fingers Ryder had around her neck, a choking gasp coming from her parted lips.

Logan launched himself at Ryder, driving his head and shoulder into Ryder's stomach, the force throwing both men over the side of the bed. The dagger clattered away across the room as they hit the floor hard. Logan quickly rolled to his feet, crouching before the bed like a panther ready to spring.

"Don't be a fool, Grey," Ryder said, breathing heavily. "She's worth more dead than alive."

"Who sent you?" Logan demanded.

"She's your enemy," Ryder added.

"No. You are," Logan snarled and swung his tightly balled fist, connecting solidly with Ryder's jaw. The force of the blow hurled Ryder backward, and his foot caught on the edge of a chest sitting at the foot of the bed. He twisted his body, trying to get his balance, but his head smashed into the bedpost with a sickening crack. He dropped like a stone to the floor.

Logan straddled Ryder's body, grabbing his tunic roughly, pulling Ryder's head up toward him. He curled his fingers into a fist. "Who sent you?" he demanded again. He raised his fist high, ready to strike. But then he lowered his hand.

He knew Ryder wasn't going to tell him anything. Not ever again. The wide, glassy stare of his eyes was testament to that. Disgusted, Logan shoved Ryder's head back to the floor and quickly turned his attention to Solace.

She sat up in bed, touching the raw, red finger marks on her neck.

Logan moved to the bed, sitting down beside her. He took Solace's chin in his fingers and turned it to him. "Are you all right?" he asked.

She nodded, leaning into Logan. He wrapped his arms around her, pulling her into the protectiveness of his embrace. Her arms wrapped around him with a surprising strength, and she clung to him.

The door swung open and William and Uncle Hugh rushed in, their eyes widening with alarm as they spotted Ryder's dead body.

Logan met their disturbed gazes over Solace's head. Cavindale was no longer safe for the lady and the falconer.

Solace spent most of the next week resting in bed. Every few hours, William came to see if she needed anything. Beatrice fussed about her like a mother hen throughout the day. Even Uncle Hugh came by to grunt his approval of her progress. Logan was constantly with her, watching her with that unnerving and exciting dark gaze. But it was always from a distance. Logan stayed well away from her, usually gazing pensively out the window.

On the fourth day, he again took his customary stance at the window, his face as troubled as his spirit.

Solace sat up in her bed, anxiously devising ways to escape the cage her bed had become.

Logan turned to her and asked suddenly, "Why would those men want to kill you?"

Startled, Solace met his gaze. "I don't know," she replied.

He removed a gold-tipped, flower-handled dagger from his belt and displayed it to Solace.

"That's Beth's!" she said immediately. "Where did you find it?"

Logan replaced it in his belt. "Ryder had it."

Solace frowned. "How? Where did he get it?"

She studied Logan's serious expression and the implication of his words sank in. "You don't think Beth . . ." Solace shook her head doubtfully. "She would know even less about hiring mercenaries than I do."

"You're probably right," he admitted, but Solace saw the disagreement in his eyes.

He moved to the door. "I'll be right back."

Solace nodded, but was lost in her own thoughts. Could Beth have wanted her dead? Would she actually hire a mercenary to kill her? Then Logan's tale came back to her. Back at Castle Fulton, he had heard two people plotting to kill her. Had one of them been Beth? But why? Why would she want her dead?

Miserable, Solace looked toward the door, searching for the comfort Logan always instilled in her. At the sight of it closed, she realized suddenly that she was alone. Alone for the first time since she had been hurt! She flung the covers aside and stood. Swarms of black dots swam before her eyes. She steadied herself on the table beside the bed, waiting for the dizzy spell to fade. She hadn't been out of bed for four days. She wanted to get up and run or ride a horse! She settled for carefully walking the length of the room. She enjoyed the movement, the stretching of her muscles.

A shaft of sunlight on the floor caught her attention. Hungrily, her eyes followed it to the shutters. Her face lit with joy as she practically ran to them and threw them open. The sun streamed into the room, and Solace turned her face to its warm light, letting it bathe her cheeks.

"Must I always stand guard over you?"

Solace whirled to find Logan in the open doorway.

"Back into bed," he commanded.

She cast a glance at the bed and scowled, then looked at Logan. When his eyes locked with hers, a bolt rocked her body.

Swiftly he crossed the room to stand before her. He lifted his hands toward her, and Solace couldn't help but gasp in expectation. Without a word, he reached around her to close the shutters.

Disappointment speared her body like an arrow. He was close to her, closer than he had been in days. So close that his arms brushed her shoulders. With that simple touch, her senses flared to life, a tingling awareness filling her body. When he shifted his eyes to her, his hot silver gaze melted her insides.

His look moved over her face, taking in every line, every curve. He barely touched her body with his, but the heat that radiated from him scorched her.

"How do you feel?" he asked in a husky voice.

"What?" she inquired in a groggy haze.

"Your head," he said, reaching out to smooth some hair over the bandage. "How is it?"

"Fine," Solace answered, a twinge of sadness pulling at her heart. She dropped her gaze to the floor. He was only concerned with her wounds, when all she wanted him to do was kiss her. Just one kiss, she thought miserably. Just one. But even as she thought it, she knew it wouldn't be enough.

His fingers smoothed a rebellious curl near her cheek, but as soon as he released it, it sprang to life, entwining itself around his finger.

His hand was so close to her face, his fingers mere inches from her skin. Desperate for the feel of his skin against hers, Solace rubbed her cheek against his fingers. His hand froze and Solace pressed a kiss into his open palm.

She closed her eyes tightly, reveling in the brief feeling of his skin against hers, his warmth touching her.

Suddenly, his arms were around her, pulling her tight against the length of his steel-hard body. His lips pressed on hers in a frenzy of reckless wanting. The heat from his mouth claimed her body, and she felt a stirring in the bottom of her stomach. She parted her lips as a groan escaped from them, and Logan's tongue gently stroked the inner portion of her mouth, tasting her.

He pressed his lips against the wound on her forehead, trailing a line of kisses down her cheek to her jaw.

She wrapped her arms around his back, marveling at the strength hidden beneath the tunic he wore. Her fingers traced the hard muscles of his shoulders as the kiss deepened.

His hand moved up her body to cup her breast, gently squeezing it. His thumb circled her nipple, teasing it to hardness, until she groaned with need.

"Logan?" The voice came from just outside the door.

Instantly, Solace pulled away from Logan. He looked at her with a gentle grin on his lips.

Uncle Hugh entered the room, and Logan turned to him with none of the embarrassment that Solace was feeling. "Ah!" Uncle Hugh said when he saw Solace out of bed. "You're feeling better. Then come and eat!" he ordered. "A good meal cures any ill!"

Logan glanced at Solace, and she could see there was promise in his eyes. But promise of what? she wondered.

"I'll send Beatrice up to help Solace dress," Uncle

Hugh said, seizing Logan's shoulder. "I'll take this rascal with me."

Logan cast a last look at Solace before Hugh pulled him out the door. Solace raised a hand to her lips. They were still wet from Logan's kiss.

Solace stared at Logan's hands as he moved them over the map of Castle Fulton. They were strong and sure and . . . What was she doing? He was explaining the secret passages to her, yet all she could think about was the power in those hands, the gentle way he had touched her, his heated caresses. They had eaten dinner with dozens of others, but Logan seemed to only have eyes for her. And she for him. She had felt like a young girl enamored of a famous knight. He had even given her a stare that sent a flush of heat to her cheeks, a stare so hot she had been certain her face was going to burst into flames from the torrid look. Just thinking of it now made her body all warm and tingly.

She turned her gaze up to his face. His brow was set with concentration; his eyes darted from spot to spot on the map, giving Solace only a teasing glimpse at their steel-gray magnificence. She barely noticed the black x on his cheek; it had become so much a part of him. She watched his mouth moving as he spoke and thought of another movement it had made, the way he had stroked her own lips with his. Gently, she ran a tongue over her lips, but could not re-create the feel of their heated kiss. Only his lips could do that.

When he swung his gaze up to hers she realized he had asked her a question. She looked away from him and found Alexander and Blade's gazes were on her, too. They had joined her and Logan after dinner to discuss possible plans for retaking Fulton. Now that winter was upon them, they had time to make a detailed attack plan for the spring. She bowed her head. "I'm sorry," she whispered. "I didn't hear the question."

"You must be tired," Blade said sympathetically.

She nodded and lifted her eyes to find an amused smile on Logan's lips. She turned back to Blade. "Yes," she agreed. "It has been an . . . eventful day."

Alexander folded up the map. "We'll finish this to-morrow."

"Good night, Solace." Blade called as she turned toward the stairs.

She bid him a good night and made her way up the steps. She felt Logan's eyes on her as she went, and finally had to turn and cast him a glance.

He stood near the table, a heated look on his face. She couldn't resist gazing at him. His body was turned to her, his large chest bidding her to come and rest her head on it, his strong arms bidding her to come and be held, his hypnotizing lips bidding her to come and be devoured. "Good night, Solace," Logan called softly. "Get some rest. I'll see you in the morning."

She forced a smile to her lips, hiding her disappointment, then turned away and went to her room.

Solace paced in front of her window late into the night. She had washed her face and body twice. She had changed into her nightdress, lain in bed and counted sheep. She had drunk a warm glass of goat's milk. Despite everything she had tried, with every move she made she sensed the ghostly presence of Logan's mouth against hers, the caress of his hands on her skin, until her body shook with the wanting of him. She would get no sleep tonight. She wanted to feel his kiss again, wanted him to . . .

She opened the door to find the hall was quiet. Slipping into the darkness, she moved through the Great

Hall like a ghost. What are you doing? a voice questioned her. Where do you think you are going? She ignored the questions and moved on. She knew exactly what she was doing and exactly where she was going.

Thirty-six

Solace opened the door to Cavindale Manor and an icy wind whirled past, seizing her in its grip, threatening to chill her to the bone. But her need warmed her against the cold. She raced across the yard and opened the barn door, stepping into the darkness of the building.

Her eyes searched frantically, desperately for Logan. Suddenly, as if her thoughts had magically conjured him from a mysterious realm, he appeared before her, sword in hand, standing tall and silent, ready for attack.

The moonlight washed over his strong chest, his muscular arms, painting his tanned flesh with a golden gloss. His dark hair fell just past his shoulders in a shimmering wave of black. His face was hidden in shadows, as was the lower part of his body. But his eyes were visible, a cloudy gray caught in a silver strand of moonlight.

She moved toward him and he dropped the sword, sweeping her into his arms, pressing his lips to hers with an urgent hunger. Solace wrapped her arms around him, pulling him close. His strong back was hot where she touched his naked skin, burning against her fingertips. She trailed her hands along the length of his torso, up to his neck, cupping his face. She wanted to touch every place on his body, feel his every muscular curve.

He shoved aside her nightdress, baring her breast, and knelt before her to take the tip in his mouth. Solace gasped, threading her fingers through his hair, pressing his mouth against her. Surges of desire filled her like the ebb and thrust of the tide. She wanted more. So much more.

He looked up from his knees and gazed adoringly at her, as if worshipping a goddess. She framed his face with her hands before lowering her lips to his. Their mouths joined together, becoming one, tasting each other's essence. She felt a hand on her ankle, and slowly it rose up her leg until he cupped her naked buttocks. She gasped, thrusting against him.

With his other hand, he touched her where she needed him, and she groaned against his lips. Then she sank to her knees before him.

"God, Solace," he whispered, kissing her neck, cupping her breast with his palm, kneading it, sending wave after wave of pleasure crashing through her.

She reached around his waist and was surprised to find that he had no clothing on, but was still bold enough to cup his buttocks as he had hers. A groan tore loose from his lips as he thrust against her. She could feel the stiff length of him against her stomach.

Logan leaned forward, pushing her back onto the hay with his weight until he lay on top of her. With a soft growl, he claimed her lips again with a possessive desire that flamed her own passion into uncontrollable want. His manhood throbbed and pulsed between her thighs, the thick, powerful muscle taunting her with soft strokes. He pushed her legs wider, teasing her soft opening with his hard shaft. At one point, it moved dangerously near, touching the small petal that hid beneath her silken folds. She gasped aloud as her body instinctively arched toward him, trembling with anticipation.

He shifted slightly to the side as his hand caressed her hip in circles, drawing ever closer to the patch of soft, downy hair between her legs.

Just when she thought he would touch her, just when she moaned and raised her hips to meet his touch, just when his predatory fingers started stalking her through the dark tangle of her hair, he pulled away. He did it again and again until she thought she would go mad with desire. With a low growl of her own, she grabbed his hand and moved it to where her passion flared. He cupped her with his hand, and his finger touched the silken folds of her womanhood, separating them to reveal the pink pearl lying in wait beneath.

The night seemed to glow brighter around them as his finger caressed her. She could no longer feel the cold air, the hay beneath her; she could only feel him, Logan, touching her everywhere, caressing every part of her body. And then he was above her again, parting her legs with his own. She felt him ease his manhood forward, felt him force his way into her tightness. He stopped, looking down at her with silvery, moon-painted eyes.

She groaned, arching, wanting more. "Please," was all she could whisper.

Then he thrust into her, his lust-gorged member spreading her wider, plunging deep. She fought back the urge to cry out. He caressed her hair, her cheek, her face, rained kisses over her jaw, her eyes, her nose. Only after he kissed her lips again did he begin to move, slowly at first.

She matched his thrusts, their bodies joining, fusing together. He unleashed something she did not even know had been hidden deep inside of her. He had taught her the true dangerous power of making love, a power that had a life of its own, a power that she could only submit to.

Then, when Solace thought she could take no more of the pleasure rushing through her, he reached between them to touch her with his finger. A whirlwind swept her up as the sky around her exploded with light. She clung tightly to Logan breathing hotly in his ear as she was buffeted with ecstasy. "Oh, Logan," she gasped. "Logan."

Finally, after a long, unforgettable journey, her body trembled with release.

He watched her with warm eyes and pressed a kiss against her temple before he began to move again. Within moments, he stiffened, thrusting into her.

Finally, he withdrew from her and lay beside her. She propped herself on her elbow to look into his face. He was so relaxed and content. Solace didn't think she had ever seen him so.

Logan saw Solace studying his face through sleepy eyes. How did he suddenly become so lucky? he wondered. His life had always been about anger and revenge. How had he managed to get Solace to . . . to care for him?

Logan sat up, presenting her with his back. "What can you see in me?" he mused out loud.

Solace brushed her fingers through the ends of his hair and trailed a path down his spine. "Right now, I see your naked back," she whispered playfully. "And your bottom."

Logan jumped as she pinched his buttocks. He whirled, catching her wrists and flipped her on her back. He captured her beneath him with his body and pinned her hands over her head. "I want to know," he said sincerely. "After everything I've done to you. Why me?"

The amusement faded from Solace's eyes as she studied his face. "I always imagined that one day I would find someone I could count on. Someone who would always be there when I needed him. I thought I could depend on my family. But they were a grave disappointment." The words died on her lips, and a strange understanding lit her eyes.

Logan frowned slightly, not comprehending the glow on her face. "That's not me, Solace," he answered, releasing her wrists. "I hurt you. I let Barclay into your home."

"Yes, you did do that," she agreed. "But it wasn't to hurt me. It was under the notion that Barclay would turn Castle Fulton over to you."

"I never intended to hurt you," Logan admitted in an agonized voice.

"Logan," Solace sat up, pushing him from her, "I know that. It's taken me a long time to understand and to realize that the person I've been looking for has been with me all this time."

"Who?"

"You!" Logan began to shake his head, but Solace took his hand into hers. "You were there from the beginning. You opened the castle gates for me when Alissa would have locked me out." Logan opened his mouth to object, but Solace placed her fingers against his lips. "You've always been there when I needed someone to talk to. You helped me escape from Barclay. And you saved my life from Ryder." She caressed the x on his cheek. "It's been you all along, Logan. I love you."

Logan froze, unable to draw a breath, stunned by her confession. Despite everything, she professed to love him. He pulled her into his embrace, crushing her to his heart. He wanted to tell her. He wanted her to know how much she meant to him. But the words refused to come. The uncertainty of their future together kept them trapped inside him. But he knew he would always love her. No matter what.

Solace snuck from the barn early in the morning. She heard a caw and looked up to see Logan's falcon perched on a tree branch nearby. It watched her with large, dark eyes. She smiled at the bird. She had begun to see the falcon as some sort of guardian angel.

She returned to her room and quickly dressed before heading toward the Great Hall. She paused at the top of the stairs, scanning the room for Logan.

Servants scurried through the Great Hall. William was wiping his mouth and pushing his trencher away from him at one of the tables. Suddenly Solace's eyes were drawn by a dark shape who stood silhouetted near the hearth, the fires raging behind him.

Her heart quickened. She stepped down a stair and almost stumbled, but caught herself on the stone wall.

He was speaking to Blade, but turned as soon as her eyes settled on him. A grin curved his lips, and a sensual look entered his smoky eyes. He moved away from Blade toward Solace as she descended the stairs. Blade held out his hand, as if he were in the middle of saying something, but then dropped it and shrugged.

Logan met Solace at the bottom of the stairs. Taking her hand to rest on his arm, he led her to the table. They ate the morning meal together, side by side, and were inseparable for the rest of the day.

That night, as Solace headed for the loneliness of her room, she cast Logan a pleading glance. She left her bedroom door unlocked, hoping he would come to her. She sat near the window, staring at the barn, wishing he was by her side. But the moon rose higher in the frosty night sky and he did not appear. Solace lay her head on the window ledge, but exhausted from lack of sleep the night before, she fell into a deep slumber.

She awoke when Logan's arms settled around her, lifting her from the seat near the open window and depositing her gently on the bed. She refused to relinquish her hold on him, even as his hands began their slow, heavenly exploration of her body. She opened her mouth and her soul to Logan, and he worked his magic over her senses, sending her to the stars and beyond.

Afterward, he pulled her against his body, cradling her lovingly to him, his hands stroking her hair slowly.

Solace curled into his warmth, letting the glow of his love wash over her and shield her.

He cupped her breast lightly, caressing it. As the spark of desire flamed in her again, she felt him grow stiff against her.

"Lord, woman, I can't get enough of you," he growled, rolling her onto her back and lying on top of her.

Solace chuckled deeply as he entwined his fingers through hers. "That's not what you would have said a few days ago."

"I was a fool," he answered, pressing his lips to hers.

Logan made love to Solace languorously, and she thrilled to the new sensations he brought to her flesh, to her mind, to her heart.

Logan slipped out of her room early the next morning, pausing in the doorway to glance back at her. She was sprawled, naked, on the bed, sleeping soundly. He didn't think that a thousand men thundering down the road on horseback could wake her. With a smile, he turned and continued down the stairs into the Great

Hall. As he descended the stairs, he saw Goliath and Blade seated near the hearth.

"Logan," Blade greeted as he entered the Great Hall.

Logan responded with a nod of his head. "What's there to eat?" he wondered. "My appetite is hearty."

Blade and Goliath exchanged glances.

"Logan," Blade said, stepping forward, "Alexander rode out early this morning."

Logan eyed the men. Nothing wrong with a little early morning ride. "And?"

"Just over the ridge," Goliath said, pointing west. "Just beyond Cavindale's borders."

Anxiety tightened the muscles in Logan's shoulders. "What?" he demanded.

"An army has camped for the night. I imagine they'll be here sometime late today."

"An army?" Logan said, tension spreading across his shoulders, anxiety swirling in the pit of his stomach. "Is it Barclay's?"

"No. Farindale's."

Thirty-seven

Lord Farindale lifted his arm so his squire could fasten the strap on his shoulder-plate armor. He stared out over the lands of Cavindale.

Behind Farindale, his army waited, all mounted, all looking toward Cavindale Manor.

He stared again at the note crumpled in his hand. A note he had reread hundreds of times since he had received it a month ago.

Farindale—
Meet me in battle at Cavindale. I have Solace.
Logan Grey

Grey. Farindale spit, the name tasting foul in his mouth. He had thought he had rid the lands of that pestilence thirteen years ago. It seemed his work was not finished.

His squire rose, holding out a gauntlet. Farindale slipped his hand inside. The squire held out the other glove. Farindale stared at the note in his hand, then tossed it to the ground and slid his hand into the other gauntlet.

I will kill this bastard who dares to hold my Solace. If she is harmed, not a building in Cavindale will be safe from my wrath. Farindale clenched his jaw as he thought of his daughter. If he has hurt her . . .

Farindale mounted his steed. The warhorse danced anxiously beneath him. He lowered his gaze to Malcolm Wayne, his first in command. "You're sure he said the western boundary of Cavindale? Where the river widens?"

Malcolm nodded. "The messenger said you'll recognize it by the crossed trees."

Farindale nodded, and his gaze lifted to the west. "You will stay here until I return," he ordered.

"But my lord . . . !" Malcolm began to protest.

Lord Farindale silenced him with a dark look. Malcolm knew better than to argue any further. Lord Farindale's orders were law, to be obeyed without question.

"My sword," lord Farindale called.

His squire raced to him, the weapon in his hand. Farindale took his sword from the youth and stared at it for a long moment. He studied his reflection in the bright silver surface of the blade. Gray hair framed his face. Shadowy lines were etched deep in his brow. The flesh on his cheeks was sagging. He was much older now than when he had faced Randol Grey. Randol had died for his child, for Logan. And now the boy had returned for vengeance.

Farindale sheathed his sword. He hoped he was strong enough to defeat the son. For Solace's sake.

He spurred his horse over the rise in the hill.

Logan threw the saddle on his horse, checking the straps and the length of the stirrups. He had thought Solace had slain his need for revenge with her forgiveness. But it wasn't that easy. Like a horrible demon, it had raised its ugly head when he heard that Farindale was just outside Cavindale. And now it was all he could think of. For years he had sought revenge. It was his life, his blood. To think that he could be rid of the need so easily had been a grave mistake. Well, he aimed to be rid of it forever. He had to face Farindale. He had to do it for his family. For his father.

He loved Solace with all his being, but this was something the monster that lived in his heart would not let him surrender.

Logan heard Solace race into the barn and skid to a halt. She ran to him and embraced him from behind.

"Where have you been?" she wondered. "I waited for you at the noon meal."

Logan gently disengaged her arms from around him. "I have to go somewhere," he said evasively, smiling glumly at her. He ran a finger along her jaw, hoping it was enough to pacify her, but knowing it wasn't.

"What is it?" she demanded.

"Nothing," Logan said, picking his sword up from the ground. He looked at the polished surface, wishing it were his father's blade. But Barclay had it now, confiscated when he was thrown into the dungeon. It will have do, he thought, and slid the sword into its sheath.

"Nothing!" Solace gasped. "Yet you have to take your sword?"

"Solace, trust me," he said, swinging himself up into the saddle. "I'll be back later."

"Logan!" she called, but he rode out of the barn.

A prickling raced along Solace's spine. She ran back into the barn. By the time she had pulled a horse from the stall and gotten the groom to saddle it, Logan was nowhere in sight. She mounted the horse and rode out of the barn, westward.

The cold wind whipped Solace's hair around her face, its frigid teeth nipping at her flesh. Her hands felt numb. It seemed she had ridden for hours, yet she still couldn't find Logan. She spurred the horse on, over another hilltop. Then, she heard it.

The clanging of swords.

She urged her horse toward the noise and rounded a bend to see Logan fighting a man in plate armor. At first, she thought they were just practicing their moves with each other, dueling for sport. But when the man in armor lunged hard at Logan and nearly skewered his thigh, she knew this was no mock battle. Why would Logan come out this far to fight someone? And who was he fighting?

The horse danced skittishly beneath her, the cold slapping its hide. She craned her neck, trying to see the crest on the man's tunic. It was white. Part of it looked very familiar. Suddenly, the man fell to his knees before Logan, and Solace saw the symbol of a lion etched on a field of white with gold trim. She gasped, frozen with terror as Logan raised the sword over her father's head, the sharp tip of the blade pointed at her father's heart.

"No!" Solace cried as Logan shoved the sword toward her father's chest. She whirled away in horror, tears blurring her vision.

Her heart tried to deny what her eyes had just seen. She wanted to scream and trample Logan with the hooves of the horse. No, her mind continued to repeat, but her anguish peaked to shatter the last shard of hope she had. She spurred the horse on, away from Cavindale, away from Logan. Every fiber of her being screamed in agony.

Her body shook; her throat closed, choking off her breath. She had thought they shared something special. She'd thought he cared for her. She had thought . . . she loved him! And that was the worst betrayal of all. Because even with all that, even with everything they had gone through, even after the last few days, he had completed his revenge.

Logan had killed her father.

Logan turned from the battle, breathing hard, his teeth clenched, and saw Solace fleeing. He quickly mounted his horse and raced after her. He wouldn't let her escape. Not this time. Not now. He quickly overrode her horse, grabbing the reins. He pulled, bringing the animal to a stop, then reached out to seize her flailing hands and managed to grab her wrist, trying to still her movements. He was furious with himself, with her.

"Let go, you bastard!" she shouted, urging her horse forward with her heels.

"Solace . . ." he began, but she turned to him with such hatred and such pain in her face that the words disappeared.

"You fool!" she howled. "You fool! It was me! I convinced my father to take Fulton! It was my fault!"

He dropped her hands as if the mere touch had scalded his skin. "You?" His eyes narrowed as he drew back from her. His vision swam before him, his mind incapable of digesting the horrible truth of her words.

"Your father was such a bastard, such a tyrant to his people. A rapist and a killer. I begged my father to stop him. And he did!" Solace explained in clipped words, through clenched teeth.

Logan had heard rumors of his father's dark methods of tax collecting, of his abuse of his power, but he had never believed any of them. No man, especially not his father, his flesh and blood, could be that cruel. He had refused to believe it. "You're wrong," he answered vehemently, but there was the slightest quiver in his voice.

"You killed the wrong person!" Solace proclaimed hotly.

Her enraged voice jarred him, cut him. He raised his open palm, ready to smash her face, ready to knock the words from her mouth. He stared into her anger, her desolation. Slowly, he curled his fingers into a fist and lowered his hand. Betrayed. His heart exploded in his chest. He drew his dagger with a howl of rage. "Then it's you I should kill!" Her bitter accusations rang in his ear. *A tyrant. A rapist. A killer.* It doesn't matter, he thought. He was my father and his death deserves to be avenged. He pressed the blade to her creamy throat.

Solace barely flinched. "Yes, do it. You've sacrificed everything else." She choked on her words. "You can't love. Complete your revenge. Kill me. It won't bring your parents back."

A muscle worked in his jaw. He blinked back the anger and the pain that swirled in him. Slowly, he dropped his hand, his eyes flashing at her like hot lightning bolts. "Get away from me," he snarled. "Get the hell out of here."

Solace reined her horse around and rode away from him without a word.

He stared after her retreating back, a broken man.

Solace rode and rode until the horse could go no further. Then she dismounted and anguish engulfed her completely. She had given herself to Logan! She had loved him! And he had destroyed the last of her family. He had used her . . . to get to her father.

She wept into her open palms. He had done more than hurt her. He had destroyed her. Her heart lay broken and bleeding. She sobbed until the sun set.

Then as the sun disappeared over the horizon and the sky turned blood red, a new resolve swept through her. A dark resolve. If Fulton was the only thing Logan could love, then she would see to it that he never got it. I will destroy him as he has me, she vowed. He will never get Fulton. I will see to that.

Thirty-eight

The Great Hall of Castle Fulton was awash in easy conversation. A large table had been set aside for the visiting monks. With the Yuletide approaching, the table had slowly begun to fill. Now there were six monks seated there, all eating quietly.

At the main table, Beth sat beside Baron Barclay. She wiped her mouth with the back of her velvet sleeve and cast a sly look at him. He was eating a large mutton leg. She ran a hand possessively over his arm. He raised his eyes to her and smiled, holding the leg out to her. She took a bite of it. Edwin had seen to it that she had everything she could possibly want. She often wondered if he was keeping her in case her father returned, as a hostage of sorts. But she knew she was far from that. She reached down and caressed her stomach, swelling with his child. Beth smiled contentedly. She had finally found her place.

Her eyes scanned the Hall. Barclay's men filled the tables, eating to their hearts' content. They were a noisy lot, but she found comfort in their presence. With so many men at the Baron's disposal, she knew the castle was secure.

Beth's gaze shifted to Edwin again, studying his handsome profile. She had often wondered why Barclay had not offered marriage. Perhaps he was waiting for the

Yuletide. She could wait. After all, was she not having his child?

She became aware of a growing silence in the Great Hall and turned her head to see two guards escorting a woman up to the front table. Dread slithered up her spine as outrage made her teeth clench.

Barclay rose slowly from his chair. He planted his hands on the table, leaning toward the woman as she stopped just before them.

Her hair was unkempt, her clothing old, the hem of her dress ragged. Besides that, there was something different about her, Beth noticed. The woman's shoulders sagged, but it wasn't from weariness. When Solace looked up and locked gazes with her, Beth noticed the resolve and the sadness in her eyes.

Barclay's lips turned up in a grin. "Nice to have you back, m'lady."

Beth cast him a sharp, annoyed glance. He had never called her m'lady! She turned burning eyes to her sister.

One of the guards who had escorted Solace stepped forward, and Barclay bent his head as the guard whispered in his ear. His brows furrowed and his eyes turned to Solace in contemplation.

The Baron retook his seat, rubbing his lower lip in thought. "Where's Grey?" he said.

Beth watched Solace's eyes cloud. She couldn't read her expression. "We were in Cavindale. But I doubt he is still there."

Beth and Barclay exchanged a glance. Barclay waved at one of the soldiers near the door, and the man immediately headed out of the Great Hall.

"Rest assured that if I knew where he was, I wouldn't hesitate to tell you," Solace added.

Barclay raised an eyebrow. "Trouble in paradise, dear?" he wondered, mockingly.

"He killed my father," Solace said, casting a glance at Beth.

Beth narrowed her eyes. The little harlot was up to something, she was sure. She bent to whisper in Barclay's ear, "Don't believe her."

Barclay surveyed Solace for a long, quiet moment. His sharp, blue eyes assessed every dark line on her face, every clenched muscle. "Then why have you returned to Fulton?"

Solace raised her chin. "To marry you," she said.

A murmur swept through the room. Beth clenched her fists on the table and almost stood, but Barclay grabbed her arm, holding her down. "Marry me?" He chuckled. "You made it quite clear last time you were here that you would have nothing to do with me."

"I would do anything to keep Fulton from Logan Grey," she said. "Even marry you. With Father dead, I am the rightful heir to Fulton. If you marry me, the lands are yours legally and without question."

Barclay rose and began to move around the table. "That's a very big price to pay, isn't it? To keep the lands from Grey. How do I know you'll make a dutiful wife?"

"I've been trained to run Castle Fulton. I know everyone's positions. I can tally the harvest, stock the pantries . . ."

Barclay stopped before Solace and smiled wolfishly. "That's not the duty I was speaking of."

Outrage rocked through Beth. He was considering it! "Edwin," she called beneath her breath.

Solace's chin raised. "I would make you a proper wife, in all ways. You have my word."

"Prove it," Barclay whispered.

Solace shifted uncomfortably. Beth watched her wrestle with the dilemma. If that little whore touches my

Edwin, Beth vowed, I will kill her with my own two hands.

Solace lifted up on her toes and pressed her lips to Barclay's.

A hiss issued from Beth. She was on her feet as Solace pulled back.

Barclay smiled. "A rather chaste kiss from a potential bride." He reached into his belt, drawing forth a dagger, and rested the blade at her throat. "Wouldn't it be easier just to kill you and marry someone more devoted to me? Like your lovely sister?"

Solace swallowed and pride soared in Beth's chest. Do it, she silently begged, leaning forward on the table.

There was no fear in Solace's eyes, only resignation. For a long moment, she said nothing. "The peasants respect me," she finally said softly.

Barclay glanced at one of his men.

A tremor of dread shot up Beth's spine. They were having a tremendous amount of trouble with the villagers. They were slow moving, even under the threat of death. Beth cringed. The villagers held her in no regard. And they liked Barclay even less. But they loved Solace. They would do anything for her.

Barclay resheathed his dagger. "A good point," he said, and returned to his seat. "I will consider your proposal."

"Edwin." Beth gasped in disbelief.

He patted her hand placatingly. "You look weary, lady Solace," Barclay said. "Beth, go attend your sister."

Beth inhaled sharply. She wasn't some servant! She slammed her hand on the table. Barclay caught her wrist. "Easy, my dove," Barclay whispered. "She is the heir to Fulton, after all. It would be wise to pacify her. At least for the time being."

Beth's eyes narrowed. She'd like to pacify her, all

right. Right over the castle wall! Beth moved around the table, her back rigid, her fists clenched into tight little balls of fury, until she stood before Solace. She stared into her green eyes, noticing that they weren't so bright any longer. "Let's go," she snarled.

Beth whirled, leading her sister through the curious gazes and whispered murmurings that spread quickly through the Great Hall.

"Congratulations," Solace said tonelessly, glancing at Beth's stomach.

Beth grunted. Like the little harlot even cared, she thought bitterly. Suddenly, she stopped and turned to her sister. Solace's clothing was dirty, her hair ragged and unwashed. There were even streaks of dirt on her face, marred with trails from tears. Beth scowled. Solace looked like a peasant, a weepy one at that. "Why have you returned? What do you want?" she demanded.

"I told you and Barclay what I want," Solace answered softly.

Beth sucked in her breath. "That's just like you, isn't it? As soon as I'm interested in a man, you try to steal him away!"

"After we're wed, you can have him all you want," Solace retorted bitterly. "I want nothing to do with Barclay, other than make him rightful lord of this castle."

Beth's chin rose. "You can die and I can make him rightful heir."

Solace just stared at her. "I guess that's up to Barclay now, isn't it?" She brushed past Beth and continued toward her old room.

"Just kill her," Beth pleaded.

Barclay raised an eyebrow at her as he lounged in his sumptuous bed. He wondered if it was jealousy making her talk so or hatred of her sister.

Suddenly, Beth dropped to her knees, taking his hand in hers and pressing kisses against his knuckles. "Please, darling. She'll bring us nothing but trouble. We don't need her."

Barclay eased his hand from her grip. In truth, he was tiring of the sniveling whore before him. Her enlarging stomach was repulsive to him. He wanted fresh flesh. And Solace fit his fantasy perfectly. A slim, spirited girl he would ride hard and tame. The thought of her struggling beneath him brought a grin to his lips and a bulge to his pants.

"You want her!" Beth exploded as she stood.

"She has her appeal," Barclay muttered, thinking of her round breasts and her full lips that could suck him dry.

Beth placed her hands on her hips. "What does she have that I don't?" she demanded.

"Her stomach is flat and smooth." Barclay took joy in watching the hurt flash in Beth's eyes. "She doesn't snivel and whine," he added, watching Beth's lips thin in anger.

Beth launched herself at him and Barclay caught her wrists, spinning to pin her beneath him. He chuckled as she tried to lash out at him. "Seems my little hellcat has a little spit left in her after all." He pinned her arms above her head with one hand, moving to undo his breeches with the other.

A crooked smile formed on Beth's lips.

Solace stared out over her lands, resting her palms on the ledge of her window. The cold wrapped its fingers around her, embracing her in an icy hug.

Logan, she thought again and again. Pain wracked her body as she remembered his smile, the safety she'd felt in his arms. It was all a ruse. It must have been. If he had truly cared for her, how could he have killed her father?

She bowed her head, her eyes narrowing. He would never have Fulton. It would be her final justice. He could go on living his life of anger and bitterness, but he would never have her home again. She tried to raise her chin, tried to tell herself what she was doing was right. It was justice.

Solace bowed her head, weeping into her hands. Then why did she feel so horrible? Why did she feel as though she were ripping her heart from her chest?

Flames danced in the hearth, casting the Great Hall in a red glow. Barclay sat in a chair before the fire, waiting for Solace. The warmth of the hearth did not reach his heart, only his loins. He heard the soft patter of footsteps and turned to see his betrothed entering the room.

He was gravely disappointed at what he saw. Her head was bowed, her hands secured by a rope, her shoulders hunched. A defeated woman. When she reached him, she lifted eyes that mirrored infinite sadness. Dark slashes underlined each eye.

Barclay scowled. He wished he could have been there. He wished he could have seen what had transpired to douse that indomitable spirit. Still, he caught a flash in her large green eyes that made him wonder.

"Good eve, lady Solace," Barclay said smoothly.

After a short moment, Solace thrust her bound hands toward him. "These are not necessary."

Barclay shrugged slightly. "After your previous escape, I have little choice."

She lowered her hands in acceptance.

"Come," he ordered. "Warm yourself by my side."

She moved, as he commanded, to his side. When he

reached out to touch her waist, she was pleasantly pliable. He grinned, wondering if he shouldn't bed her now before the fight returned to her. No. He liked a woman who fought. "I must tell you what an absolute treat it was to hear you had simply strolled into a village and found my men. I had garrisons of them out patrolling every village from here to London. And my little dove simply walks into my hands."

Solace stared at the fire. Shadows and light danced across her soft features.

"I must wonder if this is some sort of trap."

Something crossed her face, a memory, perhaps. "No trap," she finally replied. "I want you to become rightful lord of Fulton. I want no one to question your claim to these lands."

"And so they shall not," Barclay agreed. He took her hand into his own and pressed a hearty kiss to her knuckles. "Shall we say in two weeks time?"

Solace nodded once.

"I would do it at once, but Father Davis insisted we make it a Yuletide wedding," he encouraged. "That way our union will be doubly blessed."

"Solace, I can't believe you truly want to wed this man." Father Davis stood before her, his hands clasped over his large belly, his deep brown eyes staring at her with concern. His voice seemed to echo inside the cavernous chapel. "At least I succeeded in postponing the wedding a few weeks. To give you time to really think about this."

Solace noticed the elaborate renovations to the chapel. A golden altar had been added, a huge statue of the virgin Mary. It was those cold, unseeing eyes she met, instead of Father Davis's. Solace turned her back to him, wrapping her arms around her. Before her, a row of cream-colored cherub statues watched her from atop their intricately carved pedestals. And even though the stone angels had empty slits for eyes, she felt disapproving stares emanating from them. She suddenly felt a chill. She had never lied to Father Davis before and she certainly couldn't do it in the chapel.

"He is one of the most heartless men I have ever met," Father Davis added.

Solace whirled to him, her back straightening. "Did he hurt you?"

"Me?" Father Davis echoed in surprise. "No. Not me. But I'm certainly one of the few he hasn't. Have you seen any of the villagers?"

She hadn't been allowed out of her room for two days. Barclay was afraid she would run. Finally, she had been escorted to the chapel and allowed to see Father Davis. Three guards were waiting outside to bring her back to her prison of a room when she was done.

"He starves them, Solace," Father Davis said gently. "He stole the crops when he entered Fulton, and now with the weather getting cold and no food . . ." Father Davis's voice trailed off as he bowed his head and shook it. "We pray it will be a mild winter."

Solace dropped her hands to her sides. The villagers. She was glad she had returned. Perhaps somehow she could get them food. At least the sick ones and the ones with children. "That's why I'm marrying him. Perhaps I can soften his heart."

"Child, no one can soften his heart. He lusts for glory on earth and glory in heaven." Father Davis again shook his head. "He gives gold to the church, but he is cold and merciless. Look what he did to your stepmother." Father Davis raised Solace's chin with his finger. "He will show you no kindness."

A chill of doom slithered up Solace's spine. "And I ask for none."

Father Davis shook his head, rubbing his tired eyes. "Do you love him?"

Solace sought desperately for the right answer. "My sister is fond of him."

Father Davis snorted. "Lady Beth has as much sense as a jackass."

Solace couldn't resist a smile.

"It's good to see you smile, Solace," Father Davis commented quietly. "Fulton has become a castle of gloom since you left. Tell me of your journeys." Father Davis moved over to a bench and sat down, patting the stone beside him.

Solace moved to him, sitting next to him.

"Where did you go?" he asked.

"To Cavindale," she replied, glancing down at her slippered feet.

"Cavindale? That's so far from here! You traveled alone?"

"No."

She sensed Father Davis studying her face, but kept her eyes averted, running a finger across a gash in the stone bench.

"Who did you travel with?"

A permanent sorrow seemed to sweep her into a cocoon of emptiness. "Logan Grey."

Father Davis drew in a sharp breath. "Logan? Could it be?" He clasped his hands gently before him. "Peter's brother?"

Solace nodded, a strand of dark hair falling over her shoulder. "He was the falconer."

"The falconer," Father Davis echoed absently. "All that time, and I didn't even recognize him." He turned his attention back to Solace. "My prayers have been answered." He lowered his voice in a conspiratorial whisper. "He's coming to take Fulton, is he?"

"He might be, Father," Solace said. "But by the time he arrives, it will be too late."

"Too late?" Father Davis exclaimed. "But surely you can hold Barclay off!"

"I don't want to," Solace whispered. "I don't want Logan to have Fulton."

"But, child, he's our only hope."

"He killed my father," Solace said defensively, turning her head to look at him hotly.

As they locked eyes, Father Davis groaned softly. He suddenly looked decades older.

Solace knelt before Father Davis, taking his hand in her own. "You have to marry us, Father. I want you to."

"You don't know what you're asking me," he whispered. "I don't want to see another one of my beloved children hurt."

"What do you mean?"

"I've lived at Fulton for a long time. I'm an old man, Solace. I watched Peter and Logan grow up. I loved them as I do you. And when your father came, I watched their family destroyed. They were my children. The same as you are. I can not stand by and watch you do this. I can not marry you."

Desperately, Solace buried her forehead against his hands. "Please, Father."

"Go, child," he said in a steely voice. "If you still wish to marry Barclay after you see what he's done, then I will marry you." He patted her head, gently. "Go visit Peter and care for him again."

"Peter?" Solace gasped. "He's here? Where? Where is he?"

Father Davis's brown eyes darkened. "In the dungeon."

Thirty-nine

The following day Barclay guided Solace down the narrow stairs that led into the darkness of the dungeon. His large form obscured her vision of the interior of the prison, but she could hear the moans rising out of the blackness. Before her feet hit the dirt floor of the dungeon, the groans and calls for mercy were already ringing loudly in her ears. She froze, her hands instinctively reaching out to the walls for support. The smells of charred flesh and urine assaulted her, and she had to fight down the strong urge to race back up the stairs.

Barclay turned to her. In the flickering torchlight, Solace saw the smile on his lips, a smile more horrible than the cries of the tortured, more horrible than the darkness that awaited her. He was enjoying this. At the thought, terror gripped her. She now understood why he had voiced no objection to her seeing Peter. He was actually enjoying watching the torment play across her features. She froze, unable to move. She didn't want to see the transformation that the dark power of the dungeon had made in its captives. She didn't want to see her people, her men, chained and hobbled like animals.

The Baron's grin grew, his blue eyes sparkling with dark satisfaction. He wanted her afraid; he wanted to see her terror.

With this understanding came her resolve not to give in. Solace hid her fear behind a wall of resolution and a stone face. Barclay's grin slipped a notch and he moved on, escorting her deeper into the bowels of hell. The already-grotesque smell worsened as they moved into the heart of the dungeon. In the guard's area, Barclay stopped to speak to the man stationed there.

Solace looked around the small room in horror. The torchlight washed over a woman manacled and chained to the floor. Her clothing was ripped, a breast exposed in the flickering light. Her dark eyes stared at Solace without seeing. Her hair was scraggly, her face dirty and smeared with dried blood.

But what was most appalling to Solace was that she remembered the woman from the village. She was the young, bright-eyed daughter of the miller. Her father had died in Solace's arms from an arrow wound.

Solace stepped forward, instinctively moving to the girl's side. She reached out to take the woman's hand in her own, but Barclay's fingers closed over her arm, pulling her to her feet. "She has all the attention she needs," he said harshly.

"You barbarian!" Solace accused, ripping her arm from his hold. "How can you treat a woman like that? Chaining her to the floor like some animal."

"Oh, it's worse than you think," Barclay said, so softly that Solace had to strain to hear him above the moans. "She is used by my guards to make this position more . . . appealing."

Solace gasped in sheer outrage and whirled to the young woman. Barclay moved up behind her, his oily voice dripping in her ears. "Take heed, my beloved. You could just as easily replace her." When his hand touched the small of her back, she jumped, but Barclay simply guided her down the darkening hallway.

"It's a pity the dungeon is so small," he said. "I've

had to execute quite a number of people for lack of room. But I've had no trouble coming up with ways to dispatch them."

Solace lurched forward, away from his grip, but she could not escape the darkness and the stench of death.

"Here we are," Barclay said good-naturedly, halting before a door.

It was the same cell Logan had been chained in. Dread prickled the nape of Solace's neck as Barclay unlocked the door and swung it open. He ducked his head, thrusting the torch before him as he entered the cell.

Two forms lurched away from the light as the torch's glare swept over them. Like animals, she thought. Solace grimaced, preparing herself for the atrocities she was certain had been inflicted on Peter. But no matter how hard she tried, she could not have prepared herself for the sight that greeted her.

She stepped into the cell, peering around Barclay's shoulder at the huddled form he pointed to. The man cowered in the grime of the dungeon floor, covered in muck. Dark, knotted hair fell to his neck. Solace could barely make out the tattered remains of a white tunic with her father's crest on it. The man's skin was as pale as moonlight.

Solace stepped toward him, calling softly, "Peter?"

The man started. "Go away," he commanded.

Barclay lashed out with his foot, striking him with his boot. "Don't speak to my betrothed like that."

"Don't!" Solace hollered at Barclay.

"No," the man groaned, but Solace realized it was not the blow that caused him agony.

She knelt beside him, tentatively. "Peter, it's me," she whispered. "Solace."

The man turned his head so he was looking at her over his shoulder. She could see only one of his teary brown eyes. "I don't want you to see me like this," he said hoarsely.

"Peter," Solace said sympathetically, reaching out to cup his cheek. She felt his tears, his agony as if it were her own. "It's all right," she whispered. "I'm here."

Her words drew him forth from the darkness, from the blackness that had eaten away at his soul for months. He dropped his shoulder, moving into the light of the torch.

Solace's heart wrenched and she blinked her eyes against a sudden onslaught of tears. Peter's face was covered with bruises and cuts, some healing, some festering with pus. But what made her cry out in anguish, what made tears stream from her eyes, was his other eye. They had burned it out! Where his eye should have been, there was an empty socket, blackened by charring heat, swollen and bruised. She covered her mouth, gasping, "Oh, Peter!"

He looked down in an attempt to hide his disfigurement. Solace gently cupped his chin, forcing him to look up at her. "It's all right," she soothed.

Peter reached up to brush a finger against her cheek, wiping away some of her tears.

"Be careful how you touch my betrothed," Barclay warned from behind her.

His voice jarred Solace and she stood, whirling to face him. "How could you?" she demanded.

"Easily, my darling." His voice was mocking. "I was searching for you."

"How could Peter have known where I was?"

"He is a Grey," Barclay said simply. "He might have known where his brother would take you."

Solace stepped closer to Barclay, her teeth clenched, her loathing evident. "Peter did not even know Logan. You knew that. You knew he would have no idea where

Logan had gone. You did it because you like to hurt people."

Barclay held up a hand. "On the contrary, my dove. I only hurt my enemies." His smile grew; the wavering torchlight distorted it, making it look more like a grimace. His hand shot out, capturing her arm in a tight hold. "Be thankful you are not my enemy."

She narrowed her eyes, trying to ignore the biting pain coming from his grip.

"Solace," Peter groaned and shifted, but he was too weak to rise, too weak to come to her defense.

Barclay shoved Solace toward Peter. "Care for him. Then Father Davis will marry us."

Solace stared across the Great Hall at the table of monks. Their numbers seemed to have doubled, perhaps even tripled in size from when she had first arrived a week ago; almost twenty monks now occupied the table. Every Yule, Castle Fulton was host to these pious travelers, offering them shelter and food before they continued on with their pilgrimage. Most ate quietly, exchanging few words. They dined with their hoods up, solemnly, eating whatever they were given. Solace wished she could join them.

"Aren't you hungry, darling?" Barclay asked from beside her. "You haven't touched your food."

Solace glanced down at the venison. It was not the pungent aroma of the food that was souring her appetite. "I'm sorry," she whispered. "I have no appetite." She stood to return to her chamber, but Barclay seized her arm.

"I hope you're more zealous in bed than you are for food," he murmured.

Solace gently freed her arm. "You needn't worry about my duties as a wife. I will remain faithful."

She turned and moved toward the hallway, very aware that every one of Barclay's men watched her. Barclay had freed her hands of their bindings, but it was obvious that he had instructed his men to watch her every movement.

She was still very much a prisoner.

She stepped into the hall and moved toward her room. Suddenly, an overwhelming urge to flee took hold of her. She leaned against the wall and placed her hands to her cheeks. Why? Why was she doing this? It was madness! Marrying Barclay. I have to, she told herself firmly. I have to do it. I can't let Logan have Fulton. I have to marry Barclay so the lands are rightfully his.

"My child, are you all right?"

Solace looked up to find Father Davis standing before her.

She wanted to launch herself into his arms and tell him what a fool she'd been. But she couldn't. "Yes," she said, straightening. "I'm fine."

Father Davis nodded once. His brown eyes peered at her, and she had to avert her eyes before he saw the truth.

"The wedding is in a week's time," Solace said. "On the Yule."

"Don't do this, Solace," Father Davis pleaded. "He will hurt you."

Solace looked at the cold stones beneath her feet. "I did what you said, Father. I've tended Peter daily."

"You've seen what he did to Peter," Father Davis said sternly. "You can't marry him."

Solace raised her eyes, determination shining brightly in them. "I want to."

Disbelief and hurt flashed across Father Davis's face. "But Solace—"

"You gave your word," Solace argued. "I want to marry him. I have to."

Father Davis sighed. "I will not go back on my word. If it's what you wish."

Solace nodded, grasping his hands. "Thank you."

"You don't know what you're asking," he said and eased his hands from her grip. "I wish you would change your mind. Think about it." He gently touched her cheek and disappeared down the hallway.

Solace watched him for a moment. She had thought about it. Long and hard. It was the only way to stop Logan. And she would do anything . . .

Then why did she feel so horrible? Was what she was doing wrong? She rubbed her eyes. Logan's image came unbidden. His warm smile, his soft touch, his silver eyes filled her mind.

Why? Why had he killed her father?

She pushed herself from the wall, doubts plaguing her mind. Her decision was made. She glanced up and saw a monk standing in the shadows of the great doors, watching her.

She turned and headed to her room.

Solace stared at the snow as it fell from the sky, falling over the lands like frozen tears. Then she remembered Logan's face as he'd thrust the blade into her father's heart. How could she have been so wrong about Logan? She had loved him with all her heart, all her being. It was as if he had killed her instead of her father.

She heard the door to her room open and close, but did not look up to see who it was.

A cup was thrust before her.

Solace looked down at it, then raised her gaze to meet Beth's glacial blue eyes. It seemed everything around her was cold. "What's this?" she wondered.

"It will cure all your problems," Beth answered softly.

Solace's eyes narrowed before shifting back to the drink. She took the offered cup.

"It's quick and you won't be in any pain," Beth assured her.

Solace stared at the beckoning liquid. She should have been surprised and repulsed, but she was neither. She accepted Beth's offering, nonplused. In the torchlight, the dark liquid looked like blood.

"Drink it," Beth cooed. "I'll marry Barclay, have his child and he will still be rightful heir of Fulton. Everyone will be happy."

Solace licked her lips. It was tempting, so tempting. But she couldn't do it. She couldn't leave her people to Beth's care. She lowered the cup to her lap. "I can't," she said.

"Why not?" Beth demanded. "It's the only solution there is."

"I don't believe killing myself is a solution," Solace whispered.

"Then perhaps some one else will do it."

Startled, Solace raised her eyes to her sister, but Beth had already turned her back and was headed toward the door.

That night, Solace slept fitfully, if at all. Logan's mercury eyes haunted her dreams, his gentle touch and rumbling laughter plagued her senses. She awoke again and again, only to fall into a restless sleep.

She moved through the next day like a sleepwalker. A strange mist had settled about her, a mist of confusion, of depression. Then she found herself in the chapel, kneeling before a statue of the Virgin Mary, praying for guidance.

She swallowed down a lump of despair. When she felt

a hand on her shoulder, she raised teary eyes to find Father Davis standing beside her.

"Solace," he whispered, hurt by the pain in her eyes. "What is it?"

"Father, I don't think I can do this," she whispered.

The priest's eyes went wide with shock, then a frown crossed his wrinkled brow. "You have to marry Barclay," he said quickly.

"What?" she gasped.

"It's the best thing for you. I've been too harsh on the Baron."

"But—"

"I'm sure he'll make a wonderful husband." Father Davis stood, wiping a tear from her cheek. "You're doing the right thing." He patted her hand reassuringly, then turned and moved down the aisle toward the back of the chapel.

Solace couldn't keep her mouth from dropping open. Had Barclay gotten to him? Threatened him somehow? She turned back to her prayers, hoping the few other monks kneeling in the pews in prayer could not read her impious thoughts.

The monks were everywhere. There was nowhere Solace could go to be alone, so the day before her wedding she went to the battlements, seeking calm in her churning emotions. The biting wind tore at her cloak, whipping her hair out behind her. She faced the wind, letting it sting her cheeks and water her eyes.

The land was frozen, the fields barren. Tomorrow it would all be over. Solace wondered what Barclay would do when he found out she wasn't a virgin. She wondered if he would kill her. She wondered if he would care.

She wondered where Logan was. Was he continuing

to plan the attack against Castle Fulton? Was he thinking about her?

Tears rose in her eyes as she thought of the time they had spent together. She had been filled with joy whenever they had been together. She had reveled in the secretive looks they had shared. And now all that filled her soul was emptiness.

She would be Barclay's wife. And she would loathe him.

"Thinking of jumping off the battlements?"

Barclay's voice sent a chill through her, and she blinked back her tears. "No, m'lord," she whispered.

"Good," he murmured, moving up behind her. "I don't want you dead just yet." He trailed a hand along the length of her arm.

She stiffened at his touch, feeling strangely violated. His fingers moved to caress her cheek, her neck.

Solace pulled away from him. "I prefer to wait until our wedding night."

"I insist," he smiled, lowering his head to hers.

Solace backed into the wall. "And I insist we wait."

Barclay's gaze devoured her, from her toes to the tips of her long hair. A deep growl came from his throat, and Solace hid her shudder beneath a feigned chill.

"It's so cold," she said, moving forward to step around him.

He didn't budge and Solace shrank away from him. His blue eyes burned as he suddenly seized her hand, pressing it against the bulge in his pants. "I plan to take you in ways that are not natural. And you will not protest."

Solace tried to pull her hand free, but he pressed it harder against himself.

"I have plans for you that would make a whore blush."

Solace wanted to run, screaming, from him. But she

forced calm into her voice as she met his gaze, stilling her struggles. "I'm sure you do, m'lord."

"You will do everything I say on our wedding night and for every day after." He bent his head toward her lips, releasing her hand.

Solace ducked under his arm. "But until then I'll do as I please," she called, fleeing the battlements.

Barclay started to follow, a twisted smile on his lips, a smoldering heat in his eyes.

Suddenly, a hooded monk stepped into his path, accidentally bumping his shoulder, halting his movement.

When Barclay turned enraged eyes on the monk, the hooded man humbly bowed before him. Staring down at the top of the monk's brown hood, Barclay bit back his condemning remark; he ground his teeth and lifted his gaze to see that his prize had escaped.

Forty

Solace stood at the back of the chapel, staring impassively up the aisle at the golden altar where Father Davis stood. His back was to her, his head bowed. He was clothed in a brown cloak, the hood drawn up over his face, giving him the appearance of one of the visiting monks. She clutched at her hands so they wouldn't shake, only to find they were as cold and frigid as icicles.

Monks lined the pews and the walls of the chapel. Barclay's men were everywhere as well. It looked as if every visitor and every invader had come to see the wedding.

Fitting, Solace thought. She knew Barclay had placed his men in the room just to be sure she didn't change her mind. She shook her head. It was too late to change her mind. She would not turn back.

When did I become so bitter? she wondered as she started up the aisle. When did I turn into Logan? Her footing was sure and steady, even though a piece of her heart broke with each step that brought her closer to Barclay. The white dress she wore was plain, a white houppelande, belted high just beneath her breasts. The white was a mockery of her lost virginity, but she couldn't wear black, even though it would be as dark and hopeless as she felt. Not until after she had wed

Barclay. Not until the lands were his. She had to complete that one task as vengeance for her father.

The baron waited for her at the front of the aisle, dressed in a bright red cape lined with fur that made him look like one of Satan's minions. He wore a black tunic and hose beneath the cape, and his sword was belted around his waist. But it was his eyes that snared her attention as she neared; they were bright with victory.

She reached the front of the chapel and Barclay extended his hand. Solace ignored it, a final defiance, and turned toward Father Davis.

She heard Barclay's chuckle, but paid him no heed. Instead, she concentrated on the way Father Davis was clutching the altar. His knuckles were white and the veins on the back of his hand bulged against the surface skin, as if he were struggling to crush the sculptured metal of the altar in his fingers. Then he stood, rising to his full height, and slowly turned to them, the cowl hiding his face in a shadowy pool of blackness. He slowly came down the two steps before the altar.

The room was silent. Solace waited, desperately trying to still the quickening pace of her madly beating heart. In mere moments she would be lady Barclay, and there was nothing she could do now to stop it. This was sheer madness! What was I thinking? She wanted to scream as the true horror of her predicament slammed into her. She wanted to shout at the top of her lungs and drive a blade through Barclay's black heart. She wanted to yell a curse on Logan's twisted soul. But all she could do was lower her head and close her eyes for a moment, fighting the dizzying swirl of emotions that whipped through her like an uncontrollable tornado and praying it would be over quickly.

When she opened her eyes Father Davis was standing before them. Her gaze was drawn to his clasped hands. They were strong and firm.

But . . . his hands should have been wrinkled with age, puckered by his decades of service to God.

Solace looked up, her eyes wide, trying to see past the darkness of the shadows.

Suddenly, a strong hand shot forward and seized her arm, dragging her away from Barclay!

Barclay raised confused eyes, just in time to see Father Davis throw back the cowl to reveal—

Logan!

He drew the sword that had been hidden behind his cloak and pressed the tip to Barclay's throat.

Solace couldn't move. Logan. His name pulsed through her mind with each beat of her heart. Logan!

"We meet again, old friend," Logan ground out between clenched teeth.

"You traitorous bitch!" Barclay howled, his eyes locking on Solace. "You trapped me!"

She opened her mouth to deny his accusations, but nothing came out. Instead, she let an overwhelming relief course through her.

"You're a damn fool!" Barclay spat out, his eyes shifting to Logan. "You'll never get out of here alive."

"That's where I think you're wrong," Logan replied. "Tell your men to lay down their arms and surrender."

A smile split Barclay's lips, and laughter churned from his throat. "One man against dozens? I think not."

The corner of Logan's lips curled into a grin, and he nodded his head at one of the pews. The chapel erupted in a frenzy of motion as the monks in the pews and in the aisles threw aside their cloaks to reveal Logan's friends! Solace recognized Blade's blond head and Goliath's tall form in the front row.

Barclay's guards drew their swords and the thunderous clang of a hundred swords clashing rang out in the chapel. The sound was deafening.

They had come to take the castle! For a moment, disbelief rocked through Solace. Without trebuchets, without battering rams, they had infiltrated the castle. The plan was impulsive, ingenious and admirably brave.

Solace turned her gaze to Logan, a powerful pride welling up inside her . . . until the image of Logan shoving his sword into her father's chest speared her mind. Hurt and betrayal and anger replaced her joy. She clenched her teeth and shoved the traitor hard, fleeing toward the door at the side of the altar.

She glanced quickly over her shoulder to see Logan recovering from her shove, saw him cast a frustrated glance at the fleeing Barclay before turning a dark look on her. She continued to run, hiking the layers of her skirts over her knees to achieve full speed.

She reached for the handle of the door, pushing the wooden barricade open, and ran into the small, stone alcove. Spiral stairs rose up to the next floor. Behind her, the door exploded open and Logan shot through it, grabbing her wrist and whirling her around. Shocked, she couldn't move for a long moment. He was before her, staring at her with smoldering gray eyes.

Solace began to struggle, fighting to free her wrist. He glared at her, stilling her useless battle by pressing his body against hers. Fire ignited throughout her as his breath mingled with her own. "Get away from me!" she commanded.

He pressed her back against the wall, shoving his body closer to hers. "I should slit your traitorous neck," he growled, but bent to press a kiss to her tender throat. "If it didn't mean so damn much to me."

Stunned, Solace couldn't move. His head rose until

he stared her in the eye. She found it hard to breathe with him so close. She had forgotten how beguiling those silver eyes were, how warm his body was. She felt part of her fight leave her under the hypnotic effect of his presence. His laughter rumbled through her, prickling her nerves. And she missed him. Part of her was dying, for she knew she would yield to him, even though he had killed her father.

"My stubborn little Solace," he whispered. "Your plan would have worked if I wasn't so determined to claim what was rightfully mine."

Fulton. The old argument, the old vengeance that had killed her father, sparked her anger into a disconsolate inferno and Solace renewed her attempts at escape, pounding his massive chest, trying to step on his toes with her foot. Pain flared through her heel as it slammed against his hard boot. Tears burned in her eyes. "All you care about is this castle! Your revenge! Well, it's complete now! My father's dead!"

"Dead?"

"Your vengeance is complete! You should feel proud!"

"Solace, it ended in Cavindale."

She stilled her fight and stared up into his steel eyes. Pain flooded through her. She nodded. "When you killed my father. I saw you kill him." She fought back her tears. "I *saw* you."

Logan stepped back, releasing her. She knew she should run, but the weight of her convictions pressed down on her like stone. She couldn't move as he studied her face, taking in every detail. His face softened suddenly, relaxing as understanding spread across his features. "He's not dead, Solace," Logan whispered.

"What?" she gasped.

"I didn't kill him," Logan admitted. "I couldn't do it."

"But I saw you."

Logan shook his head. "I wanted to kill him. Lord, how I wanted him dead. To avenge my father. To avenge my mother. But the only thing I could think of was what it would do to you. The hurt I would see in your eyes." He shook his head. "I couldn't do it. Not in the face of that."

"My father's alive?" Solace gasped.

Logan nodded. "He's alive."

"But you could have had your revenge."

"I don't want it anymore," Logan threw back his head and laughed. "I don't even want *Fulton* anymore." He lowered his head to gaze into her eyes. "All I want is you."

Solace stared at him, her heart beating wildly, her hopes soaring.

Logan raised a hand to trace his fingers tenderly over her cheek. "You've put more faith in me than I have in myself. You loved me when I couldn't even love myself. It took me a long time to realize it, a long time to put aside my anger. You are everything I have ever wanted."

Solace opened her mouth, but nothing came out. She was so happy that tears rose in her eyes.

"I love you, Solace," Logan whispered.

Suddenly, the wall beside Solace moved and Barclay appeared beside her, grabbing her arm, entwining his hand in her hair, yanking her against him like a shield! "Is this man bothering you, dearest?" he whispered harshly.

Solace cringed as Barclay pulled her hair tighter. Logan lunged forward, but Barclay placed the blade of his sword to her neck.

"Ah-ah," he warned. "I'd hate to slip and hurt such a treasure."

Logan straightened.

Pain flared in Solace's head as Barclay tugged harshly on her hair, dragging her back into the darkness of the passageway.

"Don't follow me, old friend," Barclay said. "Or I'll kill her."

Logan watched with growing fury as Barclay disappeared into a secret passage behind the alcove wall. He crushed his fingers into tight fists, squeezing them tighter and tighter until the muscles in his arms ached with his anger, until his entire body shook with outrage. He whirled away from the wall and raced back into the chapel, speeding through the chaotic swirl of fighting men that filled the large room. One of Barclay's men stepped in front of him, brandishing a blood-soaked blade, defying him to continue. Logan plunged straight into the man, growling like a savage animal, baring his teeth in a feral snarl, swinging his sword with a ferocity that no man could match. The guard went down.

Logan sped on, racing out of the chapel and into a long hallway. He shoved aside an ornate tapestry hanging on the wall and disappeared into the secret passageway hidden behind it. His heart pounded in his chest. He had never been more scared in his life. The possibility of losing Solace forever terrified him more than anything had ever terrified him in his life, more than his first fight with Goliath when he nearly lost his own life, more than seeing Farindale's army approaching his father's castle those many years ago.

He ran through the darkness, slipping several times on the mossy floor in his frantic drive to reach Solace.

The narrow corridor reeked of mold and decay. And death. He ran faster, his breath exploding from his lungs, his blood hammering in his ears. He knew where the passageway emerged; the exit was up on the northern tower of the castle. He could reach Barclay through the battlements. He emerged from the passageway just outside the spiraling steps of the tower. He charged up the stairs and out onto the battlements.

As Logan sped across the battlements toward the north wall, the wind whipped his hair around his face. Above him, dark clouds churned in an ominous black sky. He rounded a corner in the walkway to see Barclay and Solace already emerging from the passage. Solace attempted to break free, lurching forward, but Barclay caught hold of her dress and dragged her back.

"Barclay!" Logan shouted, his angry voice rising above the shrillness of the wind.

Barclay turned to face him, keeping his sword at Solace's throat.

Logan's eyes narrowed as he recognized the blade in Barclay's hands. It was his father's, the blade he had entrusted to Logan, the blade he had given his son in recognition of his emerging manhood. Again, Logan's body shook with rage, a tremor rippling through him.

"Let her go," he ordered, surprised at the calmness of his voice.

Thunder rumbled in the sky above.

Logan approached slowly, the strong wind blowing the hair away from his eyes, slapping at his clothes, trying to push him back from Solace. But no force of nature could keep him from her.

Barclay held the sword to Solace's throat, the lashing wind blowing her hair around her face, into Barclay's eyes.

"Let her go!" Logan repeated, deadly intent in the rumble from his throat. "It's me you want."

Lightning flashed behind Logan as thick black clouds continued to roll across the sky.

"I have no interest in you and I never did," Barclay called back. "Now back away or she is dead."

Logan stiffened. If he backed away now, Barclay would escape. If he didn't, Barclay would gladly slit Solace's throat. Logan took a step back.

Suddenly, his falcon swooped down from the ominous sky, its claws outstretched, its screeching cry drowning out even the loud blasts of thunder coming from the black clouds above! The falcon clawed at Barclay's head, scratching at his eyes with its sharp talons. Barclay shrieked in shock and fear. He shoved Solace away from him, arcing his sword at the bird. The falcon fluttered away, easily avoiding Barclay's attack.

Solace screamed as the force of Barclay's push sent her hurtling toward the castle wall. A brilliant flare of lightning burned into the sky, forever searing the image of Solace toppling over the battlements into Logan's mind.

He lunged for Solace as she fell over the edge, dropping his sword as he moved. His fingers somehow managed to find and encircle her slim wrist, but the sudden weight in his grasp pulled Logan down sharply and his stomach slammed into the stone wall, knocking his breath from his lungs. He felt her flesh slide along his fingers.

"Logan!" Solace cried up at him, her face tight with pain. Below her, far below her, the ground was littered with sharp-edged stones. No one could survive a fall from the battlements.

"Hold on!" he shouted down at her. The wind whipped around them, buffeting Solace's body with strong gusts, knocking her into the stone wall again and again. His fingers ached with the strain of holding her. "Hold on!" he shouted again. Logan clenched his teeth and began pulling her up toward him, his muscles bulging and rippling with power as he tugged. He managed to pull her up high enough so she could grab onto the edge of the castle wall.

That was when he heard footsteps rushing up behind him.

Logan turned instinctively, releasing Solace, moving away just in time to sidestep Barclay's swing. The blade smashed into the castle wall, chunks of stone spitting up mere inches from where Solace clung for her life. Solace screamed as tiny bits of rock showered her, and Logan saw her grip slip as her body dropped a foot back down the outer wall.

Quickly, he put his foot to the Baron's chest and shoved him backward. Barclay stumbled away from him, then fell, the blade tumbling from his grasp.

Logan scooped up his father's sword, *his* sword, and stood before Barclay. He gripped the blade tightly in his fingers, the weapon now an extension of his being. He moved toward Barclay.

"Just back away," he told the Baron.

But Barclay grabbed Logan's dropped sword and stood tall before him, meeting his stormy gaze with a dark stare of his own.

Logan glanced to his left to see Solace struggling to keep her grip on the castle wall. "Logan," she called to him, her eyes beseeching him for help. She was between the Baron and himself. If he made a move to help her, Barclay would cut him down. He had to get him away from Solace.

"Now, we finish this," Logan snarled as he attacked, slamming his sword down onto Barclay's, driving the

Baron back, away from Solace. He fought desperately, knowing that each second that passed brought Solace closer to her death.

The wind churned around the two fighters, pulling at their clothing. Thunder rumbled in the gray sky above them. Logan drove Barclay back and moved toward Solace, but Barclay swung after him, forcing Logan to engage him again. They crossed swords, Logan's face a grimace of agony as Solace called out to him again.

"What's wrong, old friend?" Barclay wondered through gritted teeth. A flash of lightning revealed a grotesque, distorted grin splitting Barclay's face. "Distracted? You'd better hurry. It looks like she's slipping."

Logan shoved off, swinging with all his might. Barclay blocked the blow, but the force of the strike dropped him to his knees. Logan lashed out with his boot, kicking his foe solidly in the face. Barclay tumbled back to the ground as blood spurted from his nostrils. He howled with outrage, holding his fingers to his bleeding nose.

Logan turned away from his fallen enemy and raced back for Solace. He grabbed her under her arms and pulled her over the wall, up onto the battlement. "Are you all right?" he asked gently, holding her up as her trembling legs buckled beneath her.

Solace nodded, clutching at him. She looked up into his eyes—

—and screamed! Logan spun away from her, lifting his blade in time to block Barclay's strike. Again, the two crossed swords, their faces inches apart.

Lightning flashed in the sky, followed by a tremendous crack of thunder.

"Maybe you can buy your way out of hell," Logan growled.

"You've already sold your soul to the devil," Barclay spat back. "Bedding your enemy's daughter."

Logan pushed off, taking a few steps back from Barclay.

Barclay attacked immediately, swinging for Logan's head. Logan ducked and whirled, spinning rapidly in a tight circle, bringing his blade toward the Baron's knees. Barclay angled his weapon down, blocking Logan's strike.

Logan rose to his full height and glared heatedly at Barclay. A grim determination etched itself into his features, his face turning to stone. "You have betrayed me," he said evenly to the Baron. He swung his blade at Barclay and sparks flashed into the air as the hard metals collided.

"You're an idealistic fool," Barclay retorted.

"You have tortured and maimed my brother." The power behind Logan's strikes intensified. He pushed Barclay back a step under the strength of his blows.

"He's a stubborn idiot with the brain of a gnat," Barclay snarled.

"You have threatened, and risked the life of, my lady," Logan said through gritted teeth.

"She's nothing but a whore," Barclay spat out.

Logan attacked Barclay mercilessly, swinging again and again, forcing the Baron to retreat under his savage onslaught. Then Logan feinted with an overhanded blow and Barclay moved to block it. Logan thrust, driving his sword into Barclay's stomach.

Time froze for a moment, Barclay clutching his sword above his head, Logan holding onto the pommel of his weapon, lodged deep in Barclay's stomach.

Barclay lowered his head slowly, his eyes filled with disbelief, to stare at the sword buried deep inside him. He lifted his fading gaze to Logan.

Logan grimaced as he pushed the blade deeper into Barclay's gut.

Barclay pulled his sword down at Logan in one final attempt to kill him. Logan easily sidestepped the swing, and the weapon clattered to the stone flooring of the tower. The impetus sent Barclay forward onto his hands and knees, and Logan stepped to the side to let him fall.

When Solace ran to Logan, he wrapped her in a warm embrace, their gazes locked on Barclay. Barclay managed to push himself over onto his back, gasping for a breath as he moved. His fingers convulsively gripped the handle of the Grey sword buried inside him. Blood soaked through his black tunic and spilled through his fingers. He lifted his eyes to Logan. His lips curled up in a grin, and he opened his mouth to speak. But the only thing that came out was a trickle of blood from the corner of his mouth. His blue eyes rolled into his head and his body slumped.

For a long moment, everything was still. In the sky above, the falcon circled Logan and Solace. It cawed once and then flew off.

Logan hugged Solace tightly. "It's over," he groaned, burying his face in the strands of her silken hair.

The first drops of rain fell from the sky, splashing over Barclay. The cool rain splattered against Logan's shoulders, and he pulled Solace into the protective shelter of his arms. Suddenly, the sky opened and a heavy downpour drenched the tower, the castle, the lands.

Solace stepped into the chapel beside Logan to find many of his men lounging around the pews. Blade straightened upon seeing them, and a bright grin lit his face. "Grey," he exclaimed happily.

The remaining men stood, rushing forward, enveloping them in a tide of warmth.

"They've fled, Logan," Blade said. "Goliath took some men to make sure that they were gone, but most of Barclay's men were mercenaries. Looks like they didn't think he was worth dying for."

Logan slapped Blade on the shoulder. "Good work," he said, moving through the rush of men.

"Ah! Thank the Lord!"

Solace knew that voice. A feeling of anticipation filled her, and she pushed through the crowd. "Father!" she cried out.

The crowd parted like a curtain before lord Farindale as he rushed toward her. He barely gave her time to acknowledge he was alive, he was real, before he embraced her in a powerful hug.

"Are you hurt?" he asked, holding her tightly.

"No," she gasped, trembling all over. "I can't believe it. I thought you were dead." She held onto him as though at any moment he might disintegrate and disappear from her embrace.

"No, Solace," he murmured into her hair.

"Father!"

Solace turned to see Beth hobbling into the chapel, working her way past Logan's friends to where Solace and the others stood. "Oh, Father!" she exclaimed, throwing herself at him. "I thought you would never come!"

Lord Farindale caught Beth in his arms, but did not greet her with the warmth he had greeted Solace. There was a reserve to him that startled Solace. Finally, he set Beth away from him. He looked at her rounded stomach and then back at her face.

"It was horrible," Beth muttered, burying her face in her father's tunic.

Lord Farindale exchanged glances with Logan.

Solace looked up at Logan to find his eyes cold and hard.

"You never tried to contact me," lord Farindale said calmly.

Beth pulled back to look into his eyes. "I—I couldn't. Edwin allowed me no visitors. He locked me in my room. I had—"

"I've been in the castle amongst the monks for two days now, Beth," Farindale interrupted. "I saw how you fawned all over him. I saw how you willingly shared your bed with him."

"It was an act!" Beth shouted. "I had to protect myself!"

Lord Farindale reached into his tunic to pull out a dagger. It was the dagger Logan had found when Graham attacked Solace. It was the dagger Ryder had assaulted Solace with. "I gave this to you before I left," Farindale said.

"Yes! I recognize it," Beth agreed. "Where did you get it?"

Farindale's eyes narrowed. "The man who attacked Solace had it."

"It was stolen!" Beth shouted. "I swear. It's been missing for months!"

"Your lies will never again touch my heart," Farindale said stoically. "Power and greed have always run through your veins. Unlike Solace, you are selfish and unkind. I will take you to a nunnery where you will spend the rest of your days in prayer for your sins."

"Father! I beg you! I am with child! You can not do this!" Beth pleaded.

Farindale turned his back to her, signaling one of his men to take her away. Her screams echoed in the chapel, slowly fading into silence.

"The sisters will see to her child," lord Farindale explained in response to Solace's worried look. "Do not worry."

Farindale turned a severe gaze on Logan before setting a hand on his shoulder. Solace saw the unease that spread over Logan's face until her father spoke. "I owe you much, son," Farindale said. "My daughter. My castle. How can I repay you?"

Logan would ask for Castle Fulton, Solace knew. It was what he wanted most of all. And he should have it. He deserved it. A strange, melancholy feeling settled over her.

Logan's gaze swept his men, who smiled at him in triumph. Finally, his stare settled on Solace.

"Lord Farindale," Logan said. "There is only one thing I want."

Solace bowed her head in acceptance.

Logan continued. "I wish to have your daughter's hand in marriage."

Solace's eyes widened in surprise and her head snapped up, her gaze locking with Logan's. A cry of joy bubbled from her lips.

"I should have guessed as much," Farindale said. "You have my best wishes."

Solace ran forward, throwing herself into Logan's arms. He easily caught her, spinning her around, laughing. When her feet hit the ground, she reached up to press a kiss to his lips.

The men chortled, and murmurs of approval echoed through the chapel.

"Of course," Farindale added, stilling the joyous moment, "with my daughter's hand come many responsibilities."

Logan and Solace turned to him. Solace noticed the

sternness in her father's eyes, and a wariness gripped her.

"I'm away at war much of the time. I need someone to protect my daughter, someone to look after her. But I also need someone to see to my lands, my castle. It bequeaths me to have it be my heir."

"Oh, Logan," Solace gasped. She turned her gaze up into his joyful face with more passion and relief and gratitude—and love—than she had ever felt before.

Epilogue

The wind blew Logan's dark hair about his face as he stood before Fulton's main gate. He watched with a growing sadness as his brother climbed onto his horse. The falcon on Logan's shoulder fluffed its black feathers and anxiously shifted its stance.

Peter adjusted the patch over his eye before reaching down from his mount and grasping his brother's arm. "I wish you all the best, brother," he said.

"I wish you would change your mind," Logan told him. "You're more than welcome at Castle Fulton." Logan paused. "Now that I found you, I don't want to lose you again."

Peter studied his brother for a moment. "I think it's time I see the world," he finally said, turning his gaze down the road before him. He glanced back once to look at Solace who was leaning against the castle gate, waiting for Logan. He quickly looked away from her. "I can't stay."

Logan's lips set in a thin line. He nodded once. "Good luck," he said.

"And to you." Peter then spurred his horse. The animal moved off, trotting down the road that led to the village. And to the wide world beyond.

Logan watched his brother for a long moment. He wondered if Peter had felt this way all those years ago when watching him ride out of the castle to see Farindale's army. *Did he think he would never see me again?* Logan wondered.

Solace joined him, and Logan turned pained eyes to her. She had already said her good-byes to Peter, and he saw that the ache in her gaze mirrored the emotions he felt. She reached up and caressed his cheek.

Suddenly, the falcon on Logan's shoulder took flight. It soared high into the air, its magnificent wings spread wide to catch the air currents that swirled above the castle walls. The bird circled Logan and Solace once. Then a gust of wind seemed to catch it and propel it toward Peter. Logan watched in awe as the falcon circled his brother, before diving to hang in the air just above his head.

Peter swatted at it once. The falcon easily moved out of Peter's reach, then returned to hover over him again.

Logan looked at Solace, and they exchanged an amazed glance.

"Looks like your guardian angel's found another troubled soul to look after," Solace said.

Logan cast a wistful gaze after the falcon.

"You're going to miss that bird," Solace gasped.

"No, I'm not," Logan objected.

A knowing smile spread across Solace's face. "Yes, you are."

"No. I'm not," Logan insisted.

"Yes, you are." Solace laughed.

Logan stalked her and captured her wrist, pulling her to him. He stared down into her beautiful green eyes. "I am not."

Solace smiled.

Logan pressed his lips to hers, stealing her grin. "I'm not," he whispered.

Solace stood on the tips of her toes and kissed the corners of his lips, his chin, his nose and eyes. "Yes, you are," Solace whispered huskily, kissing him fully on the lips.

"All right," he agreed, holding her to his heart. "I am. A little bit." He would grant her anything just to see her smile.

Solace hugged Logan tightly, and he gazed down at her with adoration. He was the happiest man in all the land. He had everything he had ever wanted. And something he had never dreamed of . . . his Solace.

ROMANCE FROM JANELLE TAYLOR

ANYTHING FOR LOVE   (0-8217-4992-7, $5.99)

DESTINY MINE   (0-8217-5185-9, $5.99)

CHASE THE WIND   (0-8217-4740-1, $5.99)

MIDNIGHT SECRETS   (0-8217-5280-4, $5.99)

MOONBEAMS AND MAGIC   (0-8217-0184-4, $5.99)

SWEET SAVAGE HEART   (0-8217-5276-6, $5.99)

ROMANCE FROM FERN MICHAELS

DEAR EMILY   (0-8217-4952-8, $5.99)

WISH LIST   (0-8217-5228-6, $6.99)

AND IN HARDCOVER:

VEGAS RICH   (1-57566-057-1, $25.00)

WATCH FOR THESE ZEBRA REGENCIES

LADY STEPHANIE   (0-8217-5341-X, $4.50)
by Jeanne Savery
Lady Stephanie Morris has only one true love: the family estate she
has managed ever since her mother died. But then Lord Anthony Rider
arrives on her estate, claiming he has plans for both the land and the
woman. Stephanie soon realizes she's fallen in love with a man whose
sensual caresses will plunge her into a world of peril and intrigue . . . a
man as dangerous as he is irresistible.

BRIGHTON BEAUTY   (0-8217-5340-1, $4.50)
by Marilyn Clay
Chelsea Grant, pretty and poor, naively takes school friend Alayna
Marchmont's place and spends a month in the country. The devastating
man had sailed from Honduras to claim his promised bride, Miss
Marchmont. An affair of the heart may lead to disaster . . . unless a
resourceful Brighton beauty finds a way to stop a masquerade and
keep a lord's love.

LORD DIABLO'S DEMISE   (0-8217-5338-X, $4.50)
by Meg-Lynn Roberts
The sinfully handsome Lord Harry Glendower was a gambler and the
black sheep of his family. About to be forced into a marriage of con-
venience, the devilish fellow engineered his own demise, never having
dreamed that faking his death would lead him to the heavenly refuge
of spirited heiress Gwyn Morgan, the daughter of a physician.

A PERILOUS ATTRACTION   (0-8217-5339-8, $4.50)
by Dawn Aldridge Poore
Alissa Morgan is stunned when a frantic passenger thrusts her baby
into Alissa's arms and flees, having heard rumors that a notorious
highwayman posed a threat to their coach. Handsome stranger Hugh
Sebastian secretly possesses the treasured necklace the highwayman
seeks and volunteers to pose as Alissa's husband to save her reputation.
With a lost baby and missing necklace in their care, the couple embarks
on a journey into peril—and passion.

*Available wherever paperbacks are sold, or order direct from the
Publisher. Send cover price plus 50¢ per copy for mailing and
handling to Kensington Publishing Corp., Consumer Orders,
or call (toll free) 888-345-BOOK, to place your order using
Mastercard or Visa. Residents of New York and Tennessee
must include sales tax. DO NOT SEND CASH.*